# DO UNTO OTHERS

*Northern Angola, December, 1970*

## JONATHAN T MARSHALL

PAGE PUBLISHING, INC.
New York, NY

First originally published by Page Publishing, Inc. 2015

ISBN 978-1-68213-518-1 (pbk)
ISBN 978-1-68213-519-8 (digital)

Printed in the United States of America

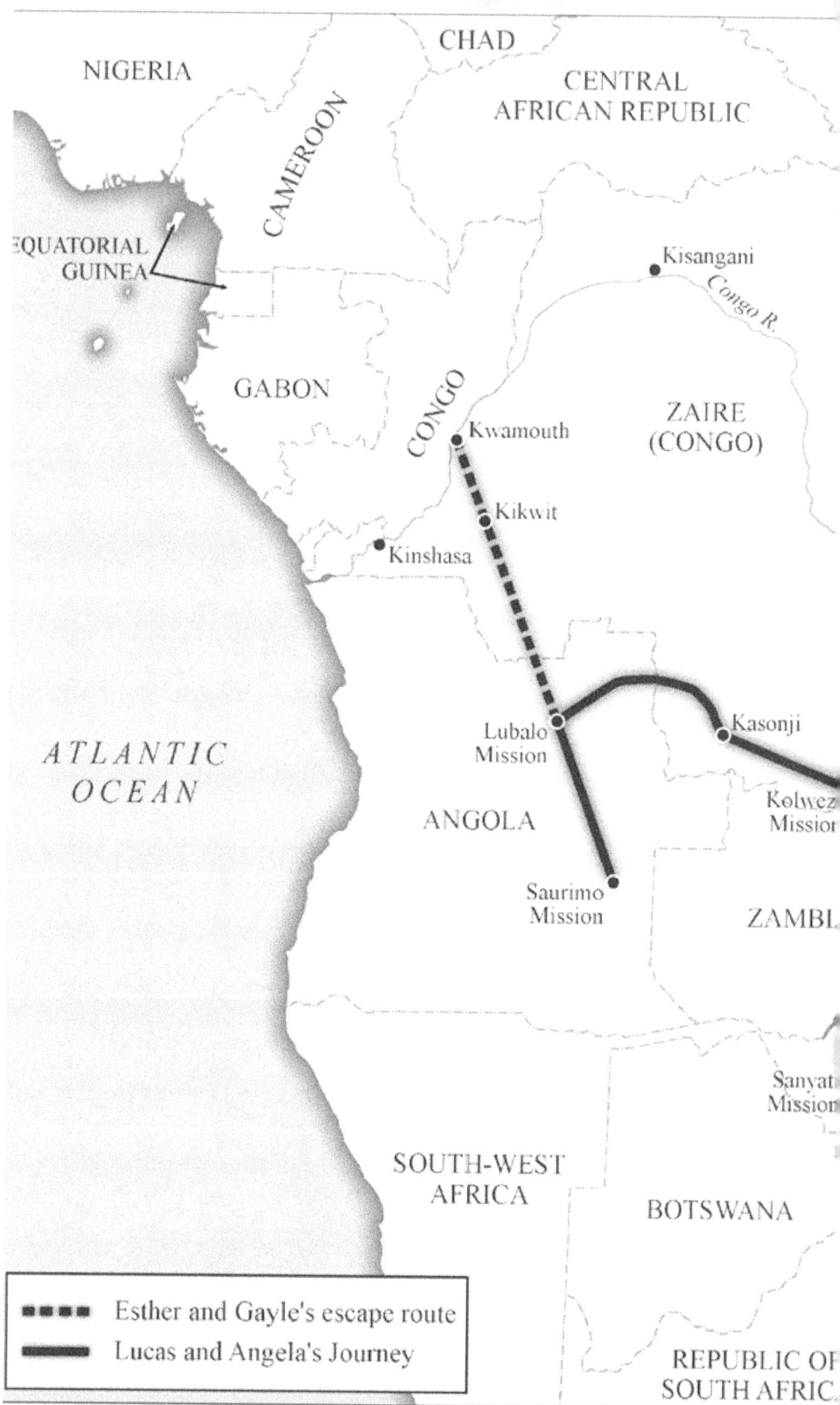

NIGERIA

CHAD

CENTRAL
AFRICAN REPUBLIC

CAMEROON

EQUATORIAL
GUINEA

Kisangani

Congo R.

GABON

CONGO

ZAIRE
(CONGO)

Kwamouth

Kikwit

Kinshasa

ATLANTIC
OCEAN

Lubalo
Mission

Kasonji

Kolwez
Missior

ANGOLA

Saurimo
Mission

ZAMBI

Sanyat
Missior

SOUTH-WEST
AFRICA

BOTSWANA

Esther and Gayle's escape route

Lucas and Angela's Journey

REPUBLIC OF
SOUTH AFRIC

SUDAN

ETHIOPIA

SOMALIA

UGANDA

KENYA

Lake
Victoria

RWANDA

BURUNDI

Lake
Tanganyika

TANZANIA

INDIAN
OCEAN

MALAWI

Lake
Malawi

COMOROS

Lilongwe

Blantyre

Nsanje
Mission

Salisbury

MADAGASCAR

RHODESIA

MOZAMBIQUE

SWAZILAND

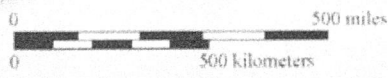

| 0 | | 500 miles |
| 0 | | 500 kilometers |

# 1
## Chapter

The soft, persistent scratching coming from his left was so faint that Lucas Stuart wondered if he had only imagined it. Turning his head, he was able to catch a momentary glimpse of the tapering end of the rat's tail as the rodent crouched behind a bamboo post. The rest of its emaciated body remained hidden by the sturdy struts of the cage that enclosed Lucas and Angela. The rat was trying to gnaw on the sisal ropes that held the poles together, hoping to obtain some nourishment from any source. Nutrition continued to be meager in this desolate place, for man and animal alike.

With a grimace that reflected his acquired knowledge of the surrounding foliage and dank undergrowth, Lucas peered deeply into the dense tropical forest that grew around his bamboo-pole prison. The growth adjacent to his enclosure, however, continued to limit his view of other survivors or possible escape routes. He wiped the sweat from his face with the back of his clammy right hand, realizing that the temperatures here were well above the forty degrees Centigrade mark (105 degrees Fahrenheit).

Each breath of the muggy, fetid air reconfirmed in his mind that the December summer of nineteen hundred seventy was not an era of moderate climate in Northern Angola, even under ideal circumstances. Puddles, remaining from this morning's downpour, sparkled on the dark, pungent forest floor, giving mirror-like reflections of the dazzling sun above them, now high in the sky. Taking another sodden breath, Lucas whispered in a soft, soothing undertone, "How are you feeling?"

Angela Abercrombe, the attractive blonde-haired woman sitting on the packed earth floor next to him in the cage, replied, "We need a plan to survive and to get free from these rebels."

Looking up from her examination of her torn and spattered nurses' scrub suit Angela continued.

"I don't feel that the situation is totally out of control yet. They haven't threatened our lives, but I *am* hot, tired, and thirsty. Most of these rebels seem surprisingly well-disciplined and responsive to their military leaders' orders. I overheard the guards discussing a plan to send a ransom demand through the American Consulate in Luanda for all of us. If I had been alone in this pen, it would have been lonely. It was quite fortunate for me that we were actually in surgery together at the time they overran the hospital, and because of their rush to imprison all of the hospital personnel during the fighting we were put into the same enclosure."

Lucas guessed that the other three bamboo-pole enclosures, hidden from view, probably contained other members of the hospital staff. Their physical condition remained uncertain. The four bamboo huts, constructed recently to store supplies for the hospital, now served the rebels as hostage prisons. In the rapid rebel advance on the mission hospital, multiple gunshots had been fired, and terrified screams had been heard. Unfortunately, his knowledge of the status of the other hospital staff remained limited to a brief glimpse he had gotten as they were forced into cages. The distance between his pen and the next was some fifty feet, but all that Lucas could see of the other captives were vague outlines lying in varying postures within the confines of their enclosures. Without the sunlight blocked by the foliage, it remained impossible to see into the interior of the neighboring cages. Yesterday, these workers, both foreign and native, had been a coordinated, engaged team of medical missionaries working diligently to mend bodies and souls. The Kongo natives had seemed to be grateful for the mission team's efforts, but now the hospital remained silent.

Turning to the nearest enclosure, Lucas called softly, using coherent Kileta dialect, as he did not know whom he was addressing. *"Kufuanana muisi?"* (Is anyone hurt?)

Rising from a reclining position, the indistinct outline of a shining black face appeared dimly through the branches behind the stout bamboo stakes of the neighboring cage. Speaking English with a distinct Kileta accent, the Angolan native responded. He was aware that Lucas spoke no Portuguese, the universal Angolan language adopted from their colonizing country.

"Ahh, Doctor Lucas, we are all fine. Doctor Maria has a few scratches and Okanna has broken his finger. The hospital patients were all left in their beds as the rebel troops flooded into the building, only the staff was taken captive. How are you and Missie Angela?"

Lucas sighed in relief. He recognized the familiar African accent of his orderly, Brightwell, who answered in English. He had learned to speak the Americans' language at a British mission school as a child, and now smiled across the ragged foliage that separated their prison huts. He was an Angola native, a confirmed Christian, and would definitely be of some help in any difficult situation.

"We are fine for now, Brightwell. Is anyone else in pain?" asked Lucas as he continued to speak in the Kileta dialect, wanting the orderly to understand every word.

"Stop the talking!" came the stern admonition from one of the insurgent guards, standing some twenty feet from the cages It startled the doctor.

Lucas knew that their guards listened to every word spoken and that they would relay the captives' communications to their guerilla officers, if other than routine conversations transpired.

"As far as we can tell, there are only some minor problems," whispered the reliable native, switching to Kileta, his native tongue. "Did you both miss the confrontation on the hospital's front lawn? Many were wounded on both sides."

All of this information from Brightwell didn't surprise Angela; she had heard stories of hospital rebel takeovers from her missionary parents since early childhood. She glanced up at Lucas as he stood at the door of their cage. Lucas was wearing a partly torn and soiled white shirt, and she noticed his khaki shorts were also deeply stained with mud. His 6'4", well-muscled frame filled the outline of the cage door, and his pigskin boots and knee socks were typical for a white physician in the stifling African climate. He *did* look older than his early forties, but the many years he had spent working as a remote mission doctor had made his life less opulent than most American physicians at that age, who were living a more luxurious life in America.

She had secretly admired his muscular body since they had first met some two and a half months ago. Lucas maintained his short-cropped hair, common to all surgeons and nurses forced to wear scrub caps daily for hours at a time. She could detect traces of his formerly light blonde hair, now speckled with grey in its usual unkempt tangle. He had arrived from the Malawi Baptist Mission at the request of the Angola Mission supervisor to help in the treatment of the poorly-fed natives suffering from injury and deprivation during the present rebellion.

"It's been 24 hours since water or food has been given to us, Lucas," she said. "We'll become dehydrated soon. Let me speak to the guard, using the local dialect to see if he will help us." Angela was familiar with most Angolan dialects and would likely be able to speak the guard's local language.

Just as Angela got to her feet, gunfire reverberated throughout the compound, its closeness startling both of them. The repeating "pop" sounds confirmed that automatic weapons were being used generously in the firefight raging to the west of their enclosure. Lucas and Angela watched as many makeshift pole stretchers, laden with African soldiers draped with blood-encrusted bandages, were rushed past their prison towards a clearing in front of the hospital. The sour stench of gunpowder filled their nostrils, carried by the few breezes that stirred the stagnant, humid air. Rising from the floor and standing near the bamboo poles, Angela could make out a silhouette, and then heard the angry voice of Reverend Brown echoing across the compound.

The reverend was a recent arrival to the Angola mission station from Massachusetts. He had very limited experience in remote jungle evangelism and no expertise whatever in dealing with rebels. Very self-confident, the self-commissioned mission-ary from his liberal Boston church had proclaimed himself an "Episcopal Evangelist" to everyone he met following his arrival in Angola a few weeks ago. He was accompanied by two female assistants from his wealthy congregation. Now, he announced to everyone in general, "I am an American! You can't put me in a cage! I'll have the American consulate file a formal complaint as soon as we get out of here!"

His tone was pompous and demanding as Angela could barely see him as he grabbed the bamboo bars, pointing between them with an accusing finger at the face of his guard. It was obvi-ous to both Lucas and Angela that this pastor from America was insecure and visibly terrified to be in an environment where he had neither respect nor any control of his fate. His outcry was answered by an almost instant rebuke, as the thump from a rifle butt was heard, followed by a groan as the reverend clutched his abdomen. The clergyman slumped to the cage floor, thrashing in agony. The blow, Angela realized, would confirm his previ-ous suspicion that there was little hope of any assistance in the immediate future.

Lucas began, for the umpteenth time, to minutely examine the sides of his enclosure. He had originally supervised the con-struction of these pens, not built to hold people in, but to keep them out. Food and grain in larger quantities were shipped from America by the Baptist Foreign Mission Board, and then stored to be available to the hospital patients and staff for consumption later. These enclosures had been constructed a few months ago under his personal supervision. Because minor pilfering and out-right burglary of food and other supply stores were widespread in the face of shortages, the enclosures had been built to inhibit indigent thieves. The enclosures had been emptied by the ravenous guards when the hospital was captured. Now they served effectively as prisons. Lucas was able to discover no defect in the construction that would allow their escape.

A short time later, every hostage and guard heard Reverend Brown's rasping voice echoing over the entire compound. Lucas was unable to see the occupant from which the voice originated, but the nearness of the decibel level informed him that Reverend Brown's pen was not far away. The indignant pastor thundered again in a high howling tone,

"This is an outrage! Free us from these indecent pigsties immediately and give us food and water!" He spoke in a haughty tone, as he would speak to a miscreant child he felt the need to reprimand. His tone of voice now began to waver, telling Lucas that he was fighting to control his fear and anger. If he could detect the change in the reverend's voice, so could the rebels, no matter what language they spoke.

Lucas was surprised that the pastor did not fathom the hopelessness of his situation. He expected that the cruel blow from the rifle butt would have made that point clear, but the pastor's continued protests belayed any expectation of change.

Immediately, Angela's soft, clear voice was heard from within the cage to the reverend's right. She attempted to give him some long ago learned knowledge.

"Reverend John! These are rebel troops that are totally in control! Your demands are out of place. I will ask them in their native language if they might give us some mercy. Please, only give me a chance to negotiate before you antagonize them further!"

She moved over to the corner of her pen where one of the unkempt rebel guards stood. His uniform, Angela noted, was composed of various remnants, probably found on the battlefields of previous encounters, and was badly soiled with dirt. His face showed extensive scars from a previous confrontation with an enemy's bayonet. He appeared almost comical in these unmatched pieces patched together.

Angela had been born and raised in Africa of missionary parents, originally commissioned from Scotland. Thus, she spoke many of the African languages from her earliest days, taught by the nanny who raised her under her mother's supervision. Angela now spoke to the soldier in perfect Kileta dialect, without foreign accent, in a conversational tone. "Friend, we have been many hours without food or water. We are not your enemies nor have we caused you any harm. Please make arrangements for water and food, such as you have, to be given to us as soon as possible."

The guard was obviously astonished to hear a "white foreigner" speak his vernacular dialect faultlessly. Turning immediately to the pen, he replied in the local dialect, "Madam, we have very little to eat ourselves, and the government troops are attacking us. I will find some water when it is safe and bring it to you. We have many wounded who are severely hurt and dying, and they also need water."

The sounds of the fighting had now moved some distance away, but the silence of the birds and lack of the usual jungle noises indicated how recently the firefight had been close to them. Only the persistent buzzing of the mosquitoes and tsetse flies around their heads was evident. The hostages and the guards had the common problem of the multiple welts covering their skin from the repeated attacks of these lusty, blood-sucking insects. Everyone was miserable in the heat. The gnats were so dense that every person had his own personal cloud that followed him as he moved about the cages or open spaces. Fear of disease from these insects or waterborne parasites was based on fact. Typhoid, diphtheria, and cholera, as well as bilharziasis cases abounded in both the military and the general populations from the total lack of sanitary facilities. These problems dated from the onset of the rebellion, which had persisted for about three years. The Peoples Socialist Democratic Union of Angola government forces were trying to suppress the Western-supported rebels, particularly by the American and South Africans. However, the mission hospital had tried to remain nonpartisan from the onset, treating both rebel and government casualties equally.

Angela felt that she needed to find some common ground to relate to their captors. She was also aware that it was common practice for the rebel troops to demand ransom for hostages prior to occasionally slaughtering the entire group after the money had been paid.

"Are you a Christian?" continued Angela to the guard, on the off-chance that her warder had been evangelized and would be willing to assist a fellow Christian.

"Ah yes, I am 'born again' Christian now," reported the guard. "I was never interested in religion until Brother Mukwa at the Saurimo Mission told us about that Jesus ancestor. Are you familiar with the Saurimo hospital?" This was the opening that Angela had been hoping to find.

Angela could see that two other guards were talking earnestly, while standing about fifty yards away in the shade of a massive Baobab tree. Seeing their comrade in conversation with one of the female hostages, the guards strolled leisurely across the gravel driveway towards the group of huts where the missionaries were imprisoned. The discussion between the two guards as they approached became more animated with each stride. Angela could hear the discourse easily, as the arguments increased in intensity and volume. The discussion was in their native Lunda Norte Province dialect, and the guards assumed that no white hostage could comprehend their conversation. A brief glance at the ceremonial half-moon cheek scars and colored skin tattoos revealed to Lucas and Angela that both guards were from the Kongo tribe.

The argument concerned the fate of the hostages. They were disagreeing on whether their forces would benefit most from the many Kwanza the Americans might pay for the white missionaries in ransom, or from using the hostages first as slaves and prostitutes prior to annihilating them after collecting the money, which had often been what resulted.

Both were animated in their ideas for the use of the captives. They were saying, "No, I hope they will tell us to use them as slaves and porters to serve us and to be mistresses for the lonely troops," argued the one on the left. "Only then will they collect the money prior to disposing of them."

Angela overheard and understood immediately that they were reviewing the fate of other captives in the past. She began to panic. Lucas, not fully understanding every word, did speak the dialect sufficiently to get the general drift of the argument. Their captors disputed harder and louder as tempers began to rise, along with their convictions. Angela, fully aware now that they were all in immediate physical danger, showed signs that she was close to losing the tight control of her emotions that she had been struggling to maintain since their capture. Her reaction to the conversation infected Lucas, as he also began to consider the threat of the sexual molestation or murder of Angela.

She quickly responded to the guard's question about the Saurimo Mission.

"Friend, we are all Christians and hospital technicians. We are in your country only to help you and your families to find the Lord and to be more healthy and happy. There is no reason to harm us. What is your name?"

The two having now arrived at their hut, all three Africans looked intently at Angela as she spoke from inside the enclosure. One by one, they began to smile, obviously becoming relaxed, until all three were grinning good-naturedly, recognizing that she spoke their dialect perfectly and without any foreign accent. The closest guard spoke, "Madam, you are not one of these white foreign missionaries, are you? You speak as an Angolan teacher from Norte Lunda would speak. My name is Manaba. What is your surname?"

Seeing an apparent opening in the conversation, Angela responded in Kileta, "Yes, Manaba, my name is Missie Abercrombe. My father is Pastor Abercrombe at the Scottish Presbyterian mission in Saurimo. Are you familiar with the mission people?"

Manaba set his Army rifle in a relaxed position with the butt on the ground. It was mutually recognizable that the tension was decreasing by the second. Seeing this, his two comrades seemed to become much calmer as well, as they leaned against one of the fence posts near the hut.

"I know the Saurimo Presbyterian Mission, but not your father," Manaba responded.

The shorter, pudgier soldier who had been arguing wore no hat and had a torn right sleeve. He now looked at Angela curiously. He was obviously a veteran of the fighting, showing a small puncture wound in his forearm. He stood with the other two soldiers, and spoke now in remarkably clear English, "Did you know Sister Joan? She taught us at the Saurimo Mission when we were children about England and Portugal. We watched Sister Joan's funeral after the great sleeping sickness, when I was young. My name is Retread, and this is my friend Biro. We are all from the Norte Lunde Province. Your father, the preacher, is a great man."

Angela felt the blood rush to her face, as she reacted emotionally to the African's statement. She could still clearly remember the gentle voice of her mother, 'Sister Joan,' as she had taught the natives when Angela was still very young. Angela had played with the other mission children as her mother taught in the thatch-covered, mud-walled classroom at the distant mission school. This memory brought back images of her parents and brothers, causing tears to glisten in her eyes as she struggled to answer the guard. While moved deeply by these memories, her practical mind remained ever vigilant.

*"So...Manaba, Biro and Retread?"* she thought to herself. *"Perhaps I can develop some kind of relationship with these guards to help us all?"*

"You knew my mother, Sister Joan? She was your teacher?" Angela used the moment, "Please try to find some water for us all, Retread, we are very thirsty," she said out loud.

Angela had responded by switching from the Kileta dialect to English. It was probable that all three soldiers had attended mission schools and could understand English. She hoped to bring back kind memories to these guards by speaking the language in which they had been taught.

A short conversation followed among the three guards. At the conclusion of their conference, Biro walked briskly in the direction of the Lubalo River, which ran near the hospital compound. He was carrying some empty plastic containers in his hands.

Suddenly, the familiar loud voice returned from the nearby enclosure, "Look! We are tired of this game. I demand food and water immediately! I am Reverend John Calvin Brown and we must have water and food, NOW!"

His voice was ignored by the guards, which Angela considered lucky for the reverend.

It had turned into early afternoon, and as was often the case, a few gentle breezes could be felt in the blazing heat. The flat umbrella-like Massasa trees rustled in the cooling rush and the ever-present clouds of gnats thinned as the insects sought shade and humidity in the denser foliage. Biro returned with water and sugarcane stalks, which surrendered sweet juices when chewed and would give sustenance to the hostages.

"Thank you so much," said Angela as she drank deeply of the dank, dirty water, knowing from past experiences that it probably wouldn't hurt her. She handed the half emptied container to Lucas. "Have the other hospital workers also received water and cane?"

Nodding, Retread attempted to resume his conversation with Angela and Lucas, only to be interrupted again by the howling, complaining voice of Reverend Brown, resounding to every guard and captive's ears.

"This water is dirty and grass is not food! We are not animals and we refuse to be treated as such. Release us immediately!"

The voice of Doctor Maria, a longtime Angola mission doctor, was now heard by both hostages and guards, speaking earnestly and sincerely from the neighboring cage in her Portuguese-accented English. "Reverend Brown! Apologize to these soldiers immediately and beg their forgiveness, or they will certainly hurt us!" Her clear, thin voice of reason seemed less of a plea than a thought she was expressing for the reverend to consider the situation before speaking.

Lucas watched as the slender, elderly lady stood at the door of the neighboring cage supported by Brightwell. He was able to see her clearly leaning against the wall of her hut as the sun shown down from the cloud filled sky in the west. Doctor Maria Portegas was an Internal Medicine physician, born and trained in Portugal many years ago. The Northern Angolan Baptist Mission had been her home for decades, and she knew the Kongo natives well, including the violence they were capable of carrying out. Their record of brutality was familiar to most Angolan residents, which had been documented in detail by the news media over the last three years of the insurgency.

In a tattered dress, shoeless, her grey hair in disarray, she stood holding onto the bamboo pole in front of her, supported by the orderly. Lucas knew that she had witnessed the results of the torture and humiliations the rebels had caused previous hostages who had been fortunate enough to escape and report their experiences.

Then, turning to the soldiers, Doctor Maria said in the native Kileta dialect, "Soldiers! This impolite American has no idea of his situation. Please ignore this ignorant emotional outbreak. Allow him to apologize for his stupidity!"

It was obvious that all three of the soldiers understood English, and they immediately reacted to Reverend Brown's disgust with the water and nutrition they had offered to him. The reverend's distaste was also obvious from the fact that he violently threw both the water and sugarcane from his pen, failing to offer any relief to the two female occupants sharing the cage with him. Seeing his contempt, the soldiers were angered. After a brief discussion among the guards, following the pastor's show of contempt, the soldier named Manabe, apparently in charge, strode briskly towards the building the rebels were using as their headquarters.

Manabe felt that he was a reasonable man, brought up in a Christian mission by parents who had insisted that the white missionary teachers were to be respected and obeyed, but this loud insolent man was without manners and undeserving of respect. Perhaps his superior officer should be informed.

They saw the guard leave, and he remarked to Angela that this was a grim signal. Lucas felt that he had not come here to Africa all the way from Philadelphia and worked all these years only to die at the hands of a group of guerillas because of one pompous man.

He mused, "What a waste of time and hard work . . . medical school, surgical residency, four years of seminary . . . for nothing?"

Looking over at Angela, he smiled tightly and whispered, "Twenty years living in remote missions, I even got a doctor of theology to be a better evangelist, and this jerk who's been here a couple of weeks isn't smart enough to be polite. Hope all of the captives don't have to pay the price of one belligerent, inexperienced man."

He began to fear most, without admitting it to himself, that these rebels might torture, rape or murder Angela. Missionaries usually are somewhat educated on the fundamentals of dealing with natives. This Reverend Brown seemed somehow to have come of his own volition with little or no preparation for native negotiations or *any* kind of emergency."

Lucas was speaking to Angela in confident tones that he did not feel. "It will probably be okay. The guard probably has to report anything that the hostages say."

Angela had more experience with the local natives than Lucas and was not deluded. She began to cry softly as she sat upon the blanket strewn on the floor of the cage, mumbling, "It's over! They will surely kill all of us . . . or worse. I know these people and they will not hesitate to torture any white hostage who refuses to beg or surrender to them. We may *all* be doomed."

Lucas took Angela gently in his arms, and after wiping her soft, tear-stained cheeks with his hand, he began to tenderly kiss her face, talking softly as he tried to comfort her. Angela was pleasantly amazed at the way Lucas attempted to calm her. His initial kiss was the first show of affection she had received since her husband died the year before. She did not reject his show of affection.

"We must try to keep our cool, Angie; maybe it's time to let you know that I'm really concerned that something could happen to you. Reverend John has put us in a rough spot, but we've maneuvered around other crises, and I'm sure this won't be the last disaster we'll see. Come on, think positive! We have figured a way out of medical emergencies together in the past; we can find a way here. You're more familiar with the Angolans than I am. Get a hold of your emotions; let's pray for knowledge, and then try to analyze the possibilities together."

He found it difficult to say that. In the past three months that they had worked together and now—confined in a small pen during thethe crisis of the past few days--his attitude towards her had become strongly positive.

It might be true that during trying times, many people turned to their inner feelings of affection to look for comfort. Angela ceased crying and began to return his caresses with increasing ardor, but she was not convinced that there was an easy solution at hand. They were well aware that a disaster for all of the hostages could be expected if no changes developed soon. These thoughts made their feelings of affection for each other more complex, complicating their circumstances.

They knew that the guard's return shortly would not bring any benefit to the captives. As he walked away, Manabe had appeared resolute rather than angry, which did not presage good for the hostages.

Lucas and Angela prayed together as they sat in the cage. Upon standing, they still were able to see only the pen next to their own, but knowing that the other two cages were only fifty yards beyond the next cage, they decided to try to find out if there were more captives in the remaining enclosures. Looking towards the neighboring pen, Lucas said in a low tone, "Brightwell, can you see to the next two enclosures?"

Almost immediately, the familiar black face appeared at the bamboo bars. He was smiling, as always, and Lucas remembered that he had never seen his orderly frown under any circumstances. Brightwell was perpetually positive. He had learned this from his mother at an early age, making it pleasant to work with him.

"Yes, Doctor Lucas, I am able to see both of the huts beyond ours. They seem occupied."

"Can you make out who is in the huts," returned Lucas anxiously.

There was a short pause as Brightwell examined the other cages. "The next hut has Pastor Brown and the two ladies he brought with him from America. The last hut has four people from the dispensary. I believe they are Jonas, Clever, and Patience. The fourth one looks like Maichipo from here. I guess the rebels just caged everyone randomly during the takeover."

Lucas and Angela now had a census of the captives. The rest of the hospital and mission staff must have either escaped into the bush or been killed. He knew that there were a total of twelve hostages. These were divided into six women: Angela, a skilled scrub nurse and assistant, the reverend's two aides, useless medically but able to assist in patient care, and Dr. Mary, a skilled physician but not a surgeon. There were also two native women, Patience and Maichipo: one an experienced scrub nurse and a cook. The male hostages were also six: two Americans, Dr. Lucas and Reverend Brown, and four Africans: Brightwell, reliable to do anything asked; Okanna, and Jonas, orderlies; and Clever, the chief mission cook. This number might become important if an escape was being considered. While no plan could be worked out in the few minutes before Manabe returned, Lucas was positive that some strategy for escape needed to be in place as soon as possible. This had to be organized before retribution for the reverend's loud voice could prove to have serious consequences.

Lucas looked over at his cellmate. He had really never observed her in detail in the close to three months they had been working together. Yes, she was attractive with her short blonde hair and trim figure; she seemed at all times pleasant and helpful as well as a knowledgeable nurse. Ordinarily they were so preoccupied with treating patients that he really hadn't had time to think about her as a woman. Under these severe conditions, he had reason to think about her as a person, and as a fellow prisoner to help him escape. He had noticed the pert swellings at the front of her attire, which the loose scrub shirt she usually wore covered. Now, wearing the torn scrub shirt, he was able to discern the taut nipples showing through the front of her displaced brassiere. She was attractive, but certainly not the most beautiful woman he'd seen. Standing about 5'3", he guessed her weight at around 105 pounds, but what he found equally attractive was her strong self-confidence and faith. Angela's quick mind, he realized, was her most attractive feature, and he needed her suggestions badly. Her knowledge of the people and terrain would be important to *any* attempt at escape.

A plan began to form in Lucas' mind. This plan would take some time to activate and he would need Angela's help to refine it, but the idea might save them all, particularly Angela. There was no time to discuss it, as he heard the crunch of footsteps on the gravel path coming towards their enclosure from the guerilla's administrative buildings. Manabe's voice could be heard as they approached, with the interjections of a much lower voice from an older man.

"This white preacher is making many complaints, but the two ladies in that pen seem to be lying on the floor doing nothing. They just sob quietly and continually," Manabe was saying.

The deeper voice returned, also in Kileta, speaking with obvious authority.

"There is no reason why we need to put up with the complaints of a foreign white prisoner, or his insulting remarks. These religious fanatics are a nuisance; let's get them out of the pen and see what they have to say then!"

Lucas and Angela could see the two men clearly from their prison as they strode past the large salmon-colored blooms of the frangipani tree shading the front of their enclosure. When the compound had been built, an open space in front of the storage buildings had been cleared for loading and unloading supplies. This was packed mud, covered by gravel, which had become worn somewhat by tires moving across the surface for the past few months. The older man obviously was an officer and carried himself with authority. The collar of his mud-spattered uniform displayed two faded gold stars of rank, and on his right hip he carried a large pistol. The worn pistol grip protruding from its holster was emblazoned with a red "U", for "Unita", the first word for the official title of the rebel army. His headgear sat low on his forehead and was as tattered as his clothing. No badge or rank was evident on his hat brim or shoulders. Manabe's uniform showed little difference in appearance from his superior, except that he carried an automatic rifle and had no sidearm. As they approached the other two guards waiting next to the cages, their conversation ceased. The superior officer now spoke again, after Biro and Retread saluted and addressed the insurgent officer as "Colonel."

"Manabe tells me that the man in the third pen is being obstructive and a trouble-maker," he said with a tight smile. "Let's get the people in that cage out of there and see just what sort of problem he thinks he has."

A distinct "click" could be heard from the lock as it was released. Lucas surmised that Reverend Brown's cage was being unlocked, from the nearness of the sound. There followed a series of grunts and cries. Suddenly, the reverend and his two assistants appeared in the large clearing. All three captives were being dragged into this open space and could be clearly observed by the other prisoners from within the other three shelters. The shocked remaining captives watched the proceedings in horrified panic as the unfortunate American missionaries were forcefully pulled into the open space.

The reverend had lost his footing and was being physically dragged backwards by his shirt collar across the gravel and into the loading area.

"What are you going to do to me?! Leave me alone! I know officials in high places who will not tolerate this usage. I want to see the American Consulate!" he pleaded in a whining voice, less sure of himself than he had been a few minutes ago. Lucas could see that the man was terrified, and was trying to cover his fear by acting outraged, hoping to intimidate the officer as he did everyone else.

The reverend's hair was now frazzled and hanging into his bright red bloated face, which was distorted in anger. The shirt he had been wearing was torn at the neck and his khaki pants were covered with mud and gravel. One shoe was missing, leaving a bright orange sock to flash from his lower pant leg. He was thrown roughly to the ground, where he remained in a disordered pile, still talking in less threatening tones.

The two women were in little better condition than their leader. They were on their feet, but a guard had grasped each by the elbow and firmly led them to a spot near the reverend. The

older lady was named Esther, and had torn her dress on a protruding bamboo splinter in her pen as the guard forced her from
the cage. This had produced a tear extending from the bottom
hem of her skirt to her waist, exposing her scrawny, white legs
covered with insect bites. Her hair hung loosely from lack of any
hair-tie and she was bleeding from her lip, which she had bitten
in terror.

Esther was moaning between her tears, "Please don't hurt me.
We came here with Pastor Brown to help evangelize the African
natives and to teach the children about Jesus. Why are you doing
this to us?"

Her companion, Gayle, was also standing, but had torn the
shoulder strap of her dress. She was trying to pull the sleeve up
while in the paralyzing grip of the guard. Her short dark hair was
mussed, but in better days, she might have been fairly attractive.
Both women wore flat-heeled tennis shoes that had once been
white. Now, they were spattered with mud and gravel. Esther
looked every day of her forty-five years. The younger Gayle was
in her mid-thirties. The three captives, now in plain view of the
other hostages, were cowering with terror, realizing that disaster
was at hand. The officer spoke in broken English, which Lucas
surmised he had learned somewhere previously,

"So you come to visit us in our country, to teach us poor
infidels modern religion and morals? Welcome! We will try to
accommodate you!" he said with ironic sarcasm. Then, with a
confident smile he continued, "We will have to inspect the goods
prior to putting you to work."

Turning to the guards, he ordered, "Strip all three of their
outer clothes. I will return in a few minutes." He then walked
briskly towards the barracks.

When this order was communicated to the helpless captives,
Esther began to hesitantly remove her clothes, sobbing and pleading as she began to loosen the top of her dress. The reverend was
in no condition to comply. He was now lying on the ground,
moaning, and in significant pain from a kick that Manabe had
viciously administered. He was roughly pulled to his feet, and
at bayonet point proceeded to loosen his belt and lower the torn

pants that had become even more mottled with debris. The reverend had a distinct stench about him, as he had fouled his pants in fear.

Gayle let out a shriek as she also understood the demand from the guard, but her anger was up and she rallied to the challenge. "I will NOT take off my clothes, not now, not ever! You have no right to touch or humiliate me! Get away from me!" she looked Retread directly in the eye.

As Retread stepped forward to enforce the order, Gayle's nerve began to fail her. But her body was not as strong as her mind and she began to sob and gasp for breath in horror of the guards' impending assault. Gayle's highly sophisticated breeding kicked in, however, and rallied her once again. Pointing her index finger at her tormenter's face she screamed, "Don't touch me, you horrible, uncouth little weasel!"

She bent towards the ground and began to vomit what little contents remained in her system. As she crouched over to retch, Retread roughly stood her up and proceeded to pull at her already torn clothes, reducing the outer garment to shreds.

Meanwhile, the reverend remained in a semi-upright stance. All that remained of his clothing was his undershirt and soiled boxers. The aggressive manner he had recently demonstrated was now missing as he slumped against the top of the waist-high wooden fence behind him. "Please don't hurt me," he sobbed out loud. Then, in a half-whisper between sobs, they heard him pray, "Please, Lord, save me from this tribulation."

Manabe, complying with his orders from a superior officer, stood threateningly before the reverend with the sharp bayonet fixed to the end of his rifle. Reverend John Calvin Brown now slumped in the fading sunlight, sobbing, utterly intimidated. All signs of defiance had fled from his manner; his only concern being to avoid further indignity and pain.

Gayle had been reduced to wearing just her brassiere and panties, her trim well-shaped body exposed. She continued to spew abuse at Retread and her other captors, and her total contempt and anger was evident in her manner. Obviously she was used to having her own way all of her life and her arrogance and temper had overridden her good sense. One of the loose, shape-less dresses that she habitually wore lay in a heap on the ground.

Esther had tried to hold onto the elastic, shaping corset she used to conceal her flabby torso. The shriek of fear and embarrassment that was heard when Biro deftly split this garment at the back with a well-aimed slash from his bayonet, had turned every head in the compound. Esther's loose flab protruded above her underwear, showing dilated crimson veins in her thin, white skin. She attempted to cover herself with her hands, but the rolls of loose tissue remained exposed despite her efforts.

Lucas and Angela had witnessed the entire episode with horror, but were not surprised. They had heard of similar treatment of abductees by the rebels and knew this was the type of behavior reserved only for captured foreigners Native soldiers captured were often instantly dispatched. Any plan to save themselves would have to be swift. The rebels had a special hatred for white aliens working in their country. Torture and humiliation, or worse, were the common reward for capture.

The colonel had returned, and stood in front of the three captives with his hands on his hips, smiling. "Let us see what you really look like," he said, staring directly at Gayle. "Remove the rest of your clothes... now."

Enraged at the thought of his audacity, her fear forgotten, Gayle rushed towards the officer. She had never been intimidated by threats to her modesty as a young girl or even as an adult. The thought of disrobing in front of the guards and mission personnel was not a possibility. With her right arm raised and her hand clenched into a fist, she wailed "You'll never see what I look like!"

Biro, witnessing this attack on his startled commander and wanting to remain within bounds of his duty, stepped forward with his fixed bayonet and caught Gayle at the level of her navel. He felt a little guilty at striking an unarmed woman, but she had no right to challenge his commander's authority. The sharp knife penetrated the skin, leaving a superficial wound that began to bleed. Gayle, thinking herself mortally wounded, fell to the ground clutching at her abdomen, "Lord, what he has done to me!" she moaned, lying on her back.

The officer, having regained his composure, calmly walked over to Gayle, picked her up as he would a dirty rag, and put her in a standing position. Turning his back, he returned to the position he had formerly occupied. Gayle continued to sob as she slumped in the standing position next to Esther. Lucas could see blood as it trickled from a superficial abdominal wound, forming a thin red ribbon down her flimsy underpants and dripped slowly into the small puddle forming on the ground in front of her. Gayle was in pain, but this was minor compared to her abject terror of the possible retribution to follow.

Esther, Gayle and the reverend were in no condition to resist any further attacks and remained silently in the open area, completely subdued. The sun had begun to sink towards the horizon, leaving a golden reflection, glowing over the western sky. Lucas had always marveled at the magnificent colors of the African sunset, wondering why this beautiful display never appeared in the western world.

"So what happens now?" he thought.

As the shadows deepened, the colonel now gave the order, "Take these three back to their cages. We'll finish this in the morning."

The officer abruptly turned, and speaking in a vernacular dialect, he walked towards his headquarters. He continued, assuming that the hostages would not understand his orders, "In the morning, the women will be sent to the barracks for soldier hospitality duties and the men will fill sandbags as slave laborers."

The guards let the three captives try to put on their torn clothing as best as they could and led them back to their cage. Gayle's wound was superficial, and with some pressure, the blood was stanched. All three missionaries were exhausted as they fell immediately to the ground on returning to their pen.

Despite the officer's assumptions, Angela had heard the colonel's remark and understood the vernacular and what he had meant. She whispered to Lucas, "We're doomed tomorrow morning; he's going to send the women as prostitutes to the soldier's barracks. You and the men are to be slave laborers filling bags with sand to be placed around their foxholes! Lucas, we have to do something before morning or all of us will be used up by these soldiers"

There was nothing further to say. The sun would rise the next morning; they had no control over their destiny.

# 2
## Chapter

Sitting quietly on the packed, mud floor of the cage next to Angela that evening, Lucas mulled over their situation. The events of the day indicated that the chance for future freedom of any of the hostages remained dim without a revision of the situation as it stood now. The prospect of slave labor and prostitution gave them little room for hope.

Lucas knew that he had to devise some plan to divert the rebels' attention away from themselves or the entire remaining mission team may be in grave danger. He was at a loss to decide what they could do. He asked himself this almost out loud. Cold logic told him that the chance of personal escape seemed small, and even if possible, he could not abandon the other eleven prisoners. He concluded that they had to out-think the rebels for all of them to escape, but time was becoming very short, and by morning it could be too late.

He and Angela had discussed many possible ideas, but each scheme resulted in the salvation of only a few of the other captives. It seemed impossible to devise a plan to rescue all twelve. As he sat silently in the sultry air, his thoughts returned to his home. His early life was spent in his parents' suburban Philadelphia residence, situated in an exclusive community, Bryn-Mawr. He remembered that his childhood had enabled him to have many privileges that most kids only dream about. Growing older, it became evident that he was a problem child. The elite private boarding schools, to which Lucas' parents had sent him, in the early years, failed to stimulate his I.Q. and resulted in failing grades and multiple disciplinary actions. His father's business, in international banking, produced few limits on the family finances. Both parents usually traveled together throughout the world, leaving Lucas without his parents to encourage or show him affection. He matured under the supervision of school officials or his parents' employees.

"Here's dinner," announced their guard, interrupting Lucas' reverie.

Manabe passed two bowls of lukewarm corn porridge through the bars to Angela.

"You better eat all of it," he said. "You'll be busy tomorrow and likely will be glad that you ate it."

Manabe did not act in an unfriendly manner, and his warning had a ring of truth that both prisoners recognized. It was the tone of a man trying to share an unspoken forewarning. Both of the hostages ate the food carefully and thoughtfully, finding comfort in the familiar taste. An empty bucket for waste was plunked down on the dirt floor through the open door, and as it slammed shut the lock was replaced with a distinctive "clack." Angela was dreading the coming dawn.

As the silence returned, so did the usual jungle sounds, again accompanied by the stampede of mosquitoes and tsetse flies looking for an evening meal. There was no way to avoid this rush, only to suffer and slap. The soft call of the night birds and the flutter of bats' wings were the only things that accented the orchestra of the nocturnal insects as they sought their evening blood snack.

"Lucas returned to his memories. He debated if he would be confined here now if he had taken his parents' advice in his younger years. After he was expelled from two private schools by the age of twelve, his parents, in desperation, had enrolled him in a military academy near Valley Forge. He opposed this institution with every cell in his young body and fought the older students' and administrations' disciplinary attempts routinely.

Military school produced two results; first, he managed to fail every subject, and second, he became an excellent physical combatant. He was not only the tallest member of his class, he daily worked fervently to develop his considerable muscular physique. This was the one activity he never failed to attend. There was no member of the entire academy, including the seniors, who would thoughtlessly antagonize him. He was dismissed from the academy at the age of thirteen, following his unsuccessful attempt to burn down a dormitory. This termination did not in any way disappoint him.

"Lucas, it's so hot and there's not a breath of a breeze," complained Angela, interrupting his train of thought.

Glancing at her silhouette as she reclined on the packed earth floor beneath the dim fractured moon light, Lucas felt a strong twinge of affection for the blonde woman sitting next to him. He gently put his arm around her shoulders and pulled her to his side, nuzzling her cheek and neck. Angela turned her face to his and kissed him fully on the mouth, surprising him. Genuine tenderness passed between them as she placed both arms around his neck and pulled him against her body. For a few seconds electricity replaced the fear she had been feeling.

"I'm not sure there will be any affection left in me after tomorrow, Lucas," she whispered, moving her entire body forward so that she was now fully against him. Her body's ability to respond to passion amidst the terror astonished her.

Her breath came in short gasps as she pulled away from his kiss. "Am I to place more importance on life or principles?" she choked. "If I don't voluntarily obey their orders, I can count on multiple forced violations, beatings, and then possible murder by those animal rebels."

Lucas silently agreed with Angela's evaluation of her situation. She had been dealing with these Angolan natives all her life and her assessment of tomorrow's probable outcome was realistic. To deny her evaluation would be foolish.

Continuing to gently kiss her lips and neck, he tried to soothe her. "The more I'm with you, the closer I feel to you, Angie.......
Maybe if we're able to get out of here and spend some time together.........." He whispered, after a short pause, "Angela, is life more important than dignity? Turn off your emotions tomorrow, if you can, and just comply. You'll still be the same to me no matter what happens tomorrow"

Angela began to sob quietly, "Who will ever want me after I've been used like that? No one will come near me. We both know HIV and other sexually transmitted diseases are almost universal in these troops."

Lucas had a dilemma. To advise Angela to refuse to obey the rebels' demands was to condemn her to violence and rape but there were few alternatives. To give her hope and encourage her to live, probably meant dishonor and disease for the remainder of her life if she survived the abuse. All of the other five women in captivity would face the same decision when morning arrived in the next hours.

"Try to rest, Angie. No matter what the decision, you will need strength tomorrow."

Lucas knew that she would not sleep, but perhaps a solution would present itself in the morning. There would be a better chance of survival if she were alert. He laid his head on the packed earth, but sleep eluded him. Thoughts of the past continued to drift through his mind.

Lucas could still clearly remember that May afternoon when he had to face his angry father. He had stood in his father's elegant executive office with the constable in charge of juvenile delinquency at his side, threatening to send him to reform school. Lucas' father had made a sizable contribution to the private military academy Lucas had been attending, so all criminal charges for arson had been dropped. However, the officer told his dad that if Lucas was arrested again he would certainly face reform school.

After his father had thanked and dismissed the official, Lucas had remained in his father's office trying not to contemplate what his dad would do next. He had indicated that the young miscreant should sit in one of the luxuriant leather chairs in front of the desk. Mr. Stuart had then said, "Lucas, what do we do now? Your grades are failing, you are a disciplinary nightmare, and nothing seems to interest you. In a few years, you'll be too old for further education and you'll end up in prison. I won't spend the rest of my life paying for you to avoid trouble. The school did that IQ test last year, so we know you *are* capable of doing the work."

Lucas sat quietly in that extravagant chair and thought. He knew that he would never be able to put up with a confined school. With his mother and father always traveling, it seemed hopeless to try to succeed in school, and who really cared anyway? Not him, and certainly not the servants who were paid to look after him, they wouldn't dare to punish him. The solution lay somewhere.

A bolt of inspiration hit him as he sat there in front of his grim father. The answer was at the farm his family owned in the northwestern hills of South Carolina, where he was free to run without all the confinement. Some of his happiest days had been spent during his summer vacations. Lucas thought that on the farm he would be under less supervision, rules and discipline.

"Why not send me to the farm, Dad? I'll get away from my reputation and I won't have to attend those stuck up private schools," Lucas returned.

By this point, Dad was willing to listen to almost any suggestion. Mom remained primarily interested in the social register and cocktail parties, so whatever they decided she wouldn't object to *any* arrangements her husband made. Furthermore, his parents were due to leave for Amsterdam in a few days, and they had made no plans to take Lucas along.

His dad had said "Schooling in South Carolina would be at the public county school. You've already failed at the private institutions; perhaps a little humility would motivate you." His father's thought continued, "We'll take any port in a storm…We can make final plans before September, and in the meantime, the ranch caretakers can look after you."

At this time, the Stuart's farm was supervised by Sally and Earl Morris, who had three older sons. The thought of Lucas staying in a rural environment appealed to his dad and seemed a tangible solution to the crisis, for the summer, anyway.

"If I can live on the farm I'll be outside in the fresh air with the animals and I won't have to live in town and go to stuffy parties." Lucas had thought.

Out loud Dad said, "Fine. You fly tomorrow to Greenville. I'll call the Morris's, and they'll meet you at the airport. We need the Learjet to travel on Tuesday, so this will work out nicely."

Sitting in the remote jungle cage, facing almost certain degradation or worse, Lucas realized that the one decision, to go to the farm, had completely changed his life forever. Whatever happened in his life from that point onward was mostly the result of the Morris's influence. They were straightforward, basic country people, uneducated by city standards, but deeply religious in thought and deed.

The Morris's three sons were all older and stronger than Lucas, whom he had learned from previous visits that he could neither whip nor intimidate. While they worked for Lucas' father, when he stayed there previously Lucas had not been exempted from hauling hay and mucking manure with the rest of the boys. Every evening after supper, the four boys played football with the other neighbor's sons who lived on nearby farms. Lucas had learned that he could compete at the same level in strength and speed as these farm lads. More importantly, he learned to love football.

"Aren't you asleep?" he asked Angela in a quiet tone as she sat up in their dusky, unlit cage and began to try to smooth out her rumpled scrub suit. This gesture tugged at Lucas, so hopeless was the effort, yet so feminine amidst the surrounding squalor.

The prisoners had no way to accurately determine the time of day. All of their watches had been confiscated after their capture and only the moon gave its dim light through the clouds making time seem to pass like thick sugar cane syrup dripping from an earthen jar. Finally a soft glow appeared in the Eastern sky, anticipating the arrival of morning, but Lucas presumed that all of the hostages were already awake, anticipating the coming events of the day. They knew that this dawn would be a tragic one, as the information that Angela overheard had been passed along to the non-Kileta-speaking whites. Lucas could almost feel the hopelessness emanating from the occupants of the cages, it was so dense.

Sitting up, Lucas put his arm tightly around Angela's shoulder to reassure her, and he kissed her gently on the mouth to confirm his affection for her, despite her coming degradation. Her soiled, wrinkled clothes still got between them as they embraced, but he was a bit less surprised now when she kissed him gently back.

"I don't want to die," Angela murmured, "Jesus is my Lord and Savior, so death doesn't scare me, but I'll lose all those years of a productive life." Speaking into his ear with sobbing breaths, and tears running down her stained face she continued "Will you still want me after they take me today?"

Lucas felt her supple body as he pressed her soft breasts against his chest. Kissing her on the neck and ear he mumbled, "Angie, our future relationship won't be based on what happens today. I admire what you are, not where you've been. Just stay alive so we can work things out together."

The crunching sound of approaching footsteps on the gravel in front of the cage interrupted their conversation. Biro's face appeared at the cage door. In his hand was a rusty bucket containing two small, green, porcelain bowls of the staple white corn porridge, this time with beans mixed into the sludgy white consistency. On the side of the bowl was a thin slice of rough barley bread, similar to what Lucas had seen in the local stores reserved for the poorest natives. Residing on top of each piece of bread was an irregular glob of lard. An old rust-encrusted mug of warm tea had been deposited on top the sticky mess in each bowl. Lucas found when he picked it up that the liquid had long since turned cold.

"Eat. We'll be back after dawn," remarked Biro in his African-accented English. He turned and proceeded to the neighboring cages to distribute breakfast to the others.

The entire meal reminded Lucas of the food rations he had seen fed to his servants' *kiase*s, or shacks when he was living in Malawi. Angela looked the meal over, and observed, "A pretty decent breakfast for condemned prisoners. No goat meat, but I'd wager that the rebel troops don't eat much better than this."

Drying her face with her sleeve and wiping her hands on her soiled pants, Angela began to eat slowly. As she had watched the African natives' custom since childhood, she used her finger to spread the lard thinly over her bread. Then, she used her other hand deftly to scoop the gruel onto the bread and deposit the combination into her mouth. Lucas followed her example. The taste was not pleasing and the rough bread irritated his tongue, but he was ravenous and grateful for any nourishment. The tea was cold and unsweetened, but effectively washed the contents of his mouth down his throat and into his stomach.

Having finished the sparse meal, Angela and Lucas sat on the packed mud and watched the orange glow in the eastern sky gradually turn into a golden ball as the sun appeared. Morning was upon them and no workable plan was in hand to escape. Exhausted from the sleepless night, and not wanting to think about the coming day, Angela asked, "Lucas, why did you become a surgeon?"

Thinking for a minute, Lucas replied, "It's a long story."

Then he realized that if he could divert Angel's attention for even ten minutes, it would keep her mind from contemplating the anticipated disastrous events of the day.

So, he continued, "Well, in the northwestern hills of South Carolina, I guess, is really where it all started, Angela." He went on to describe the circumstances of his move to the farm, telling her all about the Morrises and his problems as a younger boy, as well as that his family owned a large cattle ranch in the rolling green hills of the Appalachian foothills.

"Most of those remote areas of South Carolina are filled by pine trees and fertile pastures. I spent the next four years there, attending a county high school, working the farm and playing football. It was the first time that I had a chance to learn a little about life. The Morris family took me in and I maintained a high enough grade average in high school to stay eligible to play foot-ball," he continued.

"It doesn't sound as if you were an intellectual giant in those days," said Angela smiling.

Lucas felt he was succeeding in diverting Angela's attention from the now brightening daylight, so he returned to the dia-logue. "You got that right, Angela," he said, laughing. "My par-ents made me apply for admission to every Ivy League school in the country before high school graduation. They all turned me down even though I didn't need scholarship money. My father had insisted that I should at least try to get into a top-rated college."

Now becoming more interested, Angela asked, "But when you sent your resume to the Lubalo mission, applying to come to Angola, it said that you attended Cornell University for four years of college. How did that happen?"

"Oh, that's another story Angie. Do you really want to hear it?"

"I have no pressing plans in the next ten minutes, Lucas, so is there a reason that it's a secret?"

Lucas was not used to telling anyone about himself. He was embarrassed to tell her the whole story. On the other hand, full daylight was approaching and he realized that talking was help-ing him to relax, too.

"Well, I might not have been the greatest brain in the school, but I could play football and was awarded the All-State Linebacker Award for South Carolina in my senior year of high school. Football scholarship offers arrived from everywhere, but my parents wouldn't let me accept any of them. Dad said that if anyone accepts an athletic scholarship the coach owns him and that he could easily cough up the tuition rather than have that happen."

Angela looked at him closely, saying, "So how did you get into Cornell?"

"In America, football is a big money sport for the collages. Major funds come in from the alumni and from game atten-dance, sort of like soccer is here in Africa. I accepted admission to another West Coast school, without a scholarship, and planned to attend that school and play football for them. Two days before leaving for California there was this phone call from the football coach at Cornell. It seemed that their middle linebacker had broken his leg on the first day of practice, and the coach had no good linebackers and no more athletic scholarships either. He asked if I would like to attend Cornell. After telling him that his school had already refused my admission due to my low SAT score and low grades, he told me to send an application to *him* personally. So, I did. He called back a few days later, saying football practice was at 9:00 the next morning and to be there with my tuition check for the bursar. That's how I got admitted to an Ivy League university. I guess the Lord was looking out for me after all."

Suddenly, the sounds of automatic gunfire could be heard faintly coming from the south. The intensity escalated rapidly as the staccato sounds increased in volume and number. The fighting was coming towards the hospital compound as the Peoples Socialist government troops advanced from the south. Soon the noise was emanating from within a few hundred yards of the cages and had inflated to the point that verbal communication was impossible. Lucas observed the frightened prisoners in the cages finding space flat on the packed mud floor as they prayed for deliverance from their captivity at the hands of Savimbi's Nationalist rebels. This was not to be.

The noise of the rebels; gunfire response surged from the bunkers that had been dug around the perimeters of the hospital grounds as the rebels began to hold their ground and then advance. The Angolan government troops fell back into the foliage, retreating with heavy exchange fire. The rebels now had reinforcements arriving, but Lucas could not see from his prison exactly from where they came.

Lucas and Angela could see the flood of rebel troops as they advanced, using heavy artillery and other vehicles. The reinforcements moved toward the conflict to assist the dug in rebels' stubborn stand in the trenches. Some of these vehicles displayed faded white stars, the military hardware having come from articles of the USA military. The whole battle lasted less than an hour. Both revolutionary and government casualties lay strewn on the hospital grounds; many of these men were moaning and crying out in agony. From his limited view within the pen, Lucas could see that some of the combatants' wounds were quite serious. Whatever plans the rebels had for the prisoners would not be carried out today. The hostages remained in their pens, feeling, at least temporarily, safe as they had a front seat view of the battle. On the other hand, any chance that the government soldiers might help them faded with their retreat.

"Angela, it appears to be over for a few minutes." breathed Lucas with his arm over her shoulder.

As the rebel guerrilla forces regained lost territory, and advanced to the South, the sounds of the battle became less distinct and the noise of the conflict faded in that direction. Those rebel combatants left behind appeared to be wounded or logistics personnel. An occasional 'boom' was heard as their artillery came into the battle, but with the retreat of the government troops hope for relief from their situation also disappeared.

"I guess that I'm okay, Lucas," answered Angela. "The noise during the fighting was appalling...and all those dead and wounded soldiers we saw! What about you? Are you okay?"

The roar of conflict gone, upon standing in his cage Lucas could see unfamiliar soldiers sitting or lying in various positions on the gravel driveway in front of the prisoners' pens. They had propped themselves up or were sitting on ammunition boxes, fence posts, and fallen trees with missing limbs or other serious injuries. Those still able to move smoked cigarettes or drank from canteens. It appeared to Lucas that most of these troops, from both sides of the conflict, had been left behind due to serious wounds. There was little talk, as most of the active soldiers had continued the fight, moving South with the advance.

As he stood, Lucas pushed on the cage door, saying "Perhaps the Lord has let us survive for another day, Angela." He found the door still tightly secured. No random shots had damaged the pen. Disappointed, he carefully tested the rest of the walls of the pen, finding no damage which he could exploit for their escape.

Suddenly, Manabe, standing next to their pen, remarked, "I see you are still here, safe and undisturbed. The colonel will be most pleased that all of you prisoners are here waiting for him when he returns," the guard said sarcastically.

Turning, Lucas remarked, "Not wounded in the firefight, Manabe? How are the other captives?"

Manabe smiled a broad menacing grin and said, "All of you are safe. By tomorrow, when we are reorganized, we will find things for you to do."

His implication was obvious. Angela, however, realized that Manabe had inadvertently informed Lucas that the recent battle had bought the hostages a few precious hours to try to work out a plan for escape. After Manabe walked away, she whispered to Lucas, "Thank God all of us are safe for the time being. What sort of plan do you have in mind?"

Lucas, wanting no one to overhear their conversation about escape, realized that he had only a brief outline in mind. He decided to delay the discussion. Putting a finger to his lips so Angela would know to change the subject, he said, "Now Angie, where was I in our discussion of how I became a surgeon?"

Understanding Lucas' message immediately, Angela replied, "I think you were telling me about your university schooling and how you got admitted."

As he picked up his previous story, Lucas continued to relate his arrival from rural South Carolina at the prestigious Ivy League school in Ithaca, New York. He had been the last member of the football team to arrive that August, as pre-season football camp had begun three days earlier. Upon suiting up and walking out onto the practice field for his first morning session, the other players recognized the 'newbie'. He immediately received the usual derision and ridicule reserved for all freshmen players, especially those from the rural south.

"So this is the hick from the sticks! I'm surprised he could even find the football field. Shall we introduce our new hayseed middle linebacker to what a football looks like?" sneered one of the 'high class' cornerbacks from New York City.

Lucas explained to Angela that any experienced football player is fully aware that the middle linebacker is supposed to be the meanest, toughest son-of-a bitch on the team. Lucas immediately recognized that intimidation was the name of the game here. Without a word, he had walked over to the offending cornerback and hit him in the mouth as hard as he could. The fight that resulted lasted for ten minutes until the coaches and players broke it up, but no one on that team ever openly taunted Lucas again.

"I made my point and ended up rooming with that cornerback, another cornerback, and the strong safety for the next few years. They were all extremely intelligent and motivated, which I guess rubbed off on me. We became the best of friends and studied daily together," he remarked.

"As all four of us were from wealthy families, and *any* attempt at serious study while living in a fraternity is next to impossible, we rented a farm near the campus and lived together. When it came time to sign up for classes, the other three enrolled in pre-med courses so I did too, in my naïve ignorance."

He had learned how and what to study from his roommates and graduated near the top of the class, still the starting linebacker for all four years.

"I don't understand anything about American football," said Angela. "They only play rugby in Africa. What did you do in your spare time? Didn't you have a serious girlfriend while you were at the university?"

Lucas decided to try to ignore the question. It was now approaching noon and the rapidly rising temperatures generated the acrid smell of dead and decaying flesh as well as blood from the putrefying bodies throughout the compound. Even though the smell was familiar to Lucas and Angela, the odor of so much dead flesh was exceptionally strong, permeating the entire area. They could see Brightwell and Doctor Maria in the next cage, through the trampled brush, covering their noses with cloths to dispel the fetid stench, their eyes weeping from the aroma.

"Lunch is served, *ver stoots*" (Such as it is) remarked Biro, his voice tangy with something close to sympathetic sarcasm as he produced a bowl of unrecognizable mush for each of the prisoners. "Eat it, *kurumisa cheti*," (finish it all quickly) he said, telling them that the rebels had found no other food available.

When he had left, Lucas said in an anxious voice, "Angela! Biro speaks Shona. He must have lived in Rhodesia or Zambia to know that language. He may know people *we* know. We must find out more about him, he may be the one to help us escape."

The bowl contained a large amount of what appeared to be some sort of cold corn-meal mixed with *rape*. The cup of liquid accompanying this offering was supposed to be water, but the acetic smell of the contents told Angela that the solution possibly came from the blood-polluted waters of the Lubalo River. The strong temptation was to throw it all out, untouched.

"You must eat whatever calories you can," suggested Lucas in a loud enough voice to carry to the other hostages. "We need to keep our energy up for later trials."

What the food lacked in flavor, it made up in volume. Lucas looked at Manabe and Biro, who he could see standing nearby, around the treeless clearing in front of the cages talking to a few of the soldiers evidently wounded from this mornings' firefight. He watched as each soldier devoured with relish the same food that he and Angela had been given. He decided that if the soldiers could eat it, so could he.

The drinking water supplied to the hostages was a different matter. Most of the rivers in northern Angola drained to the north and ultimately on into Zaire. These waters originate from the hills in central Angola and are normally safe to drink after boiling, to kill the myriad of contaminating parasites, such as typhoid or cholera. The Lubalo River, which flows north near the mission, was this type of waterway, with its source near Quelele, a settlement some 75 kilometers to the south. Lucas had traveled to this settlement by Land Rover a month ago from the Lubalo Mission to treat a sick native missionary. The thin mud track followed the course of the river, but the road was almost impassable due to ditches and deep holes. A Kongo tribesman had arrived at the Lubalo mission by foot, seeking help for his invalid grandmother, a Sunday school teacher in Quelele. Without this tribesman's guidance, Lucas would have had great difficulty reaching her.

The cloudy liquid that she observed in their cups confirmed Angela's suspicion of gross pollution by mud and blood from the fighting, which now altered the crystal clear waters of the Lubalo River. Having no means to boil the fluid, the hostages were forced to choose between drinking the water without sterilization or to parch. Either of the choices was risky and most, finally, did drink it.

"I don't see Retread around," remarked Angela in Kileta to Biro as he stood near their cage. "He has been one of our normal three guards since we were captured. Has he been sent away?"

Biro glanced up from his meal and mumbled in a low voice, "Retread has gone to meet his ancestors. He fought bravely and died. His parents will receive him into heaven with glad celebration."

Having finished their meal, the guards moved away from the cages into the shade, some fifty meters from Lucas and Angela. The captives could now speak quietly without being overheard.

"If we don't do something, tomorrow we'll be sent to slave labor and prostitution," whispered Angela. "Do you have a plan?"

"The Lubalo River flows north from here into Zaire and then joins the Kwilu River, which continues further north on to Kikwit, a major town where I have some friends. The entire territory that the river flows through is desolate brush country, and from what I've been told it might be possible to successfully navigate the river by boat. My estimate of the distance is almost 250 kilometers of deprivation, but it might be better than months of slavery or being used by the soldiers. We would be moving with the current, so floating would be little work. What do you think?"

Angela was desperate, but a trip of this magnitude in their physical condition sounded ridiculous. Looking skeptically at Lucas, she whispered, "And how do we get everyone out of their pens, and what boat do we use?"

Lucas elaborated on his idea to clarify it to Angela and also to focus it better in his own mind. After a moment's pause, he suggested, "If one of the guards, possibly Biro, can be asked to consider helping us by opening our cages, we can make a run for it. There's no way by land we'd have even a remote chance of avoiding recapture, if they were looking for us. A vehicle wouldn't be of much use, as they'd find us immediately on the roads or tracks, so it would have to be overland on foot, which would be difficult in the dark.

Angela knew that Lucas was right about there not being a chance on land. The rebel guards seemed to control the roads and tracks for miles, and with the fighting the escapees wouldn't even know which direction to run.

"How do we find a boat even if we do get out?" she inquired, still not convinced. Continuing she said, "You and I might make it 250 kilometers downriver, but those American missionaries will never survive a trip like that."

Lucas said that he knew where to obtain a fishing boat large enough to hold the twelve captives; he had seen it anchored at least ten kilometers downstream from the Lubalo Mission a week ago at the town of Lubalo. Even if they managed to escape and travel by foot that far, there was no guarantee that the boat had not been moved. He surmised that there was no way, in their dehydrated and starved condition, that some of the other hostages could travel by foot through the dense brush for that distance. To attempt to travel the roads by foot would mean certain recapture.

Lucas said to Angela, "Okay, too many intangibles in the plan…but it won't hurt to try to make friends with Biro. Maybe we can come up with another plan that involves him."

It was in the early afternoon now, and the intense heat of the day was being felt all over the mission station. Every afternoon all living creatures attempted to get out of the sun to find shade and avoid its burning glare. The distinctive crunch of footsteps on gravel could be heard advancing from the mission living quarters below. The missionary dormitories had been serving as the rebels' barracks. While Lucas and Angela were unable to see the persons walking towards the pens from the barracks, they could now recognize their voices easily.

The colonel was saying, "Our soldiers have fought well in the last few days and deserve some recreation. The general has reluctantly given permission to take the two white women out and bring them to the soldiers' day room now."

Lucas and Angela were surprised to hear the sounds of the cage lock being opened, followed by the loud objections from Gayle as a rough rope was placed around her neck. "Take that rope off of my neck! I won't follow you anywhere! Ouch!"

"I really thought we'd all be safe for a day or two," Angela whispered.

Gayle was heard as she was forcibly led from her enclosure toward the mission dormitories, struggling by dragging her feet to resist the persistent pull of the rough rope and loudly gagging as it tightened around her neck. Esther, evidently following quietly, was resigned to a similar catastrophic fate. Not being able to see where the two terrified women were being taken, the worst fears of the ten remaining prisoners were confirmed by the screams and pleading that resounded a short time later from the direction of the troops' living quarters. This turmoil was followed by complete silence over the compound. All of the other captives silently prayed, bending their heads towards the mud floors of the pens, the women hoping that a similar fate would not await them in the near future.

The sounds of dragging, halting footsteps on the gravel were heard later after dusk, as the women were led back to their prison pens. Evidently, Manabe and Biro were not directly involved in this gross violation of the missionaries, as they had been ordered to remain in the area of the pens, guarding the other prisoners throughout the two ladies' ordeal. The closing of the pen doors was seen clearly from Brightwell's enclosure as the ladies were roughly thrown on the hut floor by their guards.

"Brightwell, can you see Sister Gayle or Sister Esther?" Angela softly called when the guards had left. The foliage still blocked her view in the gathering dusk.

A face appeared dimly through the failing light at the bars of the adjoining cage. He was no longer smiling. Angela could see that tears were falling from his chin and dripping onto his scrub shirt. Opening his mouth, Brightwell let out a soft moan. Trying to suppress his choking sobs, he answered, "Sister Angela?…they have destroyed them…Sister Esther is alive and barely moving, but Sister Gayle is either unconscious or dead. I can't tell from here. The reverend was left in the pen and is now trying to help them."

Pausing to regain control of his emotions, he continued, "We must pray for the sisters and ask God to forgive these soldiers. It will be difficult."

Lucas felt the urgency to escape. The strategy to sneak away down the river was implausible, but Angela must be saved from violation. They had to either get the help of a guard or force their way out. Lucas felt that if all of them were to escape, including Esther and Gayle in their present condition, his previous river plan was not going to suffice. Without access outside of their cages tonight, tomorrow would surely bring a repeat of today's nightmare that they all dreaded. Today's terrible tragedy had guaranteed tomorrow's disaster.

After a brief discussion, Lucas and Angela agreed that any possible negotiations with the guards would have a better chance of success if Angela initiated the discussion.

First, she spoke their language fluently and would understand the nuances of the Kileta dialect. Second, because she was a woman, the guards with wives and daughters might be more likely to agree to betray their own troops out of sympathy for her, and their previous acquaintance of her mother. Protection of women and children was traditional in the native custom, but rarely for non-family members.

Later that evening, Angela could make out Manaba in the bright beams of moonlight distributed widely across the loading space. The guard was leaning against his rifle and calmly smoking a cigarette as darkness enclosed the compound. Biro was not in sight. No Biro was a bad omen, as he and his family had spent much time on the Saurimo Mission. Their hopes had been with Biro.

"Manaba! Could you please come over here for a second?" Angela requested this using the Kileta colloquial dialect that she had recently discovered was his home language.

Manaba, picking up his rifle, casually ambled over to the pen in which Angela was imprisoned. Looking her directly in the eyes, he asked, "Are you ready for tomorrow?" He said this with a sly anticipatory tone in his voice. His expression carried not a trace of sympathy for the plight of the captives. Lucas noted his attitude and felt little encouragement.

Angela ignored the question. "Manabe, that was uncivilized treatment by your soldier friends today for the two American ladies. Did you see their horrible condition when they were brought back to the pens? What if those American women had been your wife or daughter, how would *you* feel now?"

Without emotion, Manabe looked at Angela and in a dead, flat tone remarked,

"My wife and two daughters were slaughtered by the government troops, for no reason, a few months ago. This happened while these troops were invading our homes. You missionary people think that we Angolans need to hear the words from the Bible of peace and love. Perhaps you should have started by telling your government friends about Jesus."

This statement brought Angela to a staggering halt in the conversation. She had heard about the government troops' needless sacrifice and rape of the rebel troops' families out in the bush, but never actually met someone this close to the massacre.

After a moment Angela went on, "We are terribly sorry for your family's demise, but that is no reason to subject *our* men and women to rape and torture. Can you not see that we are neutral in the conflict and only hope to bring medicines and teaching to your people?"

Manabe began to walk away, and as he looked down the short path towards the clearing, he said, "I don't make decisions on captive treatment, only the colonel has that authority. For my part, I think all of you deserve torture as foreign intruders. All of the soldiers look forward to seeing you in the morning."

With this final remark, all hope of salvation in the minds of Angela and Lucas, died.

# 3
## Chapter

*A*s darkness enveloped the missionary compound, food was distributed once again to the prisoners The meals remained the same as what the rebel fighting forces ate; corn gruel (*sadza*), lard on barley bread and tepid, weak tea. Cassava root appeared occasionally in the evening for variety.

When she had finished her food, Angela moved to the side of her cage and called softly, "Brightwell, are there any developments in the reverend's cage? Can you tell if Gayle survived?"

No response was heard for about five minutes. Finally, the familiar, dark outline of a head appeared at the bars. "Missie Angela," Brightwell responded, "The reverend reports that both ladies are alive. Gayle was badly misused and is wishing to die. Esther is bleeding from her rectum and is in severe pain. So far, the reverend has been left alone but he is unable to stop her bleeding. How should I advise him?"

Lucas stepped to the cage corner and said, "Have both ladies lie down and remain as quiet as possible. There is little we can do from here. Tomorrow this torture may well start again. Try to get some food and tea into their stomachs. We will pray for all of you."

Angela sat limply on the floor of their hut and sobbed, "I'll be like that tomorrow night. Why shouldn't I try to run when they come for me and just let them shoot me in the back? No pain and no torture. Then I'd be in heaven with Jesus, and not bleeding and in pain," she concluded with a sigh of resignation.

Lucas sympathized with Angela's desire to avoid trauma. The thought of her having to suffer the same degradation and physical pain tomorrow that Esther and Gayle had endured today was more than she could contemplate. But what were her choices?

"Angela," he said, taking her into his arms and kissing her wet cheeks, "We don't know what plans the Lord has for us here in the jungle. In Roman times, many Christians were fed to the lions in the coliseum for the mob's entertainment, but eventually all of the Roman Empire was converted to Christianity and that barbarism was put to an end. We don't know His purpose, but we must bravely walk down whatever path Jesus puts us on."

This was little comfort to Angela. "I still face those filthy soldiers putting their hands all over my body in the morning. When my husband was alive we made such soft, sweet love but he was taken from me. And now I have to put up with rape and sodomy? I'd much rather die intact than end up like Gayle or Esther."

Lucas knew that Angela had been widowed only a few years earlier and now had determined to let the insurgents kill her rather than violate her body. Knowing this, he vowed that he would try to change her mind. While this forfeiture might be brave, it would serve little purpose in the long term. The vision that they might have a future together tied him closer to her with each passing day, as they survived in that small cage, slowly becoming interdependent, both emotionally and physically. Over the last twenty-four hours that they had been caged together, he had gained admiration, respect, and appreciation for her. He also felt desire. It was difficult to believe that one could experience these profound emotions while locked in a cage, but Lucas felt that there must be a reason they were here together, just as there was a reason for everything else that God allowed.

He was not prepared to lose her and regret it for the rest of his life, even under these terrible conditions; they must not abandon all hope for deliverance.

"Don't give up hope, Angie. At least wait and see what happens in the morning," Lucas counseled. He had difficulty trying to express the words he wanted to say, as he looked deeply into her porcelain blue eyes, but he knew that she heard his mind saying "Please don't destroy yourself now…I think that I may be falling in love with you…"

Lucas was surprised at his developing vulnerability for Angela. He rarely made any decisions in life or medicine without first carefully considering all of the ramifications. Here he was in a pen with a woman he had known for only a short time, thinking that he might be falling in love with her. He feared that the starvation and pressure must be getting to him.

"Hold me…just hold me tight!" said Angela, turning to Lucas and putting her arms tightly around his neck.

They remained embracing for some minutes, desire surpassing the miasma of misery and desperation. Reality eventually prevailed. After a while, they sat together talking calmly as the night darkened around them. Angela did not change her mind, determined to die rather than suffer the fate of the other two women missionaries. Their talk drifted to other subjects. He began to tell about himself, which he rarely did, not anticipating the question Angela finally asked: "Lucas, tell me about the women in your life since then. Why did you never marry?"

At this point, Lucas wanted to discuss anything with Angela but his past love life. Normally he wouldn't have told her anything and would have changed the subject, but perhaps she would die tomorrow and if she knew more of his past life she would feel like she knew him better; so he said, "Angela, back many years ago, in college, I was so busy playing football and studying that I had little time for social activities," "Don't give me a story! Tell the truth," said Angela smiling. "Who was she? Come on, I know you must have had at least one steady girlfriend in college!"

His face flushed, "Oh, I met this girl from Skidmore College at a Christmas party. Her parents had invited my Mom and Dad, during my junior year, so I came too. Her name was Patricia and her father was the C.E.O. of U.S. Steel, in Pittsburgh, a major city in Pennsylvania. She was a sophomore and planned to spend her junior year studying to speak French in Paris. Some sort of program with a university in Paris linked to Skidmore. Anyway, our parents were socially familiar and we had many common friends so it seemed that we were compatible. We both had cars and eventually almost every weekend that spring, one would drive the 150 miles to see the other."

"Sounds like it was serious, Lucas. Did you fall in love with her?" asked Angela.

"No, the next year she was off to Paris and found some smooth French guy to fall in love with. I never saw her after that. Do you really want to hear all this?"

"Come on, Lucas. I want to know the whole tale. It makes sense that you would like a girl like that in college."

Now that he had begun, Lucas felt that he had to continue the story, trying to leave out many gory details, despite Angela's persistent questions. "By the time medical school came around, I was busy working in hospitals, and from then to now, almost every girl I dated was a nurse. In fact, it's been very unusual for me to be attracted to *any* women other than operating room scrub nurses. There have been women since Patricia, but only one serious relationship."

Angela now smiled, her mind fully occupied by his narrative. "I'll wager there were a few of them, Lucas. I'm a scrub nurse and my husband was a General Surgeon before he died. He also had an interest in missions. We were only married for a few years, so we had little time together because he had to work almost every night trying to care for his patients. I know how it goes with surgeons and scrub nurses; much of the time we *did* have together had to be spent trying to catch up on our sleep. I think the Cerebral Malaria would not have killed him if he had rested properly. I was devastated at his dying at only thirty-five. The past few years, since he passed away, I've really missed the companionship and affection we shared."

Her remark resonated with Lucas, as he always felt comfortable with scrubs. They seemed to fully understand the pressures and life style of surgeons, as well as most surgeons' overt sexual drive. Scrub nurses were always available as companions for any adventure. Angela's relationship with her husband brought up a deep response in his soul, causing him to be drawn closer to her.

"So who was the lucky girl to marry you, was it a scrub nurse? After all that, there had to be someone!"

Telling Angela any more was painful to Lucas. He didn't consider himself a sensitive guy, but those memories still stirred up anguish in his gut. Angela was insisting on invasion of an area of his life that he never discussed with anyone.

Sensing this pause, Angela knew instinctively that any further dialogue was not going to be easy for him. Sitting next to him, feeling sweaty and dirty with those pesky insects everywhere, Angela felt closer to Lucas than she had to anyone since her husband's death. She gently put her hand in his and looked directly into his face.

"If it hurts to tell me, you don't have to, but knowing of your heartache will make us closer." She then softly kissed him on the mouth while squeezing his hand.

Any physical contact between prisoners had been forbidden by the guards as just another way to make the missionaries feel more isolated. Kissing and fondling were not likely to occur in open view anyway. Nevertheless, Lucas reacted immediately to her caress. Perhaps he was losing it but he felt that he wanted Angela with more intensity than he had ever felt before. Sexual feelings seemed to multiply in captivity to offset the feelings of isolation and loss of emotional dependence. Then his mind reverted to the present moment.

Lucas knew that it would be diplomatic to minimize to Angela anything he told her about previous female relationships but if he did, he felt now that she might understand what he meant. His feelings of wanting to be close to Angela outweighed his fear of her perception of his past. This reassured Lucas, and gently stroking her hand he said, "When I was in residency, there was a scrub nurse named Joanne. She was about twenty years old, and we worked together from time to time, eventually getting to know each other fairly well. She was a beautiful, short-haired blonde with porcelain blue eyes...but not at all flashy. One afternoon, after a six-hour operation, we were both exhausted and she invited me over to eat supper at her apartment. Long story short, we started dating steadily."

'What's going on in there?" Biro's rough tone interrupted their conversation. The guard went on, "She's going to see all of the affection she'll ever need tomorrow. Shut up and go to sleep!" Pausing for the guard to walk on past their pen, Angela picked up the conversation about Joanne. Giving him a knowing smile, she said,

"Joanne attracted you only by the cooking, I suppose?"

Lucas knew Angela was kidding, but he felt the need somehow to be honest with her. They were on the same wavelength and he did not want the trend to break. In a lower tone, he continued, "Not only was she beautiful, but a sexual dynamo. Could go on and on for hours in the evening, and want more the next morning. I had never met anyone like her before. Heck, she routinely had sequential orgasms. That girl could sense when I wanted her and was always ready, totally uninhibited, and our relationship made the other residents in the hospital jealous."

"So what happened? It sounds as if two were meant for each other."

Lucas took a deep breath and continued, "First of all, she *was* an excellent surgical assistant technically, and knew what was going on during any case, could anticipate any complication, and was always prepared for an emergency. Nothing rattled her during a surgical procedure if anything *surgically* went amiss, a real joy to scrub with. So, we were more than sexually compatible, she enjoyed the same music and athletic activities I did, her Christian beliefs paralleled mine and she was interested in mission work. We lived together for over three years. *But* she had one monstrous psychological hang-up."

"What separated you, since the conditions were so good? Did you want to marry her?" interjected Angela.

"I *was* in love with her and she with me, but we never married," sighed Lucas after a pause. "She had one defect that I thought at first was minimal, but eventually separated us. Although she had many excellent qualities, she had an explosive temper. We could be in the middle of a surgical case, and Joanne would ask for an instrument that the technician didn't have on the table. The tech would have to ask the circulator to go and fetch it. That was fine with me, but not Joanne. She would pitch a fit, screaming and swearing at the tech, calling her a 'stupid cow' or something like that, and dump the rest of the instruments on the floor. Joanne would then order the poor tech out of the room and take over the tech's duties herself. The surgery would be faultless, but everyone not immediately needed would have found the exit. This didn't happen only in the operating room but in a store or at home. It could be over a minor thing or a major frustration. You just never knew when she would erupt. Ten minutes later, she was all butter and cream apologizing, but the damage had been done. Everyone was afraid of her, including me."

"It sounds as if she might have had a psychological problem, Lucas. So what did you do next?"

Lucas now had Angela's full attention, the following day's problems temporarily forgotten. "I thought that I was in love with her, but these tantrums really got to me. When my training was finished and the opportunity to work in the Malawi Mission came, she was set to go, too. I told her that I was going alone. The fit she had was the worst ever. Swearing like a chuck wagon driver, she called me every name she could think of and threw plates and stuff at me, breaking some of the windows in the house. You could say that our separation was somewhat 'turbulent', that was twelve years ago.

"She came to Africa once, a few months later, to try and patch things up. When she saw the Malawi mission hospital, she was appalled at the conditions and tried to convince me to return to America with her. I guess that might indicate that we weren't so compatible after all. She probably would have stayed, but I asked her to leave and she went home. We certainly could have used her *medical* talents…but on a mission…. with a vocabulary like that?"

"So do you still love her?"

"I don't really know. I've never felt a lot for anyone since then, until you."

In the gathering darkness Lucas wasn't sure he should reach for her, due to the guard's vigil on their pen. He hoped that his direct approach had affected her. This might not be the best time to exchange tender words or caresses, but with the anticipation of tomorrow's events, there might never be another opportunity. He didn't want her to face tomorrow's events without knowing the hope and love that he could give her.

Drained by the day's events, they both lay down after talking and slept fitfully for a few hours. They slept close to each other on the tattered, dirty blanket carpeting the mud floor of their enclosure. The sound of the door opening startled them to wakefulness. Biro reclaimed the waste bucket and replaced it with an empty one.

"Good morning," he said in a quiet tone, as the two prisoners sat up. "Dawn is coming and here is breakfast. Good luck to you both today."

He carelessly plopped the two bowls at the mud entrance, slopping gruel onto the blanket, and causing the tea to slosh into the food. The reddish-golden glow on the eastern horizon betrayed the darkness inside the enclosures. It was a beautiful dawn, and Lucas wondered if it was to be their last sunrise together.

A few minutes later, the approach of two guards was heralded by their loud voices as they progressed from pen to pen. "All men come out. Stand in a line on the gravel, and wear your shoes and head cover if you have them."

Lucas and Angela ate the meal as quickly as possible, unable to finish. The other captives had as little time to eat, also forfeiting any chance to finish their food. The men were being forced from their enclosures by guards, stumbling as they tried to walk on the gravel paths.

Each cage was opened and every man in the enclosure was ordered outside to stand on the gravel forecourt and wait. Lucas' turn came and he obeyed, standing quietly with the five other men. This was his first view of all four cages at once since his capture. As he left Angela, he whispered to her, "Just stay alive for me. We'll work it out together," before being roughly prodded by a bayonet point into line with the other men.

Lucas had a few minutes as he stood in line to try to examine the women remaining in the four cages. They were at least fifty meters away so he couldn't be sure, but all of the women but Gayle and Esther were standing up and trying to see what would happen to the men. He was able to make out Esther as she crouched on her knees. Her face was swollen and red, the shreds of her blood-stained skirt stuck to her knees and the upper half of the dress was badly torn. Gayle appeared to be lying prone at the bottom of the cage. He did see her move, so he was sure that she was at the least still alive. A groan emanated from Gayle, as he watched her attempt to sit up. It failed, and the moaning sound she made as she fell back down resounded in his gut. It summed up Lucas' total loss of hope. He guessed the other hostages felt the same.

A guard Lucas had never seen before pointed at the line of six hostages with his rifle, and screamed in almost indiscernible English, "Get moving! You are now slaves! If any of you attempts to escape, we will shoot all six of you useless scum."

Lucas glanced at the others as he stood in the line. They all appeared tired and dirty, but the reverend could barely stand and finally became semi-erect to a stooping position.

The guard had motioned the six terrified men to walk on the gravel path leading toward the hospital by waving his rifle in that direction. Lucas and the other five men shambled off in a ragged line, the reverend almost falling down. Lucas thought, as he was positioned at the back of the line, that the six of them probably made up the most scruffy, ragged, stumbling group of men he had seen. The reverend was having a hard time walking, so Lucas placed his hand under the reverend's armpit, lifting him into an upright position and helping him to keep up with the slow pace, as the group lurched on to the front lawn of the hospital. Each prisoner had at least one minor wound, and none had shaved for days.

As the front lawn of the hospital came into view, Lucas thought to himself that the scene that he saw was unique for depravity and neglect. He had been involved in wars and rebellions all over Africa, but he had never come across anything close to this setting.

In the dim light of dawn, Lucas could see the mission hospital and the previously well-kept green lawn surrounding it. To his left were the residence of the technicians and the nurses' dormitories, now used as living quarters by the rebel troops. His former house was out of sight behind the tall trees at the back of the dormitories. Situated on the entire foreground of the hospital were hundreds of makeshift cots and stretchers. Various uniform jackets and coats were being used as blankets for the disabled soldiers, lying in awkward positions, apparently totally unattended. Some were already dying, some with no dressings or bandages on their wounds, their open injuries exposed to the air and covered with flies and maggots. These soldiers were the veterans of the fierce firefight in the last few days. Their frayed and damaged uniforms showed allegiances to both sides of the conflict, equally left to suffer. No one appeared to be taking care of them and some were calling out for water or relief for their pain. There was total chaos.

*"There must be hundreds of wounded out here,"* thought Lucas. *"I've never seen people having to suffer so badly and totally abandoned."* Looking towards one of the guards, Lucas said aloud, in Kileta dialect, "Who is the commander of this unit?"

The guard, stiffened and said, "Our commander is General Missimo Honduro Alverez, the Supreme Commander for the Northern Angola Insurgent Military Unit."

The men were stopped by the guards from proceeding further, about halfway through the hospital grounds. From his position, Lucas was able to see into the front door of the mission hospital. What he observed confirmed his suspicions about the state of medical care being given. He saw beds and mattresses, with occupants randomly distributed in the hallways and rooms. The apparent lack of care and organization inside was similar to that out on the lawn. No IV solutions were apparent, and blood and feces littered the floors.

"I wonder where General Alverez is now?" asked Lucas in a casual voice, not wanting to sound disrespectful. As a "prisoner" he had no right to ask *any* questions about the situation. The soldier he spoke to might decide that retaliation from a bullet would answer him.

Poking Lucas so hard in the abdomen that he fell to the ground, the guard declared, "The Commander is here at the mission and will not tolerate any insolence from a prisoner like you!"

Now lying on the ground, Lucas held his gut in pain, but he was less hurt than he wanted the guard to believe. Lying there, Lucas could see another guard, a sergeant by his uniform insignias, hurrying from the front of the hospital past their location. He seemed in a panic as he appeared to be searching for someone or something. Breathing in rapid gushes, he stopped near where Lucas was slowly getting up. The exasperated sergeant, looking at the guard in charge of Lucas, asked in Kileta, "Have you seen the Commander? His first lieutenant is bleeding again and we are unable to control it. If his lieutenant dies, the General will be furious. We need medical help immediately."

Lucas' guard shrugged his shoulders, saying, "He's around here somewhere, but we haven't seen him this morning. Probably still in his bunk at this hour."

Lucas felt that this emergency had to be sent by Divine Providence. The circumstance of this soldier's hemorrhage occurring at the moment they happened to be in a location to hear it was not just chance. It was up to him to take advantage of this opening that had appeared at such a critical moment…but how to do it? He could not afford to appear disrespectful, yet he had to appear to be competent to save this man. "*The Lord has made a break for us*" he thought.

Standing up straight despite the remaining pain, Lucas took a chance and walked over towards the sergeant and guard, since the hostages were not restrained in chains as they stood waiting.

"Excuse me, sir. I couldn't help but overhear the officer's predicament." He spoke respectfully in Kileta. "It may be that we could help in this problem, as I am a surgeon experienced in the treatment of bleeding. May I assist you?"

Immediately, both insurgents turned and looked at Lucas. The guard, lowering his firearm, said with a sneer, "Get back in line with the other vermin or I'll teach you a lesson you'll remember."

The sergeant, putting his hand on the guard's rifle and pushing it away, said to Lucas, "Stay here for a minute. Don't move."

Then, looking at the guard, the officer said, "Let's talk for a minute. Walk over here." The two rebels walked a few steps away to speak in private. Lucas could hear the officer's voice as he spoke to the guard in a muted tone, but he was unable to discern what was being said.

Taking the guard by the arm, the sergeant said, "What do we have to lose? We have no doctor of our own, and the hostage may be able to save Lieutenant Makura. Either way, we win. If the lieutenant dies, it's the doctor's fault. If he lives, we saved him. There's little choice."

The guard responded in a loud voice that Lucas could easily hear, "No! This man is my responsibility! He is headed for slave labor today to fill burlap bags with sand, and no one is to interfere!"

The sergeant replied, still in a subdued tone, "Fine, I will tell the General that we found a doctor but you refused to let him save his lieutenant. What do you think will happen to you when the officer dies?"

The case was convincingly closed. Walking back toward Lucas, the sergeant said as he pointed to Lucas, **"You**, come with me."

The guard said in a threatening tone as Lucas walked towards the hospital with the officer, "He is no longer my responsibility. If he escapes, it is *you* who will answer for it!"

\* \* \*

The arrival of dawn had come slowly, brightening the surrounding vistas into early daylight. While Lucas was still being led to the bleeding lieutenant, the dawn illumination found Angela and the other female hostages alone in their pens, anticipating the worst. The men had been marched off to labor camp a few minutes earlier, but the women had, at least for now, been ignored.

*"Sometimes the waiting is worse than the event,"* Angela thought, dreading the crunching sound of footsteps on the gravel path. She guessed the time to be about seven o'clock. The warmth from the sun felt reassuring as it rose above the horizon but did not relieve her anxiety.

Looking out of her cage, Angela realized once again how really tranquil the picturesque, remote, African jungle could be at early daybreak. Trying to ignore her present circumstances, she thought back to her untroubled childhood days, living with her parents on the mission near Suarimo, only about a hundred kilometers south of her present location. War and rebellion had not interfered with her early life on that remote jungle mission. From birth, she had been isolated from conflict by living in one of the most remote areas of Angola with only nature, animals and the weather as primary concerns. Now as she sat in her prison pen she could see the soft pastel colors of the rising sun on the horizon as they blended into the white-hot heat she knew would envelop the compound by noon.

These thoughts and the beautiful sunrise brought back memories of her parents. Tears came to her eyes as she saw her mother's face in the mists of the past. Angela had played behind the mud school house from her earliest years, listening to her mother as she taught the natives about Christ and how to read and write, using the Bible as a text. Her father, who preached the gospel every Sunday from the front of the thatch-roofed church, had held Angela's full attention as she sat in the front row. Her mother's death from sleeping sickness, when Angela was only eight years old, had left a permanent scar on her heart. Often in the years after her mother died, when sleep eluded her, Angela would walk the half kilometer to a high hill near the mission early in the morning. Angela would sit on a mound and watch the sunrise, hoping that her mother was watching the same colors appear from heaven. She still dearly missed her mother.

\* \* \*

"Come along, doctor, or whatever you are," the sergeant said gruffly, as he pushed Lucas towards the front of the familiar hospital. "You'd better know what you're doing or I'll make your life a living nightmare."

They walked rapidly towards the hospital entrance, forced to detour around the many bodies cluttering the grass around the front porch. The other five male hostages were led by their guards into the shade of a large Jacaranda tree, its purple blossoms in full array, and ordered to sit and wait. The guards anticipated that Lucas would fail and they all would be returning to their former duties momentarily.

As he entered the hospital, Lucas was appalled at the changes he saw from the usually clean, well-kept front hallway. It was now littered with debris and wounded soldiers lying on mattresses. The sick and injured patients littering the wards appeared to have no organized care of any kind. The sergeant led Lucas through this chaos to one of the small rooms on the first floor, towards the back of the hospital. Inside lay two patients on beds and also two wounded soldiers stretched out on the floor. Neither patient on the floor had IV solutions or dressings on their injuries. Parts of uniforms, stained by blood and flesh, seemed to be strewn everywhere, next to used canteens and empty food trays. The sergeant led him through this litter to one of the beds where a young soldier lay on his back with a large neck wound. A grimy soldier wearing a green, blood-stained bandana around his head stood next to the bed, applying pressure with his hand on top of a cloth. His palm was grasping the throat of the wounded lieutenant in an attempt to control the blood that seeped around his fingers and onto the pillow. Lucas recognized the collar insignia of the soldier on the bed and assumed correctly that this was his patient.

The sergeant looked at the soldier holding the lieutenant's neck and said, "Jose, how is he doing? Can you stop the bleeding?"

"How long has he been bleeding like this?" asked Lucas in Kileta as he looked at Jose's hand, watching the blood ooze from the neck wound. Lucas noticed that the color of the seepage was bright red as it trickled over Jose's fingers.

"We had it stopped until just a few minutes ago. He rolled over and that started the blood coming again, He turned to Lucas. "The lieutenant is bleeding to death, can you help him?" he asked.

Walking to the bedside, Lucas put his hand on top of Jose's hand and indicated for Jose to remove the pressure. Immediately, blood began to squirt rhythmically from the lieutenant's throat, making the wounded officer begin to gag as the blood entered his trachea.

"*Yeah*", Lucas thought to himself. *"It's the left carotid artery alright! We need to get it controlled or he's a goner."* Lucas automatically began to assess the situation, as he calmly and deliberately applied pinpoint pressure on the pulsating artery with his left index finger, bringing the squirt to an immediate halt. "Give me your right index finger," Lucas said to Jose.

Lucas used his right hand to guide Jose's finger to the exact point of the bleeding and firmly pushed his finger into place, removing his own hand. There was a brief spurt of blood at the exchange of fingers, then total control. "You only need to use enough pressure to stop the bleeding," Lucas said to his new assistant. "We don't want to strangle him."

Looking the sergeant directly in the eye, Lucas went on, "This control is only temporary. The lieutenant needs treatment immediately. We can let him die or operate to repair the defect in his blood vessel. To do surgery, I'll need assistants and staff to prepare the room and to organize the equipment. This will include those nurses and assistants you have locked up in pens, and the men standing at the front of the hospital under the trees. If we expect to have any chance of success, we have to act now."

The sergeant was stupefied. He had no authority to release the female prisoners, much less to permit medical treatment. Turning to tell one of the soldiers to take a message to the General about this emergency, the sergeant bumped his shoulder into that very officer. The General had heard the story from one of the guards and now stood directly in front of Lucas. He had observed the entire episode with Jose.

"Doctor," the General said in heavily Portuguese accented English, "Can you save my lieutenant?"

The General was one of the original leaders of the rebellion forces and was concerned about *this* particular lieutenant not only because he was an excellent soldier, but also because he was the general's nephew. To have him die would be a loss to his family as well as his army.

"I'll do my best, but to have much chance of success in surgery we'll need the nurses and technicians you have as prisoners," answered Lucas.

Rubbing his stubble-covered chin with his right thumb and forefinger, the General gave Lucas' offer some thought for a few seconds. He mistrusted the doctor and the hospital staff, but it appeared that he was out of options. The lieutenant was his sister's youngest son and her favorite. She had not agreed with the politics of her son joining the revolt, and if he died it would remain on the General's conscience. Besides, his family was extremely important to him.

"If I allow this help to come into the hospital and any attempt to escape is made, now or later, all of the remaining hostages will be immediately shot. These terms are not negotiable," he said slowly, looking Lucas directly in the eye.

Lucas thought that he could speak for all twelve captives, who at this point were not anticipating a bright future. He'd find a use for the non-medical people and the General would never know who did what anyway.

"Okay, we have an agreement. We will work to save and treat ALL of the wounded with no escape attempts, but I need Angela, my nurse, right now."

Lucas had now expanded the proposition from one lieutenant to the whole mass of wounded soldiers, with this negotiation. This treaty would assure the safety of all the hostages for a while. By keeping the mission personnel busy saving lives, the rebels would feel that they were too valuable to torture. This opportunity would also give the missionaries a chance to interact with the soldiers from both sides to evangelize, which was the missionaries' reason to be there in the first place, as well as to treat their diseases and wounds. They had promised not to attempt an escape, but could perhaps still accomplish their original calling to Africa.

Turning to the sergeant, the General said curtly, "Give the doctor what he needs, immediately, and then follow the doctor's instructions. If the lieutenant dies, you are responsible. Find this Angela person first. There are many of our brave soldiers in distress needing help."

Giving a salute, the sergeant turned and sprinted out of the hospital towards the cages. As he ran along the gravel driveway, he encountered a detail of guards on their way to pick up the female hostages for "soldier hospitality" duties in the barracks.

The sergeant reported the new orders about the female hostages to the detail's captain. "We are to take all captives to the hospital immediately for duty there. The General wants me personally to bring some woman called Angela first."

The captain listened attentively to the new orders and remarked, "There's going to be some disappointment in the ranks. We were all looking forward to a little entertainment this morning after breakfast. The new directive will be followed."

Saluting the captain, the sergeant ran ahead. Standing in the forecourt of the pens, he announced loudly in English, "Which of you goes by the name, Angela?"

Fearing the worst, Angela replied in a weak voice, "I am she." Thinking, "*I hope that Lucas is alright?*" and her fear for her own safety forgotten, she feared the worst for her newly discovered love.

The sergeant immediately strode to Angela's enclosure and, unlocking the chain, he jerked the door open, saying, "You are wanted immediately. Follow me!"

Angela was certain that Lucas had been wounded or worse. She followed the guard at a quick trot down the gravel drive, past the captain going the other way. As the front lawn of the hospital came into view, she gasped at the sight of so many soldiers lying in total disorder. This sight disgusted her first as a nurse and also as a human. It appeared also to her, as she rushed past, that they had received almost no care.

As the sergeant approached the front stairs and began to ascend to the hospital entrance, Angela could smell the rank odors of ammonia coming from the hospital interior. Recognizing the smell of dead flesh, her eyes began to water but she did not hesitate to enter the hospital as the door was pulled roughly open by the nearly exhausted soldier who had run back and forth to get her. He now led her into the hallway, and seeing the clutter and disorder she said incredulously, "Have you no orderlies or medics to organize this mayhem? Most of these injured are *your own* people."

With no reply, the sergeant said, "Just follow me, Ma'am, you are needed by the doctor."

Angela noticed that he had addressed her as "Ma'am." She had become used to the brash, demanding orders of the entire rebel force until now. Suddenly, this sergeant seemed to be *asking* her to do something in an almost respectful tone. Angela was astounded.

Entering the room, she observed the disarray everywhere, but she smiled immediately at the sight of Lucas. He was standing next to a bed, which was the immediate focus of her attention. In the bed lay a patient obviously in terminal distress.

Taking the first deep breath she could remember inhaling since being taken captive, she gave momentary thanks to be out of that cage and then approached the rebel lieutenant's bed.

"What's going on?" Angela asked as she arrived at the bedside.

Lucas smiled back, and mumbled in a low professional voice, "We've got a situation, Angela. The commander is about to lose one of his top lieutenants. If we can save him, we have a chance to save ourselves. If he dies, I suspect all of us are finished."

"Is this the lieutenant? What's the problem with his neck?"

"It appears to be a GSW to the neck with an open left carotid artery. Who knows what else's damaged in there. The guy's bleeding like stink from all over his neck."

"What's that got to do with *our* future, Lucas?"

"Well, it appears that the lieutenant here is the General's nephew, and he has agreed that he will free us to work on the whole rebel army if we can save him. If not, who knows what that commander will dream up for us? I told him that we need the entire group of hostages to do surgery, so he sent for the rest of them. I need you to prepare the operating room to do this guy. Can you organize it in ten minutes?"

Realizing that their lives might hinge on one attempt to save the patient, Angela thought it best to get started now. Sterility would be out the window and who knew what instruments could be organized in this mess. Then she said out loud, "When the other hostages arrive, they can try to organize the rooms and people out front. There's no time to triage all these wounded now. Has anyone been to the OR?"

Since he wasn't sure if the primitive instruments owned by the hospital were even available, Lucas looked over at Jose, who still had a firm finger on the artery. Lucas said, "Just hold on for other ten or fifteen minutes, Jose. Then we'll relieve you. You're doin' it like a champion. I have to leave for a few minutes."

Lucas hurriedly left the room and headed for the second floor, followed closely by Angela. They had done many surgeries together in the past three months, and both thought along the same lines. "I'll look for the instruments while you find the sterile supplies, if there are any. We can use towels to isolate the field, and we'll need a bunch of swabs when that pressure comes off!" observed Lucas.

Angela was surprised when they gained the second floor and opened the double swinging doors of the surgical suite. The windows and walls were pock-marked with bullet holes entering from the outside, leaving the walls looking like a sieve with sunlight streaming through the openings. Flies and mosquitoes buzzed around the ceilings, making an intermittent drone as they landed and launched themselves again, angry at being disturbed. By a stroke of luck, no vital anesthesia or surgical instruments had been hit, and it appeared that a surgical procedure could be performed. The surgical suite was still intact, except for where the odd missile had punctured the walls.

*"What dumb luck,"* muttered Lucas to himself, loud enough for Angela to overhear him. "We need to gather the stuff together and get this thing done."

Angela began to assemble the instruments and supplies necessary for the upcoming procedure, opening and stacking them on tables wrapped in sterile towels and paper containers. She sprayed the insects, killing most of them.

Lucas returned to the first floor and requested that the mission's male employees, now on the outside, be brought into the hospital and some sort of organized program be initiated to attempt to feed and give water to all patients, although supplies were scarce. He placed Clever, one of the hostages that Lucas had barely known prior to the takeover, in charge of this request, as he had been the mission cook. If there were any reserves or outside sources of food, he would be able to locate them.

Doctor Maria now arrived with the other women, led by the captain who was leading them back to the hospital from their cages. Gayle, who was hardly able to walk, and Esther were assigned to an outpatient clinic room. Gayle was asked to care for Esther's wounds and feed her, as she remained in poor condition. The reverend was sent with them, as there was little else for him to do at this time. At least he was now able to walk unsupported.

Lucas turned to Doctor Maria. After a brief explanation of the immediate situation, he said, "Is there any way we could organize a blood transfusion for the lieutenant? We do not have a type and cross-match ability, as you know, but some of these fighters from the rebels or government do have dog tags with their blood type on them. See if anyone is O negative, the universal donor, who hasn't lost a lot of blood. We need to try to get 500 cc. from him. Forget about testing for HIV. Probably thirty percent are positive, but we have no test for it now. Perhaps one of the other hostages will volunteer, as there is minimal risk to the donor? 'O' negative might be difficult to locate."

Remembering that Maichipo had been a scrub nurse, Lucas asked her to go to the second floor and help Angela set up the operating room.

Finding Okanna and Jonas, two orderlies standing around the hospital entrance with no immediate task, Lucas carefully explained his plan to them. They must find Jose and the lieutenant and together move the lieutenant upstairs to the surgical suite, while maintaining control of the bleeding from the carotid artery. Lucas closed his instructions by saying, "I will take you to Jose and we will all move the lieutenant upstairs together. Then, he thought to himself, *"OKAY We're getting organized, but what about an anesthetist?"*

Just then, his eye fell on Brightwell, who had taken the initiative to instruct Patience to go to the kitchen and try to help Clever with the food preparation. Lucas knew that Brightwell had never given anesthesia and that Doctor Maria's eyesight was failing, so that wasn't a choice. "To get this close and fail because of a stupid absence of an anesthetist…? *"There's gotta be some solution!"* thought Lucas.

"Brightwell! Come help us to move the patient upstairs," Lucas directed.

Carefully, Brightwell, Jonas, Okanna and Lucas moved the lieutenant out of the room and up the stairs to the second floor. Progress was very slow, as Jose had to keep his finger on the carotid artery. Any slip by Jose would almost certainly result in a flood of blood and the lieutenant's demise. Finally, they arrived as a group in the surgical suite and carefully placed the patient on the operating table, with Jose still clutching the pulsing artery.

"Let me put on a glove and get a hemostat on that artery. After that, we'll be able to prep the area and try to repair the defect, if he doesn't exsanguinate first," said Lucas, as he put sterile gloves on his hands. "Angie, where's that clamp? We'll have to get the clamp on the artery before we sleep him."

Selecting a vessel clamp from the table, Lucas stood opposite Jose, and after dousing Jose's hand and the lieutenant's neck thoroughly with a sterilizing solution, Lucas quietly stated, "Okay, Jose, remove your finger quickly when I tell you."

# 4
## Chapter

L ucas used a damp, sterile, abdominal sponge to clear away the brown sterilizing solution that had been poured over the artery and surrounding tissues at the beginning of the procedure. In his left hand he held a vascular clamp that he intended to place on the blood vessel as it began to bleed. This completed, he quietly intoned, "Okay, Jose, move your finger."

Bright red blood rhythmically spurted into the air, covering the damaged muscles of the lieutenant's neck and chest. Lucas immediately found the opening in the proximal carotid artery as it emerged from behind the left clavicle, and firmly placed his right index finger on the artery, bringing the flood of blood to a dribble. Without looking up, he said calmly, "Swab."

Angela again demonstrated her expertise with this type of procedure by immediately clearing the still-leaking blood from the distal side of the artery, as the back-flow surged, making the entire arterial defect now visible. Still holding the clamp in his left hand, Lucas deftly placed the rubber covered prongs of the instrument on the proximal common carotid artery, controlling the flood of arterial blood from the heart.

With no further communication, Angela snatched another clamp from the sterile table and skillfully secured the distal carotid artery, thus stopping the backflow. It was obvious that they coordinated easily without speaking. The entire procedure took less than twenty seconds to complete and the bleeding was controlled.

"We have no time to mess around. If the blood to his brain is stopped for too long, the lieutenant will stroke, so let's anesthetize, prep, and organize the repair quickly," said Lucas in his usual calm, low voice.

Turning to Brightwell, Lucas nodded and said, "You seem to do everything competently my friend, so now it's time for you to give some anesthesia for us. If we show you what to do, can you do it?"

"Yes, sir. What must I do?"

Lucas found the intravenous line that Angela had previously put in place and connected a syringe filled with Ketavaar, a relatively short-acting general hypnotic anesthetic, to the line. After Lucas injected the drug into the IV line, the lieutenant immediately faded into a drug-induced sleep. Holding the lieutenant's mouth open, he helped Angela put in place an intra-tracheal tube, which was connected to the respiratory machine. This maintained the patient's breathing, which was paralyzed during anesthesia. A Pulse-oximeter was connected to the lieutenant's finger to monitor the oxygen concentration in the blood. This entire procedure took only a few seconds.

"Okay, guys, we've got him stabilized. Let's repair the artery," said Lucas.

He went to scrub his hands while Angela explained to Brightwell about monitoring the anesthetic and controlling the lieutenant's vital signs. She then entered the scrub room and stood next to Lucas at the sink. He finished cleaning his hands.

"Any word from Doctor Maria on the transfusion?" called Lucas as he entered the operating room, dripping water from his arms. "Ask Jonas to find out about the blood, Angie. Then finish scrubbing and come help me. What sutures have we got?"

As he finished drying his hands and arms on the towel that the second scrub nurse handed to him, Lucas said, "You doin' okay, Maichipo?" Lucas smiled under his mask at the competent scrub nurse as she held the gown for him to put on. This ritual had been repeated almost daily for the last three months and Lucas felt that his "team" was now reorganized and ready to function. This was a feeling hard to describe, but any experienced surgeon knows the trust he feels when a coordinated team is in place and there's a job to be done together.

The operation went swiftly and the arterial defect was sutured expertly. In less than thirty minutes it had been repaired. While some damage had been done to the trachea, this could be bypassed temporarily with a tracheotomy to insure adequate respiration. The 'trach' could be removed later as the patient recovered.

As the lieutenant's neck was being sutured, one of the double doors was cautiously opened and Jonas' face appeared from behind the opaque, splintered glass, "Doctor, how is it going? Do you need this blood? One of the volunteers was happy to donate and he has no history of being unhealthy."

Much more relaxed now, Lucas smiled at the technician and said, "You've got the juice? Hand it to Brightwell, and we'll start it up. Good work, Jonas! Be sure to thank Doctor Maria. She really came through."

The procedure now completed, Angela said to Lucas, "I'm so tired and there's all that disorganization to try to put into order. We might go down to the kitchen and see how Clever and Patience are doing. I could use a hot cup of tea right now."

As the two walked down the stairs to the kitchen, they noticed that there had been little change in the overall conditions of the hospital in the last few hours. It was fortunate that the hospital building had been constructed of brick and tile, as most of the grime and blood could be cleaned up without having to repair major fractures of the floors and walls. It appeared also that the roof had remained intact, but appearances in roofs could be inaccurate -- only a rain would reveal if it was undamaged.

"The next job will be to triage every patient in the hospital, in the halls and on the lawn, to set priorities on treatment and disposition," remarked Lucas. "We also need to clean the place up. What a mess they have made of our hospital."

As they approached the hospital kitchen, they heard the cheerful voice of Patience talking to Clever, "We've recovered it. I knew all that food we hid behind the back storage bin would not be discovered by the insurgents. We are going to prepare a grand meal for all the patients and staff. We can have food available by the time you've seen all of the patients."

Over tea, Lucas and Angela agreed that a conference with the General was necessary to obtain his consent for them to make changes to restore the hospital to a semblance of its former function. Seeing one of the General's aides whom he had not met before walk past the kitchen, Lucas stood up and approached him. "Major! We have just finished the surgery on Lieutenant Makura. Is there some way we could speak to the General for a few minutes?"

Saluting, as was his custom when spoken to, the Major responded, "I have just been informed by Brightwell as I passed him in the hallway that Lieutenant Makura has returned to his room from surgery. Evidently, there is no further bleeding. The General will be most pleased to hear of your success...I am at your service."

Seeing that the Major appeared to be in good humor, Lucas decided this might be an opportunity to push for some modification of their captivity. If the lieutenant survived, all the better, but if not, smarter to see the commander while the wind was drifting Lucas' way.

"Are you going to see the General now?" asked Lucas. "Could we follow you to his command post?"

The Major turned smartly on his heel saying, "Follow me. I will see if the General is available to see you now."

Lucas and Angela followed the officer out of the hospital and along a dirt path behind the mission workers' housing, which was now being used as soldiers' barracks. Dropping further back from the Major's lead, Lucas began to speak to Angela in a low voice. "So far, so good. If the lieutenant will just stay alive for a few days, perhaps we can do some good and figure a way out of this mess. Don't get nervous; just follow my lead if we get to talk to the CO."

They followed the Major as he walked into what used to be Pastor Williamson's house. As they stood in the hallway waiting Angela saw that there had been some redecorating since her last visit. The administrator's house, abandoned by the mission supervisor and his family during the takeover, was the largest house on the mission station and had been built to accommodate his family as well as occasional visitors. It had an extensive library, a study and four bedrooms. They had fled to Luanda by auto a few days after the trouble started. Now she could see the once neatly-shelved religious books and tracts lay in disorder on the floor. Angela also observed that his imposing massive mahogany desk in the hall was riddled with bullet holes. The Major told them to wait in the hallway while he spoke to the General.

"I wonder how the war is going?" asked Angela in a quiet voice as they stood in the hallway waiting. "The war must have moved further south, as we didn't hear any gunfire this morning."

"Wherever the fighting is going on, it's probably fierce and the rebel casualties will be high," replied Lucas. "The large number of casualties will strengthen our case to restore the hospital's function. I think that…"

Lucas' sentence was interrupted by the reappearance of the Major from a large door at the head of the hallway. The Major had a policy never to smile in the presence of a prisoner, but his pride and relief were evident as he came to full attention after closing the door and entering the hall. He clicked his heels smartly and said, "The *Generalissimo* will see you now." He used the Portuguese term in reference to his commander, as almost every non-black person in Angola, except the missionaries, was of Portuguese descent on both sides of the war.

Turning, still at attention, the major strode briskly as he led the two hostages into a large study. Lucas had only seen this room once, when he had been interviewed by Reverend Williamson for the vacant physician post at the mission about three months before. He had been impressed with the room then, with its polished teak paneling and hardwood floors.

Angela had been in this study many times during her life and she still remembered the polished ebony Steinway grand piano in the corner, and the large, comfortable chairs. This was where many of her friends sat, sipping tea and listening to her play the instrument as recently as a few months ago. She and her father had visited Reverend Williamson from the Saurimo Mission many times since her mother had passed away, so many years ago. Both missions had been built in the early 1900s and had thrived in their attempt to teach as well as induce the indigenous population to embrace Christianity. The administrator and her father were longtime friends. Angela only hoped that her father had escaped the war from Saurimo as cleanly as Reverend Williamson, but she had received no news these last three weeks.

Behind the teak desk sat the General, smoking a cigar and reading from a document that appeared to be written in English. Angola had been colonized by the Portuguese long before the British had taken over South Africa to the South, and that primary language remained even now.

"The doctor and his assistant are here," announced the Major in Portuguese.

Without looking up, the General said, "That will be all for now. Thank you, Major."

Not expecting a particularly warm reception from an officer who controlled his fate, Lucas, who spoke no Portuguese, said in Kileta "Sir! We asked to speak to you about a situation possibly of major importance to your war efforts."

The General continued to read, never once looking up or even acknowledging their presence. Angela and Lucas stood in some discomfort for a full three minutes as the General completed reading the papers in his hand. With no introduction or greeting of any kind, the General looked up and said casually, in Portuguese, "Can either of you translate English into Portuguese?" He assumed they wouldn't be working at the mission if they couldn't speak the colonial language, which was universally used by the non-black population.

Somewhat upset at his totally indifferent reception, Angela said in Portuguese, "I believe I could help you with that, Sir. I am Angela Abercrombe and this is Doctor Lucas Stuart."

Rising from his chair, obviously totally preoccupied with the problem at hand, the commanding officer simply handed the papers to Angela, saying, "Good, good. You did a fine job on Lieutenant Makura and we appreciate it." Without a pause, he continued, "We have just received this document from our American allies, but I need to know what supplies they are sending. Can you interpret this?"

Looking at the papers, Angela recognized it as an American bill of lading, listing many military goods. The information was in English, but the merchandise appeared to be in a number code. Only the heading betrayed the contents as it said "U.S. Army Stores". It appeared to be a list of supplies. From the letter she assumed that the U.S. government was sending aide to the rebels.

"General, I am unsure of what has been sent, but it appears to be from the United States Army, so I suppose it will be useful to you."

"Yes, Yes, I can see that, but I need specifics," said the general, as he waved his hand in a dismissive gesture sitting back down in the soft leather executive chair. "Why is it that you wanted to see me?" Angela could remember seeing Reverend Williamson swivel back and forth in the same chair only a few weeks ago.

"Sir," began Lucas, "The condition of the injured troops is deplorable. These soldiers are receiving little or no care in the hospital compound. This includes some of the slightly wounded who are becoming infected and are unable to be active in your army. With authority from your office, we might be able to improve the medical and surgical care of *all* of those patients needing treatment. We hoped to treat both your own and the government's troops…"

The General put his right hand up, as a signal for Lucas to be silent. "That's enough. You're certainly right about the conditions at the hospital, but I will not tolerate treatment of enemy troops' wounds. Fix them so they can return to duty and go back to killing my soldiers?"

Lucas saw the commander's point, but then had an inspiration." Perhaps in some cases, treatment of enemy injuries may stimulate them to leave the government army or even to join the rebellion? You are always in need of trained recruits, and perhaps you would gain some valuable information if they became part of the rebel army."

Looking thoughtfully at Lucas, the General paused for a second. "It's a thought, but retraining those government soldiers to new ideas is probably not viable. What type of authority do you want?"

"Authority within the hospital compound only, subject to your direction, of course." Lucas saw his chance, and seized it. "We need to triage the patients as to the seriousness of their wounds, organize care and feeding, schedule for surgery and discharge those ready to return to duty, sir."

The officer did not respond to Lucas' suggestion immediately, but sat quietly in his chair thinking that perhaps this American doctor does have a valid suggestion. Morale of the troops would rise if they knew that the wounded were being cared for. Under present conditions, this was not so. The doctor and his staff certainly would solve that problem, *but at what cost to my authority? They might even try to escape."* The officer wasn't positive exactly what other uses he had for the missionaries, but they seemed to be a valuable currency.

Finally, the commander looked up at Lucas, saying with a thin smile, "Who do you plan on treating and with what medications and treatments?"

Lucas had to think quickly. His whole plan rested on the consent of this commanding officer. Before he could reply, Angela's voice, next to him, confidently said, "We will treat the wounded, all of them. As far as I see it, the vast majority of them are from your army anyway, and the rest of the wounded are mostly unidentifiable as to their allegiance."

Trying to reinforce Angela's remarks, Lucas said, "General, many of the hospital's medications and supplies have already been depleted, but I'm sure with conservation of the remainder more soldiers can be helped. We'd like to try."

Getting up from his chair, the General walked over to Lucas and shook his hand, remarking in Portuguese, "I realize that these are not ideal conditions for you or my troops, but any help you and the hospital team can give, we'll appreciate." Angela continued to translate for him.

The officer leaned over the desk and pushed a button. Almost immediately, the door opened and the Major entered, and after coming to full attention he said, "Sir?"

Saluting casually back, the General said, "Major, the doctor and his staff have agreed to help us with the troops confined to the hospital compound. Whatever he asks for within the hospital complex is to be done. He has no authority outside of the hospital chain-link fencing, however. The doctor and his staff will sleep within the compound and if found outside the fence will be shot on sight. Is that understood?"

"Yes, sir," replied the Major, as he clicked his heels so distinctly that Angela flinched.

"I will return them to the hospital immediately and round up any other hospital workers that we may have picked up since our taking over the mission. Is there anything else, sir?"

As the Major turned to lead Lucas and Angela away, the General remarked, "They will need the electricity and water facilities to function to restore the hospital's efficiency. Turn them back on. You are dismissed."

The three left the building together, but the attitude of the Major showed a complete transformation. In an almost cordial tone the Major, no longer the stiff and formal puppet, said, "I'm very glad he made that decision. The lieutenant you saved this morning is a close friend of mine, as well as being the general's nephew. There are many sick and wounded men under my command who will benefit from the reopening of the medical facility, if you are able to bring it back to its ability to treat patients." Smiling, he continued, "We will return to the hospital now."

This bit of information would help to boost the medical team's morale as they re-established the hospital. Lucas was thankful to the Lord for his generous result with the lieutenant, as well as the salvation of the entire staff without further causalities.

As they followed the path back to the compound Angela and Lucas said nothing, but their stride was now quicker as they held hands and walked, smiling at each other. They both were rejuvenated by this major victory that had been achieved, and the Major's continued collegial tone. The undertaking at the hospital, however, was to be no small task. Once they had returned to the hospital compound, Lucas and Angela sat on the front steps of the clinic and talked. The sun was now high in the sky, bringing the temperatures near their daily zenith. An acacia tree guarding the hospital entrance provided adequate shade, allowing the sporadic breezes to cool them and carry the potent fragrance of the frangipani blossoms, which surrounded the building, to their nostrils.

"We'll have to come up with a plan before anything will work," said Lucas. "What do you think Angela?"

Angela was so relieved that the immediate danger had been avoided she could hardly speak Taking a deep breath, she said, "I think we will need to organize the running of the hospital first, then triage everyone and find beds and cots for the patients. By prioritizing, we will be able to save the maximum number of patients, after we first thank the Lord for His deliverance."

"True, but first, we must emphasize to the entire hospital population, including the guards, that within the hospital compound the war is over. Once the wounded recover they can rejoin their units. While they remain with us, however, no hostilities will be tolerated," counseled Lucas. "I've seen some disgusting attempts at murder by opposing patients still in clinics recovering from war injuries here in Africa."

Angela thought for a minute, passing her hand through her blonde hair in a futile attempt to flatten the disheveled mess. "We probably should clean the hospital up before organizing the patients. It will cost us a few hours, but save lives and decrease infections. Lucas, what do you think?"

"The second floor has little damage and we probably can organize the operating rooms and recovery rooms easily. There appears to be very little disorganization to the patient rooms on the second floor, so we can move the worst patients up there.

Then, to clean the first floor, we'll have to temporarily evacuate everyone. I don't know how much help we'll have, but the less seriously wounded will have to assist."

Finding Manaba, their old anathema from the guards at the pens, and a few of the other guards assigned to the hospital compound along with Biro, Lucas asked if they could find a bullhorn in the mission. "I know we used to have one in the living quarters behind the back door. Would you see if it's still there?"

While the megaphone was being located, Angela and Lucas returned to the front lawn of the hospital. Some colored tags that Angela had found were used to identify the degree of seriousness of the injuries of each patient. A tag was assigned after the patient had been superficially examined. A red tag denoted serious problems needing attention first, a yellow tag denoted less serious damage, but still needing attention, and a green tag meant that his problem could wait; the patient was ambulatory. A few of the wounded were dismissed immediately, as their wounds were not serious and outpatient treatment would suffice before they returned to their units.

Manabe brought the bullhorn just as the hospital staff had gathered at the front entrance. Taking the bullhorn, Lucas announced, "This is to inform every worker and patient that we have been given a mandate by the revolutionary authorities to treat every injured and sick person, as we can get to them. No hostilities will be tolerated between government soldiers and rebels being cared for here. Infractions of this rule will result in immediate dismissal forthwith to look after their own welfare."

Lucas then handed the bullhorn to Biro and told him to walk around the grounds broadcasting these terms to those lying outside the hospital while he and Angela finished triaging the remaining patients on the lawn and inside. "In thirty minutes, we will meet right here if we have finished seeing every patient by then," Lucas concluded their orders and proceeded into the hospital, followed by Angela.

He had found his stethoscope and bag, which had remained undisturbed on the second floor. Now he was able to complete the examination with accuracy of the rest of the wounded both inside the hospital and on the lawn, determining which colored tag was to be assigned to each wounded patient. Angela accompanied him, assisting in diagnosis.

In thirty-five minutes, the entire remaining hospital staff gathered at the front entrance of the hospital, including two nurses who had disappeared into the brush during the firefight. They had left during the takeover, and after ensuring the safety of their families, Eunice and Hilda had sought refuge near their ancestral homes. Now they both returned, hoping to find any other relatives or friends surviving near the hospital compound and to be of assistance. Gayle and Esther remained in the outpatient clinic on the first floor, as they were in no condition to assist in the cleanup and wanted to remain isolated from further attacks by the soldiers The Reverend Brown, however, now able to walk, attended this meeting. The major had personally escorted the reverend to the hospital compound, along with the other four male staff prisoners, when Lucas had concluded his discussion with the general securing their freedom.

"Okay, I think Angela and I have examined just about every patient. If you find a patient without a colored tag, please find either of us and we will evaluate them."

Every one of the staff was anxious to comply, understanding that their own safety as well as that of the wounded depended on the completion of the duty each was assigned. Lucas continued, "The red tagged patients go to the second floor, the yellow and green tags will temporarily reside on the front lawn. We will send nurses to the second floor to care for the sickest patients. Please do the best you can with what's available. Angela will supervise the care of all patients and IV solutions. Medical questions go to Doctor Maria."

Now as he looked directly at Okanna, Jonas and Brightwell, Lucas said, "You orderlies organize everyone who can help, including the wounded, guards, or aides, to evacuate the first floor of all patients to the front lawn. We need to clean up the mess inside and it appears that the Lord is thinking of sending rain. Those clouds gathering on the horizon will be here soon, and we need to finish before the rain arrives."

As the bright sunlight continued to blaze down on the front lawn of the hospital grounds, the suffering and wounded experienced severe discomfort, as they were unable to find shade. Brightwell organized some of the orderlies and stronger ambulatory patients to help those unable to move themselves into the shade of the trees and buildings. At the same time, the first floor was cleared of all patients and the red-tagged patients were moved to the second floor by those who were able to assist.

"We're beginning to show a little coordination" approved Lucas. "Now if we can just clean up the first floor and clear out the debris in time for the rest of the patients to be moved under cover. Those clouds will be here before you know it."

The dark clouds appeared to be rapidly approaching the hospital, with thunder rumbling in the distance even as the bright sunlight persisted. "It's going to be a frog-strangler, when it gets here" remarked Angela. "We'd better get every available person to help scrub that first floor to make room for those outside. If the patients without cover get their wounds drenched, many of them may get pneumonia."

Now, the bullhorn became extremely useful as teams were hurriedly designated and sent into the hospital. Each team was assigned to a corridor to sweep out the debris and scrub the walls and floors with disinfectant.

"Work quickly" requested Angela in Kileta on the bullhorn, as she stood on the lawn. "When a room is finished, tell us and then move along to the next one. Once the room is disinfected, wait for it to dry and then transfer the beds and other furniture into the room."

The work moved swiftly. Even the guards and ambulatory patients participated with good spirits. The afternoon light began to darken as the approaching thunderclouds obliterated the sun's rays. Suddenly, lighting flashed across the western sky, followed by the growling of nearby thunder. "Let's get the patients into the clean rooms, if you have finished your assignment," Angela instructed on the bullhorn. She watched gratefully as a steady stream of patients moved to the interior of the building.

Lucas and Angela quickly helped the others move furniture and patients out of the gathering wind and drizzle into hastily placed beds and mattresses now under cover. There were many more patients than facilities, so only the yellow-tagged patients were accommodated on beds. The green-tagged patients were assigned to floor space or chairs.

They ran out of time. The rain descended, blown by repeated rushes of forceful wind that sprayed everyone and soaked a few of the last to reach cover.

"Just deposit them in the halls, if the rooms aren't finished. We can move them into the beds and chairs as they become available"

Manabe now appeared to be one of the primary movers as he organized getting the last few patients under shelter from the rain. Somewhere during the roller coaster of the day's events the stoic guard's emotions had allowed him to side with the captives. Lucas wasn't sure what made it happen, perhaps saving the lieutenant's life or just feeling he had become part of the hospital squad, but it was obvious that the guard felt pride that he had become a member of the hospital team.

The downpour was ferocious, which was not unusual for Northern Angola at this time of year. Lucas stared out the paneless window in wonder at the volume of water being dumped on the hospital compound.

"I'm glad we're not still out in those pens," remarked one of the orderlies, thankful to be working again and out of the downpour. He stood panting next to Lucas, watching the lawn turn into a lake. "We'd be floating for sure without cover."

Turning to the familiar native next to him, Lucas said with concern, "Okanna, did you have a chance to have that broken finger examined?"

First examining his crooked finger carefully, Okanna showed it to Lucas, holding it out in front of him. "Not yet and it's beginning to throb," he replied. "Can you set it?"

"Come and find me after supper. We'll get it fixed like new," conveyed Lucas, after examining the digit.

As the completion of cleaning and occupation of all of the rooms was finally accomplished, supper arrived. This meal was proudly supervised by Clever, who had previously been the chief chef before the takeover. A smiling Patience and the guards and orderlies served each room full of grateful patients. The two estimated they had fed 200 patients in total.

"I need to check the patients," announced Lucas. "Angie, please be sure that there are no areas of flooding on the first floor. I think the clinic is sitting on concrete blocks and is well above the water. This is pivotal for the safety of the building and I don't trust anyone else."

Angela left immediately to see about the flooding while Lucas began to make ward rounds in the hospital. Lucas felt that he should check the second floor patients before getting to the yellow tags on the first floor, as he knew that there were some serious red-tagged patients up there that needed to be followed closely.

Ascending the stairs, Lucas encountered Eunice, a competent nurse who had returned from the bush. He recognized her as well-trained and was thankful for her help, Lucas greeted her jovially.

"Hi, Eunice! Glad to see you working again. How are things up here on the second floor? Are there any leaks in the tin roof, or any patients with immediate needs? We're certainly fortunate that so many of the staff is still here with the hospital so full."

Eunice gave Lucas a huge smile, her brilliant teeth sparkling against the dark, black skin of her face. "Ahhh, Doctor Lucas. We have things under control on the second floor. Maichipo and I always keep our hands on the switches! So far, the roof has held up well, but we will need to show you some of the patients."

Lucas felt deep concern for most of the red-tagged patients, as many had serious or life-threatening problems. He and Angela, with Maichipo's help, would probably be in surgery until the small hours of the morning.

"Okay, Eunice, let's start with the worst cases first and then move along," Lucas said, placing his arm around the shoulder of his competent nurse as they walked down the hall together. "Who has the most serious injuries?"

As they entered the first room, Lucas realized that less than twelve hours ago, he had been sitting in the floor of a pen, totally distraught about the coming hours. Now, he and Angela were trying to organize and run a hospital with over two hundred variously wounded men and with very little assistance. "Times do change quickly," he thought. He had lived a century in those twelve hours and now he had this large responsibility and he felt so tired.

Eunice took Lucas to each room. He examined again each patient from bed to bed, reevaluating the wounds and the condition of each patient. As they talked, Lucas said, "I need to make a list of all the red-tagged patients in the order we need to treat them. Then, we can proceed in some sort of organized way. The lieutenant appears stable, thanks be to our Lord, and Esther and Gayle seem to be in stable condition, so they won't need to be on the list."

The list was completed, and a copy sent to the operating room. As dusk approached, the surgical procedures commenced, continuing throughout the night with the able assistance of Angela and Maichipo. Dr. Maria remained in charge of the wards, keeping the wounded stabilized until the operating team got to them. Sometime towards midnight, Okanna appeared in the surgical suite. After a quick shot of anesthetic, he awoke, proudly exhibiting his repaired finger, now supported by a splint and cast. Thankfully, with Hilda the anesthetist back from the bush, anesthesia was no longer a problem, so Brightwell was assigned to ward duty. They continued to work throughout the night.

"What a night!" sighed Angela as the surgical team sat in the preparation room together to rest, having finished a difficult case. "Here comes the sun." Looking through the large window on the east side of the hospital they could see the first glow of orange light illuminating the horizon.

"We all need to get some sleep," Angela said. She arranged for Brightwell to fix the post-op bay with beds, and Patience to find some breakfast for them.

"The four of us can share the bay," Lucas remarked as they left the operating room suite.

Looking around at the surgical team, Angela said with a smile, "It'll be crowded in the recovery room with all of us, but it's quiet, and we can get cleaned up first. We're all adults and co-ed dorms are necessary at this point. Any shy people?"

No one objected to the arrangements. Maichipo, Angela and Lucas could well remember the previous night's accommodations and were thankful to even have a bed and bathroom for their use. Patience brought breakfast to them after each had taken a shower and put on fresh scrub suits. The warm cascade splashing on their bodies and the soapy, dirty water washing down the drain was a welcome payment for the days they had spent in the hostage pens and the long hours in the surgical operating rooms. The beds were only stretchers, but all four were exhausted and fell instantly into a deep sleep as the sun rose in the morning sky.

Angela awoke to the sound of heavy truck engines and a commotion at the front of the hospital. Looking through the window, she thought to herself, "Where are all these new patients coming from?" She walked to the hospital entrance, where new patients were arriving, after she had only six hours of deep sleep. "I thought that we had about caught up with most of the serious cases last night!" she said to Brightwell.

Looking up from the blood pressure cuff that he was attaching to a new patient's arm, Brightwell said, "Madam, the fighting continues in Cacolo and further to the south. We are famous now, and the rebels are sending many of the bad cases to us. Manaba said that the rebel leaders know of no other hospital within sixty miles that has a surgeon and nurses. We will probably receive many more cases."

Days passed, multiple operations were performed and some of the beds emptied as soldiers were released. A few went home, most returned to their units. Brightwell's words proved prophetic, as the hospital remained at its capacity to function. Dr. Maria and Esther were now helping on the first floor, caring for the patients as Gayle slowly recovered her equilibrium. Gayle was finally coherent, but would serve no useful purpose for weeks before recovering emotionally from her physical and psychological violations. Reverend Brown, now less vocal, tried to reassert himself as an evangelist, speaking to the wounded soldiers about their future in posterity. He was using as a translator a native Christian worker who had arrived at the mission, introduced himself, and obligated himself as an assistant. No one was quite sure, but he said he had come from Zaire. The reverend was heard to remark, "I wonder why so few of these soldiers are concerned about their souls?" Most of the natives in Angola had been introduced to the Christian religion, but the understanding of the actual path to salvation seemed to have been neglected.

Ten days after their release from the enclosures, Lucas quietly observed to Angela, "You know, Angie, the pastor is acting a little strange. First, he was an overbearing bragger. Now he seems *too* subdued. Do you think he's decompensated or just scared? Let's talk to him at supper tonight and find out what's going on in that mixed up mind." That night, they failed to talk to him due to emergency surgery.

The next day, a panting Okanna arrived at the outpatient ward as Lucas was setting a broken leg. As he wrapped the plaster, the native said between gasps, "Doctor Lucas, Missie Angela has sent me to ask you to come quick. We have a very sick patient!"

After completing the plaster cast, Lucas wiped his hands on a towel and looked for a moment at the orderly, who was rarely emotional but now had sweat pouring from every pore. Lucas realized that he must have run all the way to the outpatient ward. Following Okanna, he hurried to the infectious disease ward where he found gathered around a bed Angela and Brightwell in detailed examination of an obviously sick man.

"What is the problem?" asked Lucas as he arrived, "Okanna asked me to come quickly."

Angela turned and looked at Lucas with an expression of total helplessness, something Lucas hadn't seen in her before. Her countenance revealed fear and frustration. "He has something wrong, but if I'm correct on the diagnosis, we can't help him. What's your opinion, Lucas?"

Lucas looked kindly at the patient, and said as he put on rubber gloves, "My name is Doctor Lucas and we're all here to help you. What is your name and from where were you coming before you arrived here?"

The patient answered in a strange Kileta dialect, with a distinct accent not familiar to Lucas. Angela, realizing that Lucas would be unable to decipher his response, interpreted. "He says that he lives near Loubomo, in the Republic of Congo, north of Matadi. He left there three days ago and has come to see his family. His name is Teke, and he feels sick and hopes we can help him."

"What symptoms does he have, Angela? Did he tell you?" asked Lucas.

Angela blanched noticeably, a reaction from her that immediately alarmed Lucas. "He reports twenty-four hours of high fever, diarrhea, muscular pain and vomiting, all of which appear to be progressive. This morning, he noticed a sore throat and blood in his vomit as well as these large bruises on his skin. It sounds serious Lucas; I hope he doesn't have what I think he has!"

Calmly, Lucas said, "Angela, don't jump to conclusions. Let's examine him."

Lucas sat Teke up on the cot and began to examine the patient's entire body. There was bruising in irregular areas all over his body, obviously not from trauma. His heartbeat was regular, but congestion was in the left lung base on auscultation. Looking in his ears, Lucas could see blood in small amounts from ruptured capillaries.

"*That's a bad sign*," mumbled Lucas as he began to look at the retinas of Teke's eyes. "I see hemorrhagic areas in both retinas and his throat is bright red," said Lucas as he looked down the patient's throat with a tongue depressor and a flashlight.

With trembling gloved hands, Angela began to test Teke's body for areas of numbness, finding many spots that he couldn't feel as she punched him gently with the pointed handle of a reflex hammer. Angela and Lucas did not look at each other during their examinations, but by the tension in their bodies Brightwell guessed something was terribly wrong Angela whispered to Lucas, "Oh my gosh, he has all the signs. What do we do now?"

Brightwell, who had been helping on the ward, looked at both of them and said, "What is the problem? What is wrong, Missie Angela?"

Lucas looked up at Brightwell and after walking a few meters away, he motioned for the orderly to follow him. Then he said with a totally flat voice, "Teke has Ebola Virus, Brightwell. We're going to have to isolate him to prevent an epidemic involving the entire mission."

# 5
## Chapter

The knowledge of a patient with the Ebola virus within the mission hospital could have certainly spread panic, both within the entire mission compound and throughout the entire rebel army. Isolation of the disease would be the first concern to control the possibility of an epidemic. Even skin contact with an infected person or a sneeze could lead to widespread transmission of the infection. There was the real possibility that even previous casual contact with Teke could have led to transmission of the disease.

After isolation, the second step was equally important: To restrict the knowledge of Teke's diagnosis to only those persons who needed to have direct access to him. This would be on a "need to know" basis.

Lucas decided that they must control all of Teke's movements and establish total isolation of the patient. Lucas instructed Brightwell to give Teke a mask to cover his mouth and nose, and then educate him as to the purpose for these precautions, without revealing the exact diagnosis to him. "Teke must understand that he has a dangerous infection that could spread rapidly and that we are counting on his cooperation," Lucas went on. "For this reason he must wear a mask at all times and anyone in contact with him must also wear a mask and gloves."

The patient read, by the expression on their faces, the concern of his surrounding caregivers. Teke had previously understood the seriousness of any infectious plague within a compound, as he had been told of these dangers by his family in the Republic of the Congo. Looking questioningly at Lucas, Teke hesitantly inquired, "How serious is the disease? What is wrong with me and can you help me?"

Angela, who spoke his dialect well, answered calmly and smiled at Teke while saying cheerfully, "Teke, you might have a serious infection that could be passed on to others. I know that you would be upset if other mission people or hospital patients felt sick or as badly as you feel now. We will try to help you, but you must do as we ask to keep this sickness from spreading to others. Will you help us?"

Teke was touched by Angela's kind smile, and reached for her hand, but she feared to have direct ungloved skin contact, as it carried the danger of initiating an epidemic or infecting herself. Thus, she continued to smile, but moved her hand away from his sweat drenched palm.

Teke said, "I will help in any way possible."

"Thank you, Teke." But Angela continued to ignore his offer of friendship, even though he extended it openly, until she had fully gloved her hands. With both hands wearing latex gloves, Angela put her hand on his elbow and said, "Thank you so much for understanding and agreeing to help us prevent others from getting sick. We will care for you, and put you in a private room to keep the bugs from infecting others."

Walking behind Angela into a small, isolated utility room, the patient calmly stood and waited for its contents to be evacuated and a bed to be set inside. As he watched the arrangements, he said, "I like having my very own room," with a frail smile. "Can anyone come to visit me here?" He promptly sat on the bed when all the sheets and covers had been arranged and a pillow placed at the head.

"Not just now," Angela instructed. "Perhaps when you are feeling better."

"Post this as the Isolation Ward," intoned Lucas quietly to Angela, as they left the room. "No visitors. Anything leaving this room--plates, sheets, feces, urine, needles, or syringes--is to be bagged and burned immediately. Let's get an IV into his arm and try to hydrate him with Ringers before his kidneys quit. I need to see the major and let him know what's going on."

He smiled over his shoulder at Teke, saying, "You'll be comfortable in here and not be disturbed during treatments. I'll return to see how you're doing."

As the arrangements for treatment were made, Lucas headed towards the commander's headquarters. Passing the hospital entrance, Lucas noticed a small black boy with a white dog sitting on the front steps. Grinning good naturedly, Lucas asked,

"Hello, what is your dog's name, young man?"

Stooping to pat the dog's head as he wagged his tail violently, Lucas couldn't help but notice that the boy was extremely undernourished. He had sunken eyes, pale skin, and appeared to have no fat on his frame, as did many other children in that war-torn zone. "My name is Wicki, and this is my dog, Iuba," said the boy. "We are waiting for my brother to be discharged from the hospital so we can visit our grandparents. I am ten years old."

Lucas felt that malnutrition made the child appear much less mature than his age. He also knew that undernourishment over a long time period does increase disease susceptibility. As he hurried down the gravel path to find the major, he thought, *That's a nice kid, and dog, but they both need some food. I'll see to it when I return. Suppertime is near.*

As Lucas left the fenced hospital compound, he was confronted by a guard at the gate who challenged him. "You are not allowed to leave the hospital compound, Doctor. What is your business?"

Lucas immediately noticed that again the guard seemed more friendly and relaxed. His remark was more of an inquiry than an order, making Lucas feel that the insurgent guards now considered him as their "doctor," rather than a hostage.

"I would like to visit with Major Santiago, if possible," Lucas replied.

"Please remain here, and I will see if he is available." Quietly turning to enter the headquarters, the guard remarked, "We are all very thankful for the efforts that you and the hospital staff have shown to treat our wounded soldiers."

As Lucas stood at the gate waiting for the guard to return with the major, he noticed that Wicki and Iuba had followed him across the hospital grounds and now stood near him. The dog appeared to be a full-blooded English Bull Terrier, with the characteristic bent nose and slanted pink eyes, gaunt and with ribs showing prominently.

"He's a bit older than a puppy, Wicki. Where did he come from?" asked Lucas as he bent to rub the enthusiastic dog behind his ears and scratch his flea-bitten belly.

"A white lady gave him to me when my brother and I passed through the mission at Kisambo. Iuba could hardly walk then, but he follows me everywhere now," said the small, black youngster proudly. "He's my best friend!"

At this time, the guard returned with Major Santiago, Lucas straightened up and greeted the major soberly. "I'm sorry to bother you, sir. We have made some progress with the treatment of the soldiers, but I'm afraid there is some bad news."

Smiling faintly, the major put out his right hand, and shaking Lucas' return offering said, "The improvements at the hospital *do* make a difference. Morale has improved throughout our entire army. What is this bad news?"

Looking down at the ground, Lucas lowered his voice to exclude the ears of both the guard and Wicki, who had moved some distance from the location of the major and doctor. Lucas said, "I'm afraid that a very sick patient has arrived from the north with an extremely serious problem. I thought the General should be informed. I realize that most of your combatants are to the south, and thus out of danger, but a spread of the problem could be a serious threat to the indigent population as well as to the entire army."

The major became impatient at Lucas' lengthy preamble, and in frustration exclaimed, "For God's sake man, get to the point!"

Digging the sand and gravel with his shoe and continuing to look down, Lucas announced quietly, "I think we have a case of Ebola virus in our patients, sir."

This statement ended the officer's impatience. Immediately the look on his face changed to concern, as he realized immediately that this highly contagious fatal disease could become an epidemic in only a few days, virtually wiping out his entire army. A deep frown appeared on his face as he inquired, "How many cases are there?"

"There is only one case that we are aware of, sir. The incubation period is four to six days, but there appear to be no other infections at this time."

The major thought for a few seconds and then asked, "Who knows about this Ebola case at the present time?"

Thinking quickly, the doctor answered, "Angela, Brightwell, and myself, but we have already taken steps to isolate the patient, so there *are* members of the staff who are suspicious. When the patient breaks out with hemorrhagic lesions on his body and with bleeding from his eyes, ears, and other body openings in a few days, it will become general knowledge, sir."

Lucas could see that he had obtained the full attention of the major. The officer asked, "Can we treat this disease? How dangerous is it? How does it spread?"

Lucas took a deep breath before answering, "There is no specific treatment, only supportive. The mortality rate usually runs over ninety percent within a few days of the first symptoms. It spreads by direct contact and by inhaling the virus if within close range of the initiator. It spreads rapidly and is extremely dangerous."

The aide did not seem amazed at this information and Lucas could see that he was struggling to keep his composure. Having digested Lucas' response, the major asked a final question. "What do you have to do to contain the disease?"

"We must keep all patients suffering with the disease isolated from human contact as much as possible, destroy any effluents, clothes, and food containing the Ebola virus, and pray that he is the only carrier. We have already begun to do this," Lucas answered.

"Please wait while I inform the commander. He may have some thoughts," responded the officer.

The major exited directly toward his headquarters and disappeared through the door, letting it slam behind him. Lucas now rejoined the guard, Wicki, and Iuba waiting at the gate, and noticed that Angela was making her way across the forecourt of the hospital, coming in their direction. She looked worried and scared as she approached. "What's going on? I saw you speaking to the major as I came across the lawn. What did he say?"

Nervously glancing at the boy and his dog, Lucas quickly said, "Angela, this is Wicki and his dog Iuba. They are waiting for his brother, who is a patient in the hospital. Then, they are going to see relatives who live near here. Wicki came from up north in Zaire to visit us!"

"It's a long way from Zaire to the Lubalo River, Wicki. I'm so glad that you and little Iuba could make it" Angela answered kindly. She thought it unusual that both Teke and Wicki had migrated from the north to a war-torn province. Was there a movement from Zaire of refugees coming South?

Lucas noticed the immediate close connection that Wicki made with Angela, probably swayed like everyone else by her friendly smile and her soft, loving eyes. Wicki was thinking to himself, as he met her for the first time, "*This lady seems to have some of the same loving qualities I remember my mother had.*"

Lucas sensed the instant resonance between the boy and Angela. He said casually to Angela, "I guess the major will speak to the General and return with orders. Wicki and I were just talking. Is there anything new at the hospital?"

She replied in English with an equally relaxed tone, so as not to alarm the others standing there. "The patient remains in an isolation room with no access to other personnel. He's having problems breathing and is coughing up a lot of hemorrhagic sputum. It looks as if it may be a short sickness." Bending to scratch

Iuba's neck, Angela inquired of Wicki, "Where are you and Iuba staying?"

Wicki enjoyed Angela's attention and he smiled, showing his even white teeth. He was pleased greatly that she would even care that he had a place to stay. Since they had arrived at the Lubalo Baptist Mission, his brother had been hospitalized and Wicki and Iuba had foraged for themselves, sleeping in the jungle — a situation they had both become accustomed to for many months.

"Oh, we have been looking after ourselves," replied the young boy. "Iuba doesn't eat much and we always find a place to stay. Don't worry about us. We'll be fine."

Angela was familiar with this sad situation, as there were countless number of orphaned children in southern Africa as a result of HIV dissemination or the unfortunate demise of parents for other reasons. The fate of these lonely *piccinins'* and their survival often was marginal, their lives ending with starvation.

"Tell you what we'll do. You and Iuba could come and work for us as guards at the hospital entrance to keep out robbers. We'll pay you, but you would be required to sleep on the hospital porch and eat there, too, in order to do the watching. Would you do us the favor, if you're not too busy right now? Then when your brother recovers, you can resign to go and visit your grandmother."

Wicki was enthusiastically in favor of the idea and agreed to take the job. "We could do it! Iuba is a wonderful watchdog, even though he's only a puppy. I can sleep during the day and guard at night. Thank you Missie Angela! Do I start tonight?"

"We wouldn't consider leaving the hospital unprotected for another minute," said Angela laughing. "Come, we'll get you and your assistant some food and you can begin this evening."

By that time, everyone was laughing when the major appeared through the door, having just left the General. Lucas immediately grew serious by the look on the major's face, which did not convey any jocularity. "This problem will need serious steps," he said, "The General requests further consultation on a course of action and he will be in the hospital later today to discuss further precautions. He asks that you meet him there after supper at eight this evening."

"Please give my compliments to the General and inform him that Angela and I will see him in the front corridor of the hospital at the appointed time," Lucas replied.

The major saluted smartly and returned to the headquarters without giving any reply.

Taking Lucas' hand in her right hand and Wicki's hand with her left, leading them enthusiastically back up the hill to the hospital, Angela said, "Now, we need to get everybody some supper. I've asked the reverend, Gayle and Esther to join us, so, along with Wicki, we can have a nice, congenial party." Iuba seemed to agree enthusiastically by furiously wagging his tail as he followed the trio up the path to the front of the building. He was hungry, too.

In the hospital kitchen, Angela found Clever working zealously to turn out the evening meal for the patients. Since large amounts of food had been liberated from the government warehouses that morning, cornmeal (*sadza*) had to be cooked in monstrous iron pots over outside open fires. After straining, each portion was scooped out to be placed on the metal plates. As the result of a wandering herd of wild goats that had arrived unattended on the hospital compound in the morning, a goat meat side dish would accompany each patient's normal ration of cooked cornmeal that night. This was a real treat, as most of the diners had not had meat for weeks.

"Clever, what the heck is that animal I see on a spit turning over the fire outside?" Angela asked as he rushed by.

"Oh, Sister Angela, that's a feral hog that one of Lieutenant Makura's soldiers shot this morning. The lieutenant donated it to the kitchen for our supper tonight!"

The delightful smell of roast pork filled the air as the carcass turned slowly over the open fire coals. A guard hand-cranked the roasting porcine slowly, as drippings fell to the glowing embers, hissing as they vaporized in the heat. The aroma was overwhelming.

"We will eat at six o'clock sharp," called the cook as he rushed to help Patience fill the carts with the steaming metal plates. "It will be served in the doctors' dining room. Don't be late!"

A few hours later, as they sat down to supper, Wicki was heard to say, "This smells great. Just give me the chance and I'll eat the whole pig. Then we can go off to see how my brother is coming along." He sat at the table with the delightful aroma of the roast pork permeating the room at precisely 5:59 that evening. Presiding at the head of the table sat Lucas, with Wicki sitting next to him. Underneath the table huddled Iuba, waiting impatiently for the scraps of meat that he hoped would be passed from the hands of his small master.

"Would you bless this meal before we eat, Pastor?" asked Lucas. The reverend had returned to his former pomposity, and after a tortuous prayer, which Wicki feared would render the meal ice cold, the prelate finally concluded with a resounding "Amen."

The meal was nothing short of astounding, and when all participants, including Iuba, had eaten well beyond their fill, they relaxed at the table and discussed their good fortune at once more being able to be of some use.

"We can help these soldiers find salvation and peace of mind even if they *have* behaved savagely," said Esther. "I cannot forget what has happened to me, but I must forgive them and return to the work here that God has laid out for me."

Gayle was not so generous. "These men deserve to burn in Hell's fire and I won't be involved in any way with their salvation, either physical or moral. The Bible may speak of forgiveness, but I now believe in 'Do unto others as they have done unto you.'"

The reverend had recovered sufficiently from his humiliation, and was ready to pontificate on any subject, especially the one at hand. "These rebel soldiers deserve to suffer in the eternal fires of perdition. Any fate that befalls these infidels is too good for what they deserve."

Lucas looked over at the reverend, "Say, Reverend, I know what you suffered at their hands, but isn't the reason for being here to help them find salvation? Aren't you being a little unforgiving for being a Christian missionary?"

Looking at Lucas with total disgust, the reverend spat out, "You work on these idolaters, saving their lives so that others may suffer from their heathen tortures and wars. You're little better than they are! I've spoken to many of the soldiers and they claim to be of the Christian faith, but they appear not to practice any of it. It makes me wonder why Gayle, Esther, and I came here to help them."

"Reverend, I believe that there are more than a few of these 'Christians' in our own country that claim a similar religious alliance, but fail to come up to the standard of comportment that we would expect?" returned Lucas.

"It's almost eight o'clock," he continued patting his stomach, "and we really need to thank Clever for the excellent meal. Angela and I have a meeting to attend in a few minutes and Wicki and Iuba have guard duties. Perhaps it's time to adjourn the dinner. Reverend, please remember that not all indigenous Africans are savages. Many are good Christians with understanding and patience. Unfortunately, in the course of a rebellion, many irregular occurrences happen."

Lucas got up from the table, saying to Clever as he came into the room, "Clever, we all thank you so much for the meal. We wouldn't have eaten better at the finest restaurant."

Each participant left the table, thanking Clever for his culinary efforts. His smile of pride relayed the appreciation he felt for their remarks as they returned to their respective obligations. The reverend, however, continued to mumble something about pagan, African torturers and heathen rituals as he walked back to the recovery room with Gayle and Esther. While his lodgings weren't fancy, none of the hostages was allowed to leave the hospital grounds and it *did* serve as their temporary home.

Angela and Lucas had not expected that the General would be punctual, but as the clock's chimes in the front corridor struck eight o'clock, the officer walked through the front door, grimly greeting the physician and nursing supervisor.

After his greeting was returned, the General spoke, "Major Santiago reports that there may be a problem with one of the patients. Can you tell me more?" Angela had to interpret the entire conversation between the two men, as they spoke no common language.

Lucas returned the General's salutation and replied, "General, the patient we discussed with the major shows almost certain evidence of having the Ebola virus. His condition is continuing to deteriorate and I don't anticipate that he will survive more than forty-eight hours."

The frown on the General's brow deepened, as he asked, "Have you found any other similar cases up to this time?"

"None so far, but the incubation period is still running, sir."

Walking next to Lucas, the General lowered his voice. "If I fully understand the danger of a disease of this type, uncontained it can become an epidemic and then we might anticipate the possibility of widespread sickness, with an unacceptable death rate among the indigenous as well as the soldiers?"

Lucas didn't even want to think about such an eventuality. "That is possible, sir, but we feel that we have isolated this case completely at the present time."

"Where did this patient come from?" asked the officer.

A flash of understanding suddenly crossed Lucas' mind, but he showed no evidence of this revelation to the General.

"I believe the patient mentioned that he had left the Republic of Congo only a few days ago, sir. He evidently had to cross some miles in Zaire to get here yesterday."

The officer thought for a minute and then requested, "I want to see this patient. Is he on this floor?"

Lucas thought that the General was curious to see how a patient with Ebola appeared at a mid-stage of the disease, but this might endanger the isolation if there was direct contact. "It might be dangerous to have contact with him, sir. The disease is very contagious. We could see him from the window in the door, however, without the possibility of infection or becoming contaminated."

Laughing out loud, the General said, "I've been shot at and mortared more times than I can remember. A bug hardly scares me! Let's see this so-called Ebola thing."

Lucas and Angela led the General to the utility room and peered through the small, glass window in the door. Lucas was surprised at the progression of the disease in just a few hours.

Looking through the glass, the General remarked, "Good gracious, Mary and Jesus! He looks terrible!"

There was a trickle of blood seeping from each of Teke's nostrils and his eyes now had dark red bruises at the outside margins of his eyelids, which were clots. The urine draining from his catheter, which was collecting in a bag on the floor, was a deep crimson and there was a definite clot at the opening of his left ear. As the General was peering through the glass, Teke coughed up a large, bright red mass of bloody sputum from his lungs and transferred it to a gauze pad in his right hand. He continued to cough.

The rebel General turned away from the window, utterly affected by the scene in the isolated room. "I've spent my life seeing battle wounds," he finally said, "but nothing like that. How long did you say he has?"

After looking again at the suffering Teke, Lucas said, "Maybe forty-eight hours. He will soon become incoherent and then just gradually go into a coma and die."

Thinking out loud, the General went on. "You mean that if this patient's disease gets out of that room, many of my soldiers may have a similar fate?"

Lucas understood the General's concern, but he could not read his mind. "Yes, sir, that might be the possibility."

The General stood by the closed door of Teke's room and thought for a moment as he looked at the floor. Looking up at Angela, he asked, "As far as you are aware, there are no other identified cases of Ebola at this hospital, so if any more do develop it would almost certainly be from this room?"

Angela was uncertain of the General's point, but she hesitantly answered, "Ahh…That would appear to be accurate."

Frowning, the General continued, "He may live for another two days in this condition, I think you said."

"Yes"

"Did he arrive alone, or was someone with him?"

As Lucas answered, he began to see the point of the General's interrogation. "Alone."

Grasping the handle of Teke's door, the General jerked the door open. Without a word and in a split second, he pulled his revolver from its holster and shot Teke twice in the head, killing him instantly. The sounds of the discharging pistol thundered throughout the hospital, reverberating down the corridors and up to the second floor.

Lucas was astounded. "What the heck....."

Calmly, and as if nothing unusual had happened, the General ordered,

"I will have my aide see that the body of this unfortunate man and everything in his room is burned immediately. All furniture is to be incinerated and the walls and floors are to be disinfected completely. No one is allowed in this room for one week. These are my orders and they are not to be questioned. They are to be carried out immediately."

Turning, the unperturbed general replaced his weapon in its holster and strode away towards the entrance of the building, disappearing down the path to his headquarters. Angela and Lucas stood speechless, engulfed in a cloud of gun smoke as they remained standing aghast at the door to Teke's room. They had not expected cold-blooded murder. Nurses and aides came running from all directions to investigate the sounds.

Pushing shut the door to Teke's room, Lucas repeated the General's orders to Biro, who organized two other soldiers he found near them. "Put on protective gear and began to clear out the utility room, now," Biro ordered. "We have much work to do!"

Pulling Angela aside, Lucas suggested to her the thought that suddenly occurred to him when the General had asked for the location of Teke's home.

"Angela! Teke came from the Congo Republic, and I remember that Wicki said that he got Iuba from Kisambo, about halfway between Loubomo and Lubalo. Wicki has to be Teke's brother and he's in danger from both the Ebola virus and the General. If the General finds out they came together, he may try to shoot Wicki too.

"That's so," said Angela. "We'd better find Wicki immediately. He needs to be examined for signs of the virus. That poor orphan could also be carrying the disease, and if so, we need to treat him; if not, to protect him."

Angela walked calmly out onto the front porch where Wicki was sitting on a stump near the front door. Upon seeing Angela approach, Iuba got up and began to wag his tail in greeting. Wicki looked up at the approach of the friendly nurse saying, "What was that noise, Missie Angela? "It sounded like a gunshot!"

Ignoring the question, for the moment, Angela smiled non-committally at Wicki and remarked, "Wicki, didn't you tell me you and your brother came to Lubalo to visit your grandparents? I believe that you said he had become sick and is now a patient in the clinic. What is his name? Have you visited him since he came here to the hospital?"

"Yes, Missie Angela" said the grateful boy. "Teke and I came from the Republic of the Congo, and had to come across Zaire to get here. It was a long journey, and my brother got sick just as we arrived. I believe he is in a bed somewhere on the first floor."

Looking expectantly up at Angela, he went on, "Do you think we will be able to find my brother among all these patients?"

Angela's concern heightened exponentially for Wicki's life, first for his having possibly contracted the virus and second, if the General suspected that he was a carrier.

Angela sat down on the porch and motioned for the young boy to come closer. Looking directly into his face, Angela drew a flashlight from her pocket. Not wanting to alarm Wicki, she said, "Now, we have been taking care of all these patients and your brother, but who is caring for you and Iuba? We must be sure that our guards are healthy and able to do their duty."

Using the flashlight, Angela carefully examined Wicki for any traces of external blood, not forgetting to examine his enthusiastic dog at the same time. The stethoscope around Angela's neck informed her that Wicki had clear lungs. Iuba just wanted to play and would not hold still for any examination.

Lucas arrived on the front steps and sat down next to the boy and Angela. "I guess that both of our guards are healthy and ready to work," remarked the nurse to Lucas as she replaced her stethoscope around her neck and put the flashlight away.

"Wicki, we must talk for a few minutes," Lucas started. "I want you to listen closely to what I'm going to tell you and then

Missie Angela and I will answer any questions that you might ask. Is that okay?"

The tone of voice that Lucas was using had gained Wicki's full attention, and he now sat in front of Lucas listening to every word. "What are we going to talk about?" asked the boy, smiling in anticipation of some good news or reward.

"You told us that Teke traveled with you from Loubomo, in the Congo Republic, south across Zaire, through Kisambo… where that nice white lady gave you Iuba?"

"Oh, yes," nodded Wicki." She was very nice to us."

"Was Teke sick then?" asked Lucas.

"He was not feeling well, but we continued to travel, as it was only a few hundred kilometers to Lubalo and our grandparents were expecting us. A man with a large lorry picked us up by the side of the road and said he would leave us south of Lubalo at the mission. We were fortunate to find a ride so quickly, as we had only been traveling for a few days."

Lucas now paused for a minute and then continued, "Wicki, can you remember if there were many sick people back in Luobomo before you left there?"

"Oh yes…both of our parents died of the plague a few days before we left. Many people in our village became sick. That was the reason we had to come here to live with our grandparents. Our relatives live near Camaxilo, a few miles west of the Lubalo mission. As soon as Teke gets better, we will go to find them! Is he better now? Can we leave to find our relatives now?"

Angela took over the conversation at this point. She could feel tears as they welled up into her eyes, knowing that she had to tell Wicki that he was the only family member left alive. She wiped the moistness from her face with a handkerchief, turning her face so the lad couldn't see that she was crying. "Wicki, I'm afraid that Teke didn't survive his sickness. He died this evening and he won't be going with you to find your family. We're both very sorry."

Angela paused, waiting for this revelation to find its way into the young boy's mind, but there was no visible evidence that he understood what she had just said. He continued to sit there on his stump, without moving, and patting Iuba as if she had made a remark about the weather. He finally looked over at Angela and said, "I thought that Teke might not recover at the hospital. Our *boma* (small collection of huts) became infected with that bleeding plague, and Teke stayed at home with my parents to take care of them. I sought food. The infection was everywhere. Many people died."

Angela seemed more affected by Teke's death than Wicki, who had seen his entire village wiped out only a few days ago. "So you suspected that Teke had the bleeding plague before you arrived here?" she asked.

Dry-eyed and in a calm voice, Wicki unemotionally stated, "We both suspected it, but we wanted to try to get here before he became too weak to travel."

Lucas now spoke. "Did you not think of the possibility of the plague following the two of you everywhere that you traveled on your way to Angola?"

Wicki fidgeted nervously on his seat and replied, "We had no way to know if the bleeding plague had arrived in Zaire or Angola or what made it spread. Did Teke give the disease to anyone here? How does it spread? The Congo government reported that the plague was spread by witchcraft and curses."

Angela took Wicki's hand in hers, knowing that he had no disease, and holding gently onto his hand said, "We have no evidence at this time that Teke has given the problem to anyone here in Lubalo. Doctor Lucas and I were very concerned about whether or not you have the plague. If at this point there appear to be no signs, you, Iuba, are most likely safe."

"Does that mean that we can continue to guard the hospital and live here?" asked the anxious boy, almost in a begging tone.

Patting him on the shoulder in a reassuring manner, Lucas smiled and answered,

"We're not able to function here without a guard and his dog. We will continue to count on you and Iuba for security of the hospital. You may resume your duties, if you feel up to it."

As they returned to the front doors of the hospital, Angela and Lucas smiled at each other with the common understanding that since Wicki was now truly an orphan, he would have some security and a place to live for the future, at least until he found his relatives. Meanwhile, the hospital would try to survive under rebel control.

The next morning, after morning rounds, it was established that no new cases of Ebola had shown themselves, which was reported to Major Santiago following the specific inquiry from the commander.

"Let's go to surgery, Lucas. There are all those orthopedic cases to clean up and I've got the patients from whom we have kept food or drink for eight hours to prepare for the anesthetic," remarked Angela after breakfast. "Some of those cases may be infected, and debridement of the wounds could save their limbs if we can remove the non-viable flesh."

Walking briskly up the stairs together to the second floor, Lucas remarked, "I really hate this stench of dead flesh after breakfast throughout the hospital. We need to do something about it, Angie."

As they got into their scrub suits, they noticed that Hilda, the anesthetist, seemed extremely nervous. This was unusual, as she was an excellent nurse and had flawlessly put patients to sleep repeatedly over the last three months.

"What's going on, Hilda?" remarked Lucas as he entered the operating room before preparing to scrub his hands. "You don't seem happy this morning."

Without saying a word, Hilda continued her preparations, filling syringes and testing the oxygen mask for use on the first patient. Looking up at Lucas, she smiled and said, changing the subject, "I guess we all worry sometimes, Doctor S, I saw Wicki this morning as I came in and he seems to be taking his brother's death fairly well. Who is going first?"

Just then, the doors to the operating suite burst open and Biro charged into the surgery suite. Lucas was preparing to advise the guard that this was a sterile environment, and that he was not welcome with his unsterile clothes. One look at Biro's face, however, immediately changed Lucas' mind. Lowering his weapon at Angela's chest and panting in bursts of air, he growled, "Where have you hidden that bastard reverend and those two bitches he lives with? We can't find them anywhere within the compound this morning!"

# 6
## Chapter

The dense foliage along the river's edges made any passage by foot difficult. The soft ground gave way with each step as the tangled underbrush caught their feet, greatly magnifying their effort to move forward. This resistance eventually eroded the escapees' limited energy. As they tired, they were finally forced by exhaustion to remain on the paths and tracks previously worn into the ground by the traffic of decades past.

"Gayle, you're going to have to keep up the pace," said the reverend, his impatience reflected by his tone of voice. "It's going to be light soon and the rebels will discover that we've left. They will be after us. We need to find a place to hide during the day."

Stumbling as she tried to keep up with Esther and Reverend Brown, Gayle fell full length on the soft earth, wounding only her self-confidence, but considering the suffering she had already sustained, this was no minor blow. Turning around at the sound of Gayle's fall, Esther remarked, "You know, this was your idea in the first place, Gayle. Now you need to keep up. Try to stay on the path."

The runaways were miserable. They had left the hospital shortly after midnight, telling that boy with the dog on the porch that they were going for some fresh air for a few minutes before returning to bed. At first, as they had entered the brush and deep grass along the river's edge, it had seemed easy to travel. As they had progressed further from the mission, the river's edge had become a quagmire of mud and flying insects that seemed to have become concentrated in these marshy swamps, stinging any exposed skin and sucking their blood.

After some time passed, they noticed a glow of light from the eastern horizon, foretelling sunrise. This emphasized the urgency of their travel and the knowledge that daylight would not provide any respite from their suffering. They rested on the banks of the Lubalo River, out of breath and with no relief in sight.

"I was surprised that we had no trouble getting past the guards," noted the reverend," but now, those mosquitoes and tsetse flies are really torturing us. Let's try to get a little rest before we proceed. It can't be more than a few miles before we reach a settlement."

\* \* \*

Morning surgery at the Lubalo Mission had been canceled and the entire compound was scoured for the missing trio. When they could not be found, it was assumed that the reverend and his two assistants were on the run.

"But they said they just wanted some fresh air," explained Wicki to Lucas. "It was only about midnight and no one told me about the possibility of someone leaving, so I said that it was fine. They never came back, but I thought that they probably had returned through the back door."

"We will hunt them down like dogs and kill all of them on sight!" proclaimed Major Santiago upon hearing Biro's report. "They were on their honor to remain on the hospital compound and now this escape has endangered all of the hostages. Round up a detail of men and try to find some tracking dogs. I suspect that they will head north along the river, away from the fighting further south."

A party of five guards was formed and the few bloodhounds available were collected into a company. This was to be an attempt to follow the scent track that the three captives had left as they exited the complex. It took until ten that morning to organize the posse and actually find the scent at the edge of the compound where they had gone into the bush.

The porous ground was ideal for following the scent, and the pursuers moved rapidly at first as they trailed the trio. Without warning, the trail was suddenly lost.

"What happened here?" yelled Manabe as the dogs began to circle a large area without picking up the scent. Manabe, the leader of the posse, had hoped to be the first to come upon the escapees in order to prevent their assassination by the other guards. The Major had made it clear that the three hostages were not to be returned alive, but Manabe hoped to be the first to locate the runaways. He had his orders, but the guard had reservations about killing the unarmed trio in cold blood.

"We have lost the trail because the escapees have crossed the shallow water," said the dog handler. "Cross over to the bank on the other side. The dogs may pick it up again there."

As they came up on the opposite bank, the dogs were confused. In the darkness, the reverend had become totally disoriented and moved in the opposite direction for a few hundred yards. This mistake caused the pursuing group a considerable loss of time until eventually, the track was picked up moving south before looping north again along the bank of the river. Once the trail was rediscovered, they were forced to move slowly due to the dense undergrowth.

Up the river, north of the posse, the fleeing trio ran into more trouble.

"Reverend Brown, Can we afford to rest? Both of us are very tired and thirsty. We should have thought to bring a canteen or something," complained Gayle, sitting on the ground under a large frangipani tree. "I'm already bushed and it's only about noon. It's starting to get really hot again. I guess we left the mission without much preparation."

The reverend was not accustomed to any prolonged physical exertion and certainly not under these primitive circumstances. Looking around, he wondered out loud, "I assume the moving water of the river is safe to drink. We need some sort of container to scoop it up."

Searching around, he found a broad leaf from a plant that grew nearby. He said, "I've seen the natives use this type of leaf as a cup when dipped into the water. Maybe we can use it now."

Walking directly to the closest bush, he grasped a leaf to forcibly remove it from its stem. Gayle's scream made him jump back as a six-foot puff adder struck at his hand, missing his fingers by only a few inches. He fell back on the ground, paralyzed with fear as the powerful, thick, venomous snake calmly slithered away. He was untouched.

"That was close. Thank you, Gayle. You probably saved my life."

\* \* \*

As Wicki sat alone on the front porch of the hospital, he began to review the events of the past few days. He had been grief-stricken by his brother Teke's death and now, for the first time, Wicki realized that he was actually an orphan with no close relatives to rely on anywhere. Despite his positive remarks to Angela, the location of his grandparents was, in truth, uncertain. While he had been working at the hospital, the kind missionaries had tried to assist him and Iuba to survive, but now he saw no long-term prospects of any type. Large tears began to fall on Iuba's fur as the boy pulled the dog to his face and talked to him softly, trying not to sniffle as he patted the powerful dog's head.

"We're alone, Iuba. No one really cares what happens to us and there is no one to help us if we starve. They will certainly dismiss me since they will blame us for the escape of the reverend and his two lady assistants. We will have no place to sleep and food will be pickings from the garbage or what we can find on the road. Where will we go and how can I take care of you?"

Iuba knew that his master was sad and tried to wag his tail and lick Wicki's face, but nothing seemed to improve the boy's mood. The clouds that had been collecting in the western sky now grew darker and a slow, steady rain descended on them. Wicki and his dog moved to the back part of the porch to avoid the soaking cascade of water as the rain increased in volume. Despite this measure, a large amount of rain was blown by the increasing wind soaking them, and forcing them to move inside the hospital to remain out of the now- drenching downpour.

"Hey! What do we have here?" asked Doctor Lucas as he came upon the guard and his friend sitting on the floor at the front of the hospital entrance. "You two are soaked to the skin. I'm sending the both of you down to the kitchen with orders for a warm cup of milk and some of Clever's oatmeal cookies, right now! You'll need a towel and some dry clothes too."

"We can't go, Doctor Lucas. Only patients and employees can be fed at the hospital kitchen, and we must have been fired after last night's escape."

Lucas began to laugh, and putting his hand on the small black boy's head, assured Wicki that his job was not in danger since no one had taken anything from the hospital, and the escape was not his fault. Lucas realized, over the last few days, that he enjoyed this boy whom he saw every day at the mission. The children and their families, their injuries and problems made his work worthwhile, and were the original reason that he had come to Africa. "Now get a towel and dry the pair of you. Then report to the kitchen. I'm going to send Missie Angela to check on you in a few minutes. She'd better report that you both were warm, dry, and fed." Lucas turned his head away, but not before Wicki caught his smile as the doctor continued down the hall towards the ward where he originally was headed. The grateful boy, with lifted spirits, hurried to the kitchen to see about the milk and cookies.

* * *

The fugitives near the northern Lubalo River banks were not quite so jovial. The rain also had increased where they were traveling, destroying the scent track for their pursuers and giving the trio more time to look for refuge, but it also began to cause more discomfort.

"I'm being soaked and it felt cool at first, but now it's cold and wet. Where can we get out of this rain?" complained Esther.

Looking ahead to the north, the Reverend Brown exclaimed, "I think that I can see a roof about two hundred yards ahead above the tree tops. Let's try to get there. Perhaps we will find some protection and food. Come along."

Plodding through the mud and undergrowth, they eventually arrived at the building they had seen. "This place appears to have been abandoned for a long time," remarked Esther as they walked into the clearing where the buildings stood. "There's no evidence of people.... this place gives me the heebie-jeebies."

The three escapees looked around the cleared area and discovered four buildings standing within the flat riverbank clearing. All four structures had thatch roofs and were in total disrepair with their walls partially destroyed. It appeared that they had either been pushed over or burned in times past. There was no evidence of any attempt at repair.

"Look at this!" exclaimed Gayle, picking up a rusty knife with dirt on the blade that lay next to one of the broken walls. "Perhaps there was a home here. I want to look further to see if anything useful was left." Her tiredness and thirst were forgotten for a few minutes.

A closer inspection of the four buildings took only a few minutes, as there was little to see. The abandoned riverside village must have functioned as a sort of warehouse, as the buildings appeared to be primarily for storage. Only one shack appeared to have been used for habitation and the occupants must have been of meager means. The kitchen had little area for food storage or preparation, and there seemed to be only a place for two people to sleep.

"I think that I can see a water pump!" said Reverend Brown. The fractured grey daylight streaming through the crushed roof revealed what appeared to be a pump handle protruding from a broken cabinet in the back of the building that had once been used for habitation. The dim light from the overcast sky was barely enough to spot the handle in the opaque shadows of the shack.

Walking through the dripping rain, which splashed down onto the floor from between the broken thatch roof fronds, Gayle stumbled through the scattered trash of old cans and papers, grasping the pump handle in anticipation of relief of her thirst. She began to pump the handle vigorously, but no gush of water resulted from her efforts.

"Damn it! This pump is like everything else in this cursed country. Nothing works!" exclaimed Gayle as she watched the handle move up and down without assistance from her hand, showing that there was no friction below. Still, no production of liquid accumulated in the metal basin below the pump's spigot.

"We need a drink and the only water seems to be in the river. It's time we did something about our thirst," said the reverend. Stooping down, the reverend picked up a metal container lying on the ground. He estimated that it would hold at least a quart, although it was so rusty that there was a small hole in the bottom. Plugging the hole with a stem from a nearby plant, he said, "I'll get a drink for all of us right now," as he walked towards the river.

The distance from the abandoned settlement to the river's edge was only a few hundred yards. This ground was heavily littered with various debris, including empty used tin cans for oil products, waste paper from food containers, rope, soiled parts of clothing, and rotten logs. Negotiating this, the reverend noted a gradual uphill grade to the river's edge, which held the flow of water in check within the bounds of the river's bank. Upon reaching the small summit, he was able to view the flow of the water coming from upstream for a few hundred yards to the bank just below him. Gayle and Esther followed a few yards behind.

Deciding that he would have to go down to the sandy bank to be able to collect any water, he estimated that it was only about a six-foot drop to the river's edge. There he anticipated that he would be able to collect the water from the flat shore where it appeared fairly clear and should be drinkable.

Climbing cautiously down the side of the river bank, the reverend arrived at the water's edge, but a large, half-submerged log seemed to be lying near the bank at the spot where he had planned to collect the water. In response to this obstacle, he moved about three feet further along the sandy bank.

He dipped his hand into the water to taste it and to satisfy himself that the water was drinkable. Placing his water-filled hand to his mouth, he thought, "It *does* taste refreshing and cool." Bending over, he placed the edge of the metal container into the river and watched with satisfaction as the clear fluid began to accumulate in the container.

Suddenly, the half-submerged log behind him sprang from the water and firmly clamped its massive jaws on the reverend's right hand, right shoulder and face. His scaly back, looking very much like a log to the naïve preacher, the twenty-foot crocodile had been lying in the shallow water waiting for a meal.

"Aihhhh!" screamed the terrified man, as the fifteen hundred pound amphibian somersaulted Reverend Brown from the bank into deeper water. The crocodile, twisting in the water in a death roll as all crocs do, tore a large mass of flesh including part of the reverend's face and right arm, from his body. Gulping this mass in bulk, the crocodile grabbed another hold of the flailing body and plunged for the river bottom. It was all over in less than thirty seconds.

"What's happened?!" screamed Gayle as Esther ran with her up to the river's bank. Looking down on the river, they saw only a small turbulence as the back and tail of the scaled monster disappeared under the river's smooth flow, leaving only a fading red tinge in the current near the sandy bank.

"He's gone," mumbled Esther, her voice almost a whisper as the horror of the scene left her numb with disbelief. "That crocodile must have been twenty feet long, waiting at the water's edge." Now beginning to get hysterical as the incident became real to her, she sobbed uncontrollably, realizing that it could have been her at the river bank. "That thing just snatched him from the bank like a frog grabs a fly. It was horrible, and all that blood…. What do we do now? We're all alone in the middle of Africa."

The rain continued to fall relentlessly as the two women stood on the river bank, looking down at the Lubalo River as it flowed north to join with the Kwilu River some sixty miles away in Zaire. When she saw that Esther had regained some of her composure, Gayle began to speak. "Now Esther, we have to try to think as logically as possible, since we now have no one to advise us. We know that the rebels are bound to pursue us," continued Gayle. "Did the reverend ever tell you what his plans were?"

Esther and Gayle began to walk slowly back down the bank to the broken buildings together. Soon, they entered one of the empty storage houses. The roof was little protection from the steady rain, and they shivered in the cool breeze coming in from across the river. "All I know was that Reverend Brown had plans to try to get to a settlement in Zaire so he could call for help." Starting to cry again, Esther sobbed, "He never even told me where we were going or how far it was."

"Okay, okay," said Gayle, trying to calm her whimpering companion. "We know that he was aiming towards the north and that there eventually will be a settlement of some size along this river. We just have to follow the river for a bit longer, and we'll arrive there."

Placing her arm around Esther's trembling shoulder, Gayle dabbed her wet face with a piece of rag and began to lead her in the direction of the flow of the river to the north. The faint call of the bloodhounds was now audible in the wind from the south, and both of the escapees heard it simultaneously.

"Oh my God, they're coming for us. We'll be shot on sight when they find us," Esther sniveled. She began to try to run, but stumbled on the path and fell in a heap at Gayle's feet.

Gayle placed an arm under Esther's shoulder and lifted her from her fall, noticing that the cloudy, overcast sky still had enough illumination to disclose a thin pathway leading away from the clearing. This bare strip was well overgrown with weeds and foliage but had obviously been in heavy general use in previous times.

"Maybe we can find a way to an occupied village by following this path," Gayle said as she began to lead the way along the track, heading north.

They both felt cold and wet, as well as hungry, since neither had eaten for almost thirty-six hours. As they walked along the path in the rain, they discovered puddles that had collected on top of rocks and on leaves. These served as sources of drinking water, relieving their thirst.

"I'm terribly hungry," remarked Esther as she followed Gayle, who pulled a large hanging branch out of the pathway and entered a small clearing in the dense brush. The clogged pathway they were following had suddenly opened into a grassy clearing some thirty feet wide.

"Good heavens! Are they dangerous?" asked Esther as she came to the edge of the small clearing that the hanging branch had concealed. "There must be twenty of them!"

In the clearing sat an entire family of baboons, totally unconcerned by the driving rain. The apes were eating various fruits, including pawpaw, mangos and cumquats that grew on the trees that surrounded the open space. Some were grooming each other as they sat on the grass carpet that covered the floor of the clearing. A small, rippling stream of clear water flowed across the space, apparently headed for a union with the Lubalo River a few hundred meters further on.

After watching the apes for a minute, Esther asked, "Do we dare try to scare them? How do we get to the fruit? There's no way we could climb one of those trees to get our own meal."

Her answer came almost immediately. The sound of her voice startled the baboon family and they moved to the trees, screaming warnings and carrying their young as they rushed for cover. Once safely in the trees, the noise continued, followed by a hail of fruit, which came cascading into the clearing.

"Watch out! Their aim is pretty good," exclaimed Gayle, as the sound of a solid thump on her head reverberated around the clearing. "Those mangos hurt and they're throwing hard."

The rain now began to slacken and the baboons, growing tired of the game, found other interests to attend to. They disappeared into the treetops, swinging easily from branch to branch in effortless coordination. The two women watched the apes move through the treetops in utter fascination.

"There's enough fruit here to feed twenty people," mumbled Gayle as she began to pick up the fruit and taste the sweet nectar of a pawpaw plant. "We were fortunate to run into the monkeys."

\* \* \*

By this time, the pursuing group of guards had fallen well behind the two escapees and the trail had become more difficult to follow in the wet grass and dirt. .Manabe, who was still leading the guards' pursuit, said, "We do know the direction of their escape, but we can no longer actually follow their trail. Let's stop for a rest and try to regroup."

As the guards sat by the river resting, one guard suddenly pointed to the river's edge. "Look at that orange piece of cloth caught in the branch!" He said. "What is it?"

"Go and fetch it, Jose. It looks familiar," said Manabe to the guard who had originally spotted the cloth caught in a tangle of brush by the river's edge.

Climbing over the brush at the river bank, Jose had to negoti-ate the shallow water to reach the brightly colored material. Upon reaching the floating orange fabric to dislodge it, he found that it was actually a sock, still containing a badly mangled foot and lower leg. There was little blood, but the leg had been severed above the ankle with a ragged edge. Pulling it loose from the brush, the guard carried the sock with its grisly contents back to the group.

"I thought that I recognized the color," said Manabe as he calmly examined the specimen. "No doubt parts of the reverend now lie in the stomach of one of our reptile friends who lives along the banks of the river." He knew it was their habit to plant anything too big to consume at one time under a log, deep under the water to let it decompose for a while and then come back for it later when it ripened.

Turning to the other guards, he continued, "We'll take this back with us to the mission and show it to Major Santiago. I doubt that those two city women will survive for long alone in this jungle." He still felt obligated to follow his orders, but was thankful that he could rationalize not having to murder in cold blood the other two women who escaped with the reverend.

The group of guards gathered up their belongings in the slackening rain and headed back upriver towards the mission, thankful they had obtained solid evidence to show that that further efforts to follow the escapees were no longer necessary.

\* \* \*

"That was a well-needed meal," said Gayle, as she moved toward the clearing's edge, still clutching a final mango in her hand.

Esther continued to sit on the rock she had found for a resting place, remarking with a pawpaw-filled mouth, "I really never liked the taste of mango very much, but these were really nice. I believe I'll just have one more before we go."

Eventually, they stood up and resumed following the pathway, which appeared to continue in a northerly direction parallel to the river. They noticed that the trail appeared wider and more recently used, though the clearing had disappeared behind them in the dense brush.

"It seems easier walking here," said Gayle, again leading the way. "I think this part of the path is wider and more trafficked."

The pathway veered to the right, and suddenly, they found themselves walking immediately next to the Lubalo River, which now appeared much wider and deeper than it had been at the mission, further upstream.

"I think I can see a village across the river on the other side," exclaimed Esther as they came into a clearing about 250 yards from the opposite bank. "After what happened to the reverend, there's no chance that we could attempt to swim across." The women discussed whether they should continue to follow the trail in hopes of finding a bridge or a village on their side of the river.

"That's the best plan," agreed Esther.

It was now around four o'clock and, as the rain had cleared, it was a warm and extremely pleasant, sunny afternoon.

Progressing along the trail, it suddenly widened into a road with two gravel strips for the tires. The high grass growing between these tire tracks showed fresh wear from recent traffic. The women increased their walking rate to almost a trot.

"There has to be a village or town nearby," said Gayle, almost breaking into a run in anticipation of some type of habitation. "I'm sure people have been on this road recently." The vehicle tracks now led to a small collection of thatch-roofed rondovel huts in good repair. A little further beyond these dwellings the two women entered a marketplace with open booths, in which people were selling all sorts of foodstuffs and typical African clothing.

Neither of the women had considered their clothing prior to this moment, but the sight of civilization made Gayle realize that they stood in the bazaar dressed in tatters. "Now that there are all these people, I realize that we look terribly ragged and worse, we have no money."

"Perhaps we can find a mission somewhere in this town. Let's ask someone," answered Esther.

The two white missionaries began to look for someone to ask, but all of the people in the market place appeared to be of dark skin. Most of the shoppers in the market place appeared to speak only Portuguese or Kileta, as the natives bargained for a mutually acceptable price for their purchases from the vendors. Besides their white skin, the American, western style of clothing made the missionaries stand out among the crowds of shoppers, who were wearing native bright colors, loose fitting wraps, and head scarves. After they had been in the marketplace for some time, Gayle said, "The natives probably don't speak English, but over there is a man who doesn't appear to be a local citizen. His clothing and manner appear foreign. Let's go to him and ask for help. Perhaps he speaks some language we can understand and will help us."

It was now approaching five o'clock in the evening and the shopkeepers were preparing to close and go to supper, so there were fewer people circulating in the market. Upon approach, it became clear that the gentleman in question was not an African, but a light skinned Arab. He wore an elaborate robe and had on his head a red turban that was held in place by a golden rope. As she approached him, he was speaking fluently in a language she didn't understand.

"Ahhh, excuse me sir, but do you speak English?" Gayle opened the conversation shyly, realizing that it was unusual and against colloquial convention in the African society for a woman to speak to an Arab man without first being introduced.

Abruptly turning from his conversation with the shop owner, the short, obese Arab man with a full beard and dark eyes exhibited no sign of surprise at being addressed in English by an American woman. If he was, it was not evident in his polite manner or his prompt reply, "Yes, Mimsaub, I speak many languages including English. How may I be of assistance to you? My name is Hamid Hissain Abib. You may address me as Hamid."

Not expecting his polite, smooth, well-spoken answer, which was given with a cultured, obviously school-taught English accent, Gayle could say nothing for an entire thirty seconds. Esther finally answered, "I'm afraid we are a bit lost here and in dire straits to try to find our way home. Could you perhaps help us? We don't speak Portuguese or Kileta."

Bowing his head politely in greeting, the Arab said, again in too-perfect continental English, obviously not acquired from informal use, "Perhaps we could sit together and drink a sip of tea across the street at the café? You could clarify to me as to what assistance I could be."

So desperate to find any assistance, even after the experiences they had recently gone through, the women threw away normal precautions. They had gained some superficial confidence from the overly polite, refined manners of the strange Arab. Gayle and Esther followed the robed man across the sparsely populated dirt street to a café- restaurant associated with the only run-down hotel in the tiny village. As the three sat at the solitary table on the veranda, the Arab ordered hot tea and scones for all. "Now what is it that I may assist you ladies with?" inquired Hamid politely, after Gayle and Esther had introduced themselves.

Gayle was having second thoughts about telling a complete stranger of the last week's events in detail, but they were in an unknown village, somewhere in northern Angola with no friends or money. Anyway, before she could stop her friend, Esther stated it. "We're alone, penniless, and desperate."

During the course of three cups of tea and multiple sweet rolls, the entire story of their capture by the rebels at the mission, their escape, as well as the reverend's fate, was told. Their physical abuse by the rebels was not mentioned by either Gayle or Esther.

"That's a very depressing story," said Hamid after listening for a half-hour to their tale with almost no interruptions. "What are your plans? Do you even know where you are now?"

"We have no idea where this village is located, or how to leave this settlement. Could you please inform us how to contact the United States Embassy, or how we can return to Luanda, or from where we would be able to contact our families?"

The Arab smiled in a friendly manner and lowering his voice, said, "You are in the settlement of Lubalo. The only functioning roads are towards the south to the village of Camaxilo. At present, they are not negotiable due to obstruction by the rebel forces in active combat with the Luanda government. Thus, the only safe passage would be to the north, across the Zaire border."

"Where could we go from there?" asked Esther, now seeming more desperate.

Sitting back in his chair, their host continued, "There are no roads at all to the north across the border, and if there were I would have to assume that neither of you thought to bring your passports on fleeing the mission? Is that correct?"

"Our passports were taken when we were captured," answered Gayle in disgust, "So we are marooned? We appear to be without options?"

Leaving a few seconds for Gayle's thought to be absorbed by both women, the Arab continued. "I am taking a transport boat on the Lubalo River leaving here early in the morning. This boat will travel one hundred kilometers into Zaire to the Kwiliu River and then on to the town of Kisambo. I doubt that you will find any type of mission or communication for at least three days through the jungle traveling by river, as this is an extremely remote area. From Kisambo, however, you could contact the Embassy or your families quite easily by phone or wire."

Gayle, not wanting to upset this newly found friend, began to wonder about the Arab and asked "I don't mean to pry into your business, sir, but what are your interests in Lubalo? Why are you even visiting a village in this remote area? Are you from here?" It seemed strange to her that an Arab, educated enough to speak fluent English, would be in such a remote village in the remotest part of Angola.

Smiling easily, the Arab answered, "I am from Khartoum in Sudan. My business takes me to many remote places in the world. It is by the fate of Allah that we meet today so that I may assist you."

"We have no money and no place to run. Even if we could afford the river trip by boat, we have no passports and our clothes are torn and ragged. We don't even have a place to stay tonight!" said Gayle, accurately summing up their situation. Tears began to spill down her cheeks, dripping into her now cold tea.

"Perhaps you will accept some assistance from your humble servant," said Hamid, appearing to be honored if they would consider his help. "There is rarely a passport check on the river as we cross into Zaire and the boat fare is a pittance, which I would be most esteemed for you to accept."

"But you don't even know us, Hamid. Why would you be willing to help us like that?" said Gayle incredulously.

"I think we have little choice, Gayle," advised Esther. "Perhaps after having escaped from a prison camp, it would be a good idea to accept help wherever it comes from."

"You will pay me back many times over, I am sure," he said, "Now we must find a room for you to lodge in tonight and see if we can locate some fresh clothes. The boat will be leaving very early in the morning."

The two were ecstatic at what appeared to be their good luck.. Hamid took them into the hotel, registered for a room, and while it certainly wasn't the Ritz, it did have two beds and a bathroom down the hall. Once in the room, Gayle said, "Who would have thought that a strange Arab would care for us like this? I can't believe he's waiting for us downstairs to take us shopping for clothes! Let's get cleaned up a little and go get some decent things to wear."

They hurriedly cleaned the dust and dirt that had covered their bodies and hair over the past few days. While they were doing this, Esther cautioned Gayle, "Remember, he's doing this out of kindness. Let's try not to spend a lot of his money on clothes. We really shouldn't take his charity, but alone and without means we were lucky to find him."

Each lady tried to arrange her hair as best she could, after Esther found an old comb left in a drawer in the room. They hoped that perhaps the Lord was finally going to repay them for their suffering over the past few weeks. Hurrying down the rickety stairs to the main lobby, they found Hamid sitting calmly on one of the worn chairs, drinking tea as he waited for them.

"Ah yes," he said standing as they approached him. "Do you feel a little better now? Shall we go to find some fresh, dry attire? We must hurry, as the bazaar will be closed in a short time." He again touched his large nose and then his forehead as they stood before him, as was the custom of most Arabs greeting a guest.

Leading them from the hotel onto the dirt-packed street, he headed up a cluttered, tortuous side alley, which wandered off the main road. Gayle whispered to Esther, "He certainly appears to know where he is going, there's no hesitation."

He stopped in front of a small shop with Arabic lettering on the windows. "This is a good place to find everything. Western clothes will be too hot on the river trip. Trust me to find what you need," Hamid said.

Once they were inside, it was apparent that the clothes sold in the shop were all of Arab origin, which was not typical of the garments worn by the local Angolan natives. However, the tattered, wrinkled, western style clothes in which Esther and Gayle were attired when they escaped from the mission were no longer serviceable. Trying on the flowing robes of an Arab abayah in the dressing room, Esther whispered to Gayle, "Okay, it's not what

I'd choose in Boston, but he's paying for it and also our ticket out of here. Possibly he prefers robes to skirts and blouses. Let's go along with it for now. The robes *do* seem unusual, but certainly are cool in the hot sun."

"Right," replied Gayle. "When we get to civilization, we can find some real clothes. These sandals *are* comfortable though."

Having been completely outfitted, the two missionaries looked like Arabian women without face veils, as they left the shop and entered an adjoining restaurant for supper. Hamid remained as polite as ever, never protesting the cost of their clothing or supper. "Ladies, it is time to retire for the night. Remember, we have an early start in the morning and you will want to be rested for the long river trip."

They returned to the dilapidated hotel and after a relaxed bath that they had not enjoyed in weeks, the grateful women went to bed.

\* \* \*

At the mission, with the return of Manabe bringing the orange sock and lower leg documenting the fate of the reverend, it seemed a reasonable conclusion to the Major that the trio had not survived the escape attempt. While they had not been found, the chances of two novice American women surviving alone in the deep jungle seemed remote at best. This distressed the other missionaries, especially Lucas and Angela. Wicki, trying to be an optimist, said, "Perhaps only the reverend was eaten and the ladies got away. Shouldn't we continue to look for them?"

Taking his hand in hers, Angela said, "Wicki, we aren't allowed to leave the hospital grounds. There isn't a lot we can do right now. Perhaps the ladies did survive, but they took it upon themselves to escape and now they have to bear the responsibility."

Activities at the mission remained unchanged, although it was sobering to those remaining on the mission to realize that other escape attempts might well result in similar outcomes.

\* \* \*

Dawn the next morning brought sunlight and hope to Esther and Gayle. Donning their new robes after washing, they proceeded to the restaurant, arriving about seven o'clock in the morning. "My gosh, Look at all those people eating this early," said Gayle.

Without ceremony, Hamid arrived at their table and sat down. "There seem to be many people here for breakfast this morning. No doubt, most of these people will be travelers with us. The boat only leaves every other week, and since the start of the recent unpleasantness it is really the only safe means to travel. When you both finish, we can proceed to the boat."

As the three got up from the table, they encountered two men walking by, dressed similarly to Hamid. The three Arabs all greeted each other formally in the Arabic language, and after salutations the other two Arabs moved on.

Hamid then led the women to the ramp, and boarding the flat-bedded scow found a seat in the open air at the rear. The boat was little more than a motorized raft. It did have a wooden roof to protect its passengers from the blazing sun. Its appearance was similar to a picture Gayle had once seen of a river raft from the 1930s. The oil-burning motor sent black clouds of smoke curling into the sunlit sky and the "chugga- chugga" sound it emitted became monotonous in a very short time.

"These timber benches are hard," remarked Gayle after she sat down. There were more than twenty other travelers on the river flatboat.

"My seat wobbles," said Esther, "but it beats standing or walking."

At the front of the boat, as it was cast off and began to merge with the river's current thus gaining speed, were the two Arabs that the trio had encountered at breakfast.

They seemed to be in light conversation, but were too far distant to be heard by Gayle and Esther over the noise of the motor, even if they understood Arabic.

"I see that Hamid still makes his yearly trip to Lubalo to purchase slaves to provision his brothels in Khartoum," one was saying. "He usually tries to buy the youngest girls that he can and then shackles them until he can get them back to Sudan to train them."

The other replied laughing, "No luck this year with blacks? But those two whites will bring a fancy price in his establishments. He didn't even need to shackle them, so they must already be trained."

# 7
## Chapter

A new dawn quietly illuminated the horizon at the Lubalo Mission. Streaks of light induced silent shadows from the trees on the front lawn of the hospital as Wicki sat on his stump with Iuba at his side guarding the entrance. He enjoyed the magnificent sunrise that only Africa could provide. Watching the few scrawny chickens that had survived the war and now ventured from the surrounding indigenous rondavels where their owners lived, Wicki realized that the poultry were lucky to still be alive. These family huts had been built outside the mission grounds and the fowl moved around the compound pecking industriously for the scarce nutrition available.

The war had moved south. This time of the morning, Wicki easily smelled the tantalizing wood smoke from the breakfast fires being lit by the natives who had returned to their homes since the conflict had moved on. The boy had learned over the last few days to appreciate this stillness of the first light of early morning, as the mists began to clear. He recognized a few of the women as they hurried past his stump with bundles of wood on their heads as they moved towards the hospital kitchen. It was at this time that the hospital usually showed its first signs of stirring as it came to life.

"Iuba, are you awake?" he asked his friend. The "thump, thump" of the dog's tail against the grass lawn was the reply. "I think that it will really be a hot day, Iuba," continued the boy, as his growing puppy, already seventy pounds, rose up and stretched his legs, yawning.

The first sounds coming from the infirmary building were usually the nurses' voices, seeming to him to be a low, unintelligible murmur. One morning he had even overheard this report, as the night nurse turned over to the day shift. It usually took about thirty minutes and was culminated by the exit of the night staff as they returned to their quarters for breakfast and sleep.

"Hi, Doctor Maria! Did the night shift go well?" asked Wicki in English. The elderly physician, who was in charge of the hospital during the evening stint, was walking past him. She smiled and returned the greeting in her broken language, stopping to pat Iuba on the head.

"Small dog grow big now," she remarked as she then continued toward her residence at the back of the compound.

Wicki informed his assistant, Iuba, that they must know almost everyone who worked at the hospital. "The last time anyone we didn't know came by, you made it clear to them that they didn't belong here by the noise you made," he said.

Smelling breakfast cooking, the boy headed for the kitchen, followed closely by his loyal dog.

"That smells like porridge and bacon," thought Wicki as he increased the length of his stride. Iuba, smelling the same odors, ran ahead to the kitchen doorway, anticipating a treat.

Entering the kitchen, Wicki joined Lucas and Angela at the table for breakfast. They had just arrived from the hospital sleeping facilities and were preparing to start the day. No sooner did he sit down than a bowl of warm porridge appeared in front of him, as if by magic. Lucas was saying, "We will have to inform the mission headquarters of the loss of Reverend Brown and his two assistants. Is it right to have a funeral with only one foot and no bodies?"

Wicki, with a mouth full of the warm corn gruel, heard the conversation but after the severe experiences he had suffered and the loss of his own family, his emotional involvement with the reverend and the two ladies had been numbed to the point of disregard. He said nothing.

"There is no evidence that Gayle and Esther are dead. Perhaps they escaped into the bush and are still alive," Angela commented. She continued, "We may wish to report the ladies missing, but we don't know for sure they're gone. Let's wait for a while and see if anything turns up."

Lucas was insistent. "We can be sure that the reverend is gone, and common sense tells us that the ladies won't survive for long out in that jungle all alone. The longer we wait to report it, the more irresponsible we'll look, and their families need to know."

"Then, who do we inform and how do we do it?" asked Angela, reflecting again her usual logical mind.

"Perhaps the rebel hierarchy has issued an alert for their capture, or we could inform the Ira Calmsey Prayer Chain. If they pick it up, it will be relayed back to the States. I don't think we have the phone number of the reverend's church in Massachusetts, and we have no access to a phone now, anyway."

Looking at both Angela and Lucas, Wicki asked, "What is the Ira Calmsey Prayer Chain?"

"Well, it's a group of very devoted Christian individuals who pray for foreign missionaries working away from home, Wicki. They select individuals from all denominations working to spread the Christian message, and pray daily for their success. They keep in contact through a phone link."

"How will that help?" asked the boy as his last piece of bacon disappeared between Iuba's teeth. Wicki spoke and understood English surprisingly well for only studying at his home mission for a few years, but his natural curiosity betrayed his inherent high intelligence.

Angela smiled and passed more bacon to Iuba, now sitting at her feet. "I'm sure the Chain already knows that the mission has been captured and that we are held hostage, but they probably don't have accurate information about who survived and in what condition. The rebels' demands to pay for our release would most likely be over the same channels and the ransom would inform their families that we are still living." Turning to Lucas, she said quietly, "The mission has no knowledge of Gayle's or Esther's family in America, nor do the rebels."

Looking at Angela, Lucas said, "I don't think *any* information on the reverend or his two assistants was recorded in the office of the mission. It's strange that we knew so little about all three of them…they never talked much about America when they were working in the mission before the takeover."

The day Manabe had returned with the reverend's foot a meeting had been called by the Major. The entire remaining mission staff was informed that the life-saving service the group had performed on the rebel soldiers was sufficient for the General to parole them from punishment for the escape attempt, but any further attempts at escape would be dealt with severely.

On general agreement of the missionaries, a funeral was arranged for the reverend a few days later. Without the rebels' cooperation, little else could be done. Prayers were said, and the foot was interred in the mission graveyard, with the stipulation that should any more of his body turn up, it would be buried with the rest of his body. Following the funeral, Lucas remarked, "We still have no word on the fate of Gayle or Esther, and no freedom to try to search for them. If we are freed by ransom or fortunes of war we can look for them." That was the status at breakfast, as the negotiation of the ransom could not be continued because the rebel lines remained fluid and contact irregular.

Every day after breakfast, new patients from both sides of the hostilities arrived at the mission from the raging war to the south.

"Some of these new arrivals are seriously wounded, and some are badly burned by the new napalm tactics that the Luanda government has started using," said Lucas as he examined a new patient who had been transported from the fighting around Lunda Sul and Saurimo.

Angela was markedly distressed at the appearance of these new injured from the southern provinces. "My father is the pastor of the mission in Saurimo, and if there is fighting down there he may need my help. As long as we remain hostages, I'm not able to leave to evaluate if I can help his situation," Angela went on. "As I last heard, the Saurimo mission personnel were also being held under close arrest and have no freedom outside of the Saurimo Mission grounds."

Lucas put his arm on her shoulder and said kindly, "If that *is* the situation at Saurimo, Angela, your father wouldn't want you to come there or be endangered."

Care and surgery continued in the Lubalo complex over the following weeks, mostly treating wounded rebel soldiers as well as a few sick villagers. The efforts of the physicians and staff met with considerable favorable results, and the reputation of the facility grew rapidly with their continued successful outcomes. Within a short time, most of the northern Angolan armies, government and rebel alike, had heard about the Lubalo mission hospital and their compassionate, expert treatment.

One morning a few days later, as the trio sat eating breakfast, Clever made a remark: "I've just heard a rumor that Jonas Savimbi is coming in a few days to this outpost to verify the reputation of our hospital," he said calmly as he walked through the kitchen carrying a massive kettle of hot cornmeal mash.

Angela and Lucas were sitting at the table discussing the fate of the two assistants with Wicki. Lucas looked up, "Who is Savimbi and of what significance is that?" asked Lucas.

"Jonas Savimbi is the political leader of the entire rebel party and General Alverez's boss," announced Clever, as he stopped in his tracks, setting the large pot on the floor. He obviously thought that the information was significant as he continued, "The political leader can have all of the hostages shot or released at his discretion."

"If he comes, we'd better be certain that the hospital remains alert and the wards continue to run smoothly," said Angela aloud. "We don't want to have him return us to those cages and beatings."

While the medical operations continued for the next few days, major efforts were initiated to finish the clean-up of the wards, paint the halls, and straighten out the operating rooms, especially when the rumors were confirmed.

General Alverez himself made the announcement at a meeting called during the morning shift change at 7:00 A.M. "We are expecting an inspection in the near future by some of the leaders of our Independence Party. Please make efforts to appear efficient and organized."

As the appointed day approached, an air of expectation pervaded the entire mission complex. Uniforms, normally ragged and unkempt, were now neat and clean. Discipline was top priority, with smart salutes and crisp coming to attention at the appearance of any officer. Angela admired Manabe in his new uniform, all in the same color. Those controlling the hospital and mission were making a concerted effort.

"I gave Iuba a bath and found for myself a fresh pair of pants," declared Wicki. "We want the leader to see that Iuba and I are first class guards."

The letdown was profound when the appointed morning came with no helicopter settling on the landing pad near the hospital grounds. In fact, it was just another routine day as far as the complex could tell.....

At about eleven o'clock on the morning that he was expected, another shoddy ambulance rolled up to the hospital admission entrance with two wounded soldiers inside. The aide assisting with their care seemed somewhat untrained, but no one thought it remarkable. Often patients arrived from the battlefields being cared for by companions with little medical knowledge, so it passed unnoted. All eyes were on the helicopter pad, which remained empty.

"Is this the Lubalo Hospital? My friends have been wounded and need care. Can you help them?" asked the aide as he assisted the orderlies in placing the wounded soldiers on stretchers and rolling them into the receiving ward.

The receiving ward was busy that morning, as many wounded from the southern battlefields were arriving. Lucas happened to be passing through the admission ward and stopped to examine the two soldiers as the aide looked on.

"This one has a fairly severe gunshot wound to his left arm. We must send him to surgery to try to save the arm," Lucas advised the orderly as he placed a yellow tag on the bed. "There appear to be two fractures of the humerus."

Walking over to the second patient, Lucas asked, "What do we have here?"

A red-stained dressing was wound around the patient's upper right leg, and as Lucas began to unwrap the dressing, a spurt of blood emitted from the patient's groin. Calmly placing his gloved finger into the open wound, Lucas easily located the pulsating femoral artery and placed pressure on it, stopping the spurting blood.

"We'll need a hemostat," Lucas coolly remarked to Brightwell, who was standing a few feet away. "Please call Maichipo, up in the operating room, and tell her that we have a vascular case to go to surgery as soon as she's prepared."

The clamp he requested was produced almost immediately and placed on the artery, relieving Lucas from holding it. "Let's put a red tag on his bed and hustle him upstairs. I'll be there in a minute to fix that bleeder," said Lucas as he pulled off his gloves and started to leave.

"Does this happen often?" inquired the aide in English, as he watched both patients being expertly and smoothly integrated into the mission medical system.

"Only three or four times on a good day," answered Lucas. "If it gets really busy, sometimes we have to pick and choose who benefits from what is available. What training do you aides receive before they put you to work? If you want to come upstairs and follow your friends' treatment, perhaps we can help train you for field work."

"Do you mind? I'd consider it a privilege to see how you work. Anything I can learn may help save lives."

The patients were already being transferred to the surgery ward, so as Lucas was walking along the hallway and up the stairs to the operating room he and the aide had a chance to converse.

"How long have you been here?" the aide asked, increasing his steps into a trot to keep up with Lucas' fast pace. The aide was a very thin, small-boned man, about fifty, with no insignia of rank, but he appeared intelligent and very interested in helping save wounded soldiers.

"I came here from Malawi about a month ago, planning to stay only about twelve weeks. The Lubalo mission asked me to lend a hand here. I got swept up in the revolution, and now we are seeing all of these war wounds. Some of them are pretty serious."

"So, how do you feel about the revolution?" asked the aide as they approached the scrub room.

An alarm went off in Lucas' head. "What does he care how I feel about this little remote struggle in the middle of nowhere?" Lucas thought. "Who is this guy, anyway?" Out loud Lucas said, "I stay out of politics. This situation wasn't my choice and we're just doing the best we can to save lives and souls. These wounded need all of the help they can find."

As Lucas changed his clothes into a scrub suit, the aide seemed very curious about Lucas' motivation. This aggravated the surgeon, but he easily covered his emotions.

"Well, how did you and the whole hospital team get so organized and work so well together this quickly?" the aide asked. They were now inside the operating room and Lucas was scrubbing for the procedure. Since Lucas had already replaced the arterial clamp, he was ready to begin suturing the damaged artery. Their conversation continued as if they were sitting on someone's back porch, sipping lemonade. The expertise of Angela and Maichipo made the surgery seem automatic, so almost no dialogue was necessary between the team members as they worked on the repair.

"Actually, we were captured a few weeks ago and taken as hostages, but the General had such a disorganized situation with the wounded that he allowed us to be released from confinement so that the injured could be treated….."

"I don't believe we were introduced. My name is Angela," she said as they observed the pulsating artery, which no longer leaked. The circulation was now completely restored. "The foot and ankle also have a good arterial blood flow, so we can close," she concluded.

Now standing at the back of the operating room, the aide replied, "It's nice to meet you, Angela. You may call me Jonas for now. And who is the surgeon doing this repair?"

Looking up from the wound, Lucas replied, "My name is Lucas, Jonas. I'm pleased to meet you. Did all of these casualties occur south of here? How is the war going?"

Jonas now moved forward, closer to the scrub team to observe the continued closure of the fascia and skin layers. Jonas continued, "This war seems to go on forever. The price paid by each individual for freedom continues to mount daily with so many being killed or wounded. I see no end to the hostilities in the near future. The damage keeps escalating. It's quite fortunate that your team is here to help us."

As the procedure came to completion, the patient was moved to a bed, and the patient with the gunshot wound to the left arm was placed on the surgical table. As Hilda induced the anesthesia on this patient, the aide silently left the room as the procedure began.

"This arm is worse than we thought," mumbled Lucas as the gauze was removed from the open wound. "The blood supply will have to be repaired extensively to avoid amputation, and those fractures need setting."

The repair dragged on for hours. Finally, a pink color began to appear in the fingers of the left hand and a bounding pulse could be felt in the radial artery at the left wrist.

"I think we've got it," declared Angela in a tone of satisfaction.

Just then, the door to the operating room opened and the smiling face of Brightwell appeared at the opening. "How's it going?" he asked. "I heard the murmur of satisfaction in here, and hoped that you would soon be finished. It's getting to be five o'clock and you haven't even stopped for tea."

"What are you doing in my operating room?" chastised Maichipo in a joking tone. "If you have nothing better to do, I'll find something to keep you occupied."

Not moving his head one inch, Brightwell smiled and replied, "I guess that being tied up in here all day, you didn't hear that Savimbi *did* arrive and has been inspecting the entire complex all afternoon."

"Is that an excuse to barge into a sterile operating room and contaminate the surgical field?" Maichipo proceeded to rebuff the friendly assistant.

Brightwell, refusing to be intimidated by the scrub nurse, finished his announcements without interruption. "Well even if I'm not appreciated, I was told by Major Santiago that Doctor Lucas and Sister Angela are invited to supper tonight at the General's house, and to be there promptly at seven P.M."

At this pronouncement, both Lucas and Angela looked up to the doorway from their work in total surprise. "Okay. You can tell the Major that we'll be there," said Lucas as he returned to suturing the arm.

"So you have made your little notification. Now get out of my operating room, do you hear me?" said the scrub nurse sarcastically.

The black face of the orderly disappeared from the doorway to the sound of chuckling as he returned to the surgical ward.

"Kind of rough on him, weren't you, Maichipo?" asked Lucas good-naturedly.

Maichipo smiled and said, "If you give him an inch, he'll take a mile. Next week he'll be in here trying to pass instruments. Some decorum has to be maintained with these people, and I'm just the one to do it!"

The normally silent Hilda, giving anesthesia at the head of the table, began to smile at Maichipo's comments. "Watch out for that Brightwell. Next thing you know, he'll be doing the surgery!" They all had a good laugh at her remark as the operation finished.

Having completed the surgery for the day, Angela and Lucas made bed rounds on the hospital patients. This sometimes took a long time, as decisions had to be made for future surgery or change of medications. They were very gratified to find that Lieutenant Makura, their original patient, had improved considerably and appeared to be out of danger. When Angela and Lucas finally got back to their lodging in the recovery bay, they had just enough time to clean up and get dressed.

"What am I going to wear?" said Angela with typical female concern.

"Wear what you have, a fresh scrub suit like mine. That's all we have anyway. You'll look fine," replied Lucas with his usual male practicality.

As the couple walked out on to the front porch of the hospital on the way to supper, they encountered Wicki. He was sitting on his stump at the hospital entrance next to Iuba, Both immediately got up in response to the sight of Angela, as she passed down the front steps to the front lawn walking towards General Alvarez' headquarters. The dog was very fond of her and wagged his tail furiously.

"Hey Wicki. On the job already?" Iuba looks much better since he had his bath today," said Lucas as Angela led him across the lawn towards the complex gate some 150 meters away.

The soft, full moonlight shone across the well-kept sod as they continued to walk. The gentle breezes blowing in their faces cooled the warm evening air and carried the sounds of native voices singing. Lucas stopped and took Angela by the waist, kissing her gently on the face and neck. "You look as beautiful in a scrub suit as in a Pierre Cardin wardrobe."

"Lucas my love, it's true that it's not important where we are or the clothes we wear, but as long as we can be together I can be happy."

"You know, Angela, I haven't had a chance to thank you for all of the help you've given in organizing the hospital and patient care for the past few weeks. Without your help, it would have been impossible."

"Lucas, we've not had a second alone together since we left the cages. I miss being able to talk to you and being alone with you…not that I miss the cages."

He held her tightly to his chest and repeatedly kissed her mouth. She eagerly returned the passion as they stood alone in the moonlight.

"If we ever get out of here, Lucas, perhaps some arrangements could be made for our relationship to extend beyond just kisses?" Angela said, laughing as they separated and began walking again down the hill, holding hands.

Suddenly the familiar voice of Wicki rang out over the front grounds of the hospital, accompanied by the enthusiastic barking of Iuba, "I saw that! What's going on down there?"

Lucas blushed and said in a low voice to Angela as they continued to walk, "Now we've had it. There are no secrets on a mission. He'll tell everyone."

"Very few secrets," agreed Angela, "but most of the missionaries probably already suspected. Here's the gate to Reverend Williamson's house."

As the couple approached the gate of the hospital compound, the guard at the gate snapped to attention and saluted. He said, "Doctor Lucas and Sister Angela, you are expected. Please proceed to the headquarters entrance down the path."

As the two missionaries continued along the path leading to the front door of what used to be Reverend Williamson's house, Lucas asked Angela, "Do we know what ever became of the Williamsons?"

"I'm not completely sure," she replied. "During the scramble to avoid capture as the rebels took over, many people ran into the bush. Some were killed while we were captured together in the hospital. I hope that they have escaped."

"What's the rumor among the natives?" asked Lucas. "The 'jungle telegraph' almost always has the unofficial story on everything."

Angela agreed with Lucas' observation about native rumor and gossip. While not always reliable, the native version on anything often was close to being accurate.

Placing her arm around Lucas' waist as they continued to walk along the path leading to the front door of the large house, she said, "Hilda and I were talking the other day between cases in the operating room. Rumor has it that one of the orderlies saw the Williamsons and their daughter, Becky, moving west on foot towards Cuengo. Evidently, they have friends there with an automobile, and planned to head southwest from Cuengo, hoping to return through Malanje Province to Luanda, some 700 Kilometers to the west."

As they met another guard at the front door of the house, Lucas whispered, "If it's a true story, I hope they made it all the way to Luanda."

The guard standing at the door came to stiff attention when Angela and Lucas approached the front of the headquarters. "Sir and madam," he said, "what can I do for you this evening?"

Lucas smiled at the overly stiff guard, and in a cordial, relaxed manner replied, "I am Doctor Lucas and this is Sister Angela. We've been invited to supper."

"Remain here please. I will make inquiries inside. People were invited from the hospital complex and confirmation will be required," said the guard in an unemotional, rigid manner. The wait was less than thirty seconds. The guard returned and holding the door ajar formally motioned them into the house.

"My goodness," said Angela as she entered the hallway where they were led. There were considerable changes from the appearance of just a few weeks ago when they had last visited the General.

"The General certainly had the place cleaned up a bit," whispered Lucas as they stood in the hallway. The massive mahogany desk with bullet holes had disappeared and the bookshelves were neatly filled. Voices were heard down the hall from inside the study as the door to the study opened and Major Santiago, no longer frowning, entered the hall, smiling at Angela and Lucas as if they had been his personal friends for years. His metamorphosis obviously reflected his superior officer's changed attitude. "So glad you could come!" he said. "We are having hors d'oeuevres in the study before supper. Please come and join us."

Walking along the hallway to the study, Angela observed, "What is this? The place looks like it did two years ago! All polish and shine."

Entering the polished teak-paneled study was a startling revelation. The large study was filled with people. The old grand piano remained in its corner, but now the sheen on its ebony surface was almost blinding. Every bookshelf was polished and the books were in place on their shelves. Food trays were being carried and offered to the guests by waiters in rebel dress uniforms, obviously brought in from another location. As Angela and Lucas entered through the door, the hum of conversation dwindled to a halt, as all eyes turned towards the door.

"Ah, the doctor and nursing sister have arrived," said General Alverez, in perfect Portuguese, coming forward from the now silent group of guests. Angela continued to interpret for Lucas. "I'm sure you have met many of my guests previously, but allow me to introduce you."

The General asked for the full names of both Angela and Lucas in a low tone, and then announced in full voice, "May I present Doctor Lucas Stuart and Sister Angela Abercrombe, the head nurse of the Mission Hospital. They are presently administrating our hospital and have saved many of our brave soldiers' lives......." Lucas had to keep from laughing when Angela gave the interpretation in a whisper behind her hand, as he whispered back, "Yeah, and not so long ago we resided in the cages."

Polite applause for their accomplishments followed as the two were taken around the room and introduced to most of the officers they had already encountered around the hospital, under different circumstances during their captivity. There were a surprising number of women present.

"All this formality isn't normal," whispered Lucas in an almost inaudible voice. "Why would they do this after beating and raping us just a few weeks ago? Be careful, Angela. There may be a stinger with this group," he continued as they stood aside quietly and watched the guests eat their canapés and listened to their discourse, interpreted by Angela.

"Supper is served in the dining room! Please find a chair with your name at the place setting." The announcement was made in European accented Portuguese from the depth of the dining room. The guests moved to the dining room from the study.

Angela had early memories of this dining room, as her parents had been good friends of the Williamsons since before her birth. Her family had visited from their Saurimo Mission and she recognized the long table and chairs immediately as they entered the dining room. She could clearly remember racing toy cars with Becky Williamson down the length of the room many years ago.

"Look for our names on the place cards," instructed Angela as she and Lucas walked alongside of the table. Angela's card was half-way down the long table, but Lucas had been placed next to the head of the table. As Lucas held the chair for her, a gasp escaped Angela's mouth as she sat down.

Angela recognized the tableware and silver immediately, as well as the glassware as belonging to the Williamsons. "I've sat at this entire layout before, right in this room," she whispered to Lucas.

The table was set in precise Angolan taste, with the silverware in proper position. The salad plates appeared immaculate, as did the glassware, which was surprising after all of the fighting, and the tablecloth was also familiar to Angela. She had lived for over thirty years here and was well aware of Angolan customs and proper formal settings. This supper reflected the top society of Angolan culture.

It certainly appeared that they had found all of the Williamsons' dinnerware, cleaned it up and set it out properly, she confirmed as she sat at the table with the other guests. She counted eighteen place settings.

Lucas took his seat next to the host's seat. Every chair at the table was occupied except the luxurious padded chair with wood carved arms at the head of the table. Angela had sat in that chair at five years old and could still remember that the extravagant feeling of its softness and size had made her feel like a queen.

"It's empty for the host, which has to be Savimbi," Lucas had said to Angela as they viewed the large empty chair next to him on his left when entering the room. "I wonder if he'll be able to leave the fighting long enough to show up."

After all of the guests had been seated, the waiters moved along the table pouring red wine into each guest's glass, including that of the absent host. Lucas was well aware that protocol dictated that he not taste the wine before the appearance of their host, so he calmly waited with the other guests until each glass had been filled.

"That's first-class Portuguese wine," thought Lucas as he read the label showing through a crevice in the white napkin wrapped around the bottle as it was poured into his glass. "How would these rebels get access to such vintage wine?"

Further down the table, Angela remembered the wine cellar that she had played hide and seek in as a child. The house had this cellar secluded away from other missionaries' prying eyes and she surmised, "Ol' Pastor Hubert will miss his wine if he ever returns."

Suddenly the side door from the kitchen opened and all conversation ceased. A man appeared at the doorway wearing regular army fatigues and cap. He was unshaven and his army boots showed evidence of neglect. There was no insignia of rank on his shirt. Immediately, every guest stood up from their chairs and began to applaud and cheer.

"*This has to be Savimbi*" thought Lucas as he stood up along with everyone else. "Or *will the leader appear behind this man? He's not dressed as a political leader.*" No one followed the man as he entered the room.

On closer examination, Lucas recognized the man as the aide who had accompanied the two wounded soldiers who had arrived that very morning and had watched the surgery. Raising his right hand in recognition, the "aide" said, "Thank you, thank you. Please sit down and eat," as he smiled and walked to the head of the table. He sat down next to Lucas and everyone resumed their seats.

"I'm glad to see that you and Angela are here this evening," he said in a clipped English accent that Lucas recognized from their morning talk. He extended his right hand in greeting. "It was interesting to see your group work so well together this morning."

Grasping his right hand briefly, Lucas stammered, "I guess you are Jonas Savimbi. I'm sorry that we didn't recognize you this morning, but with all of the wounded…"

A blessing was said in Portuguese by a Catholic priest before they ate. Lucas had never seen this priest before. As he rose from his chair, Savimbi tinkled his glass for attention. All fell silent.

Savimbi then said, "A toast to the revolution and freedom from MPLA repression. May the victory over the Luanda regime come swiftly and with loss of few friends." Everyone toasted and the clink of glasses resounded throughout the room.

As the guests began to eat, Jonas looked down the table and acknowledged Angela with a slight tilt of his head as she picked up her fork. When Jonas began to eat his salad he said to Lucas, "Many of my own men don't recognize me. Forget not identifying me. It's a great advantage to appear as the rest of my soldiers so the enemy won't know who to aim at during combat. Is the food good? Try the wine."

Lucas was still getting over his surprise at the "aide's" identity. "Sir, the food is very good! We weren't eating this well even before the hostilities. Thank you for inviting us to eat with you tonight."

Laughing at Lucas' remark, Jonas said, "If we hope to have good medicine, we need to maintain the strength of our medical personnel."

As Angela was sitting on the opposite side of the table to Lucas, she couldn't help but notice that a younger, very attractive, dark-haired woman was sitting next to Lucas, apparently in deep conversation with him. As the meal progressed, the two appeared to be continuing the conversation. Angela asked one of the guests who this attractive young lady might be.

"Oh yes. Her name is Serrena Ruiz, a reporter for one of the Luanda newspapers that supports the revolution. She commonly travels with the upper echelon of rebel leaders, and often goes directly to the battlefield to cover the war"

Angela asked, "Doesn't her family worry about her being hurt in the conflict?"

The answer came, "Oh no, her father owns the newspaper, and they are very wealthy. She and her husband evidently recently divorced, and since they have no children the rumor is that she sometimes is at the front lines."

The main course arrived by waiters bringing in a large trays of roasted pig, a roast goat, and barbequed chicken, with an assortment of vegetables on the side.

"This is indeed a feast," said Lucas as he finished the last morsel on his plate. Everyone at the table heartily agreed.

"Occasionally we are privileged to be supplied by those civilians who support our efforts in the revolution, both inside and outside the country. Their support is both appreciated and necessary," Jonas said.

The meal finished, the leader got up from the table and moved to a chair in the large study. The other guests followed until all were seated comfortably. Angela noticed that Serrena made sure that she sat next to Lucas when they moved to the study. The reporter continued to converse with Lucas after they sat down in a low, conspiratorial whisper. Angela joined Lucas, Serenna, and Savimbi sitting around a small table sipping orange Cointreau. As they sat down, Lucas introduced Serrena to Angela, carefully citing her affiliation with the newspaper and her role in the revolution. "She travels often with Jonas to report the news of the revolution. I've told her that you are the main reason that the hospital is now functioning."

One glance at Serrena's high-priced, well-fitting, and revealing dress, expensively styled long hair, and three-inch heels made Angela conscious of her plain tent-like scrub suit and sneakers. She was mortified.

"It's a shame that war makes evenings like this few and far between," remarked Savimbi. "Before the conflict, an evening among friends and comrades-at-arms was common. Usually, one of the ladies would be kind enough to play or sing for our guests. That's all over now, however."

"Maybe not," smiled Lucas mischievously. "I happen to know of an accomplished pianist who has actually performed on the piano in this room many times. Perhaps she could be persuaded to do so tonight?"

Angela blushed bright red when Jonas and Serrena looked directly at her.

"Uh, no...... I used to play a little, but it's been a while since I've had any time to practice. Really, it would be a disaster."

Savimbi, smiling broadly at Angela said, "There seems to be few alternatives this evening. I think we all would be very appreciative of any attempts that you were able to make. Please play for us?"

Standing in front of his chair, in a loud voice Jonas announced, "We have a piano player with us tonight and she has graciously agreed to entertain us with a few selections. Please, shall we encourage her with a show of support?"

There was applause, and as she stood up, Angela thought, "Did he say 'a few' selections?"

Walking over to the familiar piano, Angela sat down on the stool. There was no music on the stand, so she would have to play by memory, which, fortunately, was not a problem for her. Thinking quickly, she wondered what she should play for a group of rebel soldiers and their friends. She selected Mozart.

For the next hour, the attentive audience heard Handel and Bach as well, and applauded loudly after each selection. Standing at the piano, Angela thanked her audience, saying, "I enjoyed playing for you." She then resumed her seat next to Lucas, to more applause.

It was obvious to Angela that her performance had deflated Serrena's self-confidence. She was glad that she had played after all. Angela was certain that there was nothing in Serrena's personality that she could trust, especially the way Lucas looked at Serrena when he thought Angela was not watching. Serrena's polished manners and appearance made Angela feel even more inclined to dislike her, not a Christian trait of which she was proud, but this lady was flirting with her man.

"You know," said Savimbi to Lucas as the guests got up to leave, "you've been here working on the freedom fighters' wounded for over three weeks, and we really appreciate your services. Don't you think it's about time for you to go home?"

Lucas thought that he had developed a hearing impediment. "I'm sorry; would you repeat that, sir?"

Savimbi started laughing as Angela gasped and sat back down in the chair she had just left. He went on, "The Bible says to 'do unto others as you would have them do unto you,' correct?"

"Well, yes," stammered Lucas, still not believing what he had heard.

The leader went on, "You have done a great service for the revolution in the past few weeks and I personally watched as you did it willingly and competently. I will order that you and your team are free to leave in the morning, and we thank all of you for your help. Evidently some of the missionaries were not treated as they should have been."

Walking back to the hospital compound, still unable to realize fully what had just happened, Angela said, "Lucas, I can't leave the Lubalo Mission without finding out what has happened to my dad, down at the Saurimo Mission. The fighting is in that area and anything may have happened to him."

# 8
## Chapter

The smooth flow of the current carried their river boat past the trees growing in lush abundance at the water's edge. Tree branches protruded out over the river's calm surface to form a chute for the scow, as the water moved seamlessly to the north. The repetitive drone of the motor, along with the passing tranquil flow of cloudy water, acted like a lullaby, soothing some of the passengers into a semi-conscious state, a dream world.

Beyond the trees, and further back from the banks of the river, the villagers carried on their everyday life, unchanged for centuries, oblivious to the people confined to the slowly moving river craft. The occupants of the vessel moved further downstream as each view of native life slipped slowly behind them. The minutes became hours and then turned into days with little change of scenery.

"See the little boys playing with a wire car on a string?" said Gayle, pointing out to Esther two small children along the edge of the water. "They have a car *and* an airplane made of twisted wire. It's quite realistic looking, but the chance of either of them ever traveling on a car or plane during their lifetime is remote."

Esther, being the elder, was more sedate and enjoyed the peacefulness of the trip as well as Hamid's polite, deferential manner. She had become homesick and was thankful to be leaving the jungle and mission. Gayle, however, was becoming bored with the inactivity on the river craft. The other passengers spoke languages that Gayle couldn't decipher and Hamid was getting on her nerves with all those polite bows and Arab hand movements. Esther was the only other person with whom Gayle could converse.

Esther felt that the natives showed skill and imagination to make such realistic toys out of a few pieces of scrap wire. She realized that she was beginning to feel hope, now that they were on their way back to the United States, and these children reminded her of her sister's children back in Massachusetts.

"This trip seems to be going on forever, Esther," said the impatient Gayle. "It's been two whole days and nights, and still we haven't come to the Kwilu River, or even a major town. I'm going to ask the captain, if he speaks English."

The travelers noticed that the Lubalo River had begun to widen as other smaller waterways joined it in its path towards the larger Kwilu River, one of the major rivers draining into the mighty Congo River from the Northwest, on its way to the Atlantic Ocean.

"The river's getting wider" observed Gayle hopefully, "Look, there must be twenty-five feet of water on each side of the boat to the shore now," her boredom interrupted.

Esther replied that she was seeing many more natives living along the shoreline and that the small villages were larger and no longer seem so far apart. The groups of round, unkempt, dirt-walled, thatch-roofed huts along the river banks seemed to be increasing in number with each mile they progressed along the river. The huts also seemed larger and a few of them even had a metal cone at the tip to reflect the heavy rain that comes seasonally.

Gayle observed, "One of the natives told me at the mission that sometimes those metal cones attract lightning, causing the entire household to be roasted like chickens if it strikes the cone. Evidently heavy thunderstorms are common here, and whole families can be killed.

Esther shook her head and replied "I had hoped that we could have been of some use to these people, but the revolt at the mission prevented that."

Esther was much more sensitive to people and their feelings than Gayle, she realized, but Gayle still felt herself more intelligent and with a stronger personality. For that reason she felt that she had to lead, as Esther wouldn't. Since they thought that they were on their way home, Gayle felt that there might be some difficulties in connecting with their families, and to plan a way to reach civilization would take finances that she was aware Esther had limited access in that area. Gayle decided that when the opportunity presented, she would have to provide the means for both of them to leave Africa.

"Esther," Gayle remarked, "when we get to a phone and can call out of this remote place, I think that we should call my Dad first and ask him how to arrange transport back to London or America. I know he will contact your people and inform them that we are OK and what's going on."

"I agree," Esther said quietly. "Your Dad certainly has better connections and can organize it faster."

It was now approaching midday and the smell of the wood fires from the riverside households drifted onto the river. The aroma, as it came to the passengers, made Gayle and Esther feel that they were ready to eat. Observing these shoreline fires, Gayle noted that the open outdoor fires were being down-drafted to hot coals as the cornmeal gruel or the fish and goat meat stews were brought to a boil. The delicious aroma reached their nostrils making Gayle's saliva glands work overtime to drip digestive juices down her throat, causing her stomach to growl in anticipation of the noon meal.

The school break for lunch must have come as they floated past. They saw the children pour from the doors of the school together, each wearing the same outfit. They guessed accurately that most African public schools require a uniform. As the buildings emptied, the identically clad children did not stop to play, but made a direct path to their respective huts for their noon meal. "Uniforms are only required in private schools in Texas," noted Esther. "What a good idea they have here."

Each child from that school wore matching colored shirts, skirts and pants and every student had a similar straw hat with a matching colored hatband so that the affiliation of each child could be identified at a glance. "A standardized school uniform must also eliminate one richer child from wearing better clothes than a poorer classmate, thus greatly aiding in discipline," said Gayle as they stared at the stream of youngsters leaving the building.

As the flat, floating scow carried the passengers further down the river, they could see how much the river had widened and the current increased. "The confluence of the Lubalo and Kwilu Rivers must be very close, so we *are* making progress," said Gayle. They also noticed that besides the speed, the depth of the river was increasing.

The two companions were encouraged by these developments on the river, but they could see that their Arab host, Hamid, remained unconcerned, being totally occupied by a high stakes card game with the two other Arabs on board. By the scowl on his face and his generally stern manner, the women surmised that their Arab host was getting the worst of the gambling. This development resulted in a very poor temper from their host, making conversation strained.

Esther pointed to a collection of huts and stalls on the river bank ahead of them. "You know, Gayle, I think that's a town right ahead of us. See the shanties and marketplace square with all of the sellers' stalls? Perhaps the boat will stop and we will be able to get a closer look at the people and the wares that they're selling."

Just then, the sound of the boat's motor slackened and the prow began to turn towards the shore. As the vessel pulled alongside of the dock, the motor died and a rope line was advanced to a native standing on the dock who promptly tied the rope to a post.

"We appear to be stopping," said Gayle. "It looks like we'll get that chance to see the people and their goods after all. Maybe there's a phone here."

The captain came on deck and announced, "An inspection of the ship's cargo by the Zaire authorities with passport registration is to be done. All passengers should have their passports available."

"Be calm, ladies," said their Arab host, as he appeared beside them. "I have certain friends here who will be able to overlook your lack of documentation."

It was as he said. No inspection of the women's passports was requested and they merely climbed up onto the dock and proceeded to the shoreline, unmolested by the Zaire authorities.

"How was he able to do that?" asked Gayle, always inquisitive.

"I believe that I witnessed an exchange of money as Hamid spoke to the inspector," answered Esther. "Reverend Brown once told me that bribery was a routine way of doing business in these remote regions."

They proceeded to walk into the town, moving slowly through the aisles of sellers' stalls, their occupants bartering almost any commodity imaginable. Each stall had its owner standing behind the counter, often hawking their product in a loud voice. The cacophony of sound reaching their ears was almost overwhelming, as the Kileta language and foreign accents varied with the owners' origins. The stall owners appeared to originate from all over Africa and the near East. Most of the vendors had migrated from foreign countries but lived locally, importing their goods from around the world.

"Oh, I like this stall," said Gayle as she stopped in front of a large display of jewelry. "Look at all of the gold and silver baubles. I wish we were able to afford some of these items."

"Yes, you can afford whatever attracts you," said the Indian owner of the stall, speaking in accented but perfect English. "Aren't you traveling with the Arab over there?"

The Indian turned and called to Hamid, who was examining some tableware a few stalls behind them. "Hamid, my friend, I believe these two beautiful ladies are traveling with you. Come over and assist them in their selection from my wares."

Looking up from his inspection of an ivory handled table knife, Hamid nodded to the jewelry seller and wandered over to where the women stood. He spoke as he arrived at the jewelry stand. "Rasheed, my friend, it has been too long since we met. May the blessings of Allah be with you? How is your family?"

Having formally greeted each other in their native language, and exchanging news of family and friends for a few moments, they began to discuss the business at hand. "Hamid, these ladies were admiring some of my jewelry, and appeared to be interested in the jewels displayed in the counter in front of them. As I noticed that only you would be with ladies of this quality, perhaps a bargain could be struck?"

Smiling at Esther and Gayle, Hamid said in English, "Was there something here that met with your approval?"

Esther replied immediately, "No, we were just admiring the ornaments in his case. We do not wish to have them. You are most kind to ask, sir."

Gayle, however, was not so timid and asked, "Those jeweled beads…what are they used for?"

"Ah yes," Rasheed replied, removing the sparkling gems in question from their resting place within the case. "A most discerning selection. These are rubies and diamonds of exquisite quality imported from India herself. For one to wear them, covering the umbilicus, demonstrates affluence and discretion."

Gayle was a bit shocked at the reply, as she thought the jewelry was either a pendant or a broach. "How exactly is this to be worn?" she asked, seeing nothing but a small ring at the back of the bauble for securing it.

"It takes only a small pinprick to the skin, a mere momentary inconvenience, to wear such finery. Would you like to consider its purchase?" asked Rasheed.

Gayle was impressed by the dazzle and beauty of the jewelry, but sensed that to have the Arab obtain such a bauble would likely obligate her to him for other possibilities that she didn't want to explore.

"It is quite beautiful, but not fitting for me at this time. Thank you for showing it to me, and thank you, Hamid, for offering. We will walk further among the sellers to admire their offerings. Have a pleasant day."

As they continued to walk among the stalls, they noticed that the majority of the offerings were cheap costume jewelry, food items, or highly discounted clothes. They also became aware that the robes they were wearing must have been costly, as the shop keepers, upon seeing them, assumed that Gayle and Esther were wealthy and could purchase any object they desired.

"That must be the boat's whistle!" said Esther as a loud shriek was heard to penetrate the surrounding noise of the market vendors. "We had better return or be left alone in the middle of Africa."

The two women made their way back to the dock, arriving just as the boat was about to leave. As they returned to their seats on the vessel, they noticed that two young black girls, who had not been seen on the boat previously, had now boarded with the passengers and taken seats. These girls aren't older than twelve or thirteen, Gayle noted to Esther, and she wondered with whom they were traveling.

As the boat moved away from the shore, the two young black girls appeared to be sitting next to Hamid on a bench near the water. This necessitated Gayle and Esther to find a seat across from Hamid facing him. The scow was suddenly jostled by waves from another ship passing close by, causing the deck of the river vessel to bounce and jerk. The younger girl grabbed for a beam to support herself from the gyrations of the deck. It was as she reached for the railing that Gayle noticed that the younger looking black girl was wearing metal handcuffs that reflected in the bright sunlight.

"Did you see that?" whispered Gayle to Esther "She's wearing restraints! If these two young girls are traveling with Hamid, something's got to be wrong. I think that maybe we need to find out what it's all about."

"How do we do that? We know no one on the boat, and few passengers speak English," replied Esther.

"Let's walk around the boat and see if we are able to overhear anyone speaking English. If so, we could ask them if they know Hamid," replied Gayle.

The two women began to casually walk around the river vessel, but of those passengers conversing, no one appeared to speak English.

"Let's just go and sit with Hamid and the two girls. He won't think it unusual, and if we can separate one of the girls from him for just a few moments, perhaps we can learn why they're wearing cuffs," observed Esther.

Continuing their stroll around the boat, they came back to Hamid sitting with the two young girls. No conversation was evident among the trio as Gayle and Esther sat on the bench facing the Arab and the girls. Finally, Esther said, "Good afternoon. Ladies, Hamid, are these girls also traveling with us to the coast?"

"Ah, ladies of Lubalo," said Hamid in his dignified, smooth voice as he stood up. "Have you enjoyed our trip so far and the stopover at the settlement? I hope that your shopping expedition proved interesting? It's a shame that my friend Rasheed was unable to entice you to purchase a trinket."

Gayle mustered a wide smile and seized the opportunity, "I see that your new companions are wearing restraints, Hamid. Isn't that a bit unusual for a river boat trip?"

"A bit of an unfortunate happenstance, ladies. I was asked to return these children to their rightful homes. It seems that they strayed from their parents' domicile and were only recently discovered at the border."

"But to be forced to return in those heavy bracelets...?" remarked Gayle.

Smiling as a crocodile might grin at an animal it was ready to devour, the Arab replied, "Sometimes these naughty youngsters need to be reminded not to leave their assigned duties. Without restraints, the lesson might not be fully absorbed. Anyway, you need not be concerned. The problem is under control."

Gayle and Esther got up and began to walk the deck planks of their vessel again.

"I doubt that that's the whole truth, Gayle," said Esther. "Let's keep a close eye on the girls. This trip lasts four days and eventually they will have to go to the ladies' room. Then, one of us will be able to find out the *real* story.

Some two hours later as the river bank, still covered with deep green growth, silently continued to slip past them, Esther noticed that the older looking girl who was also wearing handcuffs, got to her feet indicating that she wished to proceed to the ladies' room. She made a remark to the Arab, who nodded in consent, removed the constraints and allowed her to proceed in the direction of the lavatory. As she had risen to her feet, the younger girl also stood up and followed the older girl, with her cuffs still in place. Both girls had already entered the bathroom as Esther arrived at the door. The facility was barely large enough to accommodate the two girls, and it was obvious that three would not be able to occupy the washroom together. Esther was left standing alone outside in the hallway. She waited quietly outside the door for a few minutes until the girls reappeared. All three women were still beyond the sight of Hamid, so Esther tried to communicate with them in the hallway as they emerged. She had no way to guess if either spoke English, so she just started in,

"I see that you are traveling with Hamid," Esther said to initiate the conversation.

A blank, uncomprehending stare was the only response. A few words from the older girl in some dialect that Esther could not understand was finally made after a full sixty second pause. Putting her hand on the metal handcuffs, Esther looked at the younger girl and asked, "Why are you wearing these?" Trying to show the girl that she was her friend, Esther smiled and gently rattled the metal restraints.

This action produced a look of terror on the older girl's face as she rushed down the hallway away from Esther, towards her seat next to Hamid.

"What can I do to help you?" Esther said to the remaining younger girl as she looked her directly in the eyes and put her hand on the girl's wrist.

"She speaks no English and probably would not ask for help, anyway."

Turning her head, Esther saw a black gentleman, with a dark goatee and mustache, standing directly behind her. He did not appear to be Arab, but appeared by his dress and manner to be a wealthy and educated man. He was smiling as he placed his hand on her wrist and moved Esther's hand away from the girl's metal bracelets. He said a few words in some dialect and the younger girl hastened down the hallway, back to her older friend and Hamid.

"I see that you are unfamiliar with these surroundings and customs," he said. "My name is Bernard. I travel this river frequently. You appear to be in need of some clarification."

Esther recovered from her shock, recognizing the man as having already been a passenger on the boat when they had boarded at Lubalo, she now discovered that he spoke English.

"My name is Esther. I am traveling with my friend Gayle, and we are trying to return home to America. What clarification are you talking about?"

"Many foreigners believe the reports that slavery is no longer to be found in Africa. The actual facts do not confirm these stories. Slavery is common, especially in central Africa where many parents are unable to support their families."

Esther was aghast at this report. "How could *any* parent sell their child into slavery?" she asked.

"Is it better for the entire family to suffer, or for the rest of the members to have enough to eat at the sacrifice of a few? Those being sold are often well supported and fed, though their lives are commonly destroyed."

Esther was beginning to understand the situation with Hamid's two black girls. She asked, "And these two girls…?"

Bernard continued, "Probably sisters, sold to the Arab at a high price, on their way to the brothels of Khartoum. This Hamid is a well-known owner of these illegal houses and we see him in these remote areas every year searching for children to purchase."

"Thank you, sir. Your enlightenment has cleared up some mysteries," she said to the stranger, and continuing under her breath inaudibly, "…and created others."

Esther could not get back to Gayle quickly enough. She immediately suggested that they go for another stroll on the deck, and as soon as they were out of Hamid's hearing range she described the entire episode to her friend.

"No wonder he was so nice to us," said Gayle when she had heard the story. "We are marooned out here in the remote wilds of Zaire, stuck on a river and possibly being sent to be prostitutes in Sudan. Esther, we've got to do something to get away from this Arab as quickly as possible, but we have no resources or friends."

"Let's try to be calm," said Esther, trying not to panic. "Perhaps there is a solution and this Bernard may be willing to assist us. But how do we know who to trust?"

Gayle stopped walking for a second and, holding on to the railing for support, said, "This 'Bernard' may be as bad as Hamid. First we are imprisoned at the mission, then the soldiers and now this."

They continued to pace the wooden planks of the deck together as the scow followed the river, moving first northwards, and then directly west with increasing speed. There was desperation in their thoughts. They came to Africa to serve, and since their arrival they had been imprisoned, violated, and seen the horrible death of their minister after only being in Africa for a few weeks. There seemed to be no one to help them in sight. They were physically tired, but the repeated emotional stress had exhausted both of them to the point of total defeat.

"Look how wide the river has become," remarked Gayle. "With the fusion of each smaller river, more water joins the main flow and the current becomes stronger. This must be the Kwilu River. This scow has to stop somewhere, and then we must make our escape."

"We haven't stopped to load or unload passengers in half a day, although there have been a few towns and villages," observed Esther. "Perhaps we can ask where the next stop will be."

They continued to watch the banks of the river as it passed them, until a major town came into sight ahead. The monotonous sound of the motor now came to a halt and the boat began to drift towards the shore.

"We must act as if everything is the same and then attempt to escape," said Esther.

"I really don't want to wear metal bracelets. That Arab may attempt to shackle us if he suspects we know of his plans. Keep an eye on him at all times."

As the boat slowed and began to drift towards the dock, ropes were cast off and then attached to posts on the shore. These ropes were used to moor the vessel adjacent to the dock where they were secured firmly. Once the gangplank was laid, the passengers began to file down the rough planks to the dock.

"Now arriving in Kikwit," came the announcement from the cockpit.

"Do we run for it?" suggested Gayle, almost in a paroxysm of fear.

"Not now with everyone watching," replied Esther. "Play it cool and see if Hamid tries to stop us. We don't know for a fact that we're slaves yet, let's see his intent."

Hamid was waiting for them at the boat's walkway as Gayle and Esther approached the planks leading from the edge of the scow to the shore.

"Ahh, ladies," smoothly stated the Arab, neglecting his usual bow. "I have been briefed on your latest inquires. I want to advise you that any attempt on your part to refuse my hospitality will result in an unfortunate and immediate incarceration. This could include placement of wrist and ankle restraints. This would be most inconvenient for all of us, I am sure".

This terrified the women, nowho now realized that they were indeed captives of the Arab in this remote part of Zaire, with no friends or money. Bernard had betrayed them. When they were alone, Gayle asked, "What now, Esther?" Even though she considered herself in control, it was Esther she turned to when they were in trouble. Some humility, she had to admit, was needed to save their eventual fate. "We could try to run away, but to where? Without money or even knowing where to go, he would find us almost immediately." "Let's try to think logically for a way to escape," said Esther. "We should act as if we *have* accepted our fate, and when his guard is down, try to get free."

"We might inquire from the captain of the ship where the scow is headed and then plan for that. If he puts those ankle and wrist cuffs on us escape will be difficult."

Gayle thought for a minute before answering. "My family probably is already aware that something has gone amiss at Lubalo and that we're in Zaire, but I have no way to contact them or ask for help without a phone. For now we're on our own until I'm able to contact them."

Esther returned, "If you can contact them, I'm sure our troubles will be solved almost immediately."

The collection of huts in Kikwit was large and there were many people milling around in the shops and streets, enabling Esther and Gayle to put a few feet of space between themselves and the Arab. However, he kept a watchful eye on them at every moment and no opportunity presented itself for further knowledge of the scow's eventual destination or outside contact. Suddenly, they found a sign on a bulletin board that had been hung on the wall of a building.

"Look at that sign. It's in English!" whispered Gayle "It says that there is transport by river boat going on the Congo River, up to Kisangani. That's north and away from the western coast. If that's an advertisement for *our* boat, we'll never get home."

Gayle began to frown and tears appeared in her eyes, indicating her distress at thoughts of a home that she feared that she might not see again for a long time.

"Stop that," ordered her companion. "Don't cry. If he sees you, it will give our whole plan away to that despicable Arab. Lose your cool and we'll both be wearing cuffs before you know it."

Esther was right. Gayle regained control of her emotions as they returned to the ship, still followed by Hamid. They were not able to understand the conversations of the other passengers as they re-entered the vessel to sit on the deck benches. A new passenger, talking to his wife, mentioned the word "Kisangani" twice in the conversation.

"I heard that," said Esther. "We need to get off of this scow before it reaches the Congo River and begins to head north, ending our chance to go downriver to the Atlantic Ocean and Kinshasa."

"You certainly can be sure of that!" replied a voice in cultured English nearby.

A tall, white, extremely distinguished gentleman stood next to Gayle, smiling broadly at both of them. He wore immaculately tailored coat and pants, as well as a well- trimmed beard, which was not often seen on a scow of this type. His entire appearance and manner oozed of British nobility and upper class culture.

"Did you overhear our conversation?" asked Esther, startled by his remark.

He replied, "I couldn't help but hear you as I passed by. Why would you want to go south to Kinshasa?"

"Oh please don't repeat what I said to that horrible Arab. We are being forced to travel with him and we suspect that he wants to abduct us and force us to travel to Khartoum. His intentions are less than honorable."

"My name is Sir William Spencer-Johnston. I guarantee that nothing of the sort will happen to you while we travel on this vessel. I believe by your accents that both of you are Americans?"

"Yes, we are American missionaries who were taken hostage during the revolution in Angola. We have no documentation or money. The Arab has taken advantage of us and now we are helpless to stop his plans to send us into white slavery."

My name is Esther and this is Gayle." She then related their whole story. Sir William showed no surprise at Esther's recitation, but his face turned red with anger as he fully realized their situation. He said in a forceful, low voice, "Ladies, we'll see about this. Do nothing now but continue to follow the Arab's orders. I will see to it that his little scheme fails, but we will wait until the boat reaches the confluence with the Congo River at Kwamouth. It will stop to board and unload passengers going further north. The authorities will be there to assist us."

"By what good fortune do you happen to be traveling on this decrepit scow today?" asked Gayle. They naturally distrusted any stranger after their experience with the Arab, but his whole appearance and manner exuded English upper class, and partly because they were desperate, and partly just by his manner, they both felt that he could be believed and trusted.

Feeling a bit more familiar with the women now, Sir William confided, "Oh, I am a solicitor for the British government in these remote areas, and this is the only conveyance available that I could take, allowing me to reach the Congo River where I can catch a vessel south to Kinshasa."

As the British official was still speaking, Hamid walked up to the trio and said, "I see that you are interested in my two associates? Perhaps we can come to a temporary arrangement before the trip terminates?"

"The possibility is small, but I will keep your offer in mind," said Sir William as he briskly walked away and entered one of the two cabins on the scow.

The Arab insisted that the four hostages remain on deck, sitting on their benches as the shoreline continued to slip by. The bright, golden moon rose in the sky as darkness obliterated their view of the dense, green growth surrounding them. It became clear that the trees were becoming much closer to the water as the flat vessel progressed deeper into the center of the country. They had arrived in the jungle.

"It still gets cold at sunset," remarked Esther as they sat facing the breeze generated from the vessel's movement on the water. Each passenger thankfully snuggled down into the blankets that all deck passengers had been issued as they had boarded for this segment of the trip. "I will be glad when we reach the Congo River," said Gayle, not daring to mention their encounter with Sir William.

"I agree," answered Esther, as she settled next to her.

The dark brown expanse of the Congo River came into view the next morning at sunrise. At first, it appeared only as a thin sliver in the distance, but as the scow approached the massive flow of water, it became apparent that this was indeed one of the major rivers of Africa.

The river's dark flow could be easily seen as it rushed towards the Atlantic Ocean, a thousand miles to the southwest. Many means of floating transportation could be observed moving on the water as their vessel approached the confluence of the rivers. The scow turned left, joining with the flow of the current, as their little boat was now accompanied by the many larger vessels already moving on the muddy, brown waters. Fishing boats, intermingling with those carrying almost any type of freight and passengers, surrounded them as they began to move slowly down the river.

"Look! We're about to dock right here with the other passenger ships," exclaimed Gayle. She wondered what Sir William had planned, thinking as she stood with the other passengers to watch the scow being tied to the wharf.

As the scow docked they saw Sir William leave the deck first and rush off into a building towards the back of the dock. On the door of the building that he entered they saw the official insignia with a coat of arms of the army of Zaire. Hamid had also seen Sir William's destination, and before either Gayle or Esther realized it, he had produced two sets of steel cuffs from his robe and slipped them on their wrists. Once the ladies realized what he had done, they resisted vigorously, but it was too late, they were already in chains.

"You will remain with me and say nothing," growled the now hostile and not so polite captor. He had switched in a second from the smooth talking benefactor to a vicious slave master. "I think you are trying to cause trouble for me and your efforts may cause you much future discomfort."

Sir William emerged from the building a few minutes later followed by two formidable army guards in full dress uniforms and armed with holstered pistols. Each also carried an automatic weapon, and by their manner, it was obvious that they were not about to be resisted. The three, who had just left the building, immediately boarded the vessel and in a "no funny business" manner headed straight for the bench upon which the Arab and his four captives were still seated.

He addressed the Arab in English, "Sir, we have a serious complaint of attempted slavery and abduction," the corporal said in a rough tone. "What is your relationship with these ladies?"

The Arab smiled with his most disarming smile and replied, "Ah yes, the members of the Zaire Constabulary…It does me much honor to meet you. We five are merely traveling through your beautiful country on our way to the Sudan, and are hoping for no unpleasantness."

Gayle slipped her hands out from under her robe, exhibiting her shackles, and said, "We are being held captive against our will. This man plans to sell us into slavery. Please free us."

The Arab never wavered for a second, and replied smoothly, "An unfortunate situation, the two younger girls are runaways who must be returned to their homes and families in Sudan. The restraints are merely to insure their safe return home. The ladies are escaped prisoners."

The corporal stared at the four women and said, "You want me to believe that the two blacks are runaways and two whites are escaped prisoners? Do you have any documentation for all of this? I doubt it's true, especially when a member of Her Majesty's Diplomatic Corps vouches that they are being held against their will."

"Ah yes, corporal," said Hamid. "If we could just talk privately for a minute, I will produce the warrants and I believe this misunderstanding can be easily resolved."

Stepping to the side, the Arab whispered to the two guards some unintelligible remarks and handed a packet to the bigger guard as they shook hands.

"That's got to be a bribe!" said Esther to Sir William as the package disappeared into the official's pocket. "We'll never get free from that Arab," she said as all four ladies walked down the gangplank to the pier and remained standing on the dock with Sir William.

Sir William strode back into the army building's office, followed by the two guards with whom Hamid had just been conversing. The interval waiting for resolution seemed like an hour, but in actuality was only about ten minutes. The door opened and Sir William was not smiling as he left the office.

"Evidently the bribe has had its effect," he said grimly. "The decision is that the whole situation will be heard before the magistrate this afternoon at two. Since I am a solicitor in the Queen's court, I will personally represent all of you this afternoon, if that's agreeable. I can't be bribed, but the magistrate is another matter."

The group separated as Gayle, Esther and the two African girls remained shackled and were remanded to the Zaire magistrate's jail in the temporary custody of the Zaire constable until final disposition. Their case was to be heard later that day.

"We have a good chance for freedom," said Gayle to Esther. "Sir William will surely win with logic and reason, and that magistrate will side with us. I guess we stay here until they decide to whom we belong."

* * *

An hour later, they sat in a dirty jail cell without lunch, waiting for their two o'clock trial to begin. A loud clang of an unseen steel door at one o'clock signaled the arrival of a visitor. It was Hamid.

"Beautiful ladies," he began, "I just wanted to clear up the little misunderstanding that we had this morning. The two black children sitting over there are my rightful property. I have given their parents compensation for their employment and their involvement is not your concern."

"You mean that they were purchased for money to be slaves in your whorehouses with us in Khartoum?" Esther almost screamed.

Not ruffled by Esther's attack, the Arab continued, "What these children do for me is not of your concern. They are my property, to be used at my discretion."

"Slavery is illegal in every country in the world, you Arabian monster! We'll see you sentenced to prison!" intoned Gayle. "You planned to enslave myself and Esther by trickery when we arrived in Sudan, but Sir William will defeat your plan. You're only here now because you found out he is a British Official and you fear he will have you arrested."

Smiling his disarming smile, which was his habit when challenged, he continued, "Customs vary from country to country, and these children will be well fed and nicely dressed, which was not possible at their home. When this trial concludes and you are back in my charge, I see that severe discipline will have to be instituted to teach both of you respect for your proprietor. Trust me; you *will* end up in Khartoum working for me."

"Don't count on it, Hamid," said Esther with a deep frown. "We may have to murder you in your sleep, but neither of us will submit to your demands. Now, get out of here and leave us alone!"

The Arab, apparently unimpressed by Esther's threat turned and left the prison cell, gloating over what he considered his prospects of financial gain in a few days. Esther and Gayle made multiple, futile attempts to communicate with the two black girls being held in the same cell. The girls spoke only their native dialect and other attempts were rejected, except hand signals indicating basic needs. Gayle and Esther thought that Sir William was generous to include these two native girls in his lawsuit to free them all, but they felt that it was mostly the principle that directed him.

Two o'clock arrived, but nothing happened. As is customary in Africa, nothing starts on time and the four women were forced to wait patiently in the damp, dirty cell until four-thirty that afternoon. They were then informed by the guard that the trial had been deferred until the next day. Supper arrived on a rusty metal tray with a small amount of thin soup and some wheat bread that was hard and stale.

"Try to eat some of it, Gayle. There must be some nourishment in this mess, and hopefully, we will be freed by the judge in the morning," begged Esther as she tried to choke down a few fragments of the meal herself.

The two native girls ate the supper without complaint, as this type of fare was routine for them. Darkness came, but there was little sleep in the dank cell for the four prisoners, as their fate was still undecided. The hard, unpadded steel shelves used for beds made any type of comfort a fantasy.

The next morning at nine o'clock, the clank of the iron doors again foretold that someone was coming to the cell block. This time, it was the guard. He said a few words in a native dialect, and the black girls, still wearing their shackles, moved to the cell door. Gayle and Esther followed them. It was time for their trial.

# 9

## Chapter

Lucas and Angela sat in the hospital post-op bay and quietly discussed what their next steps should be. Since Savimbi had freed them that evening, they could leave Lubalo Mission at any time, either together or separately.

"We came here to serve the population's medical needs," said Lucas. "But with all of the fighting, it's more like being army medics. We haven't been able to be as much help to the common people who live in this area as we had hoped."

Angela looked over at Lucas, got up from her chair and kissed him as he sat on his bed. "Will we stay together now that we're free, Lucas?"

"I certainly hope so," he replied.

She caressed his head and face, running her fingers gently through his blond hair down to the nape of his neck. Their lips met, hovering for a moment. The passion they felt for each other was overwhelming, its seed having been planted as they sat in that dingy, mosquito-ridden cage weeks ago. Lucas wrapped his arms around her waist and could feel her heartbeat against his face as they lay back on the bed in unison. She looked into his clear blue eyes and could see the earnestness in them. As their burning lips finally joined with desire for each other, Lucas began to hold Angela even tighter, then fondled her breasts through her scrub shirt. Her sweet smell filled his nostrils as he fumbled with the ties to her scrub suit. Her hands deftly removed his scrub shirt, revealing his strong, tanned chest. She no longer had any reservations, as she knew that she had not had such strong feelings for another man since her husband died.

"I've wanted to make love to you for so long. You've been in my mind constantly. We're together all day and I've wanted you ever since we were in those cages," said Lucas.

"Oh Lucas, I need you to love me," returned Angela, as passion finally overcame their hesitations. Terms of affection poured forth, now that they finally had the opportunity and place to explore their desire for each other.

The other members of the surgical team living in the post-op bay found "urgent" matters to attend to and left them alone to consummate their love.

Finally, when it had remained silent inside the room for ten minutes, the door to the post-op bay opened slowly and Hilda walked in. "Maichipo and I need to get some sleep, if you two are finished," she said with a wide, knowing smile. "We have expected for some weeks that it was about time that you and Doctor Lucas would get that over with. We have big surgery in the morning, so it's bedtime now."

Angela blushed slightly at Hilda's remark, but felt no shame. After Lucas had left the room to follow a patient on the ward, she interrupted Hilda and Maichipo's preparations for bed by saying, "We have big news! Lucas and I were invited to eat dinner this evening with Savimbi and he has granted all of the hostages their freedom. It's hard to believe, but we can leave!"

The anesthetist and scrub nurse stopped their preparations for bed and stood looking at Angela in total disbelief at what they had just heard. "You're serious?" said Maichipo. "We can go home?"

Hilda, the thinker, said after a minute's pause, "We have sick and severely wounded people in the wards. It would be wrong to abandon them. I think it would be better to set up a schedule to leave, so the patients will be cared for."

The three operating room personnel then discussed the situation for a few moments, deciding that in five days most of the patients would be well enough to survive without further treatment. New incoming patients would be advised of the staff leaving and could choose to stay or leave.

Maichipo said, "I am from this area. My family lives a few miles from here. I'll stay and help, as will some of the other nurses and orderlies. Brightwell is our neighbor and I'm sure he will want to stay too."

Angela finally remarked that she would discuss the situation with Lucas,. "I must find my father and two brothers before I can make any decisions. They were in the thick of the fighting down south, and may need assistance. I hope that Lucas will agree to come and help me find them after we finish here in five days."

Lucas was anxious to return to Malawi and to resume work in familiar surroundings. He was hoping that Angela would accompany him to his home mission, but after he subsequently talked to Angela later that evening, he realized that she had to be sure that the rest of her family was out of danger before they could make more permanent plans.

After the discussion broke up, all of the hostages were advised of their freedom that same evening. By the next morning, almost everyone had decided to remain on duty until the five day scheduled period was over. Most of the skilled personnel would leave at that time, but Doctor Maria, who had lived in Lubalo for many years, felt that she needed to continue her work, insuring that a physician would remain in attendance at the mission after the others had left.

Two days prior to leaving, Lucas saw Angela daydreaming over her coffee in the kitchen, with a worried expression on her face. This concerned him and he walked over to her. Placing his hand on her shoulder, he said, "What's on your mind, my love. You haven't looked that worried since Savimbi asked you to play the piano at the dinner."

"How are we ever going to find my family in the middle of a war?" asked Angela. "We also have to consider what will happen to Wicki and Iuba when we leave Lubalo to search for my relatives. We have to solve these problems before we leave here."

Lucas thought for a few seconds, before replying, "I was hoping that Savimbi would give us a pass to look behind the rebel lines for your father and brothers." Wicki and Iuba will be safe if they stay here, as we will only be gone for a few days. We can try to make long-term arrangements for them when we return to Lubalo from our search for your family. Any further plans will have to wait until that point."

The five days had passed quickly, as there was much work to be done. The former hostages moved their living quarters out of the hospital and back into their previous residences. Lucas returned to his own flat, asking Angela to live with him, as it was now general knowledge that they were lovers.

"Not an ideal situation for a conservative Christian mission station, but accepted by most of us as inevitable," quipped Brightwell.

"I'm not embarrassed at all," said Angela. "I love Lucas, and though we're not married we may as well live together for the present time."

The patients were discharged as they healed. Only the worst casualties were admitted, and by the fifth day the hospital was nearly empty.

"Savimbi was most pleased to give us that pass to look for your family," Lucas told Angela on the evening of the fourth day. "He even has supplied us with a vehicle. I guess that you can't do better than that!"

On the morning of the fifth day, Lucas made extended rounds on all of the patients still in the mission hospital. He wrote down the discharge orders for each remaining patient and suggested further treatments that each might need in the near future. Following careful review of all these remaining patients in the hospital, they decided that their medical responsibilities were fully covered, since Doctor Maria had decided to stay at the mission to supervise those patients remaining in the wards. Angela felt that they wouldn't be gone for more than a few days and they both felt that it would be wise to return to Lubalo to check the patients, collect their possessions and make arrangements for Wicki prior to leaving Angola permanently.

The next morning, as Lucas climbed into the packed Land Rover next to Angela, Wicki came over to the truck, Iuba as always by his side. "Will you promise to return?" he asked in a tearful voice. "We don't want to stay here without you. Guarding is our task, but Iuba and I want to travel with you if you leave Lubalo for good."

Angela reached down from her seat at the open window of the truck and fondled Iuba's ears. "We'll miss both of you, Wicki. You can count on our return before either of us moves on permanently."

Lucas started the large diesel engine, and the truck began to move slowly southward down the poorly maintained road. As they gained speed, they heard Wicki calling out, "Good luck in your search and please return safely," over the crunching of the thick rubber knobs of the tires crushing the gravel stones into the dirt.

A poorly reinforced dirt track was the only available avenue that traveled south towards Quelele. It ran almost parallel to the Lubalo River, mimicking each twist and turn of the riverbank. Recent heavy traffic of military vehicles had somewhat smoothed the ruts, but the numerous potholes made progress slow. Lucas was only able to drive about twenty miles per hour over the first section until they reached Statico, a small collection of huts on the banks of the Lubalo River.

"If the entire road to Kinge is like this," Angela said, "we'll be all day just reaching the main road to Saurimo. I don't think we need to waste time looking for Gayle or Esther, since they went north and we're headed south."

They continued on the rutted road for another two miles, trying to avoid the deep, mud-filled ditches and overhanging branches until they arrived at a wide, swift-running creek that emptied into the Lubalo River.

"There's no telling how deep the creek is," remarked Lucas as he slid to a stop on the bank. "It appears to be about two feet deep, which is no problem, but the bed of the stream may be soft, and we'd be stuck in the middle with water rushing through the vehicle. I'd better check it."

Lucas got out of the vehicle and removed his shoes and socks. He then rolled up both pant legs and proceeded to the edge of the water opposite the Land Rover, looking for tire tracks in the dirt on the opposite bank where previous vehicle traffic might have emerged from the water. "I can see the emerging tracks!" he shouted to Angela.

Making a straight line from the four-by-four, he proceeded to wade across the rushing water towards the emerging bank, squelching the soft bottom with his feet.

Feeling the deep mud at the bottom of the wide creek with his feet, he felt almost certain that the truck would become stuck in the soft muck. He suddenly sank to his waist, about two-thirds of the way across, causing him to realize that he would have to find a more solid bottom before they tried to cross. Following the current, he found a solid gravel bottom in about two feet of water, fifty yards farther downstream. He turned to tell Angela to bring the truck to this point on the bank when he saw her wildly gesticulating and pointing to the opposite bank. Before he could wonder what all of her excitement was about, he heard a splash of water a few yards below him and guessed what the problem was without looking. Instinctively, he jumped away towards the original bank as the snapping jaws of a three-ton hippopotamus fanned his right arm.

Knowing that the animal was quicker in water than he was, but also remembering that hippos generally aren't vicious or aggressive unless they have a baby with them, all that he really needed to do was get out of the animal's way.

Moving quickly, Lucas scrambled up the dirt bank and onto the grass. The behemoth did not follow but placidly moved downstream.

As he began to catch his breath, Angela ran up to him. "Did he get you? I tried to warn you, but the noise of the water drowned out my voice."

"I was lucky I moved when I saw your frantic pointing. Thanks, you probably saved me from injury," said Lucas, coughing up some river water.

"I'm just happy you're safe. Did you find a place to cross?"

Lucas took a deep breath and said, "It's safe to cross here, but we'll give our large friend a few minutes to wander farther away before we try it. We'll need to move the truck to this spot, so we can cross."

Lucas and Angela lay on the lush, green grass overlooking the creek and made love as they waited. The smell of the blossoming frangipani flowers soothed them as they lay listening to the gur-gling water below them.

After Angela dressed, she moved the Land Rover to the spot where they had been lying. As they lay on the cushion-like mat-ted grass in the shade of a large Massasa tree, they discussed their future plans. The cooling breezes blew across their faces making them comfortable despite the hot air.

"Where do you think we should go, Lucas? Somewhere else in Angola, or possibly back to Malawi? Do you plan to return to America? Anywhere, as long as we stay together, is fine with me. The hospital as a mission no longer exists, but is now a rebel stronghold, my obligation there is over," answered Angela.

"I feel that it might be better to return to Malawi for a while. I have a contract until December of this year and that will give us time to think about any future plans," said Lucas.

They lay on the grass, enjoying each other's company, talking and just being relaxed. "Well, we better get moving," said Lucas, standing up and putting on his clothes, which had now dried. "Ole' Mr. Hippo is long gone. I'll walk across the creek in the water and you follow directly behind me in the truck."

"Did you check the exhaust snorkel so I don't stall out?" asked Angela.

"Everything is ready to go, honey. Just start 'er up and follow me down the bank to the water."

All went smoothly and Lucas led as Angela, driving the truck, followed him into the rushing current. The vehicle was on solid gravel and continued to move slowly to a depth of two-and-a-half feet of water. As the water rose to cover the floorboards, Angela pulled out the throttle, depressing the accelerator. She shifted into low gear and kneeled on the seat, enabling her to steer and stay dry.

"Hey, look out, Lucas," screamed Angela, "That hippo is back!"

Lucas looked up. Swimming towards him at full speed was the hippo, directly in his path. The beast was approaching rap-idly and now was less than thirty feet from Lucas.

"Shoot him, for gosh sakes, use the rifle!" shouted Lucas at the top of his lungs.

The reliable Land Rover ploughed on through the water at its snail's pace, no longer controlled by Angela's hand as she frantically fumbled for the rifle lying in the back seat, under a tarpaulin.

"I've got it." Angela cried out as she pulled the large bore weapon on to the front seat and expediently chambered a shell.

"He's on me," came Lucas' desperate call, as the hippo opened his mouth, engulfing Lucas' entire upper body.

A tremendous explosion erupted from the front seat of the truck followed by a huge splatter of blood and fragmented bone, covering the front of the vehicle. The massive hulk of the hippo lay on the water, covered by blood, which was spurting rhythmically from a two-inch hole in the creature's forehead.

"Lucas, where are you? Are you okay?" cried Angela as she disparately scanned the surface of the water for some evidence of movement.

The current continued to flow with no interruption on the surface. The truck had now reached the opposite bank and began to climb the grade slowly. Still scanning the surface of the waters, Angela pushed in the throttle and put the transmission into neutral, watching the lifeless body of the hippo drift downstream with the flow of water.

"Ahhhh!" came a sudden noise from beneath the floating hippo. A head appeared above the waterline next to the buoyant body, and Lucas called, "Help me Angela, I'm hurt and the weight of the hippo is dragging me under."

Without hesitation, Angela rushed into the water, grasped Lucas under the armpits and dragged him to the bank. He was covered in blood and bone fragments. She was unable to determine if the debris belonged to Lucas or the hippo, but at least he was alive.

"Where are you hurt?" she asked, beginning to wipe the blood and debris from his face and head.

Feeling his left arm with his right hand, Lucas replied, "I think the bullet may have grazed my left arm, or the hippo bit it before that shot. I can feel the ulna move when I move the fingers of my hand. In any case, thank you. That was an amazing shot under pressure and off hand."

They sat on the bank of the creek for a few minutes, mutually examining him as the water rushed by. He was well shaken up, but the damage to his left arm was minor. With careful palpation, they established that there probably was an undisplaced partial fracture of the left ulna.

"Let's get to the truck. A splint should be all that we need," said Angela. "I'm so glad that nothing else appears to be damaged."

It was well after noon by the time she had found a piece of wood to use as a splint, placed it on his arm and they set out again. The road was slightly better and, with his painful left arm, they agreed that Angela should do the driving.

"This road to Quelele is worse than I remember," said Lucas as they bumped over potholes and ditches. "The map shows that the road is a bit better from there to Cananga."

At last, they reached Quelele, a settlement of battered, thatched mud huts sitting at a crossroads in the middle of remote Angola. They wanted to inquire as to which road led to Cananga and then to Mona, at the main highway. Unfortunately, there were no signs and the war had emptied the village. A rebel sergeant appeared. After inspecting the note from Savimbi, he stated, "You don't want to go to Mona on this road. The fighting is fierce at Sacumbi. It will be safer if you travel the dirt tract to Lunvula. Then, go south to Choge to get to Saurimo."

"How long will it take?" asked Angela.

The sergeant rubbed his chin for a minute and said, "Probably a day or two. The road is washed out in places, and all of that area isn't necessarily under our control. You go at your own risk…Come to think of it, I'm not sure we still control Saurimo, although we did a few days ago."

As they started down the indicated narrow dirt tact, Angela said, "Lucas, do you really want to risk this trip in your condition? We don't really know who has military control in Saurimo."

"We'll go for it, Angie. No matter who has control in Saurimo, we're still medical people, and if they're fighting they'll welcome our help. Besides, you'll never rest easily until you know about your family."

Fortunately, the supplies of food and water that Angela had packed into the truck had not been damaged by the river, so they seemed to be able to travel without looking for supplies en route.

"Okay, Lucas. Let's go a little further and see what condition the road actually is in. We can see then who has military control of the region."

The sergeant had not been exaggerating in his estimation of the condition of the road. As they moved further from the settlement, the ruts became soft and deep, making progress difficult or impossible without four-wheel drive and the winch on the front of the truck. They were fortunate to have been given such a muscular vehicle.

"Some of the road is quite passable, while other areas are difficult," said Lucas.

After what seemed like hours, they arrived at a collection of huts that were occupied by soldiers. Stopping at a graveled, level place, Angela asked, "What is the name of this town? Are we on the right road to Lunvula?"

"This *is* Lunvula," laughed the soldier, "But if you go south, the fighting is pretty bad. Where are you headed?"

"We are trying to reach the mission at Saurimo," answered Angela. "It is my home and my father lives there, is there any way to get there safely?"

The soldier called to a lieutenant standing next to a mud hut. After explaining their problem, and rereading Savimbi's letter carefully, the officer said, "I am instructed by our commander to help you in any way possible, and this I will do. Horaldo says that you need to get to Saurimo, and tomorrow morning I have to travel there anyway. If you are willing to stay the night and leave your vehicle here, you may ride along with us in a tank to the town you seek. It won't be fun, but we'll probably get there by dusk."

Lucas spoke the local Kileta dialect well enough to communicate after living in Angola for three months and said to the officer, "We appreciate your help. I'm feeling better and there's probably no other way to get there." Then he added, "Where do we stay tonight?"

The lieutenant led them to the only undamaged building they could see. It was made of dried mud with a partially destroyed thatched roof. Inside were at least ten wounded soldiers lying on improvised cots made of grass, situated on the floor. "You may find a spot to rest somewhere in here until we leave at dawn," he said, smiling as he left them inside the building.

Angela and Lucas, evaluating the situation, identified themselves as medical personnel to one of the nurses, and went to work immediately on the wounded soldiers without waiting to be asked. They continued to work until long after dark, trying to see in the dim light shed by kerosene lanterns, which was the only light available. Although medical supplies were meager, many of the wounded soldiers' conditions could be improved by their knowledge.

At about ten o'clock that night, a soldier brought them some supper, saying in broken English, "The officer, he in charge and he say that you need this. It not much, but we gladly share what we have with any doctor willing help wounded friends. We all thank both you for help, not knowing you doctors."

"We've done all that we can tonight, Angela. Let's eat and get some sleep. We'll check them again before we leave in the morning."

The supper consisted of some corn gruel with an unidentified meat on the side.

"Not up to American standards," quipped Lucas as he vigorously shoveled the food into his mouth, "But it's a banquet when you're this hungry."

They found a grass mat and slept. Dawn came quickly, and Angela and Lucas awoke as the first rays of sun broke the darkness with orange and red streaks on the horizon. Lucas was still mystified at the multicolored sunrises seen only in the African sky.

Rubbing the underside of his left arm, Lucas said, "My left arm is still sore, but improved. Maybe it isn't broken after all but just badly bruised." He removed the makeshift splint and flexed his left hand.

"There's no telling when we will find an X-ray machine, so until we can get to the Saurimo Mission, Lucas, keep the arm in a sling, just in case." Angela said, inspecting his arm. "Perhaps we'd better make rounds and get ready to travel."

The lieutenant arrived a few minutes after they had finished seeing all of the patients. "We really appreciate the medical help.

There was no obligation, and the troops and I thank you for your kindness," said the officer. "Your reputation for care and skill at the Lubalo Mission Hospital has preceded your arrival. Two of our men reported to us that they had been treated at your mission." Without waiting for Lucas to reply, the officer continued, "Okay, let's get ready and go."

First, Lucas discovered a ravine near the camp, with some protection from the weather, to park the Land Rover. It was in the officer's compound and out of sight. He locked it, even after the officers assured him that it would not be molested. Three light tanks were lined up on the dirt in front of the town, ready to move.

"Look at the markings!" whispered Angela as they walked towards the tanks. "Those are American made with their white stars painted over and the rebel insignias in red, yellow, and green stuck on. The U.S. must be supporting Savimbi."

They climbed up and sat at the top hatch of one of the tanks looking out over the open fields as they fell away below them.

"This really is a beautiful country, isn't it, Lucas? It's a shame there has to be war. The land is rich and almost anything could be grown here with some fertilizer and labor."

The lieutenant's voice from the next tank came over the intercom. "Stay inside your vehicle. It will be much safer. We expect ambushers and snipers on this trip. Let's roll on!"

The view from inside the turret was really much better than they had anticipated, and as the tanks moved slowly down the muddy, water-logged road, they could easily see the surrounding countryside. With the upper hatch open, fresh air circulated freely, and despite the occasional bump Angela found the trip not unpleasant, but cramped.

"It's turning left," said Angela, as the heavy vehicle made a sharp turn, some two hundred yards beyond the town. "We're off the road and going cross-country."

They continued in this manner, gaining speed as they rolled over ditches and fences at about twenty miles per hour.

"Couldn't we make better time on the road?" Lucas asked the sergeant tank commander, sitting deep in the bowels of the tank and steering from its viewing point below the turret.

"The roads are heavily mined, and we'd be stopped within a few miles," he replied.

"I'm really glad we left the truck," said Angela.

About ten minutes later, a loud "ping" was heard within the tank. The sergeant immediately climbed from his viewpoint in the depth of the tank and slammed the open hatch closed.

"Government snipers!" he said. "They're everywhere behind our lines. We'll be seeing them for a while until we reach Choge. Don't worry, they can't penetrate the armor on this tank, and if we don't run into a bazooka or rocket launcher, we'll be safe."

"Great comfort," remarked Lucas sarcastically.

The sergeant smiled and said, "Not used to combat, Doctor? It might be good for you and the nurse to see what we have to go through to obtain all the wounds that you continually patch up."

The tank twitched and shuddered on, now accompanied by intermittent gunfire from all sides, but no rockets or bazooka shells were fired at them. After three hours, the tanks slowed and came to a halt. The constant gunfire had also stopped.

"What now?" asked Lucas.

"Pit stop for refueling and food," said the tank commander pleasantly. "We are at a fortress in Luangue. Everybody out to relieve themselves and to eat."

As they climbed out of the tank, Lucas and Angela noticed that the other two tanks had stopped and parked next to them. After such a long trip, they found that it was difficult to walk and staggered briefly as they tried to regain their footage.

"My ears are still ringing from the gunfire," said Angela.

"What did you say?" said Lucas laughing as he also covered his ears. "I have the same ringing!"

Everyone in the convoy had left their vehicles, ready to take a break from the swaying motion and vibrations of the rugged armored panzers. After relieving themselves, they sat down at a crate, which they used as a table, to eat the meager victuals placed before them. As they were finishing their meal, the sounds of battle could be heard in the near distance. "We're close to the fighting," remarked the lieutenant. "It sounds like it's only a kilometer or so away. We will have to go around the battle to get to Choge, and then on to Saurimo."

As the crew rested for a few minutes, a soldier with a caduceus on his collar walked up to the lieutenant and spoke to him briefly. The officer nodded. Then, the lieutenant strode over to Lucas and said, "Doctor Stuart, the fortress has some wounded soldiers here and no physician. One of the medical orderlies was asking if there was anyone in the convoy with medical experience who would mind looking at some of the more seriously wounded. We do have the time to delay and they say that it would really help to have a professional opinion."

Lucas stood immediately and answered, "Sure. Where are the wounded?"

"Just follow the orderly," he replied.

Lucas and Angela followed the corporal to a grey tent with a large red cross painted on its top. Inside were men lying on stretchers, a familiar sight by now to Lucas and Angela. Intravenous bottles hung from ropes suspended from the roof of the tent and bloody bandages covered various parts of each of the wounded soldiers. "This is almost as bad as Lubalo Mission a few weeks ago," breathed Angela. "What can we do with this mess?"

The corporal led Lucas to a patient lying on his side on a cot near the door. His uniform was covered with blood, but a colonel's star was easily visible at his collar.

"This is our unit's commanding officer and we need him badly," said the soldier. "Can you help him?"

Lucas turned the patient flat on his back, gently. The colonel let out a groan as he was moved, forcing the wound on his abdomen to ooze a small amount of blood and cloudy yellow fluid.

"He has a gunshot wound to the left abdomen," said Angela. "The entrance wound is on his abdomen and there is a much larger exit wound on his left side."

Pulling the dressing off of the wound, Lucas said, "I can see the intestines within his belly. There is fecal contamination, so he must surely have had his gut perforated. We'll have to move quickly to save him!"

Finding the lieutenant who had brought them to Luangue, Angela explained the situation. Then she asked, "How long do you plan to stay before we leave for Chonge and then on to Saurimo?"

The lieutenant grimaced and finally said, "We can't afford to lose a colonel for a trip to Saurimo. If we stay until morning, can you do the operation this afternoon? It's much safer to travel in combat zones in daylight."

The surgical operation proceeded that afternoon in the makeshift surgical suite the fortress managed to put together with Angela's help. While they had to turn down some of the many volunteers offering to donate blood for the colonel, they did use four units of the precious liquid to keep him alive. After the five hour operation was over, the officer appeared to be resting peacefully on his cot.

"There's no way we can express our appreciation for your efforts," said the lieutenant. "We do have a bottle of vintage cognac that was being saved. If you would take it, the entire unit would feel obliged."

Lucas and Angela didn't drink cognac, but they still accepted the gift with many thanks, knowing it would be an insult to refuse.

"We'd better get some sleep, Lucas. We have a long journey in the morning."

When Lucas arrived at the colonel's cot early the next morning, he was pleasantly surprised to see the officer sitting up in bed and conversing with his junior officers. He appeared alert and oriented.

"How are you feeling?" Lucas asked as he approached the group gathered around his cot.

"Much better than if you hadn't happened to be here last night," was the jovial reply. "Thank you so much for your timely efforts," he said in poor English with a heavy Portuguese accent.

The group of officers dissolved and the colonel reached out to shake Lucas' hand. As they grasped hands, the officer said to Lucas, "I understand that this morning you plan to go on to Saurimo. It's a dangerous trip. Should you perhaps consider postponing it for a few weeks?"

"I don't think that's possible," said Angela as she approached the cot, having overheard the conversation.

"Colonel," said Lucas, "this is Angela Abercrombie. She assisted me last night in your surgery."

"Thank you so much. What is the urgency of your visit to Saurimo? Why not wait a few days until we are able to solidify our control of the area?"

Angela explained that her family had been at the mission station and her concern for their safety. "I really need to find them and insure their condition, Colonel," she concluded.

"You have done me a great favor by saving my life." said the colonel. "Now I will return the favor. I am the commanding officer of the district of Saurimo and have absolute military authority. Since you feel the necessity to travel, I will send my aide, Major Puzzo, who will travel with you in the convoy leaving this morning. He will see that your family is found."

"I don't know how to thank you, Colonel," said Angela as they left the tent.

They ate some fruit for breakfast and boarded the second tank in the line of three in which they had arrived as its diesel engine roared to life. Major Puzzo sat in the turret of the first tank, commanding the three armored vehicles as they thundered south on the road towards Choge.

The trip to Choge was uneventful, as the rebels appeared to have nominal control of the surrounding area. Their convoy moved swiftly through the scattered brush covering the parched dirt. As the tanks lumbered along the rutted dirt roads, passing many burned out houses and buildings, Angela and Lucas were impressed by the ferocity of the war and the devastation that the rebellion had caused to the population of rural Angola. The colonial Portuguese government, trying to maintain control of the rural population, refused to turn Angola over to the local population. In this attempt, they had destroyed most of the rural agricultural land, turning it into a desert. Both sides were aware that some of the world's largest oil reserves lay deep under its shores and the future of the country was hotly contested. Neither side would yield easily.

"There's barely an intact house and most of the farm animals have been slaughtered or run off," remarked Angela as she and Lucas sat in the turret of their tank watching the countryside pass behind them. Many cattle and pigs lay in the barnyards, dead from the lethal crossfire. The pastures were devoid of live animals.

"There don't seem to be any crops left either!" replied Lucas "They'll starve next year."

The three tanks continued through the scrub brush covered countryside, uninterrupted by hostile gunfire from government forces. They finally reached the outskirts of Choge, marked by multiple mud houses and buildings in various stages of destruction. Fires burned inside the remains of some of the houses and a few dead soldiers lay on the streets.

"Is that thunder or gunfire we hear?" asked Lucas, as a rumble could be heard in the distance.

Even as the tanks stood still, their idling engines made so much noise that they were forced to use their radios to communicate.

"It's time to close the hatches!" the Major's voice with static came from the intercom. "It's unfriendly country from here to Saurimo."

All the tanks' upper hatches were slammed shut and locked. After a few minutes, the Major's tank could be heard to accelerate as it pulled forward and to the left, rolling over debris littering the streets. They could see his tank through the site-slits on the front of their tank.

"Hey, Lucas, they're shooting at us!" exclaimed Angela as she instinctively ducked lower inside the small space within the bowels of their tank. As they continued forward, the "ping" sound became a hail. Suddenly, there was a loud explosion behind them followed be a series of smaller "pops" echoing through their tank.

"What the …… what was that?" asked Lucas.

He immediately heard the Major's voice over the intercom, saying in a grim tone, "Scratch one rear tank. The government troops must have rocket launchers. Now we go full speed. Try to keep up with me!"

The roar of the now full-speed engines filled the interior of their tank, making conversation futile. The armorer, a silent man who was constantly firing the tank's eighty-eight caliber cannon, ejected the spent shells to the floor of the tank, making agility an asset. The constant machine gun fire splattered spent casings all over them. They were in a battle for their lives.

After about ten minutes, the roar of the engines diminished substantially as the forward speed and the firing slowed. The intercom crackled again with the Major's gravelly voice, "They're on the run. Don't bother to follow them. We have business in Saurimo. Follow me!"

Their tank made a sharp turn, following the Major's lead, and started traveling cross-country over ditches, streams, and roads.

"At this rate, we should be in Saurimo shortly," said their tank commander. "Hold on, this will be a bumpy ride!"

For an hour, they traveled at a speed of about thirty kilometers an hour over the roughest terrain imaginable. Finally, the tank ground to a halt. The intercom squawked, "Saurimo on your left, ladies and gentlemen. What is your pleasure?"

"We want to go to the Saurimo Mission, north of town, please," answered Angela. This was conveyed to the Major over the intercom.

"Follow me. It's about a kilometer away," he answered.

The rest of the trip was peaceful. The turret open, Angela and Lucas were perched on top of the tank, looking all around for some evidence of habitation. It was emotionally devastating, as all they could see was destruction of the former landmarks Angela recognized. The Anglican Church that was almost leveled and the open market place where she used to shop for food with her mother was now a tangle of burnt timbers.

"There is the mission!" exclaimed Angela, pointing to a smoldering ruin of buildings. Out front was a sign stating, "SAURIMO SCOTTISH PRESBYTERIAN MISSION."

"Oh my Gosh!" whispered Lucas. "Look at the destruction!"

Angela began to cry.

# 10
## Chapter

T he distance from the holding cell to the courtroom was short, but as they walked across the stone pathway their ankle and wrist shackles rattled, a reminder that there was the possibility they could lose their freedom. The four women who had traveled with Hamid proceeded to the hearing. They appeared subdued as they were led into the large wood paneled room. A few benches for spectators had been built at floor level in front of a raised podium at the center of the room, where the judge's plush, leather-cushioned chair was enthroned. A lone witness' chair sat near the left side of the podium, bereft of cushion or leather. It was an impressive courtroom for such a small, remote town on the Congo River.

"Look at the writing on the wall above the dais," said Gayle to Esther, once they had been seated in the front row of benches. "It's in French, and its translation says that this is the Supreme Court for this entire district of Zaire. There are no appeals of its decisions."

The handful of spectator benches remained only partially occupied, and at the table on the left side in front of those benches sat Sir William and another man, who the women had never seen before. There was also a table in front of the benches on the right side with two chairs. These two chairs were occupied by Hamid and another man, both dressed in similar garb. All four of the ladies whose fates were in question were clothed in prison clothes with orange stripes, to identify them should they attempt to escape.

"Why is everything here in French?" asked Esther. One would think they'd use an African language."

Gayle replied, "You need to remember a little history. This used to be the Belgian Congo, colonialized from the 1800s by the Belgians. Thus for a hundred years all legal documents and the legal language was in French. Since the country became free, the legal system remains in French. I hope Sir William speaks French."

"Tous les invoque," was announced by the bailiff, as everyone in the room stood. The door behind the dais opened and an elderly white man in a long, black robe entered the room. He sat in the judge's chair, and everyone in the room sat down again.

The gavel banged twice and the judge spoke English, with a low, clipped French accent. "This is case number 74625, and it will be tried in the English language, as it is the language that most of the litigants speak. There will be translators for any who don't. Are there any objections?" Esther noted what she thought might be compassion in his gaze as he surveyed the four women.

No questions were raised, and the Belgian Justice opened the case. "As this is the provincial capital of the territory, the decisions made here are final and binding" said the judge. "As I speak both languages, and the litigants speak English, we will continue."

He began by addressing Sir William, "I believe the litigation involved in this case concerns the proper custody of four ladies, found to be under the supervision of a Mr. Hamid Abib, traveling on a boat that arrived recently from Angola. The complaint has been filed by Sir William Spencer-Johnson on behalf of the four ladies."

No one stirred, as all eyes turned to the podium where the judge was sitting.

The magistrate questioned, "May we hear from the plaintiff first?"

Sir William stood at the table and requested Gayle as his first witness for the plaintiff. She arose from her bench and walked directly to the witness chair. Sitting in the chair, she gave her full attention to Sir William, after she was sworn in.

"By what authority did your supervision fall under the control of Mr. Abib?" he asked Gayle.

Looking directly at Sir William, Gayle answered, "By no authority. His claim is false. I am an American citizen and under no one's authority."

Still standing, Sir William walked a few steps until he was standing directly in front of Hamid at his attorney's table. By Sir William's manner and obvious experience, it was evident to Hamid and everyone else in the courtroom, that Sir William was a professional solicitor. It was assumed that he would feel comfortable in any trial situation, and as he moved elegantly around the podium Hamid began to feel increasingly uneasy. He was moving around in his chair as he began to sense that this hearing was going to be more of an ordeal than he had anticipated. There was no jury, as this was a preliminary hearing, and the judge would decide if the case would go on to trial.

"Then how did you happen to be traveling with Mr. Abib from Angola to this location?" asked Sir William.

Gayle related the entire episode from their capture by rebels at Lubalo Mission, their escape from the rebels, the death of Reverend Brown and the meeting with Hamid.

"When Mr. Abib suggested that he would help you, did he mention any type of Repayment, or further requirement for his services on your part?" asked Sir William.

Looking directly at Hamid, Gayle said, "None whatsoever."

"Has he *ever* mentioned any obligation on your part as a requirement for repayment for his assistance?"

"Not until we docked at a town in Zaire two days ago and he brought on board those two children, shackled and restrained. It was a disgrace, and when we asked about it, he informed me that we *also* were his wards."

"Now then, did he inform you as to why you were to be his servants and what services you were to render as repayment for his assistance?"

"I object!" shouted Hamid's lawyer. "There has been no evidence of any enslavement intentions, only employment to repay his expenses."

"Sustained," said the judge

"I suppose, he wanted us to pay him back for the money he had spent on our clothes and hotel…the boat trip too. He didn't say what we were to do, but it was to be in Khartoum. I don't know what businesses he has there."

"Yes, we'll get to that shortly," said Sir William.

"Objection!" shouted Hamid's attorney, now standing at his seat at their table.

"No connection has been established to Mr. Abib's business and this whole trial."

"Sustained," repeated the magistrate.

"But Mr. Abib did offer to pay for your accommodation and travel to this location?" Sir William continued.

"He did," replied Gayle

"And no mention was discussed about repayment or restitution for costs?"

"That is correct, until the day he told us we were his slaves."

Sir William smiled at the judge and said, "I have no more questions for this witness."

Sir William sat down and Hamid's lawyer asked Gayle a few routine questions of minor import. Then, Gayle was excused as a witness.

"We would call Tsitsi Kalumbe as the second witness for the plaintiff," said Sir William to the court.

As the name was called by the bailiff, the rattle of shackles shattered the stillness of the court room. The older of the two black girls stood and walked over to the witness chair and sat down. Immediately, the attorney for Hamid stood. "We object to this witness! She is a minor and doesn't speak any recognized language. Her testimony will be invalid!"

"I'll be the determiner of what is or isn't valid in this court-room," spoke the judge. "Sir William?"

As Sir William rose from the table, the man sitting with him rose also. Both men stood before the judge. "Your Honor, this is Horace T. Pettybone, and he has come to assist us."

Handing a sheaf of papers to the clerk, Sir William continued, "Mr. Pettybone is a certified interpreter of the local dialect spoken in the Lubalo District of Angola, Kileta. These papers will attest to his education and certification. I intend to question this young lady with his assistance."

A copy of the papers presented to the court was given to Hamid's lawyer, who examined them closely.

After waiting for a full five minutes while the judge and lawyer reviewed the documents, Sir William continued, "If there are no further objections, may I question this witness through the interpretation of Mr. Pettybone?"

"Wait a minute!" exclaimed Hamid's lawyer. "How do we know that this man is actually Mr. Pettybone? He could be anybody at all. The documents certainly certify his competence if he actually is who Sir William says he is. But how does he just happen to show up this morning at the plaintiff's convenience?"

Sir William was not in the least shaken by this question and replied, "Would the defendant's lawyer like to put Mr. Pettybone on the stand and question him as to his veracity and identity?"

"I would," said Hamid's lawyer

"Then we will proceed," said the judge, gaveling the discussion to an end.

The bailiff motioned for the girl called Tsitsi to step down and Mr. Pettybone took her place in the witness chair. Tsitsi sat on the bench again with her sister.

A brief examination on the witness stand resulted in Hamid's lawyer conceding that this *was* indeed Mr. Pettybone and that he was qualified to interpret for the young black girl. He also finally admitted that she was a valid witness, after which the judge allowed her to testify.

This having been established to everyone's satisfaction, the young black girl, still wearing ankle and wrist bracelets, dragged her chains back to the witness chair and sat again in front of Sir William. She was sworn in after it was established that the truth was required in her testimony. She had never heard of the Christian God prior to this occasion. Mr. Pettybone walked over to the girl and greeted her in Kileta.

"*Mbote na mono mpangi. Wa faso? Ku tuba bene kibeni Kileta.*" The young girl on the witness stand immediately smiled, as for the first time in days she could understand what was said to her. Her younger sister sitting on the benches also smiled at Mr. Pettybone's greeting.

"Now then," said Sir William, "Please state your name and age."

Mr. Pettybone immediately spoke, using the obscure West African Kikongo dialect of Kileta. The girl obviously understood him, as she immediately responded in the same dialect. The entire examination proceeded in this manner, from English to dialect and then back to English through the interpreter. Mr. Pettybone spent about five minutes explaining to Tsitsi that this trial was about her relationship to Hamid and whether she and her sister would go with him to Sudan. Tsitsi indicated that she understood.

"My name is Tsitsi Kalumbe and I am fourteen years old," said the girl.

"And what is your sister's name and age?" asked Sir William.

As Tsitsi answered in the dialect, Mr. Pettybone broke into a grin. "She says her sister's name is Tsabola Kalumbe and she is twelve. Tsabola is the term for 'pepper' in their dialect."

Sir William proceeded with the questions as soon as the laughter subsided. "How did you and your sister come to be with Mr. Abib?" he asked, pointing to Hamid.

"Our parents are very poor," said Tsitsi. "In Angola, our family was starving and they decided to sell Tsabola and me to Mr. Abib so that the rest of the family could eat and continue to live in our house."

"How do you know that?" Sir William queried, through Mr. Pettybone's interpretation.

Tsitsi now became uncomfortable and began to squirm in the big witness chair.

"Our parents told us that we must go to live with this strange man, as *bumpika* to save the family from starvation. This word means a slave, or *nkole,* a prisoner. Both of our parents were crying when Mr. Abib gave them a large wad of money and put these metal bracelets on our ankles and wrists. He then took us to the river and made us get on a boat with him."

Mr. Pettybone tried to conceal his own reaction to her answer by turning his head away from Tsitsi, but the judge and everyone in the courtroom were aware that her answer had affected him deeply.

"Did you go with him willingly?"

"We did not wish to leave our family, but we were told to do as he directed us and remain quiet, and so we did."

"Do you now or have you ever had a passport?"

"What's a passport?"

Mr. Pettybone explained with some considerable difficulty what a passport was and established that neither girl had now or ever had the document, thus establishing their presence in Zaire as illegal.

"We have no idea of our birth date or even the location of our birth," Tsitsi testified.

"So you were on your way with Mr. Abib to Sudan, with no documentation and no knowledge what was going to be expected of you?" continued Sir William.

Mr. Pettybone translated the question and also the negative answer. W

"I am through with the witness at this time," said Sir William.

The judge looked at Hamid's lawyer, Mr. Hassain, and said, "Your witness."

Mr. Abib's attorney stood and walked over to the witness chair. He asked, through Mr. Pettybone, "Miss Kalumbe, it is your testimony that you did come willingly with Mr. Abib at your parents' request? No force was used to get you to board the boat?"

A positive response was recorded by Mr. Pettybone, but a long soliloquy followed her answer. "What did she say?" requested the judge.

"Your Honor, the dialogue was not responsive to the question. Mostly she was complaining about her treatment by Mr. Abib and her sister's pain from the shackles they are forced to wear."

The judge said, "Do you have any further questions of this witness?" to the attorney.

"No, Your Honor," he answered.

The witness was excused and the defense was called to state their case. Mr. Hamid's attorney rose and faced the magistrate. As he stood at the table, he said, "Your Honor, Mr. Hamid Abib himself will testify."

Hamid got up from the table and walked to the witness chair. Before sitting, he placed his hand on the Bible and swore to "tell the truth, the whole truth and nothing but the truth, so help me God."

Hamid's lawyer stood up from behind the table and approached the witness chair. After a pause, he looked at Hamid and said, "Tell me Mr. Abib, how is it that you happened to be in a supervisory capacity to the two young girls Tsitsi and Tsabola?"

"I purchased the services of these two sisters, Tsitsi and Tsabola Kalumbe, from their parents. We have here a receipt, signed by both parents, for the two-year duration of their services. This is concrete evidence of the legal transfer of their services and my supervisory assignment."

"This is exhibit one," said Hamid's lawyer, Mr. Hassan, as he laid the documents on the dais in front of the judge.

The judge examined the documents and said, "These papers appear to be in order. They are signed and stamped with the magistrate's insignia from Angola."

Mr. Hassan smiled and continued, "Why are they then wearing restraints, Mr. Abib?"

"The children had not traveled previously and the restraints were instituted to insure their safety during travel."

The judge, interrupted the interrogation, and asked, "These documents seem to be in order, where are you taking them and what sort of work will they be doing? One-hundred thousand Kwanza, (about U.S. $1300), seems a high price to pay her parents for help in your office, especially when you add in transportation costs and living expenses."

Hamid answered without pause, "We are on the way to Khartoum in Sudan, for the girls to work at a hotel, cleaning up and dusting the facilities."

Gayle, sitting in the audience, whispered to Esther sitting next to her, "Then why didn't he use girls from Sudan and save the expense of travel?"

Hamid continued, "The complaint lodged by this gentleman is baseless and without grounds." He frowned as he pointed at Sir William.

"And the two white ladies?" asked Mr. Hassain, Hamid's attorney.

"The two white ladies were alone in Angola without funds. They requested my assistance. I not only fed and clothed them, but generously gave them lodging and paid their fare on a boat to this location. When I requested them to repay my generous hospitality, they refused to give me any type of remuneration. I will thus take them also to Khartoum so that they may work off the debt."

Having finished his interrogation, Hamid's lawyer sat down. Hamid remained sitting in the witness chair, obviously uncomfortably anticipating the coming onslaught.

"The plaintiff's examination?" requested the judge.

Sir William got to his feet after a brief pause. He moved elegantly across the room until he stood directly in front of the now intimidated Arab. Smiling at the twitching Middle Eastern man, Sir William asked pleasantly, "Rather warm weather we're having, Mr. Abib. Are you feeling well this morning?"

The tight-lipped answer came, "Yes, sir."

Sir William continued the interrogation in a pleasant manner, "Mr. Abib, what is your main line of business in Khartoum?"

"I am in the import and export business, and have been for years."

"Ah, yes," went on Sir William pleasantly. "What exactly is it that you import and export, sir?"

"I import goods and wares from all over the world to Khartoum for resale," said Hamid.

Sir William gave him a stern look and continued, "Do you have any other business interests in the Sudan, Mr. Abib?"

"Well, I have a few buildings that are rented to other businesses and I own an automobile sales outlet."

"That's all?" said Sir William pleasantly. "Do you own a dozen brothels in the red-light district of Khartoum?"

"I certainly do not!" retorted Hamid.

"Hmmm," said Sir William, as he walked back to the table where he had been sitting and lifted a paper from the tabletop. With no unpleasant tone, Sir William said, "If I showed the court a certified copy of your arrest record from the Khartoum police department up to last month, what do you think would be the primary reason for your various incarcerations over the past ten years, sir?"

Hamid now began to become very nervous, moving about in his chair and scratching his head. He said, "I have not the faintest idea. I am a distinguished citizen and have no blots on my record!"

"I submit this as 'exhibit one' for the plaintiff," said Sir William as he placed the paper on the Magistrate's dais. He handed a copy to both Hamid, still in the witness chair, and to Hamid's attorney, Mr. Hassain. There was a silence as the documents were perused.

"Shall we examine the report together?" asked Sir William still in a conversational voice.

"Sure, I did have some trouble. It wasn't my fault. I rented to these people without knowing their business. This can happen to anyone."

Sir William smiled and asked, "Ten different renters and you were unaware of the business they were in? I doubt it. All ten were running brothels and you were ignorant? The Sudan courts found you guilty, and I think we here can guess the truth. No more questions."

In the courts of Zaire, as in Belgium law on which all of Zaire's laws are based, the judge can question the witnesses. The judge now asked Hamid, "Tell me, do *any* of the four women in your charge have *any* documentation of entry in their possession? Do they have passports or visas? Can you show us any immigration paperwork?"

"No," answered Hamid quietly.

"Then this is an open and shut case," continued the judge. "The intentions of the defendant are impossible to determine at this point, but it is clear that all four ladies are in the country illegally." The judge stated, "I order that all four ladies be returned to Angola forthwith at the expense of Mr. Abib. Case closed," he said bringing the hammer down with a resounding 'Thump!' Then, he arose and proceeded to his chambers.

"So much for that," said Sir William. "I suggest that we retire to the local bistro, after you change out of your striped prison clothes, to celebrate. Unfortunately they won't remove the restraints until all of you are back in Angola, but you will be free when you get there."

The women were freed and returned to their hotel room to change clothes before they had the party to celebrate. Sir William selected a nearby restaurant where they could all sit to discuss the morning's successful outcome.

While they still bore the metal restraints, they no longer had on the striped prison garb. They were back to wearing the Muslim robes bought for them by Hamid in Lubalo. Mr. Pettybone came along, as did the Deputy Marshal assigned to supervise the women until they had returned to Angola. After some persuasion from Sir William, the deputy reluctantly agreed to remove the ankle and wrist restraints from the four "immigration violators."

"How did you ever happen to run into Mr. Pettybone before the trial?" asked Esther when they had found seats and had been served drinks.

"Dumb luck," replied Sir William. "I went to the English Consulate, here in Kwamouth, to report about your predicament. Horace…may I call you Horace?… was listed under 'interpreters of remote dialects', and since I was aware that the two girls spoke no European languages, I called him. We got to talking on the phone and then met last evening. I guess it was fortunate for all of us that he had the qualifications for our trial and was kind enough to help."

All of this conversation was being roughly translated by Mr. Pettybone. As they spoke, Tsitsi said, "*Munu matondo kutonda ya mono mpangi,*" (We give many thanks to our friends), trying to thank Sir William and Mr. Pettybone.

"Okay, so you got lucky on finding Horace," said Gayle smiling at him. "What about the record of Abib in Khartoum? Where did that come from?"

"My dear Gayle, did you not know that Sudan was subject to British rule from the middle of the nineteenth century to the present. Our central office in Khartoum has kept records of their jurisprudence for decades."

"You old fox," said Gayle, hugging Sir William's neck and kissing his cheek playfully. "If anyone could do it, I was sure that you could free us from that Arab devil."

All four thanked Sir William profusely as they sat at the table celebrating.

A toast was proposed by Esther, and as everyone raised their glass or mug she expounded, "To the gentleman who saved all of us from total servitude." With Horace interpreting, the entire group said "Hear, hear!" and downed their drinks.

Then, Esther asked, "So how do we get back to Angola now?"

Sir William thought for a minute and then said, "The judge ruled that Hamid has to return all four of you to Angola. It's a sure thing that he won't take you there himself, but will have the deputy escort all of you back, at his expense."

"Okay, how do we get there and to where in Angola does he return us?" asked Gayle.

Sir William got up from his chair and walked over to the deputy, sitting at a nearby table. "Sir, we know the judge's ruling on the four ladies' illegal immigration to Zaire, but where and when is Hamid obligated to fulfill his judgment to extradite them?"

The deputy smiled slowly over his drink and said, "My job is only to see that the judge's ruling is carried out expeditiously and accurately. How he does it, and to what location, is Mr. Abib's problem. The money collected by the magistrate will be a fine, decided by the court and estimated to cover the costs of fulfilling Mr. Abib's obligation."

Walking back to the four captives' table, Sir William sat down. He lowered his voice and said, "Not good. Hamid will put up to the court the smallest amount of money he can before scuttling on back to Sudan. Almost certainly it means a boat trip back to Lubalo."

"That's fine for Tsitsi and Tsabola," said Esther. "They'll be back home again. But Gayle and I want to go home to America. How do we do that?"

Sir William thought for a minute, "Hamid is only responsible to return you to where he illegally brought you into Zaire, which is Lubalo. There is no airstrip here, so the scow is the only way back to Lubalo. We will have to then get you to the American consulate in Luanda to obtain a passport and money to fly home, a difficult proposition with the war and all."

"Will you help us, Sir William?" asked Gayle.

"Let me think about it for a day, Gayle. The options to leave here are limited. For now, let me find all four of you a place to stay tonight. Maybe tomorrow we can tour this river-port town of Kwamouth, here on the Congo River. After those nights in prison, I suspect that a shower and a decent bed will be in order."

Gayle had the thought cross her mind that not only had Sir William provided expertise in law, but was now going to find lodgings for four women that he hardly knew. Why was he willing to do all this for free, unless he suspected who she really was or recognized her family name through her father? These thoughts went through her mind, but her visceral attraction for Sir William kept telling her how enticed she was with him.

Mr. Pettybone stood along with the others at the table and accepted everyone's thanks. He was on his way to Kinshasa the same afternoon and had to leave for his ship.

"We all appreciate your help, Mr. P. Please explain to Tsitsi and Tsabola that we will return them to their parents in a few days if they will be patient," said Sir William.

Mr. Pettybone explained the situation to the two African girls and they accepted the news with wide smiles. Pepper, the younger sister, seemed to accept every situation with equanimity, while her older sister was more cerebral. Then he said, "I'm on my way. There are very few people around here who speak both English and Kikongo but you can always use hand motions to communicate with the girls, if you need to tell them something."

After shaking hands all around, Mr. Pettybone said something to the girls that made them laugh. As he left to catch his boat, turning to Gayle he remarked, "I told the girls that their parents could keep Hamid's money for their time."

"He's certainly a nice man," said Esther after he had left. "We'll just have to communicate with Tsitsi and her sister as best as we can until they get home."

Sir William found the four women accommodations in a double suite at one of the better hotels. He then took them to supper. Esther noted that Sir William always managed to sit next to Gayle, or walk next to her, no matter where they went. She, however, wisely said nothing about it.

"It's getting dark and we'd better get some rest," said Gayle. "Thank you again, for all that you did for us today, Sir William."

Gayle and Esther both kissed him gently on the cheek, but Sir William put his arm around Gayle's waist and pulled her to him as she went to put her face next to his. That was enough to tip off Gayle of his feelings, and she exchanged glances with Esther as they both read the same thought. The four went off to bed, and Sir William set out to do some investigations. The deputy marshal sat on a chair outside the women's rooms and slept intermittently.

As the four ladies were preparing for bed, Esther turned to speak to Gayle, but she put her finger to her lips and whispered, "I know what you're thinking but for now let's just leave it alone and see what happens. We need Sir William and I really think he's nice, so don't say a word."

As morning came, all four women awoke and began to bathe and dress. A knock came at the door of the suite, and upon opening it Esther, wearing only a hotel robe, greeted a bellhop standing there with four large boxes, each with one of the ladies' name on it. "For you," he said, as he handed the boxes to Esther, who stood dumbfounded at the room's entrance. He also passed an envelope to her and then turned to leave, not waiting for a tip. To expect a *bonsella* would have been futile, as the four ladies did not have one Democratic Republic of the Congo franc among them.

"Open the envelope!" declared Gayle who had come from the bedroom to investigate the knocking. "Let's see who sent the boxes!"

A message was inside the envelope, which was elaborately sealed with a gold colored stamp. The envelope was addressed to "The Four New Freewomen," which was written on the front in gold lettering. Examining the boxes, they found that the four packages were tied together with a satin ribbon. Each box had a name on it and there was one for each of them. Esther opened the letter. It read: "Newly freed ladies need to appear at their best." There was no signature, but the note was written in elegant letters.

The four women proceeded to tear open their boxes. To their amazement and joy, they found that each package contained two complete new outfits, including underwear. The garments in the boxes fit each lady perfectly and were of an expensive and up to date English style. Exclamations and laughter dominated the room as they tried on their new attire, admiring each other's new looks.

"So much for the Muslim robes," said Gayle, as she threw her old, dirty cloak into the wastebasket. "We all will look great in these clothes. Let's get dressed and then go to breakfast!"

As the four neatly dressed women arrived in the hotel dining room, more than a few eyes were raised as they sat together and placed their orders. Tsitsi and Tsabola had to make hand signs, wearing modern clothes awkwardly for the first time. Their selection of food went through Esther, who ordered for them. Their new clothes made each look distinctively different; white cotton shirt and polo pants for Tsitsi and yellow for her sister; Gayle and Esther also received cool cotton outfits in expensive design. Just then, Sir William walked up to their table and sat down.

"Aren't we well dressed?" he said smiling. "Where did you get the stylish clothing? You all look great!"

"But these clothes were sent by you, weren't they? We all were just about to thank you for these wonderful clothes so we could get out of those nasty Muslim robes!"

Sir William frowned. It was obvious that he had not been joking.

"Then where did the clothes come from?" Gayle asked.

The ladies related to Sir William about the arrival of the boxes and then produced the note, which he examined carefully, with a suspicious smile. "I guarantee that this is not from me," said Sir William. "The clothes are quite expensive, and this quality of goods is not available in Kwamouth. The closest source would be Brazzaville, and most likely, even they would not have it there."

The entire breakfast was eaten with a cloud of mystery hanging over them, as there was no solution to the source of the gifts. Then Gayle made a suggestion,

"Is it possible that someone, who we don't know, saw or heard about the trial, and sympathized with our cause? There are many people who would like to see an end to slavery in the world. You never know who reads the newspapers."

Sir William thoughtfully rubbed his goateed chin. "Yes, a certified check arrived this morning from an English bank made out to me with no name of the sender. The note read something about "success in our cause" and was for a considerable sum of English Pounds Sterling. At first I thought it was from the British Government, now I'm not so sure. It didn't really concern me at the time but, with your story, the theory you propose might be possible."

After some further thought, Sir William arose from the table and walked around behind Gayle saying, "Please sit still for one minute, ladies." He then examined the labels in the back collar of each of the ladies dresses, expressing a satisfied "Humph" with the identification of each label. He then sat down again.

"Ladies, these clothes were purchased at Harrod's or another high class London store. To have arrived here this morning, after being purchased yesterday, means that only diplomatic pouch transportation was possible. We're dealing with an individual or group with extremely high grade diplomatic connections and access to major financial resources. Do any of you know of such connections?"

There was a silence for a full minute, as his announcement took effect. No one said a word. Finally Esther said softly to Gayle, "Well, aren't you going to tell him?"

Gayle blushed, but said nothing. All eyes turned to Gayle with questioning looks, upon hearing Esther's remark. Finally, Esther said, "Look Gayle, if you won't say anything, I will!"

Gayle took a deep breath and said slowly, "Okay, okay, I'll tell it. It's me. I guess I should relate the tale myself instead of Esther."

Sir William was now at full attention, and wanted to encourage Gayle because his curiosity was high, but he saw her hesitation to speak. He remarked casually, "It's not a problem, Gayle. Would you rather not say anything?"

"No, no," she stammered. "I guess it had to come out eventually."

With halting words, Gayle began, "Actually, my father is a wealthy industrialist and contributed large sums of money to help the American President win the last election. In return for his help, the President appointed him as the U.S. Ambassador to England, where my parents are now living. That accounts for the clothes and speed of delivery."

Sir William now said, "Your parents must have been frantic when they heard that the Lubalo Mission was overrun by rebels and they were unable to contact you. I *did* recognize your name as possibly the daughter of the Ambassador. After meeting you, my suspicions that you might be related to that family increased." He began to eat his eggs and toast, while sipping his morning tea.

Gayle had increasing respect and admiration for Sir William with each passing day, but her worry about his motives held her back. She hoped that she could learn more about him if she were a bit more open. She admitted, "My parents were against my going to do mission work in Angola, but because Reverend Brown was our pastor in America and they knew Esther's family, they finally consented to the mission trip this year."

Sir William was now fully engaged. "How did they find out where you were, and what you were going through?" Breakfast sat only partially eaten on their table.

"I had tried to contact them but since our capture, we have never been able to get to the outside world. I guess they heard about it in the news reports of those missing," said Gayle "I was reluctant to tell anyone before now, since the demand for ransom would have become astronomical, so I swore Esther to secrecy. We weren't really sure of you until yesterday, when you took charge of that courtroom. It was just luck that you came along, Sir William."

They finished breakfast and remained at the table, drinking tea.

"My parents took the precaution to have the CIA place a homing device, similar to a stolen automobile locater, under the skin of my forearm," she continued, putting forth her arm and showing them a fixed spot on the ventral surface with a minute scar on the skin. "I objected, but it was the only way they'd let me go. You know, blackmail from kidnappers, missing in the bush, and so forth. With satellite technology, they probably have been tracking me since my capture at Lubalo, but because of our being in such a remote location, could do nothing to help me."

Esther said, "We knew better than to let people know who she is, but without the escape from Lubalo, there was no way for her family to help her, especially in the middle of a war. We were sure lucky to run into you, Sir William. You saved us from God knows what, although at Lubalo, I thought we weren't going to make it."

"That explains a lot, including the bank draft, but now we have the Congo magistrate to deal with and neither of you has a passport. We still have problems that probably can be solved with diplomatic intervention," concluded Sir William.

"Just get me to a phone and both Esther and I will have diplomatic passports in a few hours. Maybe then, we can get back to England."

A phone was found and a short reunion over the long distance lines was accomplished. All offers of further remuneration to Sir William were politely refused, but a large bank draft to the girls was promised, which could be collected at one of the local financial institutions.

"We can travel in style now that our families can help us." said Esther. "But what about Tsitsi and Tsabola?"

"Heck," said Gayle, "they started out with us and deserve to finish the same way. We'll all take a ship to Brazzaville and fly to

England, first class. I bet the girls from Lubalo would love to see the big city."

Up to now, the deputy marshal had been quietly listening at another table, as the four ladies had been celebrating. He now spoke. "Ladies, I can't help but overhear your joy and celebration at being released from that Arab's custody. However, all four of you are under a direct court order to return to Angola at the point of your first illegal entry. That would be Lubalo. Until I have a court order to the contrary, it is my duty to see that this order is carried out expeditiously."

Gayle and Esther were speechless. Then Sir William said, "You mean that all four of the ladies must take the same boat back to Angola and perhaps be involved with the rebels again?"

The deputy looked up from his breakfast and stated, "That was the order and until changed, it stands."

"No problem. We have the right diplomatic connections," said Sir William. "We'll simply have the order modified. Give your dad a call, and he can go through diplomatic channels to get you out of here."

The second phone call was made within the hour, and Ambassador Wright, her Dad, understood the problem immediately. He remarked that changing a court order on illegal immigration might not be easy, and his fears were justified. The return call was made the same evening.

Gayle took her father's return call in her hotel room, still having difficulty believing she and Esther were in a modern first class room with bathrooms and room service. "What progress did you make on modifying the order, Dad?" asked Gayle. "We got the money you sent, and I decided not to let Sir William pay any more bills. We are living in style."

"None. The Democratic Republic of the Congo Ambassador does not interfere with local legal matters, and his government has strict policy on deportations. So far, I cannot seem to find anyone interested in letting you leave through any other immigration station."

Esther could hear the disappointment in Gayle's voice.

"But Dad, we have no time! They're taking us on the same boat in the morning. Isn't there something you can do?"

"We'll keep working on it, but it looks like you will be forced to take the same trip back to Lubalo. Once there, we'll have a helicopter at the border waiting for you and Esther. You know, that's Africa."

Gayle was devastated, as was Esther. Explanation to Tsitsi and Tsabola was impossible, but they understood that all was not going as planned by watching Gayle's demeanor. The deputy was determined to see all four to the Angola border no matter what, and Sir William's attempt first to convince the judge to alter his ruling and then attempts to bribe him failed. Africa has been well known for decades to have rules that don't make sense, and then stick to them.

As they all sat at the same breakfast table the next morning, Sir William said in frustration, "It looks like there is no alternative. They won't legalize your entry, even with the diplomatic passport you now have, and it appears you are bound to take the same boat we traveled on from Lubalo back upstream to Angola."

"When we get to Angola, who knows what they'll do?" moaned Esther. "I'm afraid to go back, but there appears to be little choice."

"That's not even the biggest problem," wailed Gayle. "We'll be all alone on that same river scow in the jungle for days. The trip upstream is slow and who knows what can happen?"

# 11
## Chapter

As the tank moved along the roads that were within the compound, it appeared that the total destruction of the Saurimo Mission as a useful entity was complete. Almost all of the buildings appeared to have been demolished or severely damaged, the chapel was a burnt out shell, and the living quarters lay in ashes.

After seeing the destruction of the mission, Angela requested the sergeant driving the tank to turn left at the next corner and then continue for a few blocks. "Our house is down that street," she said.

Angela observed the destroyed houses pass behind them as the tank moved slowly down her street. Large tears rolled down her face when she saw the buildings and houses that she remembered as a child now lying in various stages of annihilation. "The hospital used to be on this block, up the street from our house," she said as they passed a building, now leveled to only a few concrete blocks piled on top of each other. "My father was the pastor of this Scottish Presbyterian Church," she said, as she pointed to a burned-out patch of debris. It had been the mission's primary chapel. This destruction is devastating."

As the block ended and they continued on down the same street, Angela strained to see the ruins on the right side of the street. "Our house was the third on the right," she moaned. "All that's left on that spot is some burnt-out grass thatch, which was part of our roof, and I see a mass of rubble and burned timbers attached to the charred chimney. Please stop for a minute. I want to get down and examine what's left."

Both Lucas and Angela climbed down from the tank as it stopped. They walked through the pile of debris where her house had formerly stood. As they picked their way through the ashes, broken concrete and wood, a burgundy colored shred lying on the ground under a charred board caught her eye.

"What's this?" she said, giving voice to her thought. "What does this colored book remind me of…?"

Lucas turned to see Angela stoop to brush some ashes off an object lying on the ground among the charred glass and metal window frames obstructing their pathway through the remains of her house. Then he heard her groan, as he saw Angela slump to the ground. What she had found had deeply affected her emotionally, as Angela fought to control her despair. He didn't know what to do to help her pain.

"Oh, Dad, oh, Dad," she repeated over and over as she sat on the ground, sobbing. "What have they done to you? Did you have to leave it behind in the fire, or were you consumed?"

Bending from her sitting position on the ground amongst the debris, she carefully extracted a burgundy, leather-covered book that Lucas could see was a Bible. Walking over to Angela, he saw her open the book, now singed and the edges burned, to examine some pictures within the cover pages. "This was Dad's Bible. He used it every Sunday to preach. He was never without it."

"The pictures?" Lucas asked tenderly.

"It's our whole family. Here's an old one of Mother, and this is Tad and Jake with me when we were kids. It's been awhile since I've seen any of them. But what's happened to them?" she said starting to cry. "I know my father would not have left his Bible behind. He took it everywhere with him."

They carefully dug through the debris, looking for any other remnants that might have survived the destruction, but found nothing significant. Clutching the precious book to her chest, Angela finally led Lucas back to the waiting armored vehicle. Looking back over her shoulder at the ruins of her childhood home, she reluctantly turned toward their transportation back to Lubalo. They boarded the tank and began to move further down the street.

"I'm not satisfied with just some ruins and Dad's Bible," said Angela. "We need to find someone who was here. Perhaps they could shed some light on what happened to my family and the rest of the mission people."

As they continued to move further down the street where Angela used to reside, they saw an elderly black man in tattered clothes, hobbling along the road. He was picking through the debris, probably looking for food. "Please stop near him," pleaded Angela in a voice strong enough for the sergeant to hear over the diesel engines.

"Excuse me, sir," said Angela in Kileta. "Did you live here formerly?"

The man looked up at Angela and examined her features intensely through his haggard, empty eyes. A glimmer of recognition flashed across his wrinkled face and a faint smile appeared, revealing the many missing teeth in his mouth.

"Missie Angela…..? Yes! It *is* you! After all these months, you decided to come home to see all of us here in Suarimo. I know you, ever since you've grown from a little *piccanin*."

"Oh my, it's Dixon! I didn't recognize you in that condition." She turned to Lucas, excitedly informing him, "He was my parents' gardener even before I was born."

Angela, now excited at meeting someone whom she had known all of her life, hoped he would know the fate of her loved ones. She asked, "What are you doing here in all this devastation?"

"Ah Missie Angela, when your family left, a few weeks ago, they knew I would be staying here to watch the house. The war came and there is no house now, but I am still here with my wife and children. What must I do?"

Angela could easily guess that Dixon was worried and very hungry, so she reached into her canvas knapsack and pulled out a sandwich that they had brought as part of their supplies for the journey and gave him some water from a canteen to quench his thirst. "Tell me, Dixon, where did my father and brothers go?" asked Angela. She dreaded that the answer might tell of a disaster.

"Missie Angela, they all left for the west and Luanda. About a week ago, the war was approaching and Boss Abercrombe thought that they must leave. No one has been here since they all left. I was left in charge of the property, but there is nothing here now."

"Did all three leave together, Dixon?"

Dixon paused for a minute, which told Angela that there was a problem with the answer.

"Ah no, Missie. Little Boss Tad wanted to stay, but the Boss wouldn't hear of it. They had loud words."

"Now tell me the truth, Dixon. When did the Boss leave with Little Boss Jake?" asked Angela with a slighter sterner tone to her voice, knowing that the loyal servant would only tell her the truth.

Thinking for a minute, Dixon said, "It was eight days ago. They took the automobile and headed west."

"And Little Boss Tad?"

"He waited here until the fighting got bad. Then he took the motorbike, but I'm not sure where."

Turning to Lucas, Angela said, "Almost certainly, my father headed for Luanda with Jake, but Tad always was the wild one. He might have joined the rebels and could be anywhere by now. Many of the white settlers sympathized with the rebels and joined them."

"Do you want to look for Tad?" Lucas asked.

Angela thought for a minute and then said, "Tad could be anywhere. He might have made an attempt to run to Luanda to meet Dad and Jake, or he could be deep in the war, fighting the government troops with the rebels. To look for him would be futile."

"Since we now know more news about your father and Jake, perhaps it's time to head back to Lubalo," observed Lucas. "I'm glad that we have at least established that your family was well a few days ago. What do you want to do about Dixon?"

"Dixon won't be a problem," said Angela. "He was born in this area and his entire family still lives around here. He will go back to them as soon as I release him from Dad's assignment and he will help his own family."

"Dixon," Angela spoke, "You no longer need to remain with the house. There is nothing left to watch. I want you to return to your people for now and when the Boss comes home, he will give you your job back."

"Yes, Missie Angela" was the reply. "I will see them today and I know when Boss Abercrombe returns, he will give me my job again. *Tatenda*," he said, thanking her.

The rumble of the tank's diesel engines filled the driver's compartment within the bowels of the tank as it accelerated northwards toward Lubalo. For now, most of the fighting had subsided and the armored vehicle bounced and jarred the occupants as it rolled across plowed fields and creeks.

"I feel almost certain that Dad and Jake will arrive safely in Luanda," said Angela. "Dad knows the roads well and speaks the vernacular fluently."

"What about Tad?" asked Lucas.

"Tad is another story. He's wild, fearless and pro rebel. There's no telling what he might do. He might even be headed toward Lubalo looking for me!"

"How old is Tad?" asked Lucas.

"He's twenty-three, going on seventeen. Somehow he never matured like the rest of us, but maybe that's because he's the youngest and has never had to assume much responsibility."

The dirt and gravel tracks leading north from Saurimo were heavily land mined by both the government and rebel armies. This made road travel extremely dangerous without landmine detectors. The cross-country route remained infinitely slower and rougher, although it probably was relatively safe.

After an hour of rough roads, Angela finally complained. "Lucas, this bumping and twisting is giving me a sore backside. When do we take a break?"

"Let's ask the sergeant who is driving this metal box. Maybe he knows."

Inquires resulted in referral to the commanding major in the leading tank, who was not responsive to their queries. "We need to get to Chipomba before dark. We can rest there and get some food. Just stand up inside the tank and your bottom will suffer less," advised the major over the intercom.

As dusk descended on the convoy, now consisting of the remaining two tanks, an armored car, two trucks and a Jeep, they finally rolled to a stop in the middle of a field, high on a hill. "We can see and hear any approaching vehicles or troops from this vantage point. Walk around a bit and we'll try to feed you with the soldiers in an hour or so," said the Major when they had finally crawled out of their tank.

As Angela and Lucas stood looking out over the Angolan landscape at the multicolored sunset, they admired once more the kaleidoscope of pastel colors illuminating the western sky. "You know, Lucas, we may end up living anywhere else in the world, but Africa is my home. Here the wars, destruction, starvation, sickness, and suffering *do* upset me, and these problems might not be present in other places, so the small amount of good that we can do is important because it gives relief to those less fortunate than we are."

"Angela honey, the world is filled with individuals who are also able to help these people, but they are too indifferent or scared to actually *do* anything about it, so the suffering goes on. There is widespread recognition about the African situation, but to actually actively get involved in helping to solve their needs would be too expensive or, in the majority of cases, too much trouble for them."

They stood out in the remote meadow of untilled ground, holding hands as the sun faded behind the distant hills and the darkness began to eclipse the magnificent display of colors. Chipomba lay below in the shadows.

"The food's on. Come and get it!" rang the voice of the cook.

By the time they had finished supper, darkness had fallen and everyone had settled into the routine of evening army camp. Guards had been posted and tents erected. As it was late Sunday, the evening's religious services had already been attended and most of the troops were either sitting around their small camp-fires chatting and drinking beer or had gone to bed.

"I wonder if Dad and Jake made it safely to Luanda," Angela said to Lucas, as they sat on collapsible chairs near their fire.

"They know the roads and speak the language, Angela. I'm sure they had a safe journey," he replied encouragingly. "I'm really glad we could find out that your family has survived the war thus far."

They sat for a while longer and discussed the changes at Lubalo over the last few weeks and if they should take Wicki with them when they left the mission for good.

Angela said, "I realize that you are obligated to return to Malawi next week, and I want to stay with you, Lucas. How do you plan to get there? It's a long distance."

"Yes, it's probably about fifteen hundred to two thousand miles, Angela. It's a long drive or a seven hour plane trip by a Beechcraft twin engine aircraft."

"What do we tell Wicki? He already says that he wants to come with us and bring Iuba. We really will need to do something for the two of them."

"There may not be room if we all fly," replied Lucas. "Let's wait and see when we get back to Lubalo. It's time for bed; we have a long trip in that uncomfortable rattle trap tomorrow."

Angela sat thinking for a few minutes before she stood up. She walked over to where Lucas was standing, and placing her arm around his waist she kissed him repeatedly on the lips. "You know Lucas; I'd really be lonely without you beside me, not just today, but always."

Kissing her back, and holding her against his body, he joked softly, "You'd better be careful what you sign up for, woman!

This ole' boy may be plannin' to see other parts of the world that you never figured on."

"Where are you contemplating taking me, travelin' man?" she said lovingly.

"The northern parts of Zimbabwe need a doctor and nurse, I've heard. That's within my learning curve in the Shona language. Are you prepared to see Chironga next year?"

She kissed him on the mouth again, smiling, and whispered, "Anything you can stand, I'm willing to stand with you. Lead on to distant and exciting hospitals, O healing man."

"In the meantime, we'll examine the backs of our eyelids for a spell," said Lucas. "Good night, see you in the morning."

They went off to bed and slept soundly until the sounds and smells of breakfast tantalized them into wakefulness the next morning.

"I'm hungry enough to eat a rhinoceros," said Lucas as he stood at the inadequate camp mirror trying to shave. "Let's get something to eat."

Angela and Lucas sat at the table with the major and the sergeant as they wolfed down pancakes and honey as fast as the competent cook deposited them on the platter. "Okay, I've had enough," said Angela to the group, pushing away from the table. "Lucas, if you eat any more, you'll lose it inside the tank."

Then addressing the Major, whose name was Thaddeus Moyo, Angela asked, "Major Moyo, what's the plan today? Will we get to Lubalo by night fall?"

"That depends on the traffic and our government friends," he replied.

The Major was completely in charge of the convoy, and began giving his orders to the leader of each vehicle. "We'll continue to travel cross-country for the next twenty miles or so. Try to stay between the tracks of my lead tank to avoid landmines. We don't expect to have much gunfire, but a few days ago we did have some sniper fire as we came through here going south. Stay well behind me."

Camp was dismantled, and the trucks were packed with food, cots and gear. The convoy was prepared to move off from

Chipomba towards the north, but just as the Major, commanding the first tank, was ready to order them to start moving, he received a message over his radio. Lucas' tank simultaneously received the same message. The cipher was in English, sent by the South African forces, who strongly backed the Angola rebels. South Africa wanted the Portuguese to leave Africa, as the Portuguese opposed apartheid. Ironically, this put the South African government on the Angolan rrebels' side, allied against the Angolan colonial government.

It said: "A strong force of government troops has been sighted by the South African Air Force. They are moving at high speed in a North Easterly direction from Cuango, and appear to be heavily armed."

"So we're gonna have company any time now," said the Major. "I know that the enemy column will encounter our lines at Quimbonge, and that means there will be one hell of a fight south of Lubalo. Hang on, children. We're in for a bit of a scrap if they penetrate our outer defenses."

The pace of Lucas and Angela's convoy astounded both of them, as the six vehicles accelerated towards fifty miles per hour over rough terrain, moving in single file.

"I'm getting beaten to death by the rough bumps," said Angela. "I wish we didn't have to go this fast."

The sergeant looked over at them and remarked, "Rather get beaten to death by the bumps than hit by a government rocket launcher."

After an hour of this travel, they pulled onto a gravel road, which reduced the bumps dramatically. "Thank heavens," said Angela, "A smoother road."

They came to a full stop about a mile down the gravel road.

"We're in Sagumba," barked the Major over the intercom. "You have time to relieve yourselves while we refuel. If you're not on board when we're ready to leave for Caanga, you could get left behind."

"Angela," Lucas reminded her, "We left the Land Rover in Lunvula, a few miles south of here. I think we're going to need that truck. We'd better go back and recover it."

The Major, hearing Lucas' remark, said "You return to Lunvula at your own peril. It's a dangerous trip."

"He's probably right," remarked Lucas thoughtfully. "We'd better get out and decide what we want to do."

The break benefitted everyone, as the cramped space in the vehicles was confining. It also gave the missionaries a chance to stretch their legs and view the terrain. Most of the surrounding foliage consisted of scrub plant growth, mostly weeds and dirt. About a hundred yards from their stopping point on the remote trail they could see a farm, which consisted of a small mud hut with a thatched roof and a broken wooden door, standing ajar. The owners of this establishment appeared destitute, as they stood within the fenced corral that surrounded the dilapidated shack in which they lived. They were in the center of the enclosure watching the tanks pass by.

"Look at the goats and sheep inside the fence," observed Angela. "They look just like those I grew up with. But they're emaciated because they have so little to eat."

Five poorly nourished animals stood near the building in the center of the stockade near a sickly pig. The group of animals appeared to be in various stages of starvation, as did their owners.

"Lucas, we need to give those people some money so that they will be able to feed their animals better," suggested Angela.

"What about helping the owners themselves?" returned Lucas. "They look as poorly nourished as their animals."

A low growl followed by a roar of the heavy diesel engines coming to life filled the area as Lucas and Angela walked across the road to the farm house. "Positive you won't ride with us?" called the Major as the first tank, followed by the rest of the convoy, pulled out onto the gravel road and headed north. "I know your truck is only a few miles walk from here, but it could be a dangerous trip."

Angela and Lucas stopped at the farmhouse to talk to the farmer. The family consisted of a man and a woman with one small undernourished daughter, who was eleven but looked like a poorly nourished nine-year-old. As they talked briefly to the farmer, he explained that neither the people nor the animals had eaten in days and were near starvation. Lucas handed the man a few Angolan dollars, as Angela and he walked on towards Lunvula where they had left their truck.

"You know, "Angela remarked as they walked along the road, "I'm really glad we gave that farmer some money to feed his animals and family."

"Well they certainly needed some help," returned Lucas. "I am too."

"I figure it's about eight miles to get to Lunvula. We can do it in a few hours and the walk will be refreshing after that long tank ride," said Lucas as they entered the dirt road that led past the thatch-roofed farmhouse. They checked their canteens, feeling the hearty breakfast they had just eaten would suffice until they reached the truck.

"But is it safe with all of those government troops around?" asked Angela, taking his hand.

"We're taking a gamble walking out in the open like this but no one can tell by our clothes whether we are rebel or government affiliated, so we should be fairly safe. I'd rather not lose that truck, it may be useful later. Let's walk at a quick pace."

They walked at a brisk pace along the dusty, dirt road. Almost all rural Angola roadways were unpaved, winding pathways, which the wind blew into clouds of dust, obliterating the surrounding scenery. As they progressed along the dusty pathway Angela remarked, "I think I hear the sounds of the war in the distance to the north," as they increased their pace towards Lunvula. "We don't want to get involved if possible."

Darkness was beginning to close in, not only from the passage of time, but also from the increasing rain clouds that encompassed them from all sides.

Puffs of dust in the road began to kick up ahead of them, after they had been walking for about an hour. As they continued to hurry along the road, they wondered what was causing them, as they felt no rain drops. The puffs increased in frequency and appeared everywhere. Then the sounds of gunfire suddenly surrounded them, and they recognized that a firefight was in progress. They were in the middle of it.

"Get down, Angie!" said Lucas. Placing his arm around her shoulders, he pulled her into the ditch on the side of the road. The gunfire increased exponentially and explosions of rocket fire and grenades were close at hand. They could hear the "clank" of tank tracks approaching along the road, and then detonation of tank shells, as they landed near their hiding place.

"What are we going to do, Lucas? They're all around us. We could be killed."

The sounds were deafening, as return fire from beyond the road by bazooka and automatic weapons increased. From their hiding place, Lucas and Angela were unable to determine which side was rebel and which were government forces. Then a tank shell erupted only a few yards from their ditch, spraying dirt and debris over them.

"We dare not move," said Lucas calmly. "If we stand or run, a stray shell could hit us."

Just then, a ground-shaking explosion went off less than twenty feet from their hiding place. The ditch collapsed upon them and they were buried in a blanket of gravel and mud.

"Can you breathe?" asked Lucas, wiping the wet soil from his mouth and nose.

Angela didn't move. Frantically, he dug into the pile of sludge next to him, and finding an arm, he pulled her out of the ooze. Turning her on to her back, he could find no breath. Her pulse was faint. Blowing into her mouth after clearing an airway, he was able to inflate her lungs, as the battle continued to rage around them.

Ignoring the gunfire around him, he continued to resuscitate her, mumbling between his breathing into her lungs, "Come on, girl! Take a breath."

Finally she coughed up a little dirt and muck, and then coughed more times, vomiting saliva stained with brown dirt. Lucas gave her some water to rinse her mouth.

"What happened?" she sputtered

"No big deal, Angie. You just got smothered by dirt from a shell, but I'm glad to hear your voice. Lie flat next to me for a minute until you catch your breath."

Burrowing deeper into the soft dirt, both of them lay still as the fight thundered overhead. The exchange of gunfire continued for ten minutes with neither side appearing to gain an advantage until the deafening sounds began to move south, away from Lunvula.

Raising their heads, they looked south.

"That looks like the back of the Major's tank," said Lucas. "In fact it *is* his tank. We've spent the last four days following it, and those markings on the rear tread shields are definitely his," replied Angela. "The battle must have forced him to come back this way. Maybe we should crouch down and follow it for some protection as it moves down the road."

As she was speaking, a tremendous detonation ripped through the tank, turning it on its side. This was followed by multiple smaller blasts from within the tank, as the 88-millimeter ammunition shells ignited. The noise was shattering.

"The tank's gone." Angela said sadly, as the burning metal debris flew in all directions, narrowly missing Lucas. "We would have been *inside* that tank if we hadn't decided to get the Land Rover. The only way that could happen is that the government troops have acquired bazookas or rocket launchers." They now realized that their best chance to leave the area was to wait for the hostilities to decrease and then head north to recover the truck.

The battle slackened a few minutes later as the rebel forces advanced rapidly, pursuing the retreating government troops, who were retiring to the south.

"Now is the time to go," advised Lucas.

They stood up and ran along the shoulder of the road, passing many wounded soldiers from both armies. As they possessed no medical supplies, they continued to run, not waiting for the hostilities to resume. They moved north, following the road towards Lunvula, and their truck. As they approached the outskirts of town the devastation appeared to be almost complete.

"Can you locate the ditch where you hid the car, Lucas? There doesn't seem to be much left here."

They were looking for the turn-off where the path had led to the gully and the truck. "I hope we can find the drain where I hid the car…This looks like it might be the place," said Angela pointing to a flat-sided ravine.

They turned sharply off of the main road into a gully, which appeared to run at right angles to the route they had been traveling. Identification was difficult due to the devastation of the surrounding landscape, but after a few hundred yards, they arrived at a thicket of trees, hiding the view from the main highway. "Here we go!" said Lucas. "I'm sure this is it."

Walking carefully between the trees and through thick brush, both were startled by a large flock of guinea fowl that sprang from underfoot and ran away in all directions.

"Wow! Those birds startled me," exclaimed Angela. "Do you see the car anywhere?"

"Yeah, I've found it, but what a mess. Come and see what's happened to it."

Cautiously, Angela made her way through the underbrush in the direction of Lucas' voice. As she entered a small clearing, stumbling through the weeds and dangling tree branches that-which concealed the vehicle, she saw it. Its appearance was dramatically changed. "They've made a mess of it," she cried.

The truck sat undisturbed in the small clearing, but it was now covered with bird excrement, inside and out. "Angela, our guinea fowl friends found a new home and there are nests inside as well as on the roof," Lucas remarked dryly.

"But the smell is the worst part of the change," she replied.

"The smell won't interfere with how it runs, Angela. Let's get in and see if it will start up."

Placing a handkerchief over her nose, Angela attempted to remove some of the aviary fecal contamination from the passenger seat and dashboard. This attempt only resulted in a gooey mess on her hand as well as the seat. Finally, with a scrunched up nose, she simply sat in the seat, coughing from the acrid smell.

"I'm used to the sights and smells of an operating room, Lucas, but this is BAD! You know we've only left the car here a few days and look at what happened."

Laughing, Lucas said, "Only a few days? Yes, but the entire flock of guinea fowl has probably been roosting here."

Lucas motioned for Angela to get out of the truck, and reaching into the backseat he recovered the tarpaulin that had been covering the seat and rifle. Turning it upside down, he covered the front seats and then sat on the relatively clean surface.

"That'll make it a bit less messy. Let me try the ignition," he grinned.

As he was about to turn the key, the constant dull rumble of the conflict in the distance was suddenly interrupted by the louder staccato of rapid explosions.

"That sounds like mortar fire, Angela. I hope that the rebels have them on the run. The racket from the conflict is becoming softer as the battle moves further away."

Taking a deep breath, Lucas turned the key in the ignition. The motor immediately sprang to life, emitting a roar as the diesel engine started and then settling into a purr. "Well, I'll be darned!" he exclaimed. "Get in, Angie, before it quits. We need to be on our way back to Lubalo."

Putting the vehicle into 4x4 low reverse, Lucas cautiously backed out of the ditch. Once they had cleared the bushes in which the truck had been hiding, and now no longer in the ditch, Lucas changed to forward low gear and pulled out onto the dusty, potholed side road.

"We'll drive back to the main road and we can head north to Lubalo," he mumbled under his breath. "The main road isn't much, but it's enough to allow us to reach the mission."

The drive back to the main road was short but difficult due to the cavitations previously made by exploding artillery shells that had landed on the road. Some of the holes in the road were six feet in diameter and two feet deep. After navigating around the large holes on the side road, they finally entered the main road, only to discover that it was in worse condition than the peripheral dirt tracks. The conflict had taken place along this passageway and shell craters and debris, as well as destroyed vehicles, blocked their path at almost every kilometer. This made detours necessary and forward progress extremely tedious.

"I don't expect that we'll reach Lubalo much before tomorrow evening," complained Angela. "The road was always difficult, but since the conflict it's even worse."

They followed the dusty, gravel road north for an hour before there appeared to be less evidence of the conflict. The twisting and turning path finally deteriorated into a track at Chicongo, with packed dirt for the wheels and high grass in the center. This made visibility about three feet, reducing speed to a minimum.

At their reduced rate of speed, Angela suddenly remarked, "I see something on the left, Lucas. It looks like there's been a wreck over in the grass, between a large truck and another car. As they moved even slower, she continued, "Wait! I can hear someone groaning in pain, so it must be someone's hurt there. Let's go and see."

Lucas slowed their truck to a halt and leaving the truck on the track they walked a few feet through the high grass to the wreck. It appeared that both of the drivers had swerved to the same side at a high speed, trying to avoid a collision but resulting in a major disaster.

"My gosh, Lucas, it appears that there is a motorcycle trapped between a truck and a car. They tried to avoid a collision but both got off the same side."

The calls for help continued, but at a lower volume as the caller's strength ebbed.

Walking around the wreckage in the tall grass, Lucas and Angela could see the lower torso of a man protruding from under the car. The other two drivers were examined and found to be dead.

"There he is!" said Angela, pointing to the legs that were thrashing in the grass next to the motorcycle. "I guess that he was the one on the motorcycle. Let's see if we can help him."

A quick survey of the trampled grass revealed what had probably transpired earlier. The motorcycle had been traveling from the south in a northerly direction at high speed followed closely by the car. From the north, the large truck was moving south, also at high speed, on the single track dirt path. Because of the high grass, neither had spotted the other until it was too late.

Both had tried to avoid the wreck by leaving the track, but had swerved to the same side, crushing the motorcycle between them as they hit.

Angela took a deep breath and said, "*Mbote! Beno kibeni kaidi nge?* (Hello! Are you in pain?) *Mukubu ya menga? Beto munganga!* (Are you bleeding? We are doctors.)"

The reply was a bit shocking as it came from under the wreckage, and it was in perfect English. "Are you kidding me? Of course I'm in pain. I don't see any bleeding, but if you could get me out from under this bloody truck, I'd appreciate it!"

From his response, it was obvious that the injured man spoke Kituba fluently, or he would not have understood Angela's question, but was of British origin, as he spoke with an English accent. Lucas replied in English, "Hold on, sir. We'll try to get you out from under this mess as quickly as possible."

Examining the wreckage, it was apparent that the motorcycle had moved to the side immediately before the truck and car had hit, avoiding much of the crushing blow as they had collided. He was now pinned under the truck by the twisted handle bars of his motorcycle, but the soft grass and earth had cushioned his fall.

"Let's see what we can move," said Lucas, trying to push the protruding end of the handle bar.

"Ouch, damn it! I must have broken my arm or something," came the voice from under the truck. "Take it easy on moving that stuff!"

With much maneuvering and pulling, the debris from the destroyed motorcycle was removed and the upper torso of the motorcyclist came into view. This was accomplished only after much cursing from under the truck.

Angela was now able to see his left arm crumpled over his abdomen, and from its position concluded that it must have been broken in several places.

The slow progression of debris removal continued and finally the shoulders and neck came into view. A gold chain surrounding the neck with a distinctive Celtic cross hanging from it appeared from under the truck.

"I know that cross!" cried out Angela, as she stooped to see it better. She recognized the distinctive design of the cross she had given to Tad, her brother, on his sixteenth birthday. Since then she had never seen him without it dangling from his neck. Dixon, the gardener had mentioned that Tad had headed in the direction of Lubalo, but to find him here was nothing short of astounding.

"Tad?..It's Angie…Are you alright? I never expected to find you out here."

"Sis?….. I thought no one would find me for days."

Angela was totally shaken by her discovery, as they cautiously pulled the wreckage from his face and head revealing a smiling, but bruised and lacerated face. Now sitting up on the ground, he inspected his severely swollen arm, and remarked calmly, "I guess my left arm is busted, Sis. Who's this guy inspecting the rest of me like he knows what he's doing?"

"Tad, this is Lucas, a physician from the Lubalo Mission, You'll get to know him when we get you cleaned up and into the truck."

"Proud to meet you, Lucas," he said standing with assistance from his sister.

Looking under the truck to be sure no one else was trapped, the formal introductions followed Angela's reunion with her brother. Although various scratches and puncture wounds were identified, the broken left arm seemed to be the only serious damage found.

"We'll get some sort of sling arranged and when we get back to the hospital we can x-ray to determine if there is any other damage," explained Lucas. "In the meantime, let's be sure there are no other survivors."

A careful re-inspection of both the truck and automobile confirmed that there were no survivors, and since by now evening was approaching they decided that it would be judicious to wait until morning to travel on to Lubalo, as Tad was in no condition at this time.

"You know, it's been months since we last saw each other, and now to meet just when I needed you and the doctor is almost beyond coincidence!"

"Tad, I think the Lord was looking out for all of us. We might have missed seeing the wreck and driven on to Lubalo without ever finding you."

They sat around the fire, that evening and talked for hours reviewing their adventures. Tad and Lucas also got better acquainted, finding that they had much in common. Tad related that when their Dad had concluded that the Saurimo mission was no longer viable, he and Jake had decided to go to Luanda. After much persuasion failed to convince Tad to go with them, he had decided to try to join the rebels, but the war overtook him. He was on his way to find Angela when the accident occurred.

"Angela, do you know what happened to Jake and Dad? I know they headed for Luanda a few days ago, but I'm not sure that they got there."

"I only know that we saw Dixon in Saurimo, walking in front of our house, but he only knew that they had left safely."

Then, with a twinkle in his eye, Tad said, "And Lucas *Kubiba beno vanda luzolo*? (He spoils you as his loved one?)"

"She spoils *me*!" said Lucas immediately, showing that he knew enough of the Kikongo dialect to join in the laughter. It was a peaceful evening.

The next morning they ate and resumed the trip to Lubalo.

"We must get Tad to the hospital to set the fractures in that left arm. He may lose part of the left arm's function without proper treatment," said Lucas.

As they finally drove through the entrance gate of the Lubalo Mission, Angela let out a sigh of relief. "At least we're here and can make plans to travel, when we need to."

After parking the truck, the three walked across the grass towards the hospital together, but as they climbed the steps to the front porch, they encountered Maichipo leaving the hospital. She was crying, and said, "Thank God you're back, Dr. Lucas. It's a terrible tragedy inside."

# 12
## Chapter

As the sun rose the next morning on the banks of the Congo River over Kwamouth, Gayle and Esther awoke to see the sparkling color display in the eastern sky. Their oak paneled luxury suite was situated on the top floor, next to Sir William's penthouse at the Regency Hotel.

"Now that Dad has sent the money, we may as well stay at the best hotel," Gayle had suggested the previous evening after she had been to the bank. "There aren't many places to stay, but the Regency is reported to be the best."

Tsitsi and Tsabola were staying in the same suite with Gayle and Esther. Their suite included two bedrooms and a large lounge, a dining room and kitchenette. Hearing a discussion by the two sisters in their adjoining bedroom and concluding that they were awake, Gayle remarked, "We'll all get dressed and go down to breakfast together. We have plenty of time, as we have little baggage to pack for the trip back to Lubalo on the riverboat today." The two native sisters agreed with the suggestion. Communication between the four women was improving as

Gayle and Esther picked up a few words of the Kikongo dialect of the Kileta language, and the sisters began to learn English.

"As I recall, the scow leaves at noon?" said Gayle. "I guess that marshal will be with us every step of the way, all the way back to Angola."

Esther laughed and said, "That marshal is a real bulldog. I'll bet he slept outside our door last night to be sure we didn't get away."

Tsitsi and Tsabola, while not understanding their banter, did catch the spirit of the repartee and laughed along with Esther and Gayle. When the accommodations on the boat for the trip back to Angola were discussed, they found that Gayle had reserved one of the primary cabins on that river boat, so that they wouldn't have to sit outside on those hard benches for three days again. Esther was in a playful mood, kidding everyone as the four ladies entered the dining room.

Sir William was sitting at a table by himself. "Let's go and sit with him," said Gayle. At this remark, Esther began to realize, for the first time, that Gayle's feelings for Sir William went beyond just casual friendship. She watched Gayle's body language when she spotted him at the table and saw her whole countenance light up.

As the four ladies approached his table, Sir William stood and, mocking formality, said, "Four beautiful ladies. I feel privileged to have such distinguished company for breakfast. Please sit down." They all laughed.

The waiter produced the menus after all were seated. Out of nowhere, the omnipresent marshal appeared at Sir William's shoulder. Looking up from his menu, the knight said, "Is there something we can help you with, sir?"

The marshal, after pausing for a second, let out a nervous cough. Finally, he said, "The river boat leaves for Lubalo at twelve-thirty today. It will make everything easier if the four ladies appear on the dock by noon."

"Rest assured, we will all be there," replied Esther. "You don't have to hound us."

The marshal gave a polite bow and responded, "I don't like this trip any better than you do, but the deportation must proceed as the judge has ruled, and I'm afraid we must comply with his ruling."

Continuing to examine his menu, Sir William remarked, "We will all be on the dock at noon, sir." The marshal turned and walked to his seat across the room where he had ordered his breakfast, sitting alone as usual.

"You don't have to come to the dock to see us off," said Gayle after they had ordered breakfast. "We have very little luggage and the hotel porters can see that our bags are there with us. You must have a busy day ahead. We'll be fine."

"How can I get aboard the boat to Lubalo if I'm not there on time?" asked Sir William. "The British government is not about to send the American ambassador's daughter three hundred miles into the African jungle without an escort."

"Are you really coming?" asked Gayle. "That's fantastic!" she said, reaching to her left to kiss him lightly on the cheek.

Smiling broadly, Sir William retorted, "I received orders from London this morning to accompany all four of you beautiful women to Lubalo. My cabin ticket is already in my pocket. Orders are orders and must be followed, you know," he said with a wink.

Breakfast was finished and all of the travelers retired to their rooms to collect their belongings. Gayle financed a brief last shopping spree into the town, not only because she was now affluent, but because she was grateful for her freedom. Everyone purchased gifts to take back to their families. The four women, now friends after all of their mutual adventures, appeared on the dock at precisely noon. Each of the four riverboat boarders had a small suitcase in which to carry their possessions back to Angola.

"Look at that pile of expensive, leather luggage over there on the dock," observed Esther. "Whoever owns those bags must have spent a fortune and must be traveling for an extended period."

"Just a few items that may become useful on a trip from England to the Angolan bush," said Sir William silently appearing at her side. "You never know, one might have to travel deep into the bush or even to Luanda. Be prepared!" he said, laughing at her remark as he arrived behind them.

Tsabola tapped Gayle on the shoulder, as they stood there waiting on the dock. She pointed to a man with his back to them, standing on the far side of the dock. He appeared to be boarding the same river scow that they all had traveled on from Lubalo a few days ago. He was shouting and waving his arms. It was Hamid. He was continuing his trip to Kisangani, and was complaining about the way they had handled his luggage.

The scow had been delayed before it could continue its travel and was only now leaving for northeast Zaire. Evidently his luggage had been offloaded when he was sent to trial and was now being on-loaded again.

"I didn't see that much luggage on the trip from Lubalo," remarked Gayle. "He must have stored it here when he came from Khartoum."

"If it wasn't for Sir William, we'd be with him and headed for who knows what servitude," said Esther. "Thank you again for your help!"

As they were standing on the dock, an announcement came over the loudspeaker,

"*Mbote! Kutuka boma iya, masua Lubalo Kwilu nzadi kubasika!* It was repeated in English; Attention! From gate four, the boat to Lubalo via the Kwilu River is now leaving."

"That's us," said the baggage handler, "You can walk over to Dock 4 and board the ship. I'll take the luggage."

"It will be interesting to see what type of boat will be going back," observed Sir William as they followed their bags toward the end of the dock. "There's no telling what type of vessel travels these remote rivers in the peripheral locations of Zaire."

As they approached dock number four, they saw their river conveyance. The original scow that they had ridden from Lubalo was a miniature edition of this boat. The construction was similar with a large motor-house at the rear, a flat deck with benches for those who were unable or unwilling to pay for a cabin. Also there were some constructed cabins at the front. This ship, however, was at least twice the size of their former vessel.

"It's huge," whispered Esther as they approached the gangway. "But it appears to be older and not in such good condition."

224

"Let's get aboard and inspect our accommodations," suggested Sir William. "We'll only be aboard a few days, and as long as it's seaworthy, it really doesn't matter."

Once aboard, their porters brought the bags and set them on the floor of their assigned suites. The four women's lodgings consisted of a large furnished central sitting room with two adjoining bedrooms. The sofas and chairs appeared somewhat worn, but still serviceable. A well-used dining table with four wooden ladder chairs had been placed at one end of the parlor. Each bedroom contained two beds and was joined at the middle with a connecting bathroom.

"Four ladies with only one bathroom to share?" joked Sir William. "A sure disaster!"

The women walked over to see his room and found a much smaller room, similarly furnished, with two beds and a bath. It had a large desk at which to study or eat.

"We assume that you will be kind enough to dine with us?" asked Gayle. "We have plenty of room and you'd be alone in here."

Contrary to African custom, the boat left dock within two hours of its scheduled departure. The massive vessel pulled away from the dock and turned to head upstream into the strong current of the Kwilu River. It left a large wave behind it as it churned up the muddy water in its wake, the powerful engine pushing it along.

"This will be much slower trip to Lubalo," remarked Sir William. "We'll now have to fight against the strong current that helped push the boat downstream." They stood outside on the deck, holding onto the handrail and watching the slow progression of their ship upstream. As it labored to propel the ship against the current, the monotonous sound of the diesel engine was so loud conversation became difficult.

At first, the boat seemed to be barely making progress, but after a few minutes, the shoreline began to slip by more rapidly.

"It must be a hundred-two degrees out here," remarked Gayle. "I'm perspiring profusely, but the breeze is nice. Those ceiling fans inside our cabin do little to cool us."

Sir William and the four women proceeded to walk along the deck of the boat, noting that on this trip; relatively few passengers were sitting on the outside benches in the hot sun. The marshal, however, was sitting on a bench by himself, and appeared to be fast asleep.

"Look at the heavy growth of foliage along the shore," remarked Esther. "When we were going down stream the thought of captivity preoccupied my mind and I failed to appreciate the greenery."

"Because the movement upstream is so much slower, we can really better appreciate the shoreline," added Gayle.

An entirely new arrangement developed after a few hours of upstream travel. The two African sisters, Tsitsi and Tsabola, spent their time in the cabin talking, resting, or occasionally watching the panorama of land and fields slip by as they stood on the deck. Esther found a small library in their room and was absorbed in reading. Sir William and Gayle spent their time together, talking, eating or just standing on the deck when it was not too warm, usually at dawn or dusk. Many tall teak and mahogany trees grew along the river's edge and were often filled with exotic birds and monkeys. Their calling at the approach of evening was beautiful to hear as the boat slipped through the dark water.

When Esther and Gayle were getting up the next morning, Esther remarked, "I see you and Sir William everywhere on the ship talking or eating and just being together. Are the two of you really getting close?"

"He's really an interesting person and has been all over the world, Esther. He seems kind and is well spoken. Evidently, he's from the top of English society and has had an excellent education."

"Well then!" remarked Esther, "sounds to be ideal husband material? He would have an acceptable background from your parent's point of view?"

"That's not the question, Esther. Am I acceptable to him? He doesn't know about those episodes at the prison camp."

Gayle and Esther had never discussed the torture and rape that had occurred when they had been imprisoned at Lubalo. It had not been forgotten, but both had tried to suppress the memory and it was difficult to think about. Now, for the first time, it stood clearly before them in its full horrible ugliness.

"I've tried to forget that day," said Esther. "But the possibility of HIV or another disease is still present in the back of my mind."

"I've had no symptoms. Have you, Esther?"

Esther looked at the floor for a full thirty seconds before she replied, "The bleeding was so profuse for the first few days after we were misused, that there was no way to tell. Then, a yellow-green discharge developed for a week. I've had a period since then, and now, nothing."

"I've had a similar experience," said Gayle. "I did have a menstrual cycle too, so I'm sure there's no pregnancy, but I'd have to be tested to discover if I contracted a disease. So would you."

Esther sighed, and after a minute went on, "You can't make love to Sir William without knowing, if you really love him, Gayle. I'd suggest that you prepare an excuse, if it gets to that situation before we arrive at Lubalo. Doctor Lucas or Angela, if they're there, could test you without his knowing."

"I'll have to explain it to him, Esther. He'll either accept it or not. I can't just not say anything, it'd be like lying to him."

With that, the discussion ended for the time being, but the possibility of having contracted a disease continued to hang in the back of Gayle's mind. It made her reluctant to give her full affection to Sir William because of the real possibility that upon learning of her previous disaster, he might reject her, especially if she were HIV positive.

The progress upriver was slow since the recent rains had caused some flooding and the current against the boat's progress was much stronger than was usual at that time of year. Puddles of stagnant water could be seen on the land, in the fields, and soaking the grounds around the *kraals.*

"It's taking much longer to return to Lubalo than it took getting to Kwamouth," said Gayle to Sir William. "But the present company makes it seem shorter and much more pleasant."

"I feel the same, and it allows us a better chance to become acquainted. We can use the time to get to know each other better."

The boat continued to plough its way upstream at a slow steady pace, finally arriving at Kikwit around noon, after a two day struggle. Those passengers departing at Kikwit had left the vessel hours before but it still remained tied to the dock while the crew worked on the engine. Finally it pulled away from the dock to continue the journey upstream, south to Lubalo.

"Why the long delay?" Esther had asked the captain. The ship had been sitting at the dock for what seemed an extended period.

The captain, an aged black man who spoke English, had obviously been a riverboat pilot for decades. He merely shrugged his shoulders and said, "This is Africa; delays are normal, often for days. Now that the engine is fixed, we'll be leaving."

Finally, the boat began to slowly pull away from the dock to continue its journey upstream towards Lubalo As it entered the main current, the passengers could hear that the engine was missing some beats. The steady "chug" of the motor was no longer monotonous, but was irregularly missing beats more and more frequently. This continued for three hours before the missing sounds became full time. Then, the engine stopped completely.

"This is serious," said Sir William. "With no engine, we have no control of steering, and we are helpless in the current. We'll wash downstream." This thought was obviously not lost on the other passengers and crew who hurriedly gathered at the stern of the boat, anxiously awaiting resumption of the engine. The engineer had lifted the cover of the engine and appeared to be working frantically to restart it.

As the vessel's momentum upstream slowed and its forward progress stopped, it began to float backwards, totally out of control in the strong current. One of the male passengers began to run to the front of the ship, shouting in a terrorized voice, *"Benu kufua masua!"* This caused the other passengers to panic also. Just as it appeared that total chaos would reign, the engine coughed to life for about thirty seconds, and then died again. The boat continued to float downstream with the current.

"What will happen now, Sir William?" asked Gayle. "We could crash into anything."

Sir William grasped her hand and said in a totally controlled voice, "Just hold on, Gayle, we're safer on the boat than in the water for now. If we have to jump I'll tell you when and get us to the shore."

The ship, floating downstream with the current, began to gain momentum as the seconds passed. It was being pushed rapidly towards the shoreline with no steering control and at a sideward angle.

"Grab onto a handrail on the opposite side of the deck." advised Sir William. "If we hit anything on the river's edge, we'll want to be away from the point of contact."

Sir William, Gayle, and Esther moved to the port side of the rapidly moving vessel as it neared the rocks lining the banks of the river. There was a loud scraping sound emitted from the hull as the bottom of the boat dug into the gravel at the river bottom. They had reached the handrail just in time to brace themselves. This sound was accompanied by a jerk of the vessel as its momentum slid to a stop, giving any passenger not anchored to a solid support, a severe jolt towards the rear of the ship.

Sir William was concerned about how much damage has been done to the ship, as well as the depth of the river at this point. He also remembered that he had seen a group of large crocodiles along this bank a mile or so further downstream, and that they remained responsible to see that Tsitsi and Tsabola were safe.

Walking briskly to their cabin where the African sisters had last been seen, Gayle opened the cabin door to find the entire contents of the room pushed against the posterior wall, furniture, beds, and luggage all in a heap from the impetus of the ship's grounding.

"Are you all okay?" she asked, finding both Tsitsi and Tsabola calmly sitting on the floor. While the sisters didn't understand her words, they read on Gayle's face her concern for their safety.

"*Nduku, Mpesi kibeni nkatu!*" was the prompt reply as the Africans stood up and brushed themselves off. They were unhurt.

The group of passengers leaving the suite walked across the deck together, among the milling passengers, to the starboard side of the vessel. Panic and pandemonium reigned everywhere, with confusion increasing as the water level had begun to rise over the deck of the sinking ship. The hull began to fill with water, causing the boat's right side to sag under the pressure, spilling the cargo stacked on deck into the river. Fruit, sisal, and cotton were scattered over the water. Fluid rushed inside of the hull, crushing the supporting structures and collapsing the deck, causing a loud cracking sound to echo throughout the vessel as much of the right side of the ship disappeared.

"This boat will go under in a few minutes," warned Sir William in a calm voice. Gayle noticed that his voice remained steady as he realized that failure to act promptly could result in some passengers' demise. "We had better get as many people on to the shore as soon as possible," he continued.

By voice and hand signs, Sir William, Gayle, and Esther led Tsitsi and Tsabola, as well as many of the boat's passengers, onto floating wooden crates from the ship's cargo and then to the shore. This was a distance of only twenty yards from the shipwreck to land, across deep water. The captain and the crew also made multiple trips between the sinking ship and land. Eventually all of the passengers were safely on shore.

"That captain is a true hero," remarked Esther. "He saw that everyone got to shore before he left the ship."

"Okay, all are safe. I guess that we have about twenty people out here on a wilderness shore who have lost their entire luggage and have no food or drink. What do we do now?" asked Gayle.

Walking over to the captain, Sir William said, "You seem to be the only person who speaks English as well as the local dialects. What is your plan for rescue?"

The captain scratched his head for a moment and said, "We sent a message by shortwave to Kwamouth before she sank. They will send another boat, which will arrive in a day or so. We really only have to wait until it arrives to continue our journey. I am just now preparing to instruct the other passengers."

After his announcement, the stranded passengers realized that they had neither blankets nor food, so they decided to try to set up a sort of camp to organize their remaining assets. This was decided as a group, since the majority of passengers had lived in the bush most of their lives anyway. The ship's crew established a fire and some flat places to lie down. The problem was that the area was in the deep jungle, populated by animals, mosquitoes, and tough bushes with long, sharp thorns.

Making camp, however, was much easier than if the passengers were a collection of town people. Now that the possibility of drowning was past, they organized their wait with a full sense of intelligence and cooperation, not to mention experience.

Sir William mentioned that they were really fortunate to have Tsitsi and Tsabola with them. They already had made makeshift chairs and beds for the five of them after a few hours and Tsitsi had caught some birds and found some edible greens. Esther watched Tsabola weave a fish trap from the thorn bushes and it appeared that she was going to cook a supper stew with her fish and vegetables.

A few of the other passengers were less fortunate, and simply stood on shore and looked out at the river, or sat on the ground bemoaning the loss of their goods. The captain and his crew did their best to help the other passengers, but Sir William and the four women appeared to be in a more tenable situation.

"Tsitsi has communicated to me that at dusk, the mosquitoes will come in force," said Gayle. "She has gathered some leaves and has found a gourd to cook them; making a paste that she is indicating to me we should rub over any exposed skin as soon as the light fades."

"I don't doubt her one bit," said Sir William. "She has lived in this environment her whole life, and any food or concoction she makes I'll use as she suggests. You know, Gayle, I'm impressed with the progress you have made in your ability to communicate with Tsitsi. In the last few days the two of you are starting to understand each other and you don't even speak Kileta."

As the light faded, Tsitsi's anticipation became true. The gnats and mosquitoes arrived on schedule in an unbelievable number, virtually overwhelming the people on shore. The swarms of biting insects came from the stagnant puddles of water, which had resulted from the recent rains.

"The buzzing is so loud, it's almost deafening," said Esther. "I've not had a single bite. The smell of Tsitsi's repellent is terrible, but it's worth it."

The other members of the castaways eventually requested some of Tsitsi's formula until there was none left, leaving the unfortunate remainder to slap and scratch in agony for the rest of the evening. Supper came and went, maybe not the best meal, but better than anyone else could conjure. The children in the company were invited to share Tsitsi's dinner, but the majority of adults went with less. It was obvious that the other passengers would have to make arrangements of their own for food, and most were able to find something. The marshal remained sitting alone on the bank, still watching the four deportees, and saying little.

The following morning Esther said, "Since another boat is on the way from Kwamouth, ascending the Kwilu River as we did, it should arrive by tomorrow morning. We really only need to wait another day."

"Don't count on it, Dearie," replied the captain, overhearing her remark as he was passing by. "There are ships, and then there are ships. I suspect that they sent the old *Bana ya Congo*," that is, the People of the Congo, to get us. She's old and slow, so I'd not spend a lot of time looking downstream for her smokestack for another three days. By then, we'll all either have starved to death or been carried off by those damn bugs."

The first morning after the shipwreck, Sir William noticed Tsabola had selected a thin teak tree branch, about six feet long. Having borrowed a knife from one of the deck hands, she was carving it into a curved piece of wood.

"What is its use?" Lucas mimed, so she understood the question.

Standing up, Tsabola held the branch in front of her and acted out its use as a bow.

Sir William pantomimed that there was no string or arrow to go with the bow, but she showed him a thin straight branch she had carved as an arrow and a vine to string to the bow.

"I'm amazed how resourceful these girls are," Sir William said to the captain, who was seated on a tree branch that he had managed to use as a seat. "But even if Tsabola *could* construct a bow and arrow, there's no way it would have enough accuracy to use it hunting."

The old sea captain just sat on a tree branch that he had adopted as a seat and smoked his pipe. "I'm sure glad I could save this brier from the wreck," he observed. "By the time this pipe is empty, we'll have us a mess of fish and fresh game for breakfast, mark my words."

While he was still speaking, Tsitsi went to the river's edge and recovered the fish trap she had dropped into the water the previous night. The trap was so heavy that her sister had to help her lift it from the water. Inside were many fish, almost all edible. A group effort cleaned them. After a stick had been placed lengthways through the mouth to the tail, the aroma of roasting fish soon filled the air, as they were turned over hot coals.

"That really smells delicious," said the captain. "I believe I'll have one of those myself."

Tsabola then walked into the brush and a while later returned with a pig that she had caught by the leg with a wire snare. It was duly killed and skinned. After sectioning, it was roasted along with the fish. There was enough food that everyone had sufficient to eat.

"I think we could say that we've had a minor banquet here, thanks to the girls' skills," said Sir William as he licked the drippings off of his fingertips, sitting on a log near the fire.

"While living like this isn't exactly like the hotel, we can survive," remarked Esther. "Waiting for the substitute ship will be easier. Are Tsitsi and Tsabola going hunting with that bow and arrow?"

Sir William surmised that the captain had faced similar problems before and thus realized that the sisters were used to surviving under difficult conditions. "You didn't see her cook those leaves this morning, did you?" remarked the captain, still smoking his pipe after his breakfast. "If they can find a kudu or antelope to nick with a poison tipped arrow, we'll all be eating roast meat for supper. Those leaves the girls cooked made a paste, to smear on their arrows."

Two days passed on the shoreline, with everyone benefiting from the girls' knowledge of woodcraft and insect repellent. However, the stranded people were getting nervous about the failure of a relief ship to appear from downriver.

"I spoke to the dispatcher over the shortwave before she sank," repeated the captain. "He said he would send a substitute ship, or we could have someone go by foot to Kikwit, but it would be two or three days' walk through uncharted jungle and thorn bushes. I don't think we'd have many volunteers for the trip."

Boredom was as much of a problem as anything, as the time weighed on the stranded passengers. The trees and bushes surrounding their campsite were so dense that a short path of a few hundred yards could take hours to clear, so a trip of thirty miles would be exhausting and dangerous. Sir William and Gayle, who in the meantime spent every day and night together, enjoyed each other's company and were becoming more attached daily.

"Tell me, Sir William, how you happened to obtain a knighthood?" asked Gayle one evening as they sat before the fire, quietly talking.

"It's a long, dull story, Gayle. There's no point in giving you a lot of insipid details."

"Sir William, we have no pressing appointments here in the bush, and I'm really interested," returned Gayle. "Please, tell me."

Sir William shifted in his seat. It was obvious to Gayle that he was uncomfortable talking about himself and especially about this subject. Finally, he began, "Without getting into a lot of detail, Gayle, my family was deeply involved for generations in financial and agricultural connections in the Falkland Islands. As you may remember, this is a group of islands off of the coast of Argentina which they attempted to annex a few years ago. The islands are a possession of England, which decided not to support their efforts. A short period of hostilities existed between England and Argentina over the administration of these islands. As a young man looking for adventure, I had enlisted as a fighter pilot in the Royal Air Force just before that incident."

"Yes, I remember that war," said Gayle, encouraging him to tell more.

"Well it just so happened that at that very time, the RAF sent me to fight in that southern Atlantic conflict. In the short version, I was involved in the war and was fortunate enough to be of some use to Britain. For my efforts, the Royal family saw fit to reward me with an Order of the Garter Knighthood. It's really a lot about nothing."

"They don't award knighthoods in the Royal Order of the Garter for nothing," said Gayle. "I'm sure you earned it. Were you wounded in any way?"

"Only some minor scratches, Gayle. And you can stop calling me 'Sir.' My friends call me William, which will do nicely."

The evening progressed, and as the hours grew late Gayle and William became more intimate in their conversation, leading to a discussion of the seizing of the Lubalo Mission by the anti-government rebels and her captivity.

"The reverend, Esther, and I were placed into a cage together, and the next day, all three of us were seriously misused, William," said Gayle. "Since we escaped, I've not had a chance to see a doctor or to find out if I contracted any sort of disease or serious damage, although I feel fine"

Sir William was instantly empathetic to Gayle on this subject and her wanting to be fully honest about the possibility of subsequent problems. If their relationship progressed over the near time period, as he hoped it would, the answer to her questions might be pivotal to their future, but out here in the wilderness, no answers were available. Sir William appreciated that Gayle had told him of her rape, but he knew that the less he made of it now the better she would feel, so he acknowledged her remark and changed the subject. Answers would come later if their relationship deepened.

"Tests should be done as soon as possible, Gayle, probably at Lubalo." Then, changing the subject, he said, "I would imagine that your family is aware by now that we are marooned on this river bank. That microchip in your arm will indicate your location and they will be looking for you soon."

Sitting next to the dim, fading glow of the fire's coals in the early hours of the next morning, Gayle and William lay on the grass, exchanging caresses and soft whispers until each drifted off into peaceful sleep. This sleep, while deep, was rudely interrupted at first light.

One of the native passengers had been scrutinizing the western horizon over the river ever since the sun had risen in the east and illuminated the sky. He now began shouting to the camp, "I can see black smoke on the horizon rising from the river! Is it the relief ship?" Every eye in the camp was instantly open. Gayle thought she saw a thin trail of black smoke rising from the river, far down stream.

The gruff voice of the captain, speaking in English, replied almost immediately. "Relax, it could be any ship and I don't expect our relief for at least a few more days. Someone may be cooking breakfast. Go back to sleep everybody."

But no one returned to his sleeping post. All eyes were glued to the river on the western horizon. After fifteen minutes of uninterrupted observation, it was confirmed that there was indeed a cloud of black smoke rising from the west, over the river. Its source was not discernable due to the distance of the cloud. While all attention was focused on the river, a faint whirring sound coming from another direction, grew louder and louder.

"It's a helicopter!" exclaimed William to everyone in general. "I'd recognize that buzz anywhere."

All eyes moved to the sky as a huge American combat chopper, complete with rockets hanging from its fuselage, rose from the river and hovered overhead. It bore no national insignia, but was, without question, an American built aircraft with an eagle painted on both sides. It had no stars on the fuselage. From the open sliding side doors appeared protruding fifty caliber machine guns, which were manned. Two pilots, with dark sunglasses, were at the controls. They wore no official uniforms, but only unmarked flight gear. The noise and wind from the propellers was shattering as the gunship hovered over the camp.

"I hope they're on our side!" remarked William, "The amount of damage they could do would be unholy, and they're obviously not here to view the scenery."

As the aircraft hovered overhead, a cable was thrown from the main section of the helicopter, landing in the water and immediately four fully armed men dropped from the craft into the water near the cable. All four men swam ashore and appeared on the edge of the water, dripping river water onto the ground. William, recognizing their methods and their form of arrival, walked forward to them and said, "Navy UDT Unit, I presume, sent for Miss Gayle Wright? I am Sir William Spencer-Johnston, special agent for Her Majesty's Service."

The commanding officer of the unit saluted, and with a pronounced South Texas accent said, "I am Captain Joshua Leadbetter, sir! Actually we're originally from the Tenth Unit of the 125th Commandos, but now we're private. Is Miss Wright about?"

"Pleased to meet you," smiled William as he pointed to Gayle standing next to him, "She's here. What can we do to assist you boys?"

"Well, sir, we weren't sure what the situation would be and we were sent to facilitate her return. We thought that she may have been recaptured by rebel forces, or encountered other problems. I see that she is safe. Her parents are waiting for her in Luanda."

"Are you official U.S. Navy, or mercenaries hired by a private contractor?" Sir William wisely asked. He had noticed that the markings on the helicopter were American but not Navy, and he felt that to hand Gayle over to anyone not official might be dangerous for Gayle. In practical terms there was little he could do anyway.

"At present, we have been employed by Miss Wright's family to return her to them," replied the Navy Captain. "They became concerned when she appeared to be stranded in a remote area of the Kasai-Occidental Province of the Republic of the Congo. The fact that we knew her exact location should verify our veracity."

"And if I *want* to take the boat back to Lubalo and not fly to Luanda? What then?" asked Gayle.

"Our instructions were to bring you to safety. It appears that a boat is now arriving here that can transport you; I will radio for further orders, ma'am."

The captain radioed his helicopter for further instructions, as William whispered to Gayle that this was her chance for a nice helicopter ride to Luanda. "I don't want my parents messing up my life again, William. I want to stay with you!"

The refugees had now gathered as a group around the rescue team, but were largely unable to understand what was happening. In the meantime, the relief ship was fully in view, with its black smoke curling up into the sky from a half-mile downstream.

It blew its whistle as the arriving boat captain spotted the little crowd on the riverbank and the helicopter hovering over the group.

Suddenly the marshal, who had witnessed the entire episode, stepped forward and addressed the captain, who was waiting for a reply on his phone. "Sir, I am a Republic of the Congo Marshal on official business. These ladies remain in my custody until released legally at Lubalo on the Angolan border. If you transport them before I release them, we will have an international incident. They must accompany me to the border, as they are under a court deportation order."

There was a pause as this information was transmitted by the captain to the helicopter, and then on to Luanda. Captain Leadbetter finally put his phone down and stated to Gayle, "It's your choice, Miss Wright. We can certainly take you and your friends to Luanda now, but there may be repercussions for the Marshal. The river vessel to transport you all to Lubalo has arrived, and you could travel in a day or so there. If it is your choice to travel by boat, we are instructed to meet you in Lubalo and then transport you to Luanda."

"It's fine either way, Gayle," said William "No big problem if you fly."

"But I want to stay with *you!*" replied Gayle.

The replacement boat had arrived and a gangplank was lowered to the shore. The stranded passengers were boarding, and after bidding goodbye and thanks to Captain Leadbetter and his crew, Gayle and Esther, as well as the two African girls, boarded the boat along with Sir William. Everyone watched in fascination as the helicopter recovered the four commandos on the ground before it moved swiftly off to the east.

"So, I ride the spanking new *Bana ya Congo*," said the old captain, his pipe still stuck in his mouth. "They told me that she was being built, but I never expected to ride her as a *passenger*. They must have retired that other old tub."

The ship that had now picked up the castaways was new and its powerful engine moved the vessel rapidly upstream against the current. The accommodations were similar to the older models, but brand new and luxurious. Everyone enjoyed the ride, but Gayle grew anxious, knowing that this portion of the trip would end rapidly and she might never see her William again.

"There's Lubalo!" remarked Esther as they rounded a turn and the village came into view. "Now we can go home," she said happily.

Gayle failed to see the joy at their arrival as she and her friends walked down the gangplank to the dock. The helicopter was not in sight, but a new Land Rover truck was waiting for them as the Marshal filled out official forms and discharged the four women from custody.

"Well, we're all here," said William.

Just then, Brightwell walked over to the five arrivals. His usually smiling face now appeared somber as he said, "I'm glad you finally made it safely. Doctor Lucas and Sister Angela have sent me to take you back to the mission. The helicopter crew advised them that you would be arriving shortly and have sent me to assist you. There's a problem there."

# 13
## Chapter

L ucas and Angela were not surprised that problems had
developed when they returned by truck from Saurimo.
Having expected some sort of dilemma when they
returned, Angela was nevertheless surprised at the grim welcome
that greeted them as they walked through the front door of the
mission hospital. Tad had already been sent to the emergency
department for examination and X-ray of his arm.

"What's going on?" Angela asked Hilda, the first nurse she
saw in the darkened hallway on the first floor. "The hospital staff
seems subdued or upset about something... it's so quiet. Are
there any problems here in the hospital?"

Hilda stopped in the hallway, almost in tears, addressing
Lucas and Angela quietly. "You've been away and so you didn't
hear. Wicki was sitting outside the front entrance on his stump
early this morning, about three, when Iuba started barking at
something next to the front stairs. I guess Wicki had dozed off
for a minute, and awoke at the noise. Anyway, by the time he had
become fully awake, Wicki realized that Iuba had discovered a

large snake near the front entrance of the hospital and was trying to attack it. It was a King Cobra, and it had already extended to its full height and was hissing at Iuba. Without stopping to think, Wicki tried to reach over to hit the snake with a stick before it could hurt Iuba and ended up being bitten himself."

"How is he?" asked Lucas, his voice gravely filled with concern for the boy. They all knew how serious a bite from the snake of that type could be.

"He's in a coma, Room 230," replied Hilda. "Iuba is unhurt and lies under the bed, but he growls at anyone approaching Wicki. We're afraid Wicki will die if he doesn't respond to treatment."

Lucas became even more concerned. "Do we have the antiserum for cobra on hand?" He told Hilda that they had sent Tad to the emergency room and that he and Angela would investigate Wicki's accident. Tad's X-rays wouldn't be ready for an hour, and this was a crisis that they needed to evaluate immediately.

"We've given him what we have, but he's not responding. He's been going in and out of coma since the morning. We've used all the antiserum available and prednisone too. His right arm is swollen and purple, and the discoloration is approaching his neck. Doctor Maria has tried everything, but he just lies there."

"That's not good. I think we'd better go up to Room 230 and see if we can help," said Angela.

They walked rapidly up the stairs to the second floor, and cautiously opened the door of the recovery room, which was serving as an intensive care unit. Inside there was only one occupied bed, which stood against the wall. As the door opened, a low growl, which changed into a snarl, was heard from beneath the bed.

"Iuba! Is that you, my boy?" whispered Angela.

A white streak came from underneath the bed and jumped on Angela. He was wagging his tail furiously and whining. When Angela bent over to scratch his ears, he responded by enthusiastically licking her face. "I'm glad to see you too, Iuba," said Angela. "How's your master?"

In the meantime, Lucas had walked over to the bed, and began to examine Wicki, who was not responding to tactile stimulation.

"He's certainly in a deep coma now," said Lucas grimly. "He doesn't even respond to pain," he said, pricking the bottoms of his feet with a pin.

Just then, Lucas looked up, hearing the roar of a turbine engine overhead. It gradually got louder as the helicopter landed on the front lawn of the mission hospital.

"We've got company. I wonder who would be coming here by helicopter?" he said.

As the rotor blades slowed and the chopper came to rest, it was immediately surrounded by rebel soldiers. Captain Leadbetter appeared at the helicopter doorway as the door slid open. He announced, "Relax, friends. We're neutral. We've only come to pick up a few arrivals that will be here in a few hours."

He walked from the helicopter, followed by the three commandos from the Congo encounter with Sir William. The other men were dressed in similar Special Forces clothes, now dry. Spotting Major Santiago, the rebel leader who led the troops surrounding the combat helicopter, he greeted him warmly in fluent Portuguese. "Santiago? Man, how are you? Haven't seen you since Vietnam, we fought out of the same air base! Remember, you were in the 13th United Nations, and we supported that raid."

They shook hands and ended up laughing as they recalled the past battles fought and adventures in Saigon a few years previously. Lucas heard their laughter and emerged from the hospital. Major Santiago introduced him to the captain and his crew.

After all of the introductions were over, Lucas grew serious and said, "Captain, we have a crisis here; perhaps you could help. A young boy has been bitten by a King Cobra, and we're out of antiserum. Do you have any on board?"

The officer paused for a second before replying, "No, we don't carry that with us, but there might be some antibiotics on board. Would that be of some help, Doctor?"

Disappointed, Lucas said, "It might help. Could we borrow it?"

After the medication had been given to Angela for administration to Wicki, Lucas, Major Santiago and the Captain sat down in the hospital cafeteria and talked over a cup of coffee.

"What brings you here now?" asked Santiago of the captain. "That chopper you're flying is heavily armed and could be a big help in our battle with the government. Have you come to help us?"

"I'm afraid not, Major. I quit the United States Navy after Vietnam, and now am a self-employed mercenary. It pays better and I can pick my own missions."

"So, what is this mission?" The Major continued to question him.

To the utter amazement of Lucas, who sat listening without uttering a word, the captain related the adventures of Gayle and Esther, following their escape from Lubalo.

With the revelation that Gayle's father was a wealthy industrialist, Ambassador to the British Government, as well as a personal friend of the American president, Lucas was astounded.

"So this wealthy American Ambassador to the British government has hired me to bring his daughter home, along with her friend," the captain concluded. "I heard that the rebels had a little unpleasantness going with the Angolan government, so I came prepared to protect myself. We met the two ladies a day ago on the river in the Congo, but they elected to take the boat here to Lubalo. We're waiting for them now."

After a pause, the major said thoughtfully, "You know, Captain, when the daughter arrives tomorrow, you will be on your way to Luanda as a neutral aircraft. If some foreign power, like the Angola's government troops, happened to fire on your helicopter, could you retain your neutral position if you merely protected yourself?"

The obvious implications of an excuse to use Captain Leadbetter's tremendous fire power to help the rebels amused them both.

They laughed loudly at the ironic humor of this idea. Then the Major went on, "We have nothing in *our* army like that monster parked out on the lawn, and you might be able to help us briefly on your way back. It would be totally illegal, but you're a mercenary now and no international incident would result."

The Captain replied, "If you were to mention where my rockets would help your efforts the most, I could check the area out on my way to Luanda and, if fired upon, 'protect myself' as needed."

The discussion ended after much rehashing of past mutual battles. It was late when they all returned to their quarters. Upon arriving at his apartment, Lucas related the story he had just heard to Angela, adding that Gayle and Esther would likely arrive the next morning.

"I thought they both had perished during their escape," said Angela, as surprised as Lucas had been. "And an ambassador's daughter? What a relief that they are both alive."

"What about Wicki?" asked Lucas.

Angela grew serious immediately. "If he stays alive long enough to be flown to Luanda in the morning, he may have a chance. I doubt he'll make it through the night, Lucas." Angela began to cry. As she wiped the tears from her cheeks, she realized that Wicki's condition had really affected her.

"I think that there is someone knocking at our front door," said Lucas, rising and walking towards the entrance of their living quarters. "I'd better see who it is. It's almost midnight."

Opening the door, he saw the desperate face of Dr. Maria. "You and Miss Angela are needed at the hospital, sir. Wicki has come out of his coma and is asking for both of you. He's very weak, and I think there's little time for him. Please come."

Angela and Lucas ran across the front lawn of the hospital and up the stairs to the recovery room. A small cluster of nurses with tears in their eyes stood around the solitary bed in the darkened room. As Lucas and Angela entered, Iuba, who was lying in the corner, got up and walked over to Angela, whining as he approached her.

"It's us, Wicki, Angela and Doctor Lucas," whispered Angela in a caressing tone. "We're here to help you. Can you hear me?"

Wicki's closed eyes fluttered open, and a look of recognition appeared. "I'm glad you are here," he said, attempting a weak smile. "My right arm hurts ever so much."

Placing her warm hand on his sweat-drenched face, Angela answered, "Wicki, I'll get something to help the pain, but the pain meds will slow your breathing. You're very sick. That cobra bit deep."

Turning his head, Wicki recognized Lucas standing next to Angela, and mumbled, "Doctor Lucas, is Iuba all right?"

Without a word, Lucas picked Iuba up from the floor and held him in Wicki's view, over the bed. Iuba wagged his tail and attempted to lick the sweat off of the boy's face. "Hi, my friend," whispered Wicki.

He attempted to stroke the dog's head with his left hand, but he was too weak to reach out and his arm fell back on the bed. "Promise me, if I don't make it that both of you will adopt Iuba and take care of him for the rest of his life."

Angela was crying openly and Lucas felt the tears welling up in his eyes and, struggling, he attempted to hold them back.

"We promise, Wicki," they said in unison, as Lucas placed Iuba on the floor next to the bed.

A weak smile crossed Wicki's face for a few seconds, and then his whole body relaxed as he passed on into another world.

"He's gone," Lucas choked out after he felt Wicki's pulse and listened to his chest. "There's nothing else we can do."

A mournful howl filled the recovery room after Iuba lifted his head to the side of the bed and licked Wicki's motionless hand.

"We'll all miss you a lot, Wicki," sighed Doctor Maria. "You were the bright light guarding the entrance of the mission hospital."

"The dog was his only worldly possession," murmured Hilda. "No wonder his last thoughts were for Iuba."

There was no hospital chaplain, due to the war, and Lucas felt that Wicki deserved a prayer before his body was removed for burial. Bowing their heads together, the group of nurses and orderlies prayed. They were really the only acquaintances he had for the past weeks, so Lucas led the prayer. Iuba continued to whine softly as he licked Wicki's limp hand.

"Dear Lord," Lucas began, "we are here to ask You to receive our friend into your presence. Wicki wasn't a profound Christian or evangelist, but his smile and love for all people was appreciated by every member of the hospital staff. You saw fit to send him and Iuba to come into our lives for only a very short period of time, but we will all remember his bright smile and willing nature for a long time. As You receive his spirit, we are sure that his kindness and helpful attitude will be a blessing to those above already with you. Amen."

The small gathering in the recovery room dissolved. Hilda wrapped Wicki's body in bed sheets and had the orderlies place it on a stretcher, moving him to the mortuary. During this entire activity, Iuba never left Wicki's side, continuing to wait for his master's voice to call his name. He sensed the sadness of the people surrounding Wicki's body, but as a dog was unable to understand the finality of death.

"We all will miss him," said Angela as she sat with Lucas in their quarters. "Entering and leaving the hospital will never be the same without his big smile to greet us."

"We promised to take care of Iuba, Angela," quietly replied Lucas. "Tomorrow, after Wicki is buried, do you want to bring him to live with us?"

Angela sighed, and after a moment of thought said, "Every time we see that dog, we'll be reminded of Wicki. He's only a young dog and will be around for a long time, Lucas. I don't know if that's good or bad, but Iuba will be safe with us. Yes, we'll take care of him."

They kissed and retired for the evening with heavy hearts.

The next morning, arrangements were made for Wicki's funeral and burial. As no pastor was presently serving at the mission, Lucas agreed to substitute. A small plot underneath a Massasa tree, near the front of the hospital, was selected for his gravesite and a coffin of teak was built by a local carpenter, using pegs rather than nails to secure the sides and top. This was the custom with Kileta burials, due to a historical tradition of a lack of iron.

"Iuba won't leave Wicki's side and continues to whine and cry," observed Angela. "He hasn't eaten anything for two days."

The funeral and burial were to be held at the graveside around one o'clock that afternoon, and as the hour approached a somber crowd gathered outside the hospital entrance. Not only was almost every nurse and orderly in attendance, but many of the rebel army personnel who had known Wicki also stood quietly by the open grave. As Lucas walked over to the silent gathering, a Land Rover drove up to the front of the hospital, bringing Sir William, Gayle and Esther. On the short drive from the town of Lubalo, Brightwell had explained the situation to them and they silently joined the gathering. Even Tad attended the ceremony, his arm now comfortably casted.

"I only heard about the little fellow," whispered Captain Leadbetter to one of the other three mercenaries, as they joined the silent mourning assembly. "But I understand he was a real spark to the whole hospital."

Wicki's body, now inside the polished teak coffin, was carried by four of his hospital orderly friends and set down on ropes draped across the grave's opening. The only sound, as the hushed crowd gathered around the deep, wide pit that had been dug earlier that morning, was the soft whining of Iuba as he lay at the edge of the grave.

Lucas took a deep breath and began, "We are here to consign the body of a good friend of the hospital staff, patients, and everyone who knew him, to his final resting place." He continued with the dedication as the group listened in silence.

At the conclusion of Lucas' remarks, the ropes across the open grave were loosened and the box began to descend slowly into the ground. As the teak coffin was lowered, a most pitiful whine emitted from Iuba's throat as he pawed at the edge of the coffin's top boards, trying to stop its progress. He then stared despondently down into the grave, crying out.

"I think he finally understands that Wicki's gone," whispered Angela, loud enough that most of those gathering heard. "He'll miss his master for a long time."

After the grave had been filled, Iuba sat forlornly next to the burial site by himself. He finally moved to the center of the mound of dirt and lay there, whining softly.

"I don't have the heart to try to move him," said Angela. "He looks so totally abandoned. Maybe after dark he will come over to our residence."

Upon returning to the hospital, Lucas politely greeted Gayle and Esther. They all sat down with Angela and Sir William in the hospital cafeteria. The newcomers reported on their adventures, and explained that Tsitsi and Tsabola had returned to their family. Lucas found Sir William to be both knowledgeable and pleasant. A positive rapport was established between the two men. It was one of those situations where the two men functioned on the same "wave length" at their first meeting.

"We found a foot of Reverend Brown in the Lubalo River and thought all three of you were eaten…or drowned," exclaimed Lucas. "We were happily surprised to hear from the mercenary troops last night that both of you had survived," commented Lucas. Turning to Gayle, he continued, "I never would have guessed that your family had high political status. It's good to know that someone with your connections is interested in mission work and helping others. The blood tests and smears for infection Angela will have done in the morning."

"Do you have some sort of connections yourself?" Gayle retorted. "I noticed the new Land Rover that Brightwell drove to Lubalo to meet the boat. How did a vehicle like that suddenly appear on this remote mission?"

"We learned that the mission administrator, Pastor Williamson, was the recipient of a donation from the United States just a few months ago," said Angela. "He left in such a rush when the rebels overran the mission that his new truck was left behind. The staff discovered it hidden in an old abandoned building a few kilometers north of here."

"The old boss abandons his post and you are able to now use his truck?" joked Gayle.

"I'm sure that riding back from Lubalo seemed more comfortable than the long hike up to that town when you escaped," retorted Angela.

"Point taken!" said Esther "The escape through the bush was no fun and we aren't interested in any repeat escapades."

Angela sensed that Gayle had now survived a whole array of troubles, but her spirit remained undaunted. This toughness perhaps would make her able to leave the privileged background she was from to serve the Lord wherever He chose to send her, as He might actually do.

They sat and discussed future plans of all parties until suppertime, the mercenary soldiers as well as the missionaries getting acquainted better and some levity coming into the discussion despite the gravity of the day.

"Here's Iuba!" said Angela, as the dog trudged slowly over to his water bowl and drank for a considerable period of time. Ignoring the other occupants in the room, Iuba walked over to Angela and silently lay next to her.

"You've been adopted, Angela," observed Sir William. "It appears that the dog has chosen you to be his mistress."

"I'm a little surprised," said Angela, as she placed her hand on his head and gently massaged his ears. "I would have guessed that Iuba would have picked Lucas to follow, but it really doesn't matter since Wicki asked both of us to care for him."

"We'd better make some plans for the morning," suggested Sir William. "That helicopter is here to take Gayle and Esther to Luanda in the morning, and I hope to travel with them. Are you and Angela planning to travel with us or have you made other plans?" he asked Lucas. "You're very welcome to come."

"We've been discussing our options," broke in Angela. "I asked Tad if he wanted to go to Malawi with us when we leave in the morning and he won't even discuss it. Since he rode back to Lubalo with us in the truck, he seems intent to go to Luanda. When he's well enough to travel, he's determined to try to find Dad and my other brother, Jake. That means that he will probably ask to hitch a ride with you on the helicopter."

"We have enough space for you too, so please come if you want to," said Captain Leadbetter.

Lucas thought for a moment, and then replied thoughtfully, "I have an obligation to be in Malawi as soon as possible to fulfill my contract there. The question is whether to drive the three thousand miles all the way back to Nsanji or drive partway to Kolwezi in the southern Congo and then try to get a lift on a Beechcraft flight from the Kolwezi Mission in Katanga. I guess the quickest would be to drive to Kolwezi, and then fly."

You came to Lubalo that way, didn't you, Lucas?" said Angela. "I'm sure they'll be happy to take us back by plane from Kolwezi if we drive there."

"That's still a six hundred mile drive through the bush, mostly on dirt roads," remarked Captain Leadbetter, always trying to be helpful. "What about a lift to Kolwezi by helicopter?"

"Hardly practical…it's exactly in the wrong direction that you would fly to Luanda. I drove here over those roads only a few months ago. They're not really that bad. Besides, there's no war going on there. Thanks anyway for the offer," returned Lucas to Captain Leadbetter. "I'll have company with Angela and Iuba, so it will seem a shorter distance."

"So I guess everyone has sorted out his destination," said Sir William. "The Lubalo Mission hospital will continue to function under Doctor Maria's leadership and the rest of us will be leaving in the morning.

Sir William asked, "Lucas, are you going to commandeer the pastor's new Land Rover truck to drive to Kolwezi? I'm sure he would not object and we can inform him in Luanda when we see him."

"I think not!" said Lucas, appalled at the thought of seizing property not belonging to him. "Angela and I still have the truck that Savimbi gave to us a few weeks ago and it will serve nicely to take the journey through the Democratic Republic of the Congo to the Kolwezi Mission."

"I'm sorry, ol' man. I didn't mean to intimate that you would expropriate a vehicle not belonging to yourself," apologized Sir William. "I didn't realize that there was another possibility of transportation to Kolwezi."

"No offense taken," laughed Lucas. "If we needed it, we'd have asked. Do you care to take a little three day ride with us into the deep bush of the Congo tomorrow?"

"No, not really," William answered promptly.

Everyone was smiling as Sir William retorted, "I've seen quite enough of the Congo bush along the Kwilu and Lubalo Rivers in the last few days, Lucas. I'll pass on your offer and substitute a nice, quick helicopter trip to civilization and Luanda, thank you."

Tad appeared at the door of the cafeteria with his arm casted and in a sling. "The pain is about gone, so I'm ready for a nice quick comfortable ride to Luanda on that huge helicopter..... Lucas, I really want to thank you and Sis for the help. When I see Dad and Jake, they'll want to know that you're safe." Tad had been recovering in the emergency room and was now was ready to travel to Luanda to find his father and brother. Angela hoped that either or both of her brothers wouldn't return to the war on the side of the rebels but just fly to London with her father.

Supper was served. As the group sat down, each diner's thoughts turned towards tomorrow's activities and the upcoming journey that each anticipated. Iuba, still lying next to Angela's chair, accepted a few of the tidbits she offered him from her plate. He sorely missed Wicki, but he had begun to nibble a few bits from Angela's hand. There was something about her he felt he needed to protect.

After supper, Lucas and Angela returned to their living quarters. As they sat and discussed the day's events, the subject of leaving Angola permanently in the morning and returning to Malawi with Lucas, caused Angela some serious thought.

"You know Lucas, when we're no longer here, there won't be a surgeon for hundreds of miles of the mission. Doctor Maria is an excellent physician, but she does no surgery and has little competence in orthopedics. These indigenous people will be without those services, and I'll be leaving Angola for the first time in my life."

"Yes, that's true, but prior to my coming from Malawi, it was the same situation for months. What did you and the mission do before I came?" asked Lucas.

"Well, Lucas, when there was no war, we shipped the surgery and serious cases to Saurimo. If the problem was serious enough, they could be life-flighted to Luanda from the Saurimo Mission for treatment at a government hospital there. Now, the rebellion prevents that route, so they will have to find other alternatives, like before."

As they spoke, Angela got up from her chair, made a cup of hot tea for both of them, and sat next to Lucas on the couch. Lucas placed his arm around her shoulder and kissed her gently on the mouth. A low growl came from under her chair, followed by a snarl as Iuba emerged and confronted Lucas.

"Easy boy, there's no danger here to her," replied Lucas as he reached out to pat Iuba.

The dog snapped at Lucas' hand, narrowly missing his thumb. Angela jumped from the couch and grabbed Iuba.

"No Iuba! He's our friend. Lie down and stop this aggression."

The dog obeyed, but his tail did not wag. He continued to growl in a low tone, never taking his eyes from Lucas' face.

"Lucas, what's gotten into him? He's always been friendly to everyone and especially you. What's going on?"

"He's lost Wicki, his master, and he now fears that something might happen to you. He wants to protect you now that you're his mistress, Angela. He'd certainly make a formidable antagonist. An attack from him would not be fun."

Iuba continued to watch Lucas and Angela from under the chair, but his growling stopped as they continued their discussion.

"You know, Lucas," said Angela. "When we leave, there will be no surgeon for a hundred miles in this area. This vacuum could be eliminated if there were other doctors from America or Europe who volunteered to fill the gap. They could help for two or even four weeks without substantial economic loss, instead of vacationing."

"It's not even a permanent commitment, and it's surprising how much help they could give to people who would really appreciate their efforts," replied Lucas. "Not many are willing to do it, unfortunately, even though it's tax deductible."

"I'll really hate to leave Lubalo Mission, Lucas. Maybe we can return when the war is over and it's safer. We'd better get some sleep. It's a long drive over rough roads in the morning."

They retired to the bedroom, but not without having to isolate Iuba in the kitchen, as he was not going to allow Angela to leave him willingly.

"This could become a nuisance, Angela," said Lucas. "We can't isolate that dog everyplace we go."

"I think with some time, he'll relax and understand that you're not a threat," said Angela. "The English Bull Terrier breed is known for its single-minded devotion, though, so you'd better not aggravate me, or I'll sic him on you."

They both chuckled as they went off to much needed sleep.

At sunrise the next morning, the activity around the helicopter sitting on the front lawn of the mission hospital had reached a crescendo. Major Santiago was briefing Captain Leadbetter on the possible weakness of their lines near Saurimo. They had a large map draped over the front seat of the combat helicopter, and the Major was pointing out the problem. Sir William was selecting luggage as it was being loaded into the aircraft, as were Gayle and Esther.

"We've got to get this group into the air," remarked one of the mercenaries sitting inside the chopper, holding the fifty-caliber machine gun, which protruded from its side. "Reports are that the government troops are coming to try to capture this machine."

Angela and Lucas had already finished packing their truck and had parked next to the hospital to make final rounds on the patients remaining within the clinic before they left. They also came to bid farewell to Captain Leadbetter, but most importantly to Tad, Sir William, Esther and Gayle.

"We had to leave Iuba locked inside the truck," Angela explained to Sir William. "Since Wicki has passed on, he has become aggressive to almost everyone and we certainly would not want anyone bitten."

Most of the hospital staff had come out onto the lawn amongst the flowers and trees on this bright, sunny, cool morning to bid their farewells to Lucas and Angela. A few of the staff also had become acquainted with Gayle and Esther, so the gathering became a large farewell exercise, with hugging and hand-holding, which was within the African custom of separation.

"You know," Angela whispered to Lucas, "I've known some of these people most of my life. I wonder if I'll see them again once we go to Malawi."

"Don't worry," he replied. "We can come back any time you want to see your family, if they return to Saurimo and then come up here to Lubalo and visit these workers at the same time."

Brightwell was the last to bid farewell to Lucas and Angela. He had tears in his eyes and thanked both of the missionaries solemnly, still with a smile on his face. "Missie Angela and Doctor Lucas, you have saved all of us through the crisis, and I don't know how we will function after you leave. Please come back to visit. We all will miss you."

Finally, when Captain Leadbetter and Major Santiago had finished their discussion, the rest of the mercenary team boarded the helicopter. Sir William, Gayle, Tad and Esther were secured inside the aircraft and warnings were given to clear the lawn. Slowly, the blades began to turn, gaining speed with each rotation, until the roar of the turbines and the wind made all speech impossible. The massive body began to shake before the shock absorbers released their pressure and the helicopter lifted from the lawn and moved away from the hospital. It was an awe-inspiring sight to watch as the aircraft, capable of untold destruction, moved gracefully over the small mission hospital and headed west toward the horizon.

"I wouldn't want to be in a field where that thing showed its anger," said Lucas as they watched it move into the distance. "Its destructive power is awesome. We'd better think about leaving too."

Angela and Lucas walked over to the truck where Iuba had been enclosed and opening the door, let him out for a short run before they began their long road trip.

Iuba immediately ran to the front of the hospital and, locating Wicki's stump, promptly lay down beside it in his usual spot.

"He's looking for Wicki," murmured Angela.

"Listen to him whine, Angela. I can hear his whimpering all the way over here," Lucas said.

Angela walked over to the dog still lying by the stump and rubbed his abdomen when he turned over, patting and consoling the dejected animal. As she snapped a leash to his collar, she implored, "Come on ol' guy. We have to go for a long trip. I'll take you for a leg stretch and then we have to leave."

As Angela walked around the front lawn for the last time with Iuba, she bid a last farewell to her many friends still outside the hospital. However, she now had to be careful to keep the dog a good distance from other people, as Iuba no longer recognized anyone as a friend. He remained extremely protective of his new mistress.

"Goodbye, Major," said Lucas shaking hands with the rebel administrator, who had remained on the lawn as the helicopter lifted off. "Give my thanks to Savimbi and Generalissimo Alvarez when you see them. We must leave now."

Angela loaded Iuba into the back of their truck, and after Lucas started the engine the grimy vehicle moved slowly down the gravel road, moving east towards Chaua. It was the start of a long, tortuous, six hundred mile trip over dirty, dusty, poorly repaired roads with little population or possibility of assistance. However, Lucas was confident that he would manage it a second time easily.

The roads in northeastern Lunda Norte Province were not paved, but the gravel was graded and there was a clear pathway ahead. The first fifty miles to Chaua and on to Mungo were fairly pleasant, as the sun had not yet reached its zenith and the temperatures hovered around seventy-five degrees Fahrenheit. Fording the Cuilo River was without delay, despite the lack of a bridge. The water-sealed engine and snorkeled tailpipe allowed the powerful diesel engine to run smoothly through the deep flowing river and they arrived in Mungo in about two hours.

"This trip may become slower due to the poor roads, Lucas, but it gives us a chance to just be together instead of rushing somewhere. With no adverse events, we should reach the Kolwezi Mission in a few days."

They stopped on the other side of Mungo to eat the sandwiches that the hospital cafeteria had packed for them, and continued on. Forcing down a sandwich, Lucas admitted, "You know, Angela, I've been feeling some nausea and I seem to have lost much of my appetite over the last few days. Maybe it's that food we ate on the way back to Lubalo two days ago. We'll need to stop to eat supper somewhere and then go on to Cassom before we cross over into the Democratic Republic of Congo. Do you want to drive for a while?"

After lunch, Angela took over the driving duties while Lucas slept. The quality of the roads deteriorated rapidly as they moved further east, with dirt tracks turning into rocky soil. Angela was now driving over or around mud holes six inches deep filled with water from the last rain. The climb was occasionally steep, with thorn bushes growing out over the roadside, capable of flattening any soft tire. Angela looked out over the hood of the truck and noted the beautiful panorama as she ascended the final mountain range separating Angola from the Congo.

"How are we doing?" said Lucas, waking as she drove over a particularly steep rock.

Before she could answer, Lucas began to shiver, as a hard chill convulsed his entire body. This was followed immediately by profuse sweating, soaking his shirt and shorts. They both recognized this symptom immediately, as she stopped the truck in the middle of the track and reached over to touch his face.

"Yes, it's a fever of at least one hundred and two, or higher, Lucas," she mumbled. Then she said "My bet is Falciparum Malaria!"

Lucas took a deep breath and said between the reoccurring chills, "There's nothing for miles but bush, honey. We both know what comes next so just drive on. Please go into my pack and get the Chloroquine pills first. It could be a week before this thing passes."

Letting the truck idle, Angela threw the transmission into neutral and set the hand brake. She walked to the back of the truck and dug into Lucas' baggage. "Here they are!" she called from the rear of the seat. "But it will be at least three days before the medications work and I'm not losing you to any cerebral extensions."

"Angie, I'll lie in the back of the truck and wrap myself in blankets until the chills pass. The parasites will finish being released in an hour and then the fever will break for this cycle. There's nothing to do but wait, so just keep driving."

Climbing onto the back of the truck, Angela wrapped his entire body in blankets, but the chills continued. He lay shivering next to Iuba.

"Looks like a bad occurrence," whispered Lucas. "This one was fairly mild, but the next one will be a real cracker. I'd better take a few aspirin with the Chloroquine before I sink into a coma."

Angela remained cool and deliberate. She'd seen this parasite disease many times before and realized that there was little she could do except give him support. After helping him swallow the pills, she opened the emergency medical kit that they always carried and expertly put together the intravenous administration set. Angela started a solution of sodium chloride dripping into Lucas' veins to counteract the fall in sodium that would develop in Lucas' blood.

"Okay, that's done. Are you comfortable enough for us to continue?" she asked.

Lucas was unresponsive but appeared stable, so she returned to the driver's seat and started to move down the mountainside, talking to herself as she jolted over the fractured road.

She was wishing that they had that new anti-malarial intravenous drug, Artemisinin. It would clear him in twenty-four hours. But where could she obtain the drug? She knew that there was no hospital between here and Kolwezi. Lumbalo Mission didn't have the drug, so turning back wasn't an option. If she could radio ahead to the Kolwezi Mission, they could probably get some from Lubumbashi and have it waiting when they arrived.

Angela found a level spot in the road after another thirty minutes of driving. She checked Lucas' condition, which was unchanged. Then climbing onto the roof of the truck for maximum carrying distance, she turned on the shortwave radio. There was the familiar crackle of static as she hurriedly switched channels to try to find any reception, but there was no response.

"Emergency calling!" she pronounced over each channel, but there remained only the static to answer her frantic call.

# 14
## Chapter

A ngela tried to use the truck's shortwave radio to reach someone for help. Lucas groaned, and slowly sat up in the back of the truck as she remained on the roof, receiving only static in reply to her transmissions. Weakly he asked her, his mind still clear despite his fever, if she was able to raise anyone on the shortwave radio out here near the Angola-Congo border. This location, he knew, is one of the most remote areas in the world. Even with satellite capabilities, the radio was of a small size and the power was limited by the truck's battery.

Looking down at him from the roof of the truck, she replied, "Not much luck so far, honey. I see that the first cycle of the malaria infestation has passed, and you're awake and functioning again."

Lucas' long experience with malaria told him that the chills and fever usually cycled every few days. By the next cycle he hoped that they would have some Artemisinin sent ahead to the Kolwezi Mission and that it would be waiting for them before they arrived there. If not, these cycles would continue to reoccur, more violent and dangerous each time.

"Yeah, thankfully, the malaria sporozoites that invaded my red blood cells from a mosquito bite a week ago won't be released again for twenty-four to forty-eight hours, so I should be OK for awhile," said Lucas. "Hopefully we have time to get to the Kolwezi Mission before that. The chloroquine will only stop the malaria parasites *outside* the red cells. I could develop Cerebral Malaria or Blackwater Fever if the original inoculation by the mosquito was large enough."

"We'll drive on," said Angela, "after I'm able to contact someone who can get that medication to Kolwezi."

Turning again to the shortwave radio, the sharp crackle of static was the only answer to her repeated inquiries until finally she heard a faint response to her emergency calls on the radio.

"This is Abercrombe in the Congo," she called, "Can you hear me? I have an emergency."

"I am barely receiving your transmission," was the faint response. "This is Kloppie van Rensburg in Cape Town, South Africa. How can I help you?"

"We have a malaria emergency," responded Angela. "Please write this down. We need a vial of the drug, Artemisinin...that's a-r-t-e-m-i-s-i-n-i-n... sent to the Kolwezi Baptist Mission in the Congo as soon as possible."

"How do I get it there?" he replied, his voice fading through the static. Then, contact was lost.

It was a full five minutes before the South African contact could be reestablished. Upon its return, the connection was much clearer, as it was customary for African weather conditions to frequently change precipitously. For a few minutes, the contact seemed better.

"Van Rensburg, this is Abercrombe again. Did you receive the name of the drug and destination clearly?"

"That's a roger, Abercrombe. I have it written down. How do I get it to you?"

"Contact the South African Baptist Foreign Mission Board in Cape Town and relay the message that Doctor Lucas Stuart needs the medication immediately at the Kolwezi Mission in the Congo, please," Angela replied.

"Will do it immediately. Is there anything else we can assist you with?"

"That will be a big help. I will try to contact you again at 1730, same frequency if convenient, to confirm the request. Thank you. Out."

Angela was greatly relieved by the success of the contact and climbed down off of the roof of the truck. She spoke briefly to Lucas, who was still too weak to drive, but now was able to sit up in the truck next to Iuba. He soon fell asleep. A half hour later, as Angela drove on, Lucas awoke and asked for their progress. His rehydration now complete, Lucas removed the intravenous fluids from his arm as they drove.

"We've crossed the border into the Congo," informed Angela. "No guards or passport inspectors on these remote dirt tracts, so we'll have to see an immigration inspector in Mastrika when we get there, in order to be legal. I was able to contact someone in Cape Town by the shortwave and there should be medicine in Kolwezi by the time we get there."

"Yes, that makes sense," replied the sleepy doctor. "We seem to be moving downhill a lot, so the flatlands will be coming up soon. Contact could be more difficult with South Africa at a lower altitude. I feel a bit better."

They left the mountain range separating Angola from Republic of Congo, and were able to ford the Cassai River, which defines the border between the two countries. The landscape now became undulating, and Angela noted that the muddy, dirt roads were poorly maintained. As they turned south, progress was only slightly facilitated by the flattening topography as there was standing water everywhere.

"It's about three hundred miles straight south to the main paved road at Kasaji," said Lucas in one of his more frequent waking spells. "Don't expect much there. The pavement is missing for long stretches and the potholes are a real threat."

At 5:30, as agreed with their contact in Cape Town, Angela brought the truck to a halt. The stop in Mastrika to stamp their passports had been brief, and they had encountered no available medical facilities as they passed through the largely uninhabited, densely vegetated territory. Her second Cape Town contact was attempted from the top of a hill with wide open spaces surrounding it to try for the best reception.

"Abercrombe to Cape Town," she said over the shortwave on the same frequency as previously agreed.

Immediately, she clearly heard the response, this time with no static.

"This is Cape Town. Van Rensberg, to Abercrombe. How are you making out? I hear you loud and clear."

"The doctor's a bit better. Any success obtaining the medication?"

"Not much, Abercrombe. We were able to reach the Baptist Foreign Mission Board...a fellow named Pepperridge. He recognized the name of Doctor Lucas Stuart immediately, but says the medication is scarce, new, and too expensive. They are unable to supply it or transport the drug to Congo. Any further suggestions?"

Angela asked Cape Town to stand by. She turned her head and looked at Lucas. "Lucas, what do we do? Without that drug, you surely could have a serious relapse, with possible progression to cerebral malaria or Blackwater fever." She sounded worried feeling that Lucas appeared weaker.

Lucas was still in a state of semi-sleep. Thinking for a minute, he smiled weakly to himself and asked Angela for the short-wave speaker. He established contact with Cape Town again, and said, "Kloppie my boy, I don't know you but this is the doctor himself. We really appreciate your help, but we'll need another favor, if you'd be so kind."

"Shoot Man, South Africa is at your service, Doc," came the wry reply.

Smiling as he spoke into the speaker, Lucas said, "Locate the most elaborate, expensive hotel in Luanda, Angola. Call the reception desk and ask for the room of a Sir William Spencer-Johnson. He'll be there for sure. When you speak to him, explain our situation and be sure to mention my name. Also, be sure that he has the right location to send the medicine, the Kolwezi Mission in the Democratic Republic of the Congo. That's all you need to do, please."

"Okay, Doc. Who is this guy?"

"Kloppie, he's a wealthy diplomat friend of ours who can make the right connections. I sincerely appreciate your help. We'll call back in an hour to find out how it went."

After signing off, they started the truck and Angela continued to drive south. The surrounding territory was now a virtual watershed with a lush growth of bushes and trees surrounded by waterways and small lakes, mostly draining to the north and west. These rivers and streams eventually emptied into the mighty Congo River, hundreds of miles away.

As they proceeded on their way, Lucas awoke suddenly as she slowed to a crawl, almost throwing him into the front seat. "Look! A whole herd of elephants and their babies standing on the road," she exclaimed.

Looking up, Lucas replied, "In as remote a place as this, the tourists and hunters haven't been around to kill the animals. I suspect that we will be seeing many herds for the next day or so."

After an hour, they crossed the Lulua River, which was in full flood stage. The river was rife with crocodiles and hippo, and the surrounding grasslands teemed with undisturbed wildlife. After crossing the river, when Angela stopped the truck to contact Kloppie, Lucas felt better and dropped a fishing line into the water. He was rewarded almost immediately with two large fish suitable for their supper.

"Cape Town, this is Abercrombe calling, come in," she spoke into the shortwave speaker.

The answer came as a loud enthusiastic laugh, "Abercrombe? Man, you have some friends, alright!"

"Why? What happened?" asked Angela with some wonder in her voice.

Kloppie came back, laughing as he spoke, "That stud is staying in the hotel penthouse. He offered to personally fly out to Congo with the medication. All he wanted to know was if the doctor, and some *stekkie* named Angie, were okay."

Angela was now laughing too when she answered, "Kloppie, tell Sir William and his friend, Gayle that we'll be fine if he can get the medicine. There's no need to come out here."

"He's on the phone now and says he will guarantee the medicine will be at the mission before you get there. Gayle, his woman friend, sends her love!"

"Thank him again and thank *you*, Kloppie, for your help," replied Angie. "Without both of you, we'd have been in a fix! Over and out."

"What a character," laughed Angela as she started up the truck. Most all South Africaaners were very friendly whether they knew you or not, but this Kloppie was over the top. Angela and Lucas decided that if they ever got to Cape Town they would be sure to look him up to thank him for his help. Lucas had now finished scaling and gutting the fish, placing them into a canvas water container on the fender to stay cool until suppertime. Iuba examined the fish carefully.

Lucas remarked to Angela how the Lord managed to see that everything worked out for the best.. If Esther and Gayle had not been arrested and helped by Sir William, they never would have met the Englishman at the Lubalo Mission. Now it appeared this man would save Lucas' life.

As they resumed their trip southwards, the profusion of wildlife and plant growth was remarkable. Herds of wildebeest and antelope, probably never seen by white men, nibbled the dense greenery peacefully near the roadside, not fearing the truck or its passengers as it passed by. The settlements of Sandoa and Sakanga lay in a small valley near the head of the Kashile River, which Lucas selected to use as a camp for the night.

"Sometimes I worry about camping out alone here in the bush," remarked Angie. "Anyone could sneak up late at night and rob us, or worse."

As the sun sunk to the west, a glowing golden orb behind the multicolored horizon, the sounds of night began to swell with the light's disappearance. A low growl could be heard from under their truck.

"I doubt that anyone or anything will surprise us tonight, Angie. We have a full-time night guard on duty, fearful of nothing. Let's cook dinner and sleep. We have a long drive tomorrow."

The roasted fish were delicious when consumed with the green onions and cassava root that Angela had discovered growing wild a few meters from their campsite. Iuba had a rabbit that he caught as it was passing their truck just before dinner.

"Angie, you still know how to live off of the land better than anyone I've met. That dinner was really nice," said Lucas as he kissed her softly on the mouth and neck.

"Look, sport," replied Angela affectionately, "you're due for that malaria relapse cycle tomorrow, so don't get too frisky. You may be on your back with chills and fever, wrapped in blankets in a few hours. Get some sleep."

Sleep came easily as they were both exhausted.

Iuba's loud barking woke Angela from her deep sleep at about four a.m. As she rolled over in her sleeping bag, she could hear the chattering of teeth next to her, along with loud mouth breathing from Lucas' bedroll. Iuba had noted Lucas' relapse and alerted his mistress.

She climbed out of her blanketed, comfortable nest thinking, "It sounds like a relapse of Lucas' malaria." She patted Iuba, as she rose to stand by her sleeping bag.

"Okay, I'm up, Iuba. You can relax." she said as she adjusted her clothes and turned Lucas onto his back.

Just as she placed her hand on his arm to turn him, Lucas had a seizure with convulsions, reflecting possible central nervous system malarial involvement. His arm was profusely wet, as was the rest of his body, sweat soaking his clothes. Angela felt his head, she estimated that the fever at least 102 degrees.

Angela, having seen tertiary malaria in Angola, realized that she could to lose him if he wasn't cooled immediately. In past times she had seen people arrest during these convulsions, so she knew action was needed immediately.

Running to a nearby creek, Angela soaked a large cloth in the cool water and returned to the comatose Lucas, who lay on the ground quietly. Iuba had stopped barking and lay silently under the truck watching her every move.

She thought as she placed the cool cloth against his body, *"What would Lucas do if I were in this phase of the malaria?"* but he then came out of his coma as suddenly as he entered it.

The chills returned to wrack his body and his eyes opened. Looking at her with a weak smile, he said softly, "Maybe we need to get some aspirin into me and more chloroquine, eh Angie?"

"Yes, Lucas. Just don't have any more seizures. I'll get the medicine right now."

After swallowing the medications, Lucas continued to relapse intermittently into a sleep-like state for another hour as the seizure wore off. There were no intravenous fluids left, so Angela attempted to try to help him drink fluids whenever he awoke, but the chills and fever made this difficult.

"I've got to stay hydrated, Angie. This cycle will end in a few hours, and the drugs will kill the free sporocytes in my blood stream. Only the Artemisinin is capable of killing the parasites *inside* of the red cells and stopping the cycle completely. You've got to get me to Kolwezi in the next forty-eight hours, before the next cycle begins, causing a new round of symptoms. I could be in danger of serious complications."

Angela continued to try to cool his fever and hydrate him for the next two hours when, as predicted, his fever broke and the chills slowed. Lucas was awake and lucid, but in no condition to take the wheel of the truck.

"I'm so weak after that malaria cycle that I'm not sure I can sit up in the truck," he said as she loaded all the gear and helped him into the front seat of the vehicle. He had little control of his dozing off and waking up.

By now it was daylight, and the truck continued to follow the ragged track south towards the main road at Kasaji, some 150 miles away. They drove in silence, with Lucas sleeping most of the time, waking occasionally to drink water and question their progress. It had begun to rain again.

"Here's a village!" exclaimed Angela when they arrived at Zala, some three hours later. Looking through the mud- and rain-spattered windshield, Angie could make out that the town consisted of a small group of concrete block huts with thatched grass roofs. There was a general store in the center of the village, which sold dry goods, beverages, and fuel, but no hospital or medical facility was available for many miles. Angela was able to communicate with the vendors to buy fuel and some warm carbonated drinks by using a locally used Kikonga dialect. She promptly encouraged Lucas to drink as much as possible. That accomplished, they continued on their way towards Kasaji through the pouring African rain, splashing mud and debris in all directions from the soft, mushy track.

"This second cycle usually is similar to the first cycle," remarked Lucas. They both knew that it had been only a few hours since the last cycle and he could expect to be much improved for a day. They feared the third cycle, which often was devastating, with widespread dispersion of sporocytes into the blood stream, setting up the possibility of liver, spleen and cerebral extension.

Angela and Lucas had seen the third cycle many times, and, if they were able to get to the mission and Sir William was able to get the medications to Kolwezi, their hope was that the third cycle would never occur.

Noon approached, without any letup of the downpour. The soft dirt roads turned into a quagmire of sloppy mud, but their reliable truck seemed to be able to overcome all threats, as it moved southward at a reduced speed.

"See that sign?" exclaimed Angela. "It says only twenty kilometers to Kasaji and the main highway. We're almost there."

"Don't get excited, Angie. I drove this way a few months ago and the road is little better than this messy goop we're in now. Just steady as she goes until we get to the town."

Due to the weather and poor road maintenance, it was almost two in the afternoon before they drove onto the five-mile concrete road leading into the town of Kasaji.

Lucas could remember that this town was divided by the four-lane highway that ran east to west, from Lobito, on the Atlantic Ocean in Angola, all the way to the city of Lubumbashi, deep in the Central African Congo."

"Thank goodness the rain has let up," sighed Angela.

"This road is in theory only," joked Lucas. "The highway is actually paved through a major part of Angola, but once it crosses into the Congo, it is either mud or small paved segments with potholes deep enough to bury people."

"Can we actually follow it to Kolwezi?" asked Angela.

"Let's just say it consists of a few hundred miles of graded mud pathway, full of deep holes, that runs from here to the mission. By following the flattened mud tract, you will eventually arrive at Kolwezi, if the tires hold up."

They stopped and ate an extremely tardy midday meal in an outlying district of Kasaji, near a petrol station. By now, Iuba had fully accepted Lucas and freely took all tidbits offered during lunch from either party. He seemed to enjoy the chance to run freely, as he had been confined to the backseat for hours during the rainstorm. The warm sunshine that was bearing down on the travelers lifted their spirits and increased their energy levels.

"I'm feeling a little better again Angela, so I'll drive for a while and you can rest in the flat back bed of the truck."

"Sounds good. I can sleep for a few hours this afternoon, and then if you need to stop driving I'll be fresh to take over the wheel," replied Angela.

They were near one of the rare petrol stations in this part of the Congo, so they filled their gas tank before Angela and Iuba carved out a nest of blankets and pillows on the flat seat at the back of the truck. Lucas resumed the driving at around four p.m.

"I don't mind the bumps, Lucas, we can stretch out in the warm sunshine," called Angela as she settled down next to Iuba.

As the truck moved forward, Lucas tried to keep the tires on the intact, smooth part of the road, but time and weather had destroyed much of the highway, so Angela and Iuba had a bumpy ride anyway. By six, darkness had begun to overtake them and they looked for a resting place.

A level outlet to the highway appeared and he pulled the truck off of the road and came to a stop some few hundred yards onto a grassy knoll. Angela and Iuba climbed down from the back of the truck and stood watching the road.

"There is a lot more traffic than we saw out in the remote bush of the Congo. A vehicle of some sort passes every few minutes, compared to seeing something once an hour when we had little or no highway," observed Angela.

Lucas agreed, but he also noted that there was a constant stream of people on foot passing by with donkey or ox carts. He suggested that they should camp further from the road, as it might be safer.

Angie thought for a few seconds and then said, "I'm pretty tired, Lucas. Couldn't we just drive across this field to the other side, where we can't be seen from the road, and camp there?"

"It sounds like a good suggestion."

They climbed back into the truck and drove to a spot next to a stream on the other side of the pasture. Angela cooked a rudimentary supper while Lucas and Iuba set up their night's camp a hundred yards from the banks of the stream. The sun was setting and the stillness of the surrounding countryside soothed all three of them.

"Hopefully, we can get to Kolwezi by tomorrow evening, before the malaria cycles again. At least you'll be over that problem," suggested Angela as she sat next to Iuba on the ground, eating and sharing her supper with the ever-attentive dog.

They estimated that they had to drive a few hundred miles to get there, if they shared the driving over those potholed roads. It was no fun because trying to save the tires they had to swerve every few yards to avoid a six-inch hole in the pavement.

The fire reduced to glowing embers and Angela and Lucas lay down on the ground to sleep. Iuba assumed his normal position under the truck, but by midnight the ever-alert canine guard jumped up into the bed of the truck and settled down again on the blankets to stay warm in the cool night air. The gentle night sounds of crickets and frogs tranquilized them as they slept.

Lucas awoke from his deep peaceful sleep to find Iuba staring into the darkness and barking. "What's wrong, Iuba?" asked Lucas as he sat up to the sound of the dog's warning.

Iuba stood on the bed of the truck, barking loudly as he looked towards the bank of the stream. Angela, now also awake, stood up, holding her blanket to cover herself, after seeing that Iuba was concerned with something coming from that direction. A large African man walked slowly from the stream and stood next to the still smoldering fire. He appeared to have arrived in a small boat beached on the riverbank.

"Can we help you?" asked Lucas in Kikongo dialect, as he sat on the ground, still covered by his blanket.

The African moved next to Angela, as she stood with only the blanket to cover her underwear. The man placed his left arm around her shoulders and produced a large gleaming knife in his right hand, announcing, "Oh yes, you can!" in heavily African-accented English. "I'll need the truck and the lady, and I may decide to play some games before I leave." The strong odor of alcohol mixed with sweat came to Lucas.

The man moved his left arm up around Angela's neck, making her struggle to breathe, and began to pull her backwards toward Lucas and the truck, placing the large knife at her throat. This African man had made two mistakes. The first was a minor one, invading their camp. The second mistake was a fatal one, attacking Angela.

Iuba gave no further warning as seventy-five pounds of unrestrained fury launched itself from the bed of the truck. The Bull Terrier, with no hesitation in his mind, catapulted across the few feet between the bed of the truck and the African's back, landing on his right shoulder and neck. It still remained completely quiet as Iuba sank his teeth as deep as possible. Due to the impetus of his jump, he tore a fist sized piece of flesh from the African's neck. Caught totally unaware, the African lost his balance and fell to the ground, releasing Angela and dropping his weapon. A gurgling sound came from his neck. He was now on an eye level with Iuba as he lay defenseless on the grass, bleeding profusely from his wound. The odds were in Iuba's favor, and the dog did not lack any resolve to defeat his mistress's attacker.

Growling for the first time, he grabbed the African immediately across the face, destroying his left eye and cheek bone, and exposing the left half of the man's teeth as he ripped the flesh from the intruder's left cheek and lower jaw. Blood covered the grass, Iuba, and what was left of the African's face. The entire combat was over in less than thirty seconds, and the African lay comatose on the ground, blood spurting from every wound.

"We can't save him," stated Lucas calmly as he slowly stood up to examine the man, who was still breathing shallowly and then stopped altogether.

Iuba moved in front of Lucas, still protecting Angela, and let out a low growl, showing his teeth.

"It's alright, Iuba. The problem's over," said Angela as calmly as she could. She patted his head and stroked his back, pulling the animal close to her body, her blanket dripping with the blood on Iuba's body.

"We'd better check Iuba for wounds," said Lucas. "I doubt that he has any, as the African never resisted his attack."

Taking Iuba into the stream, she washed him thoroughly, examining him carefully for damage and finding no major lacerations.

The African man was dead, causing Iuba little injury, but both Lucas and Angela were horrifyingly impressed with the single-minded ferocity that had defeated her attacker. While this incident had served them well, they discussed the possibility that any attack by Iuba in the future could result in a similar disaster to a friend or acquaintance.

"Remind me not to even play with you roughly, Angela. An attack by that animal is devastating." It took a half hour before Iuba completely calmed down and returned to normal behavior, but neither of them would ever forget what Iuba could do if he thought that his mistress was challenged.

"We'd better pack up our camp and then stop in the closest town to report this to the authorities, Angela. They'll want to know what happened."

"How far is it to Kolwezi, Lucas?" asked Angela as they crossed the open pasture and re-entered the four lane highway, turning west, back into town.

"From what I remember when I drove here, as the crow flies just under one hundred fifty miles. This concrete highway only lasts for another ten miles or so and then it's back to potholes and dirt for much of the rest of the way. We can drive faster than on those mountain tracks, but it's still a long way on these terrible roads.

They entered the town of Mutshatsha and stopped at the constable's office to report the incident. After filling out multiple government forms, they were permitted to leave, with one of the assistant constables following on a bicycle. They had been asked to show him the location of the body.

When they arrived at their camp by the stream, Lucas drew back the blanket that they had left covering the attacker's body. The face of the constable turned into a grim smile as he said, *"Kuzaba beto kufua mdombi"*

"He knows the man," said Angela. The assistant constable went on to explain that the man had a long criminal record of arrests for assault and robbery, as well as rape. No charges would be pressed against them at this time, but their location must be known, in case further inquiries were necessary. Even though they had explained to the constable the conditions around the African's death, he seemed hard-pressed to understand the amount of damage that Iuba had done to the man's face in so short a fight.

"We'll be at the Kolwezi Mission, if you need us," answered Lucas.

This business now resolved, Lucas and Angela returned to the main highway and turned east towards Lubumbashi. It was around 10:30 in the morning, and they had a long drive ahead of them. Iuba now sat between them wagging his tail and cuddling with his mistress while Lucas drove the truck.

"You know, Lucas, it was great what Iuba did to save me, but in all reality he's a very dangerous animal and should be trained so that we can control him."

"Absolutely, Angie. He's still young and exceptionally smart, so that shouldn't take a lot of effort. I've had dogs most of my life, and almost any pet can be trained. We'll start when we get to Malawi."

"So in the meantime, we try to hold his attacks down to a few killings a day," joked Angela.

"Quit it!" smiled Lucas. "We can just be sure he's on a leash or confined to the truck when we stop. Teaching him to lie down or accept strangers will be more difficult, but before Wicki died Iuba liked everyone."

The flat dirt road stretched endlessly to the East, the concrete having ended ten miles east of Mutshatsha. Potholes were still everywhere in the roadway as the large lorries carrying all sorts of goods tried to avoid these deep pitfalls, which was often difficult or impossible. The full streams and deep rivers repeatedly tested their sealed engine and snorkel as they tried to increase their speed. Still, they were able to average better than forty miles per hour as they drove with their backs to the sun. The deep green foliage along the fringes of the road that surrounded them testified to the rainy season's abundance of water. It really would have been a pleasant drive if the road had been maintained.

"Lucas, without the attack this morning, this might have been a pleasant journey. I hope we can arrive at Kolwezi and get the medication before you have another malaria cycle."

"Don't remind me. Right now, I'm feeling fairly normal, but this next cycle is reported to be the worst…if it comes."

They continued to make fairly good time, entering the Katanga Province of the Republic of the Congo. Fatigue was avoided by taking turns driving in two-hour shifts.

Lucas was impressed again by the surrounding countryside, which remained mostly grassland and scrub-brush, with occasional lightly dense woodlands. The few rural villages they encountered appeared to be carved out of the hills. These villages consisted of a group of thatch-covered, round mud huts, never fewer than five and rarely more than twenty. He also noticed that these groups of huts were usually surrounded by poorly constructed, dilapidated wooden fences, trying to hold the settlement's goats, pigs, and cattle.

"Yeah," replied Angela, when he pointed out an upcoming village, "And every little house we see owns chickens, which try to cross the road in front of the truck."

They passed many stalls at the side of the road with vendors selling the local agricultural products; cassava, bananas, corn and yams. This produce was now available in abundance since the rainy season had started. The many rivers and ponds were rife with fish, appearing on ropes in the hands of individuals hawking them to traffic as it passed by.

"Oh my gosh!" exclaimed Angela, who was driving at the time. "Look at that."

By the side of the road in a ditch lay an extremely long flatbed trailer truck on its side, with all twenty-two wheels off of the slick mud road. A long sliding mud track on the road documented the driver's attempt to avoid a collision with a donkey cart, which lay mangled under the front tires of the truck. The lifeless donkey was still lying on the road and a large group of onlookers had gathered around the wreckage, making a way to drive past them impossible.

"We'd better stop to see if anyone is hurt," suggested Lucas.

Once their truck was parked, they walked over to discover if there were any injured. A small sign by the roadside had been knocked down, but it was in a language they didn't know.

Many of the crowd was busy trying to gather up the cotton, which had fallen from the truck trailer's bed and now lay soaking up the water in the ditch. A smaller group was gathered around the driver, who had been helped from the cab of his truck and now lay on the wet grass. The donkey cart driver was some thirty feet away and obviously had not survived the wreck.

"The truck driver has a broken left leg," observed Angela. "Look at the awkward angle it's taken."

"He may have an obstructed trachea from the steering wheel, too," remarked Lucas. "He seems to be having difficulty breathing."

Attempts by Lucas to examine the driver as he lay on the ground were met by loud objections from the crowd.

"Please get my stethoscope from the truck," requested Lucas. "I need to hear if he's moving enough air through his lungs."

Upon seeing Angela handing the scope to Lucas, all of the crowd's objections ceased immediately, and realizing Lucas was a physician everyone tried to assist him.

"He's crushed his trachea and broken his left leg," announced Lucas when he finished his examination. "He'll die soon without a tracheotomy. He can't breathe."

The dialect spoken in this area of the Congo was Lunda, not familiar to either of the missionaries, but by holding up his stethoscope and indicating to the crowd, Angela and Lucas surmised that there was no physician closer than Kolwezi, some one hundred miles farther east up the road. By sign language, Lucas obtained a stout stick and managed to place a makeshift splint on the driver's leg before moving him into the shade of a hut.

"Now, we'll have to put in a tracheal tube before he suffocates," Lucas mumbled out loud. "More fun."

"I heard that remark!" retorted Angela good-naturedly. "Come on, Lucas! 'We can do anything with nothing' has always been the international motto of all missionary doctors, so let's do it!"

"You're right. First, we need something hollow, with rigid sides to use as a trocar; an old fashioned pen will do, or even a thin pipe. Somehow we need to communicate to these people what we're looking for."

"We have a few ballpoint pens in the truck," replied Angela trying to visualize Lucas' need. "I can cut off both ends and it'll do for a few hours to hold the airway clear."

"Good, then we do have a scalpel in the medicine kit to make the stab wound, but no anesthetic."

"How do we communicate with the patient what we're about to do, and keep the crowd from lynching us while we do it?" said Angela.

Lucas thought for a second, and then suggested, "By dumb luck, there might be a school teacher or someone who speaks French or a European language here." He was thinking of the fact that the Congo, until recently, was colonized by the Belgians, so French had been the primary language here for many decades.

"Sure, if there is someone who speaks French, they could translate the French into Lunda, and the patient will understand, as will the crowd, meaning we won't be lynched," said Angela with a sarcastic tone of voice. "What are the odds?"

"At least not until he dies afterwards," said Lucas with an ironic twist and a smile.

The patient was now having considerable trouble breathing, so while Angela prepared their primitive equipment, Lucas shouted to the surrounding crowd, *"Parlez-vous Francais?"*

At first there was no answer, but after a few minutes, a little old black lady walked up from the back of the onlookers to Lucas and said, *"Oui."*

"Thank heavens for that," sighed Lucas. *"Merci."*

In a few basic French sentences, Lucas explained the situation to the lady and what he and Angela were about to do. She immediately turned to the patient and translated his words into Lunda. There was general approval, and the patient was laid on a blanket in the sunlight with four men to hold him. Iuba continued to watch calmly from inside the truck as the crowd now cooperated with Lucas and Angela.

"Try to get some sort of sterile prep on the throat skin with alcohol, Angie, and we'll proceed," Lucas grimly murmured.

By this time, a large, curious crowd had closed in around the patient to watch the daylight surgery. Angela signaled the crowd to spread out to give them light and room to work. They did this, but not a single person left the viewing. This was a once in a lifetime opportunity, and no one wanted to miss a single part of it.

Once the skin was prepped, Lucas made a swift, deep incision in the trachea at the base of the neck, releasing a gush of blood and air from the hole. Placing his finger into this opening to hold the airway open, he deftly inserted the plastic sheath of the pen into the trachea, establishing a pathway for the truck driver to breathe. He only wished that the emergency kit was better stocked, but this had to suffice.

"That should hold it until we can get him to the Kolwezi Mission Hospital," mumbled Lucas.

The patient never moved during the procedure, most likely because he was almost comatose from lack of oxygen. With the release of the obstruction in his airway, he began to take large breaths of air, and revived. The crowd stood silently and then applauded loudly when it was apparent that the driver could now breathe.

"Tell his family that we will take him to the Kolwezi Mission to set his leg and repair the neck," said Lucas to his impromptu lady interpreter. "We'll need help to load him onto the bed of the truck and we'll start for Kolwezi." The lady's interpretation lasted for five minutes; obviously she was taking the opportunity to embellish his request.

The patient was loaded gently onto the truck, but they were unable to leave until every member of the crowd shook their hands and thanked both Angela and Lucas. Iuba was barking loudly inside the truck, but calmed down as Angela drove away. Lucas remained with the driver in the truck bed to insure no slippage of his tracheal tube.

The trip to Kolwezi took a few hours, but the last fifty miles was on a hardtop tar road, making it smoother and faster for the patient.

When they had finally arrived at the mission about eight o'clock that evening, Angela said, "What a day! Attacked in the morning, surgery by daylight and driving in between. I'm ready for a decent meal and a really hot shower after we collect the malaria medicine."

# 15
## Chapter

Their admission to the Kolwezi mission was expedited by the need to treat the injured truck driver and put a permanent tracheotomy in place. Once this was accomplished, an anesthetic could be administered and the broken leg set with a cast placed to insure proper healing. This was done efficiently and accurately by the hospital staff. Lucas and Angela were assigned separate living quarters, as it was a Christian mission and they were not officially married. Both Lucas and Angela, being devout Christians, felt some guilt from their previous associations, but at this time nothing was said about it. Since the administrator was to meet them in the cafeteria in a few minutes, Angela deferred her anxiety to find out about the malaria medication.

"The dog will stay with me," stated Angela to the mission room clerk. "He's had some traumatic experiences recently and will be unhappy without me."

A meal was prepared and Lucas and Angela relaxed in the dining room alone, since the hour was long past suppertime. She brought Iuba along as they walked to the cafeteria, as he had not been fed. Iuba, sensing no danger, behaved himself as a gentle-man and lay under Angela's chair.

As they were finishing their meal, the mission administrator joined them in the dining room. "Good evening, I'm Reverend Wilson. Doctor Stuart and I met on his previous trip to Angola a few months ago. I don't think that I've had the pleasure to meet you, ma'am," he said as he sat down with them at their table.

"Oh, good evening, Reverend Wilson. This is Angela Abercrombe," explained Lucas. "She's a scrub nurse from the Lubalo Mission, and she has decided to spend some time with me in Malawi, due to the rebel war in Angola."

After exchanging pleasantries, Angela asked, "By chance, Reverend Wilson, has a package addressed to Lucas arrived in the past twenty-four hours? It contains some malaria treatment for Lucas, but we don't expect his disease to cycle again for twenty four hours, so it's not terribly urgent."

"Why, yes! You're asking has reminded me. I have it here with me," he said, drawing a small package wrapped in brown paper from his pocket and handing it to Lucas.

"Strange circumstances on its arrival earlier today. A jet fighter plane landed on our runway around three this afternoon. We never had a jet fighter out here before and thought that our little landing strip was too small for a plane of that genre, but I know the Navy only needs a small strip on a carrier."

"Did you happen to notice where it came from?" asked Angela.

"No one mentioned it," responded the minister. "But the insignia on the plane were South African Navy. The pilot never shut his engine off, but the co-pilot in the back seat had an American Navy Captain's eagle on his jacket. He jumped down from the rear of the plane and I only spoke to him for a minute. He was definitely American."

"It had to be Joshua Leadbetter," said Lucas laughing with Angela. "Mercenaries always find a way. Where on earth did he find a pilot and a fighter jet from a South African base? It must have been a friend's plane."

"All he said," continued the confused preacher "was 'Please get this medicine to Doctor Stuart. He'll be along later today.' He got back into that jet and it made a terrible noise as it took off."

"Thank you so much, Reverend," said Lucas as he opened the package and held up the vial of Artemisinin for Angela to see. "This is exactly what we need!"

"We had planned to go on to a Malawi mission hospital. Is there a plane going soon, Reverend?" asked Lucas. "Can you help us?"

"There's no jet due in anytime soon," said the preacher smiling. "But a Beechcraft twin motor will be here in a day or so bringing supplies, and I believe that it will likely be heading on to Rhodesia at some point. I'll see if there's room for a few passengers. He may even be going on to Malawi."

"We'd really appreciate it if we could go with them."

"You two must need some sleep after that trip" concluded Reverend Wilson.

"We thank you for the hospitality, and in the meantime, while we're waiting for the plane trip on to Eastern Africa, please ask if either of us can help in the hospital," said Angela, getting up from the table. Iuba walked slowly from beneath the table, still trusting no one but his mistress and following close behind her. They again thanked Reverend Wilson and agreed to meet again in the morning.

Before they left the dining hall, Angela took the vial from Lucas and said, "This medicine is long overdue. We're going to start the Artemisinin right now."

After she had administered the medication right there as they sat in the dining hall, Angela could finally rest easy knowing that another cycle of chills and fever would not occur. There was still the possibility, however, that Lucas might develop an allergic reaction to the powerful medication.

"Hopefully every sporocyte in my body will be killed and released into my bloodstream in a few hours," remarked Lucas as they walked back to the residents' quarters. "I haven't used that drug often enough to anticipate any reaction," he reassured her.

"But what *could* happen?" asked Angela.

"I only know that many of the guys in Malawi used to get stoned drunk after taking it so that they wouldn't feel the reaction," he replied. "Maybe if you checked on me in a few hours, it would be a good idea."

"How do you feel now?" she asked

"Just a bit warm, otherwise, okay."

"Well then, maybe we need to find some booze!" joked Angela. "I've no concept of you being drunk."

They separated at the entrance to the dormitories, and after a brief kiss, each went to their own residence. Iuba followed Angela into her apartment and found his accustomed spot on the blanket she had placed next to her bed. Angela set her alarm for 3 a. m. "I'd better check on him around then," she thought to herself as she turned out the lights, reaching down and patting Iuba's nose first. "Good boy!" she said before she turned over to sleep.

The soft buzz of the alarm brought Angela awake. She had been in a deep sleep and now sat up on the edge of the bed to clear her mind. She wanted to just go down the hall and check on Lucas. Putting on her sweat suit, she opened the door of her room. Iuba, awake instantly, stood by her side. She whispered gently to him, "Not this time, Iuba. You guard the room and I'll be back in a few minutes."

Walking along the dimly lit hallway, she came to Lucas' room and listened at the door. She could hear nothing, so knocking softly she opened the door and peered inside.

"Is everything okay?" she murmured.

Inside the room, all was quiet except for the soft, even repetition of Lucas' breathing. Her inquiry, soft as it was, brought him immediately and fully awake. Having to take call for many years at various hospitals had conditioned him to awaken quicker than the flick of a cow's tail.

"What's happening?" he responded as he sat up and placed his feet on the floor.

"Not much, Lucas," she said as she entered the room. "I just stopped by to check on you. It's three o'clock. Are you noticing any reaction to the medication yet?"

"Hi, Angie. Glad you came by. I was getting lonely in here by myself."

"No, you weren't. You were sound asleep with no thought of being alone, you dog," she said laughing, as she sat next to him on the bed.

"So far, no reaction to the medicine," he replied. "The stuff must be working, since the third cycle never showed up.

He now began to kiss her softly on the face, moving downward to her neck and then gradually, on to her abdomen and breasts. She began to breathe rapidly.

"Let's make love, Angie, honey," he whispered as they lay back on the narrow bed.

They caressed each other but the constraints of bed space made any movement difficult. Finally, Angela stood up and pulled all of the sheets and blankets to the floor, making a large flat space on which to lie. Angela didn't return to the waiting Iuba until some time later.

At 7:30 the next morning, Lucas and Angela sat in the mission cafeteria at a table, talking over bacon, eggs, and coffee. Iuba lay under Angela's chair, taking tidbits as offered.

"If Reverend Wilson ever finds out about last night, Angie, we'll have to live in town," remarked Lucas. "I hope no one heard us."

"Lucas, I do enjoy lovemaking, but as unmarried Christian medical missionaries, it's not a good example to set, is it?"

Then, putting a fork-full of scrambled egg into her mouth, Angie smiled sweetly and after swallowing, said, "You could always make an honest woman of me, Lucas. Then we wouldn't have to worry about sneaking around."

Trying not to choke on his bacon, Lucas thought quickly and said, "Are you saying that you'd even consider spending the rest of your life with a broken down, old sawbones like me?"

"You'd have to ask to find out if I would," she said as she slopped coffee on the plate in front of her. "Have you lost all of that courage that you show every time you cut a patient in the operating room?"

The discussion was interrupted by a cheery greeting from Reverend Wilson as he approached the table, breakfast-laden tray in hand. "Well, I see that the two of you survived the dormitories last night. Do you mind if I sit with you?"

"Of course you're welcome to eat with us," said Lucas, standing up. He moved a chair to the table for the reverend to sit on. A low, soft growl came from underneath Angela's chair, but with the wave of her hand in front of Iuba's face, it ceased.

"Have you made plans for today?" the reverend asked.

"What news from the Air Mission Transport System?" asked Lucas.

"Yes, early this morning a transmission was received by our office that the supply plane planned to arrive late this afternoon with a shipment. When it does, we can find out where it plans to travel next."

"That's great," answered Angela. "In the meantime, we're at your service."

The reverend finished his breakfast and stated, "As far as I know, the hospital has nothing for you to do right now, Lucas. Both of you could just relax and sight-see around Kolwezi, not that there's much to see here."

"Thanks, we'll do just that. We'll be back for lunch."

After breakfast, the pastor excused himself as he left the table. Lucas and Angela sat for a minute conversing quietly as they finished their coffee. "Now, about what we were discussing before the reverend interrupted us ..." said Angela.

"You know, Angie, if we plan to see Kolwezi we're going to have to have a leash for Iuba," said Lucas laughing.

"Don't change the subject. We were discussing making me an honest woman."

"Come on, honey. You know that we can't do much here. We're miles from civilization and don't have a friend who lives near here. Hadn't you better check on your family in Luanda to see that everyone is okay?"

Angela realized that Lucas was not ready for the discussion on marriage yet, so she decided that maybe it *was* time to check on her family.

"If I can reach the mission safe house in Luanda," she said, "probably, they will be able to tell me if my father and brothers are there. I'll ask the mission office here in Kolwezi if they have a way to contact Luanda."

In a sense Angela was relieved that she didn't have to worry about her mother, who lay sleeping for the last ten years at the Saurimo Mission Cemetery. Had she still been alive, certainly she would have worried about her daughter being halfway across Africa on a trip to Malawi and staying at a remote mission.

"That's a good idea," said Lucas, happy to change the subject to anything but marriage.

Lucas and Angela, with Iuba now on a rope borrowed from the mission kitchen and substituting for a leash, returned to the main office of the Kolwezi mission. After a brief search, the very helpful secretary, Linda, produced the phone number of the Scottish Presbyterian Central Mission office in Luanda.

"Is there a phone here that I can use to speak to Luanda," asked Angela.

"Oh yes," Linda assured her. "It costs twelve American dollars a minute, if we can get the connection, payable in cash before making the call."

"Isn't that a bit steep?" Angela asked.

Linda smiled and said, "That's what it costs us when we're able to call out. Many times, we are unable to even reach Lubumbashi, which is only a hundred miles away."

Lucas came over to Angela and whispered into her ear, "This is in the Congo bush, Angie. Just make the call and I'll pay for it."

The antiquated phone system in the Congo was still from the 1950s and a call was necessary first to the long distance operator, who would take the number and the location being called. She would then disconnect, until the party had been reached. The wait for a connection could be anywhere from five minutes to hours. Many times, the connection was not available for days.

Once she had reached the operator, Angela attempted to give the number that she wanted in Luanda, Angola, to the local Kolwezi operator, who seemed quite pleasant and cooperative. The Kolwezi operator, however, did not speak English, but only the local Congo language, Lunda. The secretary then had to give the long distance operator the number to be called and location in Lunda dialect. This satisfied the local telephone operator, and after confirming the phone number of the Kolwezi mission office to call back, she disconnected.

"Now we just wait to see if a connection can be made," said Linda. "It may take hours before she calls back."

Two hours passed and there was no return call from the international operator. Lucas sat quietly reading some medical journals while Angela was crocheting. As they sat in the office waiting for the return call, Lucas asked Angela, "How did it come about that a Presbyterian mission nurse from Saurimo has been working at the Lubalo Baptist Hospital?"

"No big deal," she answered. "My father is a close friend of Pastor Williamson, and we used to visit Lubalo frequently during my childhood. They were short of surgical nurse assistants in Lubalo, so I volunteered."

Lucas answered, "It's lucky for me that you did."

Finally after waiting patiently in the office, Angela said, "Is it possible to call back to see how they're doing?"

Linda replied, "Yes, they may tell you where your call is in line, but it's only been two hours, so don't be surprised if there are still calls in front of yours. I'll call back and see."

Lifting the receiver, Linda connected to the long distance operator, and was informed that today was a better day than most, and calls seemed to be going through. Their call to Luanda was now third in line, and probably, a connection would be made within the next hour or so.

"In America or England, this would be intolerable," said Lucas. "But for a remote place like Kolwezi, it's fairly good."

After thirty more minutes, the phone in the office rang, and Linda was informed that the call was ready to be made. Gripping the phone to her ear, Angela heard the connection go through the Luanda operator, and after a pause she heard the double ring of the phone in Luanda. The phone in Angola was answered in English, "This is the Scottish Presbyterian Central Mission. Can I help you?"

"Yes, this is Angela Abercrombe, calling from the Kolwezi Mission in the Congo. I wish to find out if Reverend Abercrombe, from the Saurimo Scottish Presbyterian Mission, has arrived there? This is his daughter calling."

"Oh yes," came the reply. "He arrived a few days ago and I believe he is leaving for the United Kingdom tonight."

"Could I speak to him, please?"

"One moment," came the reply.

The voice of her father came over the phone after a few minutes. She felt a rush of relief at the sound of his voice. "Angie? Are you alright? The secretary here said that it was my daughter calling."

Angela had known that the Presbyterian Mission house in Luanda would be the logical first stop of any of the missionaries in the country having to leave suddenly, as did her brothers. Still, she was comforted to speak to her father. He had completed over six-hundred miles through dense jungle and washed-out roads, in the middle of a war, and now sounded safe and happy at the mission house. He confirmed that Jake was fine and that Tad had arrived a few nights before, after traveling by helicopter. Tad was still in bed, but his arm had not been hurting and appeared to be healing nicely. The smile on her face as she received the comforting news informed Lucas, as he heard her side of the conversation, that her whole family was safe. He reached out and kissed her cheek, smiling too.

"Dad, I'm on my way to Malawi with Lucas, a doctor from the Lubalo Mission. We hope to fly in the next few days and I'll call when we arrive. Are you leaving for London tonight?"

"Tad told us about Lucas and the problems at Lubalo, Angie," her father replied. "Yes, the Presbyterian Foreign Mission Board in Glasgow has ordered me back to London. I'm not sure if they'll send me back to Angola soon, or how long I'll stay in Britain. Tad is coming with me tonight, so you can reach us there. Jake seems to want to return to the war to help Savimbi, but I'm trying to convince him to come with us."

"That's great, Dad. You do need the rest, and Tad should have his arm X-rayed again before you leave for London to confirm the break is set properly. Do you know if Reverend Williamson and Becky arrived in Luanda?"

"Funny that you would ask that, Angie," he said with a laugh. "We were walking down the Rua Dierita de Luanda to get supper at the Grand Hotel Universo last night and here comes Hubert and Becky, walking the other way."

"That's quite a coincidence," Angela replied. "Are they okay?"

"We stood there on the street and spoke for a few minutes. Evidently, they had a wild time getting here when the Lubalo Mission was overrun by the rebels and they had to flee. They're at the Baptist Central Mission House and doing well. They're leaving for London or Johannesburg in a day or two."

"I'm glad they're safe and that the three of you are taken care of, Dad. When we get to Malawi, I'll call the Glasgow Mission Board to find out where you're staying. Have a good trip to England! Love to the boys, goodbye."

"We'll look forward to hearing from you in a few days, Angie. 'Bye!"

When Angela hung up the phone, there was a distinct wetness in her eyes, which Lucas saw her wipe away. He knew that she was happy and really missed her family. The relief of hearing that they were all safe had lifted a substantial burden from her mind. "Dad and Jake made it safely to Luanda, as did Tad. Dad and Tad are leaving for London tonight," she related to Lucas. "The Williamsons also are safe for the time being. It's really going to make Dad's life different now that there has to be such a major change. He's not so young and will have to start over again no matter where they send him. With Tad there, he will have fewer problems adapting, but as people grow older, new circumstances are sometimes difficult."

She kissed Lucas and then sat down for a moment just resting, relieved that everyone was safe. Actually she wasn't really surprised, experienced missionaries rarely make mistakes in a crisis that newer ones might make.

After Lucas paid for the call, Angela and Lucas decided to have a look at the rural town of Kolwezi, an isolated mission in a very remote location in a midsized town.

They knew that Lubumbashi, one of the major cities of the southern Congo, was a hundred miles to the east, with a population of around half a million. Kolwezi, with about 100,000 people, remained much more primitive.

"It still will be interesting to look around and see the town, Lucas."

They walked down the main street of Kolwezi, which had originally been paved some twenty-five years ago with hard-top tar and gravel when the highway had been put through to Lubumbashi.. Lack of maintenance and rough use had reduced this road to interval segments of potholed tar and eroding dirt. On either side of the road, the broken, concrete sidewalks had spaces occupied by small merchants peddling anything from tires to food, cooking on small mobile grills. These were stationed some ten feet back from the highway, with signs in Lunda advertising their products.

"Quite a capitalistic effort," noted Lucas as they walked past. "The barbecuing food smells delicious, Angie, but you are well aware of being cautious about eating anything here. While the heating might help make it safer, these peddlers often sell rat meat masquerading as pork or beef."

The small shops lining the main road of the town were almost exclusively owned by merchants of Middle Eastern or Asian heritage who had been living there for generations. Lucas and Angela entered one of these establishments, advertised by a large sign on the front proclaiming "Hassain's Haberdashery." They noted that every square inch of space within the shop was being utilized to display goods for sale.

"If this is supposed to be a haberdashery, Lucas, it means if it were in most countries that they would sell clothes. But it doesn't look much like a clothing store. There are bicycles, hardware and anything else you could think of that a villager might need."

"Yeah, Angie. The store is only about thirty feet deep by twenty wide, and it's like a country general store in America, and nothing sells for more than a few dollars."

"The price tags are only the starting point for haggling," reminded Angela.

They enjoyed looking through the various shops selling many varieties of goods. Some of the vendors specialized in only one or two products, while others demonstrated such a wide selection of merchandise that they only had a few of each type.

"I need a pair of sunglasses," said Lucas "There's a shop across the street that specializes in that area. Let's look there."

As they entered the shop, it was obvious that any conceivable type of eyewear could be purchased at this establishment. As there was no doctor present, it was left to the purchaser to try on the various spectacles and then select the pair that allowed him to see the clearest of the writing on the walls. It was a unique system of eye testing.

"I just need a pair of sunglasses," he said, looking through the selection that ranged in price from a few dollars to three hundred. Lucas selected a polarized pair marked at seventy-five dollars. Knowing the barter system of Africa well, he casually held up the glasses he had selected.

"How much?" he said in English.

"A very fine selection," said the Indian proprietor in poor English. "And it's a bargain at only seventy-five American dollars!"

"That's a reasonable starting price, my friend. I'll give you forty-five for them," responded Lucas.

"Oh no! Those are from Europe with Polaroid lens. I am not able to let them go for a cent less than sixty-eight American dollars!" said the vendor.

And so it went. Nothing in rural Africa had a set price, and he knew that any experienced purchaser must be prepared to spend ten minutes to an hour negotiating the final price if he wants to pay a reasonable sum.

He finally got the glasses for fifty-five dollars, but he was well aware that if he was from Kolwezi and spoke Lunda it would have been considerably less.

Laughing as they walked back to the mission, Angie agreed, "Maybe, say...about thirty dollars or so. Oh well, let's have lunch."

As they walked back towards the mission, Lucas and Angela discussed the unique combination of modern and traditional transportation and dress to be seen in this rural town in the Southern Katanga Province of the Republic of the Congo.

"Now, look at the different means of transportation we can see from this corner," said Angela, as she pulled sharply on Iuba's rope to avoid a large truck from running over his front paws.

"Over there is a donkey cart loaded with yams for sale, and across the street we can see that lad on a bicycle selling sugarcane stalks."

Lucas noticed that the girl selling yams wore a long, brightly colored, cotton dress, obviously made at home. She had a traditional hair style with ornately carved ivory pins to hold the strands of hair in place. Standing barefoot on the hot tar road, she held her yams out to passersby, as she loudly advertised her wares. "Now that boy selling musical CDs and sugarcane next to her is wearing an L.A. Dodgers sweatshirt over his Levi's and new Nike tennis shoes," noted Lucas.

Standing on the street corner, in a matter of just a few minutes they watched a new Mercedes-Benz convertible pass by, followed by a man pushing a handcart full of cheap pots and pans. It was Saturday morning and the traffic was busy, as shoppers appeared to rush to finish shopping before the shops and vendors closed at noon.

Angela explained to Lucas that here, as in most of Southern Africa, all stores and shops close on Saturday at noon for the weekend, so everyone hurries from eight until noon to finish their purchases. "Saturday afternoon, for the wealthier city people, is for soccer games, horse racing, or social tennis matches and golf," she said.

"So what do the poorer, rural people do on Saturday afternoons and evenings?" inquired Lucas.

"Not always the same, Often, they just rest or procreate. Their opaque beer has extremely high alcohol content and dancing or celebrating with friends at the local beer garden helps to pass the time. This is usually associated with various stages of intoxication."

"Do the races mix or are they separated in this area?" he continued to inquire.

"Here, there has never been legal apartheid, but certain customs have prevailed. I would say that separation is more on the basis of finances and education, as it is in the rest of the third world," Angela answered.

Lucas thought for a moment and concluded that Malawi *was* similar to Angola and the Congo, but the European colonizers in all of the African countries remained mostly in the top echelon of the social and economic strata until the country gained its freedom. He also felt that now another class has developed; the expatriates who have come to Africa with certain skills, like doctors, administrators, and engineers. They often form a separate class based on education, unrelated to finances, social status, or color. This class, while growing, really never becomes part of the population, as they leave when their services are finished. In apartheid countries, like South Africa and Rhodesia, the races are separated by law, producing class based on color of skin.

In his thoughts, he concluded that this is the situation all over Eastern Africa, where, even if they've spent twenty years here, these people are usually financed from outside the country and remain socially connected to their own friends and workers from their country of origin. "Here we are back at the Baptist mission."

It was time for the midday meal and they made their way to the cafeteria, which was serving the standard cornmeal mash with gravy and bread. Many of the mission employees, both black and white, were sitting in the dining room. After Lucas and Angela had passed through the cafeteria-style line, a Congolese mission nurse came and sat with them.

"My name is Sister Phoebe. I believe you are Doctor Lucas," she said with a broad smile, placing her tray on their table.

"That's right," said Lucas, standing to hold her chair. "Please sit with us. How did you acquire that beautiful English accent in this remote corner of the Congo?"

"Thank you. I was trained in England and had to learn the language there." Without a pause, Sister Phoebe continued, "We seem to have a small medical problem, and I thought since you were here, perhaps you might help."

"I'll be happy to try. This is Sister Angela, and she is traveling with me back to Malawi. What can we do to help you?"

"Recently, we have seen a growing number of patients with certain skin conditions. They seem healthy enough, but the skin on their arms, legs, and body is scaly. Also, their tongues are white, as well as changes in the mucosa of their mouth or vagina."

"That's interesting," said Lucas. "Are there any other findings?"

"Well, in some of the patients, there seems to be a loss of coordination and inability to walk, with joint pain and loss of appetite."

"Hmmm...." replied Lucas

"And what percentage have diarrhea?" asked Angela

"Funny you'd ask that," replied Phoebe. "Many of these people *do* have diarrhea."

Lucas started laughing, following Angela's train of thought, "No flies on Angie today!" he said. "Perhaps we should have a look at some of these patients before giving an opinion, Phoebe. Are you through eating?"

They gathered up their trays and followed the inquiring nurse into the clinic and on to the medical ward. The ward was a typical mission hospital room with clean white walls and twenty beds neatly placed in two rows lining the walls. Every bed was occupied by a patient, the medical problems mixed but only male patients in this ward.

"It's apparent that the dermatitis is photosensitive, as you can see the rash on the skin where it's not covered by clothes," remarked Lucas, as he carefully examined the first patient that Phoebe introduced to them.

"The rash is sharply demarcated to hands, back of the neck and face. It appears to be associated with some bruising, scaling and there are vesicles that are easily felt by running your fingers lightly over the skin." Lucas demonstrated this to Phoebe, who immediately ran her fingers over the patient's skin.

"Yes, I can feel the vesicles, even though they're not visible," she agreed.

Angela asked Phoebe, "May I ask the patient how often he's had the diarrhea in the past week?"

"He says that it comes intermittently," answered Phoebe after inquiring from him in Lunda. "He's also having problems swallowing."

"Let's get him up and see how well he walks," suggested Lucas.

The patient was able to stand, but his gait was halted and he staggered after a few steps, grabbing onto the bed to steady himself.

"He also is showing some neurological involvement," said Lucas. "Ask him how long this unsteady gait has been bothering him."

Through her interpretation, Phoebe was able to relate that the unsteady gait had been present for a few weeks.

Lucas looked at Angela and smiled, saying, "So you already have the diagnosis, I'll wager? The question about diarrhea tells me that you're way ahead of me."

"Only a guess, Doctor Lucas, but I imagine some niacin in his diet will likely solve the problem after a few days."

"Right on, Phoebe, Pellagra is common in poorer people whose diet is restricted to cornmeal and is low in vitamins and meat. In Angola, the problem is common and I see that you're familiar with it too, Angie. It's rarer here where the soil is better and the diet varied."

A brief discussion with Phoebe on modification of diet enlightened the nurse's mind and she made a note on the patient's chart to begin vitamin therapy. This disease is widespread all over the Southern African continent so Lucas and Angela had seen it in many places, but this problem was not as common in the southern Congo where the diet is better and the people mostly get the vitamins they need.

"In a few days, his condition and those with similar signs should be markedly improved. If we're still here, we can check on them."

It was now early afternoon, and a message came to them that Reverend Wilson had invited them for supper that evening.

"Is an evening invitation to supper a formal event?" inquired Angela. "Should I get all dressed up, or what will be expected?"

Lucas laughed about her typical woman's anxiety over dinner attire. "This is an African mission, Angie. Wear something informal and simple, so as not to embarrass Reverend Wilson's wife. I'm sure she's an extremely relaxed lady. I'll wear a shirt and cotton pants."

At seven o'clock that evening, Angela and Lucas walked over to the unpretentious, one story, concrete-block house surrounded by a simple but large flower and vegetable garden. Reverend Wilson's name was on a sign at the driveway. On the porch, on a swing supported by chains, Reverend Wilson sat with a pleasant-looking older, rotund, grey-haired lady. She had her hair in a simple bun and wore an unadorned cotton dress.

Lucas thought as they walked up the path to the house, "Mrs. Wilson looks like every kid's idea of what he would expect his grandmother to look like."

"A pleasant evening to you, Reverend," Lucas greeted them as they climbed the steps to the porch. "Angie and I were happily surprised to receive your invitation to supper."

Standing as Angela gained the top step to the porch, Reverend Wilson smiled and said, "We're so glad you could come on short notice. This is my wife, Agatha. Won't you come inside?"

The house was the same as the Wilsons themselves, simple, clean, relaxed and pleasant. The overpowering aroma of freshly baked bread permeated the living room as it drifted in from the kitchen. There was no sophistication here, compared to the Williamson's mansion at Lubalo. Having taken a comfortable seat on the overstuffed couch, the discussion between the four revolved around their recent trip from Angola and Lucas' and Angela's plans to return to Malawi. After ten minutes, a pleasant black lady appeared at the dining room door to announce dinner.

"Please come into the dining room," announced the black cook. "Dinner is served."

Dinner was simple and delicious, with the freshly baked bread in a basket beside each plate. The wholesome portions of the meal of beef and vegetables were prepared without any elaborate flourishes.

"I can't remember a more tasty meal, Mrs. Wilson," remarked Angela as they got up from their chairs and returned to the living room. "Thank you so much."

As they were sitting talking after the supper, a sharp knock came from the front screen door. A black boy, around the age of eight, handed a message to Reverend Wilson and then, after bowing to each person, left.

"We have received a radio cipher from the pilot of your airplane, stating that he will arrive here in Kolwezi later this evening. I expect that you will want to be leaving tomorrow morning. I'll talk to the pilot and see about arrangements for your trip."

After a pleasant evening with the Wilsons, Angela and Lucas decided to take Iuba for a walk before returning to their dormitories. They enjoyed a leisurely stroll, arm in arm, around the darkened mission station with Iuba investigating every nook.

"You know, Lucas, a lot has happened in the past few weeks. We've been held captive, organized an entire hospital in the middle of a war zone, found my family and seen that they got to safety. We've tried to treat numerous patients with anything from bullet wounds to natives with Ebola virus and snakebite."

"Yes, Angie, honey, not to mention sending an agent of the English government, Sir William, and an ambassador's daughter to Luanda. Heck, you probably saved my life when I had malaria. We really did it all together."

"Now we're about to go to East Africa and fulfill your contract in Malawi," continued Angela. "What does it all mean? Where does the Lord want us to settle, and what are our long term goals?"

"As I see it, Angie, there's no map set out for anyone's life that they can see ahead of time, so we must just push on doing our duty as we see it from day to day. We pray for guidance along the path of life and proceed with our lives, succeeding sometimes and failing often. If we want to be together, as each challenge confronts us, perhaps we should consider getting married. You already know that I love you, Angie"

"If that's a proposal of marriage, you'd better get down on one knee!" Angela replied with a giggle, letting go of his hand.

"Yes, it's a proposal, Angie" said Lucas, as he got down on one knee and tried desperately to keep a somber face, but failing, broke into a huge smile.

"Will you marry me when we get to Malawi?"

Angie took Lucas tenderly by the neck and kissed him gently on the mouth. Then, she whispered into his ear, "Yes, I love you too, and I'll marry you once we're organized in Malawi. Now, it's late, and Iuba needs his rest, so we're off to our dormitory. Good night, my love."

"But I don't have a ring!" exclaimed Lucas.

"Details, mere details," called back Angela over her shoulder, as she and Iuba headed for their quarters. "A hazard of being a bush missionary doctor's wife. Go to bed."

The next morning at breakfast, Angela and Lucas met the bush pilot. He was in his early sixties and a retired commercial pilot with many years' experience flying charter planes for Southeastern African missions.

"My name is Chauncy O'Sullivan," he introduced himself, "and I believe you're planning to fly with me to the Sanyati Mission in Rhodesia later this morning. We leave at eleven sharp, so be sure you're packed."

# 16
## Chapter

The monotonous drone of the two engines as they propelled the Beechcraft airplane through the clear, cloudless sky over Zambia made Lucas and Angela sleepy. Iuba lay on the floor of the plane, trying to keep his eyes from closing as the pilot steered the well-appointed aircraft by sight, rather than by homing beam. Africa sparkled in all of its emerald glory as they watched the rivers and lakes glistening below in the bright sunlight. They were approaching Eastern Africa as they were leaving the Congo Republic, crossing Zambia and entering Rhodesian airspace.

"It's really beautiful in the rainy season," observed Lucas. "Everything appears so green and prosperous from this height."

"Yes, you can't see the poverty and disease from up here," replied Angela. "You have to actually be among the natives to really appreciate *those* qualities."

Turning in his seat at the front of the aircraft, the pilot, Chauncey O'Sullivan, grinned widely and remarked, "I see we have no tenderfoot missionaries aboard. Most of these new enthusiastic missionaries we see coming to *save* the continent never have a clue as to what 'Mother Africa' is going to deal them."

At Angela's request, Chauncey flew the plane lower for a few minutes so that they could watch the massive herds of wildebeest as they stampeded across the grassy plain in fear of the noisy plane as it passed.

"Are you only going as far as Sanyati Mission on this trip?" Chauncey asked, watching the landing field as he banked the plane over a group of one-story buildings and made a low pass above the landing field to clear off the antelope and wild hogs that had been peacefully grazing there.

"No, we're on our way back to the Shire Valley in Malawi. Do you know the Nsanje Mission?" asked Lucas.

"Sure do! It's the worst landing strip in the country, no grass, lots of rocks and those dang birds everywhere. Monkey Bay is much nicer, with a concrete strip and a central tower."

"Sounds as if you *have* been to Nsanje." laughed Lucas.

After landing, the plane taxied up to a metal Quonset hut with a sock above it, blowing in the wind. Chauncey cut the engines as the plane rolled to a stop. There was a tattered, wooden sign hanging at an angle below the sock that read:

### Sanyati Baptist Mission

### Sanyati, Rhodesia

"So here we are in the middle of guerrilla war territory," mentioned Chauncey. "I guess you've heard and read about the ten year war going on here?"

He went on to explain that a ferocious conflict had been going on since the Ian Smith government refused to turn the country over to the black majority when the British Colonialists pulled out in 1964. This action left the white settlers of Rhodesia to try to govern themselves independently of Britain. On one hand, it had resulted in an extremely prosperous country. Rhodesia, which they knew exports more food than any country on the African continent, had prospered but the war raged on by some of the indigenous to give the country back to native rule. Chauncey had been involved in these food and supply exports to Zambia or Malawi and other countries for years, despite sanctions against Rhodesia by many of the European countries and America.

Angela had read that there was total apartheid by law here in Rhodesia, and the law is supposedly strictly enforced. However, there was no starvation and almost no unemployment among the blacks. "Is freedom more important than a full belly?" she wondered out loud.

They walked from the plane into the hangar, and Chauncey immediately greeted a tall, thin man in his early thirties, wearing a brown uniform. No insignia or rank was visible, but a casual glance by Lucas and he knew this was a formidable soldier. Iuba made no sound, but promptly showed his teeth and moved next to Angela.

"Hello, Sean! It's been a few months since I've run into you. Have you been ill?"

"Hi, Chauncey!" the tall Rhodesian said, shaking his hand enthusiastically. "No, I've been off in the bush doing my National Service duties and fighting 'terrorists' for the last few months. How've you been?"

"This is Sean Handley," said Chauncey introducing the Rhodesian.

After the introductions, all four adults sat around an informal card table, pouring Fanta or Castle Beer from brown bottles into glasses supplied by the airstrip personnel. It was totally spontaneous, and Lucas and Angela began to realize why the Rhodesians had such a widespread reputation for friendliness and hospitality. Even Iuba seemed to relax after a while.

"Say, Sean, I'd better anchor my plane and fill the tanks, before I'm so soused I can't do it," the pilot said after three or four beers.

"Forget it, Chauncey. The *houtie* already did it and he'll roll the plane into the hangar before nightfall."

The easygoing conversation continued for the next hour. No one seemed in a rush to leave the airstrip or to find lodgings. Shortly after four o'clock, with no notice given, an African lady appeared at the doorway with a tray. On the tray, neatly arranged, were four cups, a large teapot, and a plate piled with freshly baked soft buns and jam. "Tea is served, sir," she said as she set the sumptuously prepared tray on the table.

The arrival of the servant never interrupted Sean's train of thought. Glancing up for a split second, Sean nodded to the lady and said, "Thank you, Lucy," and then resumed his conversation. It was obvious to both Lucas and Angela that the arrival of the tray by a servant was expected here at this time of day.

"Help yourselves," he said as he passed the plate bearing the buns and jam around to each person at the table. He looked expectantly at Angela. She smiled, and remarked,

"Since I have lived in Africa all of my life, I know that as the only lady present it's customary that I be the 'mother' and pour the tea."

Taking the cups individually, Angela poured the steaming liquid from the pot, inquiring from each cup owner as to his preference for sugar, honey, or milk. Last, she poured her own as the men waited to drink. When all had been served, Sean lifted his cup and proclaimed, "To Rhodesia, may she remain strong and independent!"

The conversation continued for a half hour or so until finally Sean said, "It's getting on toward sundowner time, so we'd better get you a place to stay and to get cleaned up. This may be a Baptist mission, but we don't let that interfere with Rhodesian hospitality. Chauncey, you and Lucas can stay with me at my house, as usual. I'll ask Lucy to find a room for Angela."

Looking at Angie, he asked, "Do you mind staying in the white nurses' quarters? It's next to our house and the dog is welcome, if he's house-trained."

Angela laughed, "He's trained alright, and that arrangement will be super. We just need to find a place that Iuba can get in and out unmolested. He sometimes gets a little cranky if he feels his access is restricted."

They left the landing field and all four walked down the path to the mission together.

The evening was spent with Sean. His girlfriend had left with a convoy for Drifontaine Catholic Mission that morning, some sixty miles away. As guerrilla terrorists were overrunning the bush, it was not safe to drive through the bush without a military escort. She was expected back late the next morning when that convey returned.

During the course of the evening's discussions at the sundowner and supper, Lucas asked, "How long will you be here in Rhodesia, Chauncey? Do you plan to go on to Malawi soon?"

Working seriously on his third glass of Glenlivet whisky, he replied, "Well my boy, I am scheduled to leave in a few days for the Mount Darwin area, in the north of Rhodesia. There's a Baptist mission in Chironga that needs some supplies and seems to be having some problems with the 'terrs. After that stop, we can fly from there over Zumbo to Blantyre, Malawi. Hey, but there's no hurry. We can fly any time this week. Why?"

Taking a deep breath, Lucas replied, "Well, we have to register our passports with the immigration officials in Salisbury, and pick up some medical supplies. I have some personal business, too. Is there a good jewelry store in town?"

At this remark, Angela broke into a smile and kissed Lucas lightly on the cheek. Seeing this, Sean started laughing and said, "I see…it's that way, then! On Jameson Avenue, there are a few of the better stores that carry wedding rings and custom-made diamonds. You'll be able to get anything you want there."

Everyone congratulated Angela and Lucas on their engagement, but Angela insisted that there was to be no celebration until she had the ring on her finger. "Who knows?" she laughed. "He may change his mind before then."

Sean offered the use of his truck to travel with the army convoy leaving Sanyati at 9:30 the next morning for Salisbury, the capital of Rhodesia and its largest city. When Chauncey volunteered to go with Lucas and Angela, Sean said, "What the heck, I've got nothing else to do and my girlfriend won't be back until late tomorrow morning. We can all ride in my truck together."

No one got to bed early that night, but all four were fresh and ready for the trip in the morning. As they stood in front of the

Sanyati Mission by the road leading to Salisbury, Angela asked Sean, "Is this a usual event if anyone wants to travel through the bush in Rhodesia?"

Sean smiled and replied, "Angela, this guerilla war has been going in some degree since 1964. Only since 1972 has it intensified enough that travel by individual vehicles has become dangerous enough to warrant the formation of armed convoy travel. Landmines are planted in the roads by the rebels and often individual autos and trucks are ambushed by rebel groups, sometimes numbering up to twenty or thirty."

"Gosh, Sean, how do the crops and farmers get to market? Rhodesia's economy is dependent on exportation of agricultural products, isn't it?" asked Lucas.

Sean explained that they had developed a system of armed convoys that travel on set days to certain main locations throughout the country. These consist of an armed Hippo vehicle with mine detectors leading the convoy. The rural white residents travel in heavily armed trucks, some with fifty caliber machine guns and rocket launchers, but still, incidents occur. While airplane transport is a possible alternative, it is very expensive and loads are limited. Since all white males between the ages of eighteen and seventy are members of the armed forces, well accustomed to combat, the guerilla bands have less chance to do damage to convoys and are often destroyed."

"That's a difficult way to live," remarked Chauncey. "I'll stick to airplanes, if possible, as a safer way to travel."

By now, a collection of various vehicles had gathered at the departure point. Lucas counted some fifteen cars and trucks parked by the side of the road. Two buses filled with civilian Africans and a large lorry loaded with cotton bales also stood in line, waiting for the arrival of the army "hippo" to lead the motorcade.

"It's amazing," Lucas remarked. "It's almost like a social event. Everyone knows everyone, blacks and whites alike, and they all stand and converse as if nothing unusual is going to happen. I thought the blacks were in revolt, but most of the African men are armed to the teeth and prepared to defend the convoy."

Sean was talking to a lanky black male, who looked to be in his mid-twenties, with an AK-47 over his shoulder.

"This is Prosperous Makiewa, Lucas. He is the Sergeant Major of our Sanyati Unit of the Rhodesian Police and is traveling with us to Salisbury today."

Prosperous was dressed in Army fatigues, with the stripes of a sergeant major on his sleeve. The gold stripes on the arm indicated that he had been decorated for bravery more than once, and he spoke clearly in perfect English. The amazing thing about the Rhodesian war was that blacks and whites fought side by side despite apartheid.

He introduced himself and then said, "Much of the Rhodesian army is composed of Africans who enjoy the affluence of Rhodesia and understand that majority rule will result in abject poverty for the entire African population. Socialist or communist dictatorships have destroyed many other African countries."

As he was speaking, a large truck with a V-shaped body arrived at the roadside. Inside the truck were well-armed police of both races. On top of the canvas-covered truck sat an African soldier, controlling a large cannon mounted on top of the cab. Mortars were set on the tailgate, ready to do business if the need should arise.

An elderly white captain alighted from the driver's side and was greeted warmly by everyone. He appeared to know almost every traveler personally by name, as well as their family members. He spoke slowly and clearly in English.

He explained about the organization of the convoy that morning. "Okay, we need to get coordinated before we start. The trip will take five or six hours and we will not stop except at towns, so use the bathroom now if you need to," he said with a friendly smile after being introduced to Lucas, Angela and Chauncey. "Each vehicle will get a number in line according to available arms and personnel. Odd numbers disperse to the left of the road and even numbers to the right if we're attacked. This likely will not happen as there are a large number of people and we appear to be well armed."

"The Rhodesian war is so different from Angola," remarked Angela. "Here, the rebels have no organized army but only a series of independent guerilla bands of ten or fifteen men, scattered throughout the countryside making raids. In Angola, there is an organized rebel army."

Sean explained that it was because an organized rebel army would be defeated in a week in Rhodesia. Most of the rebels trained and organized in neighboring Zambia or Mozambique, and then crossed into Rhodesia to cause trouble.

"I understand," said Lucas. "No organized army means no actual war, but a series of raids on farmers and the population, undermining the economy from within. These are terrorists' tactics, because they're too disorganized to fight an actual war."

The individual cars and trucks began to line up in the order of the numbers they had been issued. The "hippo" led off, driving at a moderate pace down the dirt road, followed by a truck with multiple rocket launchers. The others in the convoy followed at a distance, with a few car lengths between. Iuba sat quietly in the back of the truck.

"For the next hundred miles, out here in the bush, landmines are the biggest problem," said Sean as they got in line in the number seven slot. "This convoy is armed to the teeth with many men, and the result of an actual guerilla ambush would devastate any terrorist raiding party."

"And after we finally get to the tar road?" asked Angela.

"From Gatooma, we will be on hardtop roads, patrolled by the army with shortwave radios. They can call in helicopter or jet defenses with napalm from Salisbury in a few minutes. The terrorists learned long ago that initiating raids on the main roads amounts to suicide."

As they drove through the peaceful countryside, they saw widely separated small groups of grass-thatched mud huts gathered into *chikwata imba*. Lucas said, "You know, it looks so tranquil, with the gatherings of five to ten huts and small plots of land under cultivation. Seeing the farmers working their crops with those *badzas*, you'd never know there was a major war going on."

"Yes, but the guerrillas have to lie up at night and eat. Those 'peaceful natives' that you're admiring are providing shelter and sustenance for the rebels every day."

The long line of cars and trucks progressed at a relatively fast pace for about two hours. A cloud of dust rose from the dry dirt road, making vision difficult as they drove past the tall grass and flat-topped trees. The convoy had completed almost the entire hundred miles to Gatooma when they came to a sudden halt. "We can't see anything up front with this dense dust," said Sean, "But I don't hear any gunfire."

As they looked through the settling dust cloud, a passenger from the car in front of them left the car and came back to their vehicle. Sean rolled down the window and a gust of hot air, carrying dust and extremely dry warmth, hit him in the face. The passenger was breathing hard, and said, "We're being delayed. Part of the road has collapsed. It may be a trick of the terrorists, so stay in your truck. Pass the word on back."

Sean rolled the window back up and grasped his rifle from between the seats as he prepared to inform the truck behind him. "It's an old trick to blow up the road so the traffic has to stop and the guerrillas can attack the stalled line of cars," he said. "Be ready to head for the ditch on the left side of the road with your firearm at the first sound of gunfire."

Sean opened the car door and, clutching his rifle to his chest, he proceeded in a low, crouching, position, darting to the rear and using their truck and then the following truck as a shield from a possible attack. No gunfire was heard, and in a short time he returned to the truck.

"The Robinson family is in the truck behind us. They're maize farmers from Hozheri, on their way to Salisbury. They will inform the car behind them and so on to the back of the line."

After a five-minute wait, a loud report from the cannon on top of the "hippo" vehicle at the front of the convoy informed the rest of the travelers that a guerilla unit had been spotted. The fact that there was no subsequent rifle fire suggested that the guerillas had observed the convoy and had decided that the convoy was too well protected to attack and had probably melted back into the bush.

"Here we go!" remarked Sean as the car in front of him began to move. He followed at a few car lengths' distance. They picked up speed rapidly and were soon traveling at forty miles an hour, closely followed by the Robinson's truck. As they passed the area where the road had been blown up, the wreckage of a native cart could be observed where it had been pushed to the side of the road. A large crater in the road bed marked where the land mine had been planted.

"Ahh, the reinforcements!" announced Chauncey, as the sound of helicopters could be heard rapidly approaching from a distance. "They'll have rockets and will look for the guerrillas from the air. The Hippo must have called in the rapid response team when they saw them and that's why the 'terrs broke off their attack."

The convoy now was approaching the outskirts of a fair sized rural town. Running through the center of the town was a main paved road, lined by shops and gas stations. It was around noon and the streets were busy with automobiles and trucks occupied by people going about their business. No one seemed concerned about the raid that had just occurred a few miles outside of the city. Their confidence in the armed forces to control the situation had been cemented many months ago when the war started.

"Listen to that rocket-fire!" announced Sean, as they drove along the crowded hardtop road that divided the town of Gatooma. "Those helicopters must have found the guerillas and are giving them a headache."

The convoy came to a complete halt in the center of the town to allow those going no farther to get out of line, new arrivals to get into the convoy, and a brief break for the passengers.

Rhodesia was at the height of its prosperity at this time, despite economic sanctions in place from around the world. These sanctions were now bypassed by the underground purchase of their tobacco, maize, cotton and peanuts, as well as chromium and coal in exchange for arms, ammunition and foreign products of all sorts. The stores' shelves, even in a small rural town like this, were fully stocked with provisions and even some luxuries. The thought that "nothing moves without petrol" was valid, but South Africa's regime had continued to support the Ian Smith government fully, and with the importation of these products, it allowed the farming to thrive and transportation to remain unhindered. The guerilla attacks, still causing disruptions, were fought off by the well-armed farmers co-operating with each other.

Lucas and Angela decided to take a few minutes to look around the shops. After walking, Iuba was confined to the truck. On entering a small department store, they were stopped and searched for possible explosives. This involved a brief delay and was done by a polite police officer, after an explanation that some of the stores had been bombed recently by terrorists leaving packages inside the store.

"The search might make me nervous while shopping here," said Angela as they walked leisurely around the counters. "But no one here seems to mind the inconvenience and the inspection seems routine for the other shoppers."

The assortment of products amazed both Angela and Lucas. Clothes and tools from around the world were displayed for purchase, including many from America and Europe.

"The high prices prohibit the common person from shopping here, but I've never seen this diverse selection in Angola," remarked Angela as she inspected a cashmere sweater from France.

"If you notice, most of the shoppers are non-blacks, Angela. They appear well dressed, speaking English, rather than Shona," observed Lucas. "Evan Malawi doesn't have these things. People come to Rhodesia from Blantyre and Lilongwe to shop or to have medical treatments, but only the wealthy can afford it."

Having finished their perusal, they returned to the convoy as it was preparing to leave for Salisbury. "This will go much faster. All of the rest of the way is on tar roads with a military escort," remarked Sean as he climbed into the driver's seat and secured his seatbelt.

The trip over the last sixty miles was as rapid and uneventful as Sean had predicted. The dense, bright purple flowers blooming on the massive jacaranda trees that grew around the shrubbery highlighted their arrival at Cecil Square, in the center of Salisbury. They were now in full bloom, marking Rhodesia's spring season in October. The peaceful traffic in the streets seemed far removed from the bloody war going on in the bush. All of the stores appeared to be open for business and the clean streets were bustling with both black and white shoppers, all of whom were mulling through the crowded shops. Mercedes-Benzes and other luxury cars were commonly seen, both being driven and parked along the wide avenues. There were no armed soldiers patrolling the streets, but both men and women seemed to carry a sidearm in full view.

"Look at that hotel!" exclaimed Lucas as he alighted from the truck.

The large letters on the two white towers gleaming in the African sun proclaimed that this was the Meikles Hotel, landmark of the Salisbury skyline. It was directly adjoining the central square. Many vendors displayed fresh flowers and hand-carved artworks. Opposite the hotel, on the other side of the square, rose the granite edifice of the Anglican Cathedral, rock solid in its influence of the English colonization of Rhodesia in the late nineteenth century.

"This is supposed to be a small African country at war, in its final stages of penury?" asked Angela. "I see no signs of it here. This is much more prosperous than Luanda in its wildest dreams."

Sean smiled and said, "Capitalism at its full bloom, Angie. Let's see if we can find the immigration office before it closes at 4:30."

The walk down Jameson Avenue revealed more goods for sale, as the Bata Shoe Shop window displayed a large selection of footwear for both men and women in the latest fashions. Other shops displayed men's suits and women's dresses, as well as books and furniture. There was even a Wimpie's Hamburger store, with tables and chairs outside on the busy sidewalk.

"This is amazing, Sean," exclaimed Angela. "It's almost like Johannesburg, not like Central Africa at all."

The Immigration Office was open, and after a short wait, all passports were stamped and approved. As they walked along Selous Avenue, Angela asked Sean, "I don't see any supermarkets or food stores. Where do people shop?"

"First, we'd better get checked into the hotel, then we can tour the town," said Sean. "We've been invited to supper tonight near Borrowdale, and on the way I'll show you the suburbs."

"That's good," remarked Lucas. "We still need to stop for some medical equipment and there was one other place we have to stop. I just can't remember where…."

"You'd better remember! I'll assist your failing memory," joked Angela.

They entered the front door of Meikles Hotel, as the uniformed doorman held the door and warmly greeted them. They now stood in a large entrance hall with an open restaurant on the right, for fifty years a well-known meeting place for white Salisbury residents. On the left was a large registration desk with a smiling white lady behind it. She said to Sean, "Good afternoon, Mr. Handley. We have the rooms reserved that you requested." Looking over to Chauncey, Lucas and Angela, the receptionist asked, "Would you like to sign in please?"

The formalities having been completed, a uniformed bellman conducted the guests and their luggage to the luxurious rooms on the tenth floor. There was a moment when the hotel manager had to be consulted about Iuba's residence in the hotel, but after assurances as to his manners, it was decided that he was accepted if he remained on the outside porch of the room.

"Heck, these accommodations equal anything I've ever seen in Africa," remarked Lucas. "I should have been staying here before when I came to Salisbury instead of the old Monomatapa Hotel where I usually stay. Even Iuba has been accepted on condition of good behavior and house training."

Having enjoyed a hot shower and some relaxation, the three travelers gathered in the tea lounge around a table on the ground floor of Meikles to await Sean, who was scheduled to arrive at six that evening. He had gone to visit relatives living near the town center, where he was staying. Iuba had elected to spend the evening asleep on the bed, ignoring the rules.

"We can drive around the northern suburbs on the way to Doctor Burns' house, our host for supper, so you can see how the wealthy Rhodesians get by," said Sean as they boarded his truck.

"How are you employed here?" asked Angela as they drove up Second Street, passing the large, new Andrew Flemming General Hospital on the left.

"I'm in the tobacco business, as a go-between for the European companies and the Rhodesian Government," Sean replied. "International sanctions have sometimes made it difficult for these companies to purchase tobacco or other products directly from Rhodesia, so my job is to be a middle man to facilitate transfers of the funds for the product. However, as is every Rhodesian citizen, I am required to spend at least two months a year in the military, where I am in a 'special forces' unit."

As they drove north, Lucas noticed an extremely well-kept golf course on the right side of the road, with dark emerald fairways and greens. "You have a golf course here too?" he asked.

"That's the Royal Salisbury Golf Course over there," said Sean. "The professional golfer Nicky Price, learned to play golf on that course. It's one of the highest rated courses in the world."

"Do the locals play there?" questioned Angela.

Sean paused for a minute before answering, turning right and passing a large university campus on the left side of the road. "That's the University of Rhodesia," he remarked. "Their Godfrey Huggins Medical School graduates are recognized by England and the rest of the world as producing highly trained doctors."

Then, he said, "Angela, Rhodesia, as you know, is a total apartheid country. We have some of the finest hotels, sports facilities and schools in the world, primarily because they were conceived and financed by the colonial powers. None of the clubs, hotels, restaurants, or schools is integrated at this time, but if apartheid is ever abolished, they will still be here for integrated use. Our neighbors, the Malawi, Zaire and Botswana governments have all been taken over by the indigenous population and thus suffer because nothing was ever built to a high standard."

"Yes, but what about African people living here?" returned Angela.

"Good question," replied Sean. "The white Ian Smith government took over the country in 1964 to prevent indigenous rule, and in that respect is successful, but it can't last. Sanctions by the rest of the world's governments are slowly strangling the economy here. The sad thing is that, while the African population does have work and enough food to eat, they have no say about their government."

Chauncey, rubbing his chin thoughtfully, finally came into the discussion. He remarked that the society here is similar to every other third world country. There is a very small upper class and the mass of the population are terribly poor. In this type of situation, the lack of a middle class is solidified by apartheid, leaving little or no chance for the lower black classes to climb as they are denied education and access to financial resources. If apartheid were dissolved, the situation would become fluid, with improvement in class based on merit rather than color.

By now, they were driving along Borrowdale Road, a lighted, four-lane highway bordered on the right by spacious park with grass and trees.

"That looks like a racetrack." remarked Lucas as he observed the track and stands as they passed.

"Yes," continued Sean. "Horse racing is a very popular pastime here and one place that is totally integrated in the stands. The Jockey Club, however, only admits whites, so the horses are exclusively owned by them."

As they continued along the road, a large shopping center came into view. The evening was now approaching, but they stopped long enough to go in to a large supermarket with a red "T M" on the front.

"This is one of the major supermarket chains here in Rhodesia," Sean remarked as they entered the store. "It's similar to the ones in Johannesburg, but the fresh products are usually from Rhodesia. Have a look around."

In form and layout, the store was similar to any other supermarket, except that the food was African. Almost any food item they could imagine could be purchased there. After a short look around, Sean said, "We'd better be on our way to Doctor Burns' house or we'll be late for dinner."

The drive was only a few short few miles from the Borrowdale Shopping Center, and they arrived at the doctor's home punctually at seven. Surrounding the house and property was a high fence, made of concrete block and topped by barbed wire. This type of enclosure appeared to be the custom, as evidenced by every other house in the neighborhood.

"Why the fence?" asked Lucas as they arrived at the gate and waited for the African gardener to open the main entryway.

"It's the custom in the English colonies all over the world; first, to preserve privacy, and second, to prevent break-ins. Many of the homes have dogs running loose inside the fences, as it's quite common for attempts to break into the homes if they're not protected."

The garden inside the gate was amazing. The lawn was immaculately groomed with fruit trees distributed around the five acre grounds. Flowerbeds containing roses and bushes of other types abounded and the long, curved driveway passed immaculately maintained tennis courts.

"So glad you could come!" said Doctor Burns as he met the four guests at the front door.

Sean introduced Chauncey, Angela, and Lucas to their host and they walked through the house to a substantial back porch overlooking the expansive swimming pool at the back of the house. Sitting in a wicker chair, in the cool air of the gathering dusk was a lady in her late fifties, dressed in casual clothes with short, grey hair and glasses. Lucas thought, as he greeted her, that she certainly must have been beautiful in her twenties, and now appeared distinguished with those reading glasses halfway down her nose.

She looked up from the book that was nestled in her lap, and was introduced as she came to her feet.

"This is my wife, Sarah," said the doctor.

"We were so glad that you could come this evening." Sarah greeted them.

"Oh, hello, Sean. It's good to see you again," said the now-standing hostess.

"Please, if all of you will have a seat, supper will be here in a few minutes."

Looking out over the pristine garden and grounds as they sat talking, Lucas wondered if this standard of living prevailed in the Salisbury suburbs of the white upper class. He asked, "Do many of the Europeans live like this in Rhodesia?"

"Well, the wealthier people have servants to do the house-work and cooking, as well as take care of the grounds. The Africans need the employment and the help allows us to have our homes maintained for a relatively small expense," answered Sarah.

"I assume that the white middle classes can't afford to hire many Africans, as it is in Malawi?" Lucas continued.

"A few do, but most live in smaller houses and yards, so the assistance is less important," answered Sarah.

Dinner was served on the verandah by the African cook. It was delicious and consisted of an appetizer, a main course of lamb, garden salad with fruit, and dessert. While the entire meal was accompanied by South African wine, and the meal was fol-lowed by after dinner port, Lucas and Angela deferred on the alcohol. They enjoyed the meal, as it left nothing to desire.

During the supper Lucas established that Sarah was a native Rhodesian and that Dr. Burns had been born and trained in South Africa, migrating after his training as a cardiologist. The married couple had lived in Rhodesia many years.

"Truly a memorable meal," remarked Lucas, after they had finished. "It is interesting to contrast Rhodesia to Malawi. We have no cardiologists at Nsanji Hospital in Malawi. Perhaps you and Sarah could come and visit us after we get settled?"

Doctor Burns smiled and related, "You know, we've never traveled to Malawi and I've heard that it is a very beautiful coun-try, with mountains in the northern part and rolling hills further south."

Lucas now became enthusiastic at the chance of a possible visit to his hospital from a cardiologist. There were none in the entire country, so a visit from Doctor Burns would be a real benefit.

"You could make a working holiday of it and stay with us and still see the country. I'm not saying there wouldn't be a few EKGs to read, but we'd try to keep the work to a minimum."

"Sarah and I may just accept the offer, Lucas. We'll get in touch in a few weeks after you return."

It was now getting late, and after profuse thanks to the Burnses for their hospitality, the four guests returned to their hotel. Sean drove off to stay with his relatives.

"We have a bit of shopping to do in the morning before we return to Sanyati," Lucas told Chauncey as they parted that evening in the hotel lobby. "Nothing important, mind you, just some medical stuff."

Angela punched Lucas softly in the stomach and smiled. "I think there was another item you've forgotten that we need to pick up."

Laughing, Lucas said, "Yeah, but I've forgotten what it was… must have not been important, so maybe we'll just forget about it."

"I'll remember for you in the morning," said Angela as they got on the elevator.

Iuba was ready for a short outing prior to retiring for the night. He anointed Cecil Square's grass and trees repeatedly before they returned to the hotel, where he found a comfortable spot on the bed for the night.

# 17

## Chapter

At seven-thirty the next morning, all four travelers sat comfortably eating breakfast around white linen-clothed tables in the elite reserved dining area on the eleventh floor of the Meikles Hotel. The large windows and plate glass doors facing out onto the viewing deck displayed the bright purple beauty of the jacaranda trees below. As they sat at the table and ate the sumptuous tropical fruit and the English breakfast served by the efficient restaurant waiters, the calm streets contrasted the violence of the Angola that they had recently left behind.

"I think we need to collect some things today before we join the convoy returning to Sanyati this afternoon," said Chauncey. "I have a whole laundry list of things to pick up for the Chironga Baptist Mission, and I believe the two of you also have business in town to attend to."

They finished their breakfast and set about their separate tasks after Lucas, Angela, and Iuba had spent some time exploring the vegetation in the spacious park across the street from the hotel.

Although Iuba had only had a little bit of formal house training, Angela was delighted by the success he had made in adapting to hotel life. Giving strict instructions to the housekeeping supervisor about abandoning any effort to revisit their hotel room that morning, Lucas and Angela left to investigate the jewelry stores of Salisbury.

"Iuba should be content to sleep there and not cause trouble," said Angela as they left the hotel and turned up Angwa Street, walking towards Barbour's Department Store.

The streets bustled with road and pedestrian traffic, but a remote sense of impending collapse could be felt throughout the metropolis. Increasing economic sanctions by the world's nations had begun to undercut the psyche of the citizens of Rhodesia.

"We are still able to obtain the necessities of life and there are certainly few shortages of food or goods, but the costs are rising and certain scarcities are beginning to appear," Sean had said at breakfast. "Priorities of arms and ammunition are beginning to impose shortages of other items."

As Angela and Lucas walked along First Street, they noticed that the overall appearance of prosperity was marred by some of the white shoppers' apparel. Their clothes were in good repair, but the less wealthy wore rural styled clothing, like boots and rough shirts. Yes, there was no shortage of automobiles, but there were also many older models that had been well maintained. Some of the high end cars were of the newest production, but they were fewer in number. Even the autos over twenty years old, shiny and running smoothly, were usually driven by the older residents.

"Here's a jewelry store," remarked Angela as they came to a large shop at the corner of First and Speke Streets.

They looked at the extensive display in the window and found a selection of wedding rings with diamonds set in gold and platinum. No prices were shown.

"Let's go in and price them," said Lucas.

As they entered the store, a polite, well-dressed white man immediately came to their assistance. Rhodesia was known worldwide for its mining of gold and diamonds, so Angela expected a plethora of choices. However, they found that the choices were fewer than expected, as many of the affluent residents of the country had decided to entrust a portion of their financial means in jewelry, making their assets both mobile and internationally exchangeable.

"Lucas, they do seem to have an adequate selection anyway," murmured Angela, as she tried on a sparkling bridal set of two rings.

The search went on for two hours as they walked from store to store, all of them within a few blocks of each other within the large city. Finally, they reached agreement on a set of engagement and wedding rings that, while beautiful, were not ostentatious.

"This set will do nicely and it won't look like I'm married to a rich doctor," smiled Angela as they left a store on Jameson Avenue with the gems in Lucas' pocket. "We need to meet Sean and Chauncey for lunch in a few minutes at the Meikles' Mezzanine Restaurant and I'll be wearing my new jewelry!"

"Let's wait until we get back to Sanyati," suggested Lucas. "It will give us a chance to do it all formally, and we may even have a celebration."

"Okay, it's your deal and I can wait," she said as they kissed in the hotel elevator on the way to lunch.

Sean and Chauncey had already found a table outside on the verandah when the couple arrived. The four friends sat and talked after ordering their lunch.

While they were waiting for their lunch to arrive, the discussion moved to the situation in Rhodesia. Sean, a longtime resident, felt that the people of Rhodesia were in a struggle to protect their traditional way of life. He felt that while apartheid would not last forever, at the present time the country had been extremely prosperous and their way of life had remained good, for not only the ruling white Europeans but also for the native Africans, who on the whole were living at a considerably higher standard than those in any other African country.

Angela replied that there was no question that African natives here in Rhodesia lived on a scale of prosperity that she not seen anywhere else in Africa. But she went on that they still remained in the bottom segment of society and had no input as to their government's policies. Compared to other African countries without apartheid, they had almost no starvation and the people were well clothed and at least got a basic education.

Sean took a deep breath and continued, "I foresee that the international sanctions will eventually strangle the Rhodesian government into submission and democracy will prevail, but it will be a slow process and could possibly end with a black dictatorship ruling the country."

"How has Rhodesia survived for the past twelve years?" asked Lucas.

He replied that almost all of their trade, import or export, came through South Africa. Rhodesia also required fuel to function commercially and for agriculture and manufacture. Petroleum products were also being transported through South Africa due to their sympathetic white-dominated apartheid regime. Until recently, few international trading countries had placed sanctions on South Africa, so there remained almost no pressure on Rhodesia's economy, as it continued to produce large amounts of salable products and sell worldwide through South Africa. War materials also flowed freely through South African ports into the country, paid for in hard currency.

"So that's why we see a full capacity society with almost no unemployment here," said Chauncey.

"Yes," replied Sean, as their lunch arrived on an opulently appointed tray with crisp napkins and cutlery. The neatly dressed waiter placed their lunch on the table and, after inquiring if there were any further needs, left the four travelers to their meal.

"The problem here," continued Sean, "is that the entire population is at war, with every male between eighteen and seventy having an obligation to the National Service for two to three months a year after serving his original two-year service. Many women volunteer for military service, too."

"Wow," commented Lucas. "So virtually every family is affected by the war. Casualties and death can occur anywhere in the entire the population."

"Right." Sean became grim as he said, "It's surprising how united the Rhodesian population has become with this reality, both black and white. Apartheid remains the official policy, but in reality, if the man standing next to you in a firefight to protect your back happens to be black, there's little chance that you will follow much of the official policy."

They finished their lunch and checked out of the hotel. Loading their luggage and newly purchased supplies into Sean's truck, they proceeded to the fairgrounds, where the convoy was to congregate for the trip back to Gatooma early that afternoon. The members of the convoy remained a pleasant, convivial group, although fewer in number, standing next to their vehicles calmly discussing the raid on a previous days' convoy to Karoi.

"I heard that the raid involved over thirty 'terrs attacking a ten truck military convoy armed with police and light artillery. Evidently, the guerrillas were misinformed and thought the convoy was civilian," said one farmer as he leaned against the door of his truck, chewing on a cigar.

"Yeah," commented his friend, standing near an automobile with two rocket launchers protruding from the back of his trunk. "The 'terrs really caught it that time. Killed almost all thirty of 'em with no loss to our side, but they'll be at it up there again in a few days, just wait and see."

The Hippo arrived, and after preliminary preparations, left for Gatooma on time, with a mounted machine gun on a tripod and a soldier in the back bed of Sean's truck. Lucas was amazed at the amount of ammunition they carried with them.

"Why do you suppose that they picked our truck for the machine gun?" asked Angela.

"It probably has something to do with their knowing that I'm a Selous Scout in the Rhodesian Army," replied Sean.

"So what is a Selous Scout, anyway?" she replied.

"You've never heard of the Scouts?" he asked incredulously, laughing. "Well, we're probably the most elite infiltrating military unit in the world, far above the American Navy SEALs or the British SAS units. We're supposed to be able to eat Green Berets and the French Foreign Legion for breakfast," he said with a sly smile.

"What makes this unit so special?" she asked, laughing along with him.

"We not only can live off of the land for months, but we actually infiltrate the terrorists' teams, masquerading as Africans and, in some cases, actually hold rank in their forces. They are convinced we are black members of their guerrilla units. Our mission is to warn the Rhodesian army about the 'terrs' plans to attack or raid major installations, like electric plants and ammunition factories, ahead of time."

"That must be one of the major reasons that the guerrillas have had so little success," remarked Lucas.

"We speak their language as they do, and blacken our skin, going into the bush to join the 'terrs. We then attack them from within their camps, not having to venture out looking for them, as do other units of the Rhodesian Army."

"That really takes a toll on your nerves, I would guess," she replied.

"It's taken years of training and steady nerves to do it. We've had some real successes, but some disasters too. If you make even the smallest mistake and they catch you, they'll really make your life miserable before they kill you."

The road opened out before the convoy, as they traversed the same roads that they had just traveled two days before. The extensive fields of maize and tobacco stretched on both sides of the road as far as the eye could see, in full array of color and fertility. Chauncey noted that it was obvious that the latest agriculture techniques were being used in an attempt to squeeze the last morsel of production out of the fertile Rhodesian soil.

"Well, here we are in Gatooma again," remarked Sean, as he slowed the truck and came to a stop with the other members of the convoy. "There don't seem to be many trucks continuing on to Sanyati this afternoon."

When the convoy reconvened fifteen minutes later to travel into the bush, only three trucks lined up behind the Hippo.

"This isn't good," said Chauncey, as the four vehicles began to roll slowly past the outer town limits, traveling on the same dirt road where they had encountered the landmine crater only a few days before. Vendors along both sides of the road displayed their wares of carved wooden and stone art, as well as a large selection of foodstuffs.

"This is better than traveling alone through the bush," replied Sean, "but be ready to move from the truck to the periphery of the road or into the grass if any gunfire starts.

"I will man the machine gun on the truck bed, but everyone must be responsible for his own safety if a group of 'terrs attacks the convoy."

They drove at a fairly fast pace for an hour on the dirt and gravel road, causing another cloud of dust to rise far behind them. The dusty road ended abruptly and they were now following a track consisting of two dirt strips through the dense grass. This grass had grown so high and thick between the two trodden strips flattened by the wheels, that only the rear tailgate of the vehicle ahead could be seen. This plentiful vegetation, which continually brushed the front bumper of the truck, made a constant swishing sound as their truck rushed past. The lead Hippo was forced to slow, causing its large bulk to obstruct the view of the path ahead.

"Heck, we can't see anything ahead of that Hippo," remarked Sean as he blindly steered his 4-by-4 wheeled truck behind the massive military vehicle twenty feet in front of him.

The Hippo slowed to a stop as the Marimari River came into view, flowing directly in front of the pathway they were following.

"It appears that it must have rained pretty hard last night, so we'll have to ford the river this time," casually remarked Sean. "We'll be glad that our truck has a snorkel and a sealed engine, as the river appears to be at least five or six feet deep in some places." He appeared not the least bit rattled by this development.

The occupants of the four vehicles stood at the edge of the white foaming river and surveyed the water as it swirled past them, making a soft gurgling sound as it passed over the rocks buried below the rippling cascade.

The lieutenant in charge of the Hippo remarked, "Crossing the river is an ideal opportunity for an ambush. Stay as close to the military vehicle as you dare while we remain within the river bed. My men will try to anticipate any terrorists' fire from the opposite side as we cross."

Four armed Rhodesian soldiers dismounted from the Hippo and set up a perimeter at the water's edge on the near bank. They also removed the tripod and machine gun from the back of Sean's pickup truck, setting it behind a fallen log at the water's edge. Sean decided to man the machine gun himself. Lucas took over the driving duties, as he had much experience driving through deep water, and the other three trucks lined up closely behind the Hippo as it was pulled up to the water's edge.

"Okay, here we go!" said the Hippo driver. "We'll make steady forward progress at about ten miles per hour, and we don't stop for anything. If a truck in line is disabled, drive around it. We cannot defend ourselves from the middle of the river."

The roar of the powerful diesel engine in the Hippo preceded the slow steady movement of its huge body down the near bank of the river and into the water. They had about fifty meters of water to negotiate. This would mean that all four vehicles would be in the water at the same time for only a few minutes, but during that period, they would be in the most vulnerable situation. Instructions were that as the last truck descended the near bank and entered the water, the four soldiers with the machine gun would climb into the back of this last truck to be ferried to the other side. While in the water, the automatic weapons would be useless to defend the convoy from hostile fire if it came from the bushes and trees on the far side. Lucas had volunteered to drive Sean's truck as the fourth and last in the convoy, carrying the soldiers and machine gun.

"This is all very dramatic," said Angela, sitting next to Iuba in the front seat of the truck with Lucas. "We don't even know if there are any terrorists across the river waiting to ambush us."

"True," replied Lucas. "But if they're waiting for us, we are prepared to defend ourselves with a good chance of survival."

The four trucks proceeded at what seemed a snail's pace into the water so that the last truck, Lucas driving, now was at midstream and the leading Hippo was only a few yards from the far bank. "All seems to be going well, so far," called Sean, sitting behind the machine gun in the truck bed at the back of their trailing vehicle. "We're almost across."

That was the last thing Lucas heard him say, as the bushes bordering the far bank came alive with automatic weapons, firing at all four of the water-surrounded trucks. They could not move quickly when the ambush started, due to the rushing water and soft river bed, causing their wheels to lose traction. It was a potential disaster.

Lucas realized that from the bed of his truck, at the back of the line, Sean would have to direct his return fire over the other three trucks in front of them, as well as the cab of their own truck to inflict any damage with his machine gun. Without consideration of the possible consequences, Lucas made a ninety-degree left turn midstream, into the current. This accomplished two things: First, it gave Sean a clear shot at the far bank, only thirty yards away and, second, it exposed Lucas, Chauncey, Angela and Iuba inside the truck to a clear shot by the terrorists on their side of the truck.

He need not have worried.

Later, Lucas said that the stream of fire from the back of the truck by Sean's machine gun, as well as the rifles of the four colored soldiers back there with him, was deafening. Every leaf and thorn on those bushes along the river bank had disappeared when they looked later. Sean and his friends counted twelve dead bodies riddled with bullets. It was a mess.

Sean added, "That rocket launcher on top of the Hippo gave them such a scare that all we had to do was mop up as they ran for cover. Good thing we were prepared, or it might have been a different situation."

No one could speak to Angela for ten minutes after the firefight, as the noise had made her temporarily deaf and her ears ring. Iuba simply sat next to her in the truck and snarled at anyone who approached them. Thirty minutes later, the convoy had re-established its integrity and was moving northwest at fifty miles an hour through the bush towards the Sanyati Mission.

"That was the most amazing fight I've ever seen," remarked Lucas to Sean as they resumed the convoy, following the other three trucks, plowing through the tall grass and thorn bushes. "Is that what usually happens in an ambush here in Rhodesia?"

Keeping his eyes on the leading truck as it twisted and turned between the various obstacles in the pathway in front of it, Sean replied, "It rarely goes so well, Lucas. That was a gutsy move you made, exposing yourself and all of us to direct fire, but your timing was perfect and the 'terrs never expected such a move. It was fortunate that we had so much fire-power where it could do the most damage right when we needed it. You can fight with me and my men in the bush *anytime*, Lucas!"

Thoughtfully, Lucas observed, "You know, Sean, I noticed that the weapons the terrorists were using appeared to be of Russian or Chinese origin. Would that indicate support in this war by those countries for the guerrillas?"

"Absolutely, Lucas. Not only that, but those communist countries are supplying troop training in Mozambique and Zambia. We expect that in the near future easy victories like today will become rare, as the terrorists become more sophisticated and organized in their raids."

The low purple silhouette of the Sanyati Mountains now could be distinguished as they stood out on the distant western skyline, the convoy having reached a hilltop. This indicated that the line of trucks was nearing the Baptist mission, which was embraced and shielded from the dry seasonal African winds by that extensive barrier.

"Glad to see that ridge in the distance," remarked Sean. "We'll be at Sanyati in an hour or so. I'm ready for a rest."

They entered the mission gates about an hour and a half later and parked their truck, as the fading light of dusk dimly outlined the mission buildings. They had waved goodbye to the convoy, which was proceeding on to the Chenjiri Army barracks, some thirty miles to the west.

"Seems pretty quiet for only seven o'clock in the evening," remarked Chauncey as they got out of their truck and began to walk along the dirt path to the front door of Sean's residence. No lights or sounds could be seen or heard from the residence.

A low growl followed by a snarl from Iuba was the only warning the four travelers received as they proceeded along the dirt pathway leading to the front steps up to Sean's porch. Angela stopped immediately, grabbing Iuba's collar. Sean removed his rifle from his shoulder and, dropping the suitcase from his other hand to the ground, whispered from a crouched position, "Everyone get down! Angela, release Iuba; he'll investigate for us."

Angela released the now-pulling Iuba from her grasp as she assumed a low position near the ground next to Lucas and Chauncey. Whispering in a soft tone, she said "Go, Iuba! See what's in there."

Iuba needed no further encouragement, as he tore up the remaining pathway to the residence and jumped the two steps to the darkened porch. The four people, now lying prone on the grass, could scarcely make out the outline of his white fur in the fading light as he turned to the right and attacked, making no sound. The unmistakable laugh of a hyena rang out from the porch, followed by snarls and growls as Iuba tore into the animal. A fight to the death was on.

Standing up, Sean said, "He's got a hyena trapped on the porch. It must have been looking for a meal. They're strong and dangerous in this darkness. One of us could have been seriously hurt as we approached."

The fight was now reaching a crescendo, as the sounds grew in fierceness and a ball of white and speckled red intertwined fur broke through the handrail surrounding the porch. They continued in the dusk to fight on the grass for a death grip, as Sean lifted his rifle.

"No!" You might hit Iuba!" called Angela. "He can take care of himself."

Suddenly a gurgling sound emerged from the combined mass of fur, and the struggle slowed to an intermittent shaking, finally coming to a full stop. The bloody head of Iuba could be seen in the dim light as he opened his jaws, releasing the hyena, now-strangled, to the grass. He approached Angela, but he was able to only walk on three legs, as he limped across the lawn covered with gore, and collapsed at her feet.

"Good boy! You saved us from a possible major catastrophe," she said as she repeatedly stroked his blood-soaked fur. "Where are you hurt?"

Sean just stood there dumbstruck, rifle in hand, and repeated in a dazed voice, "Never saw a dog tear up a hyena in my life. Iuba must be an extremely strong dog to successfully kill a wild hyena."

Chauncey stood near Angela with a cloth he had found, to help her wipe the blood and gore from Iuba's stained white coat.

They climbed the steps and upon entering the residence, Sean turned on the porch light from the front hall. "Unbelievable mess of fur and blood," remarked Chauncey. Then looking down at Angela as she inspected Iuba, he said, "Those hyenas have an extremely forceful bite. What damage do you see?"

Angela was in tears. "He's been torn up badly and I believe he has a broken left forepaw. It's a miracle he's even alive, he's lost so much blood. We'll have to take him to the hospital right away."

At the hospital, the damages to Iuba were found to be mostly superficial, and after X-rays, a splint was provided for his left forepaw. He was placed on an examination table at the hospital for suturing of the multiple wounds, which covered his body. IV fluids were administered with antibiotics to prevent infection from the contaminated mouth of the hyena and he was given a rabies shot.

"Well, we've finally got him stabilized and we'll rest him on the couch in Sean's living room," said Lucas. "Thanks so much, Sean, for allowing us to use the Sanyati medical facilities as well as your own."

Sean smiled and said, "Really, I should be thanking Iuba for saving *me*. If he hadn't spotted that hyena, it may have attacked me when I got to the porch and there could have been some nasty injuries. That's the first time we've seen a wild animal inside the mission compound."

After taking care of Iuba, Lucas and Angela walked along with Sean and Chauncey to Sean's house and sat alone on the large swing on his front porch while Sean and Chauncey were in the house organizing supper. "With all of the excitement, Angie, there's something that we haven't had time to discuss," he said.

"I haven't forgotten," she murmured as she put her arms around his neck and gently kissed his mouth with her soft lips. "Is this the time to make it official?"

Lucas knew that this was supposed to be serious discussion, but the humor of the situation couldn't escape his notice. Here they sat on Sean's porch, amidst a myriad of blood, gore and torn fur, having just worked for an hour to save her badly wounded dog, and he was going to try to ask her to marry him.

"This isn't the most romantic situation in the world, Angie. If you weren't a nurse and used to the bush, I'd try to make it a little more sentimental, but you know that I have loved you for some time now. We just seem to be in unusual situations all the time, so opportunities are few and far between," he said, trying to suppress a smile.

Angela now sat directly facing Lucas on the swing, turning so that, while she was still sitting next to him, she faced him. "Lucas, after what we've been through in the past three months together, I've gotten to know you much better than if we had been dating or just working as associates," she said laughing out loud. "If this would have happened under any other circumstances, it wouldn't have fit, anyway." Then, after a pause, she said, "I love you, too, honey, very much."

Sean's voice now resounded from the doorway of the house, in obvious humor.

"Okay, okay, the advertising's over! Get to the chase Lucas. Dinner is getting cold and Chauncey and I are hungry."

"Can't we have a minute's peace and privacy?" asked Lucas, laughing. "I'm trying to do something here!"

Sean stepped out onto the porch, so Lucas and Angela could see him. He had been standing out of their sight for the past few minutes, and had overheard their conversation. "Look, you love her and she loves you, Lucas. Get to the question, you're holding up dinner," he said as he walked back into the house, chuckling to himself, and letting the screen door slam behind him. The two were now alone again on the swing.

"What a character." Lucas continued in a quiet voice. "Angie, you know how much I love you, and I want you to be my wife for the rest of our lives. Will you marry me?"

"I can't think of anything I'd rather be than Mrs. Stuart, with the Lord's blessing. We must see that our marriage remains under His oversight," she said, kissing Lucas softly for a long time. She held his face in both of her hands as he hugged her tightly.

Lucas slipped the engagement ring that had been purchased that morning on Angela's finger as they got to their feet.

"We'd better go inside for supper before we have both of those guys out here on the porch supervising us," Angela wryly remarked. And they went inside.

As they entered through the front door, applause resounded throughout the house. To the amazement of both Angela and Lucas, there were at least twenty people standing in Sean's living room, dining room and kitchen, all giving the couple an ovation. On the dining room table sat a huge three-tier cake with the inscription, blazing in red frosting, "Congratulations, Lucas and Angela."

"Who are all these people?" whispered Angela to Lucas.

"We anticipated the successful engagement of you two when you bought the rings in Salisbury, so Chauncey and I radioed ahead to arrange a celebration when you arrived." announced Sean. "What we didn't anticipate was the uninvited doorman on the front porch. Congratulations on your engagement! When is the wedding?"

"Unbelievable!" remarked Lucas. "We don't even know these people and they've given us an engagement party. Rhodesian hospitality and friendliness really isn't just a rumor."

The celebration, including buffet, cake and fresh fruit, started immediately, although there was no alcohol since it was on a Baptist mission. The entire medical staff and missionaries were introduced and an offer was made to marry them right there, as there were three pastors present at the festivities.

"We'll have to have our relatives present for a wedding," said Angela, thanking the friendly ministers for the offer. "Mine live in Angola and Lucas' family is in America."

There were doctors and nurses, as well as aides and visiting missionaries from America at the gathering. All seemed genuinely happy for the couple and, though they were strangers, it didn't take long for them to become friends. Finally, when the celebration had ended and all of the guests had returned to their living quarters, Lucas and Angela sat quietly in the dining room with Chauncey and Sean and had a glass of champagne, which Chauncey had produced stealthfully from his suitcase.

"To the successful and happy union of these two friends!" said Sean, lifting his glass into the air. "May God bless their marriage and support their efforts wherever they go!"

Having finished the bottle quickly, all went to bed. The lights were not turned out, however, until it had been established that Iuba was stable and in no pain.

* * *

"So how's Iuba this morning?" asked Sean at breakfast.

Angela sat quietly spooning her porridge into Iuba's mouth as he hungrily devoured every offering.

"It looks like he's ready to move on. The cast on the forepaw will hinder his walking for a while, but he appears fit to travel. Has Chauncey appeared yet this morning?"

Sean grinned at Angela and answered, "I think he may have imbibed more bubbly than the rest of us. We haven't heard a sound yet from his room this morning."

"Maybe because I don't make a lot of noise shuffling around," he answered from the doorway, as Chauncey took a seat at the table and helped himself to some porridge and eggs. "Are we ready to fly on to Chironga today?" he asked.

Chauncey was an interesting character, Lucas observed, as he studied him sitting at the table, eating breakfast, wearing loose fitting blue jeans, cowboy boots, and a sweatshirt with the words "Australia's Nightmare" emblazoned across the front. He had told them a bit about himself as they traveled to Salisbury a few days before: That he had been married for a short period of time during the Vietnam War to a nurse back in his native Australia, but she had found other interests while he was absent for extended periods and had divorced him. He evidently had been busy flying military transport planes for the Americans.

"I developed friendships with many Americans during the war, mostly from Texas, and eventually moved there to fly commercially for Eastern Airlines after the war," he had related. "I never married again and when the opportunity to fly African mission planes and fight rebels came, I left Eastern Airlines and came here. Been doin' it ever since."

Sean's story, on the other hand, was fairly typical for a Rhodesian male in his mid-thirties. Born on a remote farm in the Vumba, (the eastern mountains of Rhodesia), Sean could speak the *Shona* and *Chichewa* languages before he spoke English. He was drafted at eighteen into the Rhodesian Army, after completing his schooling, and because of his knowledge of the languages and his familiarity with African customs, he was a natural candidate for the elite Selous Scouts. He was taught how to survive under the most extreme deprivations and sent into the bush to fight alongside of the rebel guerrillas, informing the Rhodesian government of their hierarchy and planned raids. In between army stints, he worked for the Tobacco Board trying to bypass sanctions. The army work was extremely dangerous, as he faced detection from the rebels as well as being shot accidentally by the Rhodesian army. Now on leave for six months, he had a well-deserved reputation for extreme bravery and daring throughout the ranks of the Rhodesian army officers, but his leave was over.

Lucas and Angela had finished breakfast and were in the process of packing their belongings to fly on to northern Rhodesia when Angela asked, "Is there any way that I could call England from here? I need to contact my family, both to confirm that they all arrived safely from Luanda and to tell them of my change in location and of the fact that Lucas and I are getting married."

"Engaged, is the word," Lucas corrected, "Just tell them that we're engaged and that we're planning to marry in a few weeks, after we get settled in Malawi. I doubt that a long distance call will be easy before we get to Malawi. I saw no phone lines out here, and, if we fly to Chironga today, that place is more remote than Sanyati!"

They never got a chance to look, as Chauncey arrived to announce their game plan. "Okay, we need to get that plane out of the hangar and pack it for the trip to Chironga," he said. "The medical mission needs all sorts of medicines, and the army has us hauling some ammunition too."

"I'm authorized to travel with you, if you have space," said Sean. "I'm to be deployed in the Rushinga area in a few days, and it will save me a trip over those roads to get there."

With his usual casual manner, Chauncey remarked, "The more the merrier. We may need some assistance when we land. I hear the 'terrs are out in force up there, and you can help them if they decide to cause trouble," he said jokingly.

"Yeah!" replied Sean. "Sort of point out where they should aim, maybe?"

Sean disappeared into his residence for about an hour as the preparations for take-off were being completed. When he emerged, the transformation was astounding.

"Give me a rifle!" exclaimed Chauncey. "We've got a bloody guerrilla in the compound."

Sean was no longer recognizable. All of his visible skin was now dyed black, and his close-cropped black hair had been modified by a heating iron to look like that of an African.

The clothes he wore were tattered and his cap was pulled low on his forehead with a disfigured lieutenant's bar above the brim. Even his gait had changed from the crisp stride he usually used to a shuffle. He was indeed a guerrilla fighter, down to the AK-47 in his right hand.

"We ready to go?" he asked, as they began to board the twin prop Beechcraft, whose motors now roared to a crescendo as Chauncey tested them. Iuba was still only partially recovered and had to be lifted into the plane. When all were aboard, they slammed the door of the plane and headed for the end of the short runway.

The trip north to Chironga took about three and a half hours and was enjoyable except for about ten minutes when a Rhodesian jet fighter plane flew next to them, inspecting the occupants. Sean had to crouch to the floor so the air force pilot would not see him and think they were carrying rebels.

"There is the Ruya River!" pointed out Chauncey. "The mission buildings lie directly next to the water. The landing field is that meadow just beyond the mission, and we can put it down if the strip is clear of animals and people."

Circling low over an open field some twenty hectares long, Chauncey set the small plane down faultlessly on the markers and brought it to a stop, short of the trees surrounding the pasture. The strip was overgrown with tall grass.

"We're here, and I don't plan to stay longer than an hour, so don't get lost," ordered Chauncey. "The rebel activity here is extreme and nothing's safe."

Sean left the plane after saying good luck to everyone and melted into the tall grass and was not seen again. He simply disappeared. The plane was unloaded and exchanges of greetings and introductions concluded efficiently. When all had returned to their seats, the plane was ready for takeoff. Suddenly, the dense, dry grass at the other end of the field erupted in flames. The plane was trapped, with their runway now burning furiously.

# 18
## Chapter

T he rebels had started a raging grass fire at the other end of the airfield to prevent the plane from leaving the Chironga Mission. Chauncey now had both engines roaring at full throttle, but as the gusting wind was driving the flames rapidly towards the plane, the Beechcraft was forced to taxi across the open field to avoid incineration. Chauncey's ability to maneuver the aircraft was markedly limited by the swiftly approaching grass inferno approaching from the opposite end of the pasture and the Ruya River, on his right, which ran parallel to the edge of the landing field.

The Australian's sense of humor never faltered; "Great! This is all I need this morning, to be burned by a bunch of bloody rebels," the pilot said sarcastically, as he turned the plane back towards the river. "Well, you'll have to get up earlier than this to stump me, you bastards!"

Lucas and Angela were becoming increasingly concerned, as both could easily see the possibility of incineration as they crouched over Iuba in the cabin of the Beechcraft. Giving full throttle to both engines and cursing under his breath, Chauncey ran the plane directly toward the river and onto the sandy bank, which had been partially smoothed by recent flooding. The water had now receded, leaving a narrow, dry strip next to the stream. He came to a complete stop and turned the plane parallel to the rushing water. Gunning the engines again, he ran the plane at full acceleration on the sandy bank along the river's edge, gaining speed with every second. It had to be the bumpiest ride any of them had ever experienced, but the reliable two-motor craft was moving into the wind at a terrific tempo.

"Okay, you rebels, look up and see what a *real* bush pilot can do!" he exclaimed, as the plane became airborne and began to gain altitude.

Because of the heavy foliage and rolling hills surrounding the mission, Chauncey had to keep the plane directly over the river as it lifted for some distance until he could gain enough speed and height to turn north.

"We'll turn back in a minute and fly over the mission to see what's going on. In the meantime, I can radio the Rhodesian Air Force to send help to put out the fire and repel those rebels. With Sean leading them, because of his rank as a rebel officer, I doubt he'll allow them to remain long in the vicinity, anyway."

Chauncey's radio crackled as he reported the flames and possible raid on the Chironga Mission to the Salisbury Central Military Response Center. The reply was almost instantaneous: "We have the problem already reported. A helicopter and troops have been sent."

"That was fast," remarked Lucas. "There must have been a report from the mission as soon as the fire was spotted."

Chauncey first headed south to fly over the mission, and seeing that the fire on the landing field had now largely burned itself out, they all felt more relaxed. A Rhodesian military helicopter could be seen approaching the mission as the rebels, still likely led by Sean, faded into the trees and bushes.

"I'm sure that Sean wanted to get his guerrillas out of there before the Baptist mission suffered any damage," remarked Angela. "He probably used the excuse that the military response would come immediately to fool the rebel troops. I can't imagine how he manages to keep the guerrilla irregulars misled by his orders. I'm sure he wouldn't order that fire to be set in the first place."

Having insured the safety of the Rhodesian missionaries, Chauncey turned the plane north and headed for Zumbo, a town on the Zambezi River where the borders of Rhodesia, Zambia and Mozambique meet. It lies on the far northeastern border of Rhodesia.

"We'll fly over Zumbo in a northeasterly direction and then cross Mozambique and Zambia to reach Lilongwe, the capitol of Malawi," Chauncey informed the couple. "We can do our immigration and passport duties at the Lilongwe airport and then fly to Chileka Airport in Blantyre, farther south. Right now, immigration facilities don't exist at Chileka."

The flight to Zumbo, at the northeastern tip of Rhodesia, crosses one of the most desolate areas of Africa. This district is also a very beautiful and in a dense jungle region, named the Mwanzamtanda Mountain Range. It borders the mighty Zambezi River to the north, and has only one small settlement, Kanyemba, in the entire territory.

All three occupants gazed out of the window. "I've only been to Kanyemba once," reported Lucas. "At that time, we were traveling down the Zambezi River by canoe, from Kariba to Lake Cabora Bassa, in Mozambique and spent just one night in the village."

"What was the settlement like?" asked Chauncey. "I've only seen it from the air."

"Not much to see," replied Lucas. "A few scattered huts and a general store on the riverfront. As I remember, there was no electricity and not even a Coca-Cola to be found anywhere. Mostly river trade in poached ivory and hemp, not much else."

They were now a few thousand feet above the Zambezi River crossing into Mozambique air space, and had a good view of the terrain below. "It's breathtaking!" remarked Angela, as she peered from the plane's windows at the dense jungle passing below her. She saw waterfalls from the mountain streams as they emptied in to the Zambezi River, with no trace of human existence as far as the eye could see.

"This is still God's land, Angie. No man has had a chance to tame the jungle or harness the rivers. Few natives ever penetrate into the forests and the native animals still rule supreme," said Lucas. "It's probably similar to how it was a hundred and twenty years ago when Livingston came here to search for the source of the Nile."

They flew low enough to easily observe the hippopotamus and crocodile as they lazed on the banks of the Zambezi and wallowed in the river's cooling pools. Scores of small birds sat in the treetops, watching the river waters for fish to surface, so they could catch them. Fish eagles spread their magnificent ten-foot wings to gracefully snatch their dinner from the huge rushing river. Crags on the face of steep cliffs, served as nests for these large fish eagles. Their young could be seen as they groped, mouths open, waiting for the return of their parents with dinner clutched in their talons. The flat-topped Massasa trees in the valleys served as natural umbrellas, shading the ground for the ever-busy baboons, resting from their perpetual forage for food.

"You know, from up here, you'd never know that God had placed humans on the earth," said Chauncey, as he made a sharp turn to avoid hitting a large eagle as it flew by grasping a snake, writhing as it attempted to free itself.

"Not a good place to lose your sense of direction or be forced to crash-land," observed Lucas. "But inaccessible areas like this are becoming very few now-a-days and are extremely interesting. It gives me an idea of what the Garden of Eden must have been like."

They continued east, following the twisting course of the Zambezi River from the air for the next fifteen minutes before turning northeast, as Cabora Bassa Lake came into view to the south. They had now crossed into Mozambique airspace.

"Just need to cross over the corner of Mozambique and we'll be in Zambian air space," said Chauncey, as he returned to flying at an altitude of ten thousand feet.

Suddenly the radio crackled. "This is Mozambique, Zumbo Airfield calling. We have tracked you on radar over our airspace. Proceed immediately to Zumbo Airfield for inspection and immigration clearance."

"Nuts!" exclaimed Chauncy. "If we do that, it will take hours and they'll find a reason to either fine us or arrest us. By continuing north for thirty miles we'll be over Zambian airspace in a few minutes."

Switching on his radio, Chauncy replied, "This is air flight 7743 out of Chironga to Lilongwe. We are presently over Zambian air space and will proceed to Lilongwe as directed. You are mistaken, but we apologize for any intrusion tracked by your radar."

"Can you get away with this?" asked Angela

"Do it all the time," said Chauncy, after he turned the radio off. "We're now only a few miles within Mozambique and for them to scramble their aircraft from Beira would cost too much for fuel. We'll be over Zambia anyway by the time they get to us."

Turning due north, their plane was inside the Zambian border within a few minutes. By flying over the Petauke to Chipata highway, they arrived at the Malawi border within the hour. It was a shortcut to Malawi, saving forty-five minutes of flight time.

"Safe at last!" remarked Chauncy. "The Mozambique authorities would have thought twice about chasing us into Malawi air space and offending President Banda. He's a tough old bird and would raise Cain about Mozambique fighter planes over his country."

The steady "hum" of the airplane motors continued as the passing scenery gave way from the woods and mountains of Zambia to densely planted farms and cultivated plots.

"Malawi has a very densely crowded population, as the country is only a thin strip of land bordering Lake Malawi, and it has a population the size of Texas squeezed into it. Every square foot of dirt is used for sustenance or profit," explained Lucas.

"Yes, it's about 850 miles long and 150 miles wide, and yet it does manage to produce enough food to support its own people. That includes those in the mountain and forest regions in the northern part of the country," remarked Chauncey.

The mission plane obtained clearance for landing and promptly set down on the airport runway a few miles north of Lilongwe. Customs and immigration formalities were carried out by a pleasant Malawi woman, who did not delay their progress.

"It's amazing what a large, modern airport this small African country has to offer," remarked Angela. "Are we going to have enough time to explore the capital city itself, or must we hurry on to Blantyre?"

"The actual city is some thirty miles to the south of the airport, usually with heavy road traffic. Better to explore the capital later," remarked Lucas.

While Lilongwe is the capital and main government headquarters of Malawi, Blantyre is the largest city and the center of commerce. In order not to delay Chauncey from getting back to his schedule, they decided to make the Lilongwe stop as brief as possible, since he had been kind to bring them this far out of his way.

A brief tour of the Lilongwe airport informed Angela that coffee, tea, and cotton products were some of the primary exports of Malawi. The airport shops had a myriad of these products of many varieties for sale in their pleasant, clean establishments. She was impressed by the products and reasonable prices sold in Malawi Kwacha.

After rounding up Lucas, Angela and Iuba, Chauncey said, "It's time to get back to the plane and fly to Chileka Airport in Blantyre." As they walked across the cement walkway to their plane he concluded, "The boys have refueled the plane, and it's getting late. I'm not anxious to land in Blantyre in the dark."

Once in the air, the distance from Lilongwe to Blantyre was about 150 miles as the crow flies. This distance could be flown in under an hour easily, but Chauncey flew low and slow. Because of this, Angela could follow the lay of the land from the air.

"Look at Lake Malawi!" she exclaimed, as the plane flew east over the shoreline at Salima and then turned south, following the shoreline. "I never expected a lake to be almost pristine with little or no commercialization. Is there no tourism?"

"Monkey Bay, at the southern end of the lake, has some hotels, but mostly the shoreline remains in the hands of farmers," replied Lucas. "There *are* some rather nice, small hotels all along the coast from Chipoka to Mangochi, but they're primarily for small fishing expeditions on the lake."

They continued to fly south, passing over a major city of Zomba and arriving at the Blantyre airport before dark. The airport landing strip was paved, so the landing was smooth, but Chauncey's remark about the safety was accurate, as the lights on the strip were few and far between.

"Chileka Airport isn't exactly an international destination," Angela remarked, "even if it serves the largest city in the country. No wonder you had concerns about after-dark arrivals."

Chauncey parked the plane and, after disembarking, the passengers had to carry their own luggage into the small concrete block building that served as a terminal. It was marked "Chileka Airport." From that point at the airport, it appeared that almost every African, man or woman, immediately recognized Doctor Lucas. He was greeted by name, universally. As the group entered the building, they were assisted by everyone. Iuba had to be restrained on a leash.

"Ahh, Doctor Lucas, we are so glad to see you again! The mission hospital has been empty and there is no one to treat the sick. Are you going to be working tomorrow? We will help to get the supplies and luggage into your truck."

Lucas had left his truck with a friend three months before, when he left for Angola. He now recovered it in pristine condition under the metal roof of the airport car rental garage, washed, polished and fully fueled. His friend was on vacation but had made arrangements for it to be there when Lucas returned. Angela was amazed at their reception in the airport. "Do you know everyone in the whole city? I thought the mission hospital was a hundred and some odd miles south of here."

Chauncey had decided to spend the evening in Blantyre before his next flight to South Africa, so he traveled with Angela and Lucas from the airport to the city.

When Lucas was finally alone in the truck with Chauncey and Angie, as he was driving the twenty miles along the Nyambadwe Highway into Blantyre, he explained, "Angie, this is the situation.

The country of Malawi has about twelve million people living here, and there are a few major government hospitals, but the people here are generally very poor."

He went on to explain that most of the residents couldn't afford to pay for healthcare, so they had to make use of the government and mission clinics, which were free or for a small donation.. There were some private hospitals that *did* work for cash, if one could afford them. The private facilities had doctors, but there were only about fifty physicians in the whole country who worked for the government or missions, and they had to care for ninety-five percent of the population. These relatively few non-private doctors were well known and appreciated wherever they went.

As the truck traveled along the paved road from the airport to Blantyre, Angela was observing the farms and houses as they passed in the gathering dusk. There were many people walking along the roadside and in carts drawn by oxen, carrying their produce to the city to sell the next morning.

"I see that most of the people are well dressed and wear shoes," she remarked as they entered the city limits. "In Rhodesia, this was also the case."

"You have to remember that the city people are generally better off than the rural population. Their houses have electricity and many, here in town, have indoor plumbing, but when we drive on to the rural mission tomorrow, it will be different."

"How many people live in Blantyre?" she asked.

"No one really knows for sure, as there is no census and the population is mobile, depending on the rains. With good rain, the people stay in the country, as there is a plethora of food, but in drought they move to town in search of sustenance. My guess is a few million people live here right now in Blantyre."

The truck came to a stop at a major traffic circle. Heavy movement of large conveyances, as well as bicycles and pedestrians carrying multiple goods, could be seen as they moved energetically about their business.

"It really appears that we're seeing a cross-section of the country by just sitting here and watching the traffic pass by," Angela remarked. "These people appear to be very industrious, prosperous, and committed to commercial endeavors."

Lucas turned right from the traffic circle and headed up a steep hill on Robins Street, arriving at the entrance of a large open brick building, with a sign proclaiming:

### "Mount Soche Hotel"

"Home away from home," he remarked, as he drove into the expansive, paved parking lot and stopped at the entrance. "This hotel is my headquarters for activities when I come to Blantyre from the Nsanje Mission where I live. I visit here occasionally and you couldn't hope for a more hospitable place."

Having greeted Lucas warmly by name, the doorman emptied their luggage from the truck and led the trio to the front desk. "Doctor Stuart! Glad to have you back from your visit to Angola," announced the desk clerk. "What can we do for you tonight?"

"Good evening. We need two rooms for tonight, Albert."

Lucas and Chauncey roomed together, and Angela roomed with Iuba in a single room next to them. After a brief clean-up, they regrouped for soft drinks on the large external porch, which served as a dining room at the back of the hotel. The view from the elevated porch overlooked the entire city as well as the mountains in the distance. The twinkling lights of the city from this height were mesmerizing.

"It's really a beautiful view of Blantyre stretching below us, and of the surrounding rural vicinity," remarked Angela, as she sipped her drink. "Can we take a brief walk around town tomorrow morning before we travel on to the Nsanji Mission? Since we only have a few hours' drive before we go on to your house at Nsanji, I'm sure Iuba would appreciate the exercise."

"Good idea," returned Lucas. "I have to stop at the Mwaiwanthu Seventh Day Adventist Mission Hospital, here in Blantyre, for a minute anyway in the morning, and it's only a short walk from here. There's a great Chinese restaurant on the way back, and I suspect we'll all be ready to eat lunch by then."

The next morning after breakfast, they took a walk through town. It was interesting to both Chauncey and Angela, as neither had seen Blantyre previously. They walked past many shops and banks, as well as food stores and businesses.

"This seems to be quite a modern city, for such a small African country," Angela said as they left a dress store.

The two packages under Lucas' arm testified to the purchases they had made as they turned and began to ascend one of the steep hills behind the Mt. Soche Hotel, in front of the Adventist Mission Hospital. They had left Iuba and their purchases in the hotel room after their walk.

"Do you work here too?" Angela asked as they climbed the hill.

"No contract or anything, but a good friend of mine, Ron Zatthea, practices here and I thought I'd stop and introduce you. There are so few physicians in Malawi that we all know each other and help when we can."

The cobblestone drive to the mission hospital appeared in fair repair, but there were missing stones and potholes along the way, slowing their progress. "When there are few doctors and many patients, I guess you end up working anywhere they need you, Angela," he replied.

They entered the front door of the building and approached the admissions desk.

"Good morning, Doctor Stuart. What can we do for you?" was the immediate response from the receptionist.

"Is Doctor Zatthea about?" Lucas asked.

"I believe he's been called to the theatre to treat an emergency, but it will only take a second to confirm that," was the pleasant reply. "Please have a seat and I'll find out."

They sat waiting for the receptionist to make the call, and heard her inform the Operating Room that Doctor Stuart was in the waiting room. Evidently it was an opportune visit because after a brief pause, the receptionist looked up and said to Lucas, "Doctor Zatthea is tied up in surgery, but he says that he is trying to handle a gunshot wound from last night and would appreciate a hand, if you have a minute."

"We'd be happy to help him," replied Lucas standing immediately and moving toward the doors leading to the interior of the clinic. "Come on, Angie. Perhaps he can use another extra hand."

Chauncey stood also, saying, "I know how to get back to the hotel. See you there," as he turned and moved towards the front entrance. "I've had all of the gore I need for a while."

Lucas knew where the operating theatre was located from numerous previous visits, and he led Angela directly to the changing rooms. After they had both changed into scrub clothes, Lucas leaned into the door where he could see his friend Ron deep into a patient's belly and up to his elbows in blood and debris. Lucas remarked, "Looks like you're having lots of fun this morning, Ron, ol' buddy. Just hang in there for a minute until we can get scrubbed. Help is on the way."

Without looking up from the wound, Ron said, "Good to see that you're back from Angola, Pilgrim, and just in time, too! Get in here and help me to clear up this mess, and we'll get lunch together, my treat."

After a complete scrub, Lucas and Angela entered the operating room and donned the offered gowns and gloves. "Ron, this is my scrub nurse from Angola, Angela. She's also my fiancée. What can we do to make this operation an even bigger problem?" said Lucas, laughing.

Ron looked up for the first time since their arrival and after a brief glance, returned to the gaping hole he had been working in. The wound seemed to be leaking blood from everywhere, so Ron's assistant stepped aside to take the scrub table and Lucas assumed the position of first assistant, opposite Ron. Angela immediately grasped the suction device, and in a few seconds the wound was dry enough to see that the vena cava had a small puncture hole spurting blood rhythmically at the base of the blood vessel.

"There's the problem!" exclaimed Ron, as he extended his right hand towards the scrub nurse standing at the table. "6-0 suture," he said calmly and the slap of the needle holder against his gloved hand resounded across the room. "Lucas, can you hold that piece of intestine a little higher, so I can get to that spurter easier?" he mumbled.

Sweat now began to appear on Ron's black forehead as he concentrated on closing the leaking hole in the friable tissue of the finger-sized pulsating blood vessel at the bottom of the wound.

"You're getting it," encouraged Lucas, as he held the now-dry blood vessel to one side as Ron finished the neat, even row of stitches across the defect. Putting a damp sponge across the now-dry wound, Ron looked up and greeted Angela, "Nice to meet you Angela. You seem to know your way around a wound, but this might have been a different result if you and that big clown hadn't arrived at that exact moment. Thanks Lucas, we can finish this thing up now and go get something to eat."

As Ron finished the procedure, assisted by Lucas and Angela, Lucas gave a running soliloquy on Ron's rise to becoming a physician. "You see, Angie, Ron was born here in Malawi and raised locally on his parents' farm. He was a bright lad and succeeded in school way beyond the other children."

"Yeah," remarked Ron as he continued to suture the wound. "I was so bright that they threw me out of the country."

"No," continued Lucas, "that was a social issue. Ron seemed to have a problem with some of the government policies, and felt that there might be a better future in England. He migrated there to finish his education and medical school before he returned to work here at the mission."

"Sure," continued Ron, "that way I can work for almost no pay and get assistance from other starving doctors, like Lucas."

Angie was now laughing, as were the rest of the operating room staff. "Have you two always been like this?" she asked.

"Only since this big American showed up ten or twelve years ago and I needed to keep his ego under control," said Ron, stripping off his gown and gloves, as they finished the operation. They shook hands warmly in the recovery room. "Good to see you again, man. Let's see about some Chinese food for lunch." It was early afternoon.

"What about Chauncey?" asked Angela.

"He's probably eaten and headed for the airport to check out that beloved plane, before leaving later this evening," replied Lucas. "We'll see him for tea before he leaves."

The trio walked down the hill a few hundred yards and entered the Hunan Restaurant to eat. It became evident to Angela by their easy repartee that the two physicians, though living in the same country and knowing each other for years, were only actually able to meet occasionally.

During the meal Ron asked, "So how long have you two been engaged?" Most of the rest of lunch was taken up with the story of their adventures. When they left the restaurant, their parting words were an invitation to Ron to bring his wife for supper and to come to the wedding, which he would have attended anyway. After eating, Angela and Lucas returned to the hotel to find Chauncey sitting comfortably in the hotel bar, overlooking the swimming pool at the rear of the hotel. He was sipping a cold beer and watching the other guests as they sat around the swimming pool below him with their families.

"What's going on?" asked Lucas as they walked over to his table and sat down.

"Are you two finished saving lives?" he joked. "I'm just relaxing for a few minutes before I have to fly south this evening. Evidently, there's a load of supplies that needs to be sent to Angola from South Africa and I've been asked to get it there."

"Are you going near Lubalo?" asked Angela after she ordered a Coke for herself and root beer for Lucas. "We'd be interested to hear how it's going."

"Don't know for sure...Probably not, as there isn't a landing strip for hundreds of miles. More likely, I'll be flying to Luanda."

They finished their drinks and Chauncey went to pack his luggage. The three friends met at the front desk of the hotel and walked together to the entrance where a taxi was waiting to take him to the airport. Iuba strained at his leash to reach the potted plant sitting in the foyer, but was unable to convince Angela that it was necessary. He got his chance a few minutes later on the hotel's expansive lawns.

"I guess we've seen some of Africa together," Lucas said. "I'm sure we'll meet again."

Throwing his baggage into the back of the taxi, Chauncey put his arm around Angela's shoulder and kissed her on the cheek. "Look, Angie, I know that you two will be tying the knot in a few weeks, and I'd better get an invitation to the party. Just call the home mission in Johannesburg and leave a message as to the time and place. You can count on me being there."

Lucas shook Chauncey's hand and said, "We'll do it. Have a safe trip back to South Africa this evening. You know our address. Thanks again for everything."

Chauncey climbed into the front seat of the taxi and was gone.

"Time to get our truck and load it Angela," said Lucas. "It's a long drive to Nsanje, and I'd feel better if we got there before dark. If we get to bed early, we can leave tomorrow morning after breakfast.

Supper and the evening were spent relaxing in the hotel. Ron brought his wife and the four enjoyed dinner at the restaurant on the top floor of the Mount Souche Hotel. As Angela got to know Ron's wife, Rhonda, and Ron better, she could understand how the friendship of all four of them made life more sociable in this remote corner of Africa. In Angola, Becky Williamson and her father did the same. Angela genuinely liked the pretty, intelligent Rhonda and looked forward to having her as a friend. There weren't many doctors' wives with whom to socialize, and she had no practice moving in that type of society. She worried that she might need help getting along with the local wives.

Next morning, the brief drive through Blantyre was pleasant, as they passed the Blantyre Sports Club. The tennis courts were busy as usual, and the club's extensive golf course extended the luxuriant green carpet next to the Rangely Botanical Gardens to the south on the Joachim Chissano Road.

"Iuba seems to enjoy having his head outside the window in the breeze," observed Angela as they continued moving towards Mpemba, on the outskirts of Blantyre.

"If we had taken the road to the east," commented Lucas, "we would have gone into the Malawi highlands to see the extensive

348

tea estates up in the mountains. Remind me to take you to Thyolo…Really an interesting place."

"Where are we going?" asked Angela.

"We're heading due south to follow the Shire River Valley in the lowlands. We'll get to the river in a few kilometers at Kanjedza. When we come out of the mountains the view is breath-taking, as you can see the river and valley for many miles!"

"Oh yes," replied Angela. "David Livingston described the view in his notes. I guess he was the first white man to see the valley and describe it in 1859."

The road from Blantyre seemed to twist forever between the hills and mountains until they arrived at a police check-point on the road near another mountain pass. After a routine police inspection, they continued to travel along the narrow hard-topped highway for another few kilometers. A sharp bend in the road brought them to a high overlook of the entire Shire Valley, giving them a view for a hundred miles of the tortuous river as it gleamed in the sunlight below them. The surrounding hills and valleys stretched before them for hundreds of miles.

"That's amazing," said Angela, as they came to a stop at a roadside stopping point. "No wonder you enjoy Malawi so much; it's a beautiful country. I can see the river shining in the sun for miles. The valley is entirely divided into individual farms as far as the eye can see."

They sat in the truck for a few minutes admiring the view of the dark green valley expanding below them. Iuba had a chance to explore the bushes and Angela remarked as she and Iuba walked along the overlook, "The river seems to twist and turn as it moves along the valley towards Mozambique, but there are many areas where the water expands, causing wide, glistening areas that must mark areas where the river is few miles wide."

"Yes," replied Lucas. "The river at present is in flood stage due to the recent rains, and flooding of the valley in certain low areas is common this time of year. Three months from now, the river will be confined to its banks again. Those wide areas of flood water are only a few feet deep, but can be occupied by crocodiles and snakes, as well as fish. When the water recedes, they will leave fertile land for the farmers to plant."

"How long is the Shire Valley, Lucas?" she inquired.

"At least another 150 miles," he answered. "It runs all the way to Nsanje and on into Mozambique. At this time of year, it's a beautiful drive."

"I really never imagined what a beautiful country you have been living in, Lucas. Southern Malawi appears to be fertile and well-watered, not unlike Angola."

"Yeah Angela, but this is still Africa, and with the same diseases and problems of other African countries. As you well know, there are still many poor people and wide-spread disease, but it's a place that you can feel the rewards of your invested time. I think you'll find that the general population is extremely friendly and receptive to our efforts to help them."

Loading Iuba, they drove south from their elevated perch on the mountain peak overlooking the valley. As they came to the base of the mountain, a barrier across the road prevented their proceeding along the flat river road.

A black member of the police force greeted them in a friendly tone of voice and addressed Lucas by name, as he approached their truck.

"I see you have returned to us, Doctor Stuart. We've missed you at the Nsanje Clinic. There's a bunch of sick people here in the valley who will be happy to hear of your return."

Reaching out to return the officer's offered hand, Lucas said, "Mambo, I've missed the valley and all of you very much. It's always nice to return home to my friends. You'll pass the word, I'm sure, that we're returning back to the mission hospital and in a few days we'll be happy to see any problems that the valley people might have."

Looking up from Lucas, Mambo spotted Angela's smiling, amiable face as she sat next to him. His entire countenance lit up into a huge genial smile, showing his even teeth between his large lips. "So you have acquired a wife on your travels, Doctor Lucas? Ah, she is very beautiful. I must inform the population of her beauty."

Lucas began to laugh gently. "Mambo, you will have the jungle telegraph sending false messages in a minute. The word will reach Nsanje Mission, all 120 miles away, before we even arrive."

"This beautiful lady is not your wife?" he quickly answered. "But she wears the ring of marriage on her left hand, and also shows a pin of medicine on her collar."

"Mambo, please meet Sister Angela, my intended. She is a great nurse from Angola who has come to help us at the mission and has also agreed to marry me."

Reaching across Lucas' chest, the captain shook Angela's hand, and maintaining a wide grin remarked, "Doctor Lucas is not as insensitive as I feared. Sister Angela, we welcome you from the whole valley as we need medical assistance. More importantly, the doctor needs someone to care for him and to assist in the care of the people of the valley. When is the marriage ceremony?"

"Be careful how you answer, Angie," smiled Lucas. "Whatever date you give, the entire population of the Shire Valley will be there."

Fully understanding the system of African rumor and transmission of information, Angela said, "Mambo, it will be sometime in the next three weeks, and we formally invite everyone to come and celebrate with us. We will get the word out for the exact date so that everyone will know."

As they drove away, following the roadway beside the fully flowing river, Lucas said, "You have no idea what you have just done, Angie. There won't be a person in the valley for two hundred miles who won't know the whole story, and everyone will come for the free meal and the marriage celebration." Kissing her cheek, he continued, "It will be fun, and the dancing and singing will be unique. Everyone will come to meet the new nursing sister. You're going to have to prepare for many gifts and being adopted into the valley's family. Incidentally, when *are* we getting married?"

"If this is going to happen," she said as they proceeded along the river road, "we will have to get organized. My family needs to be invited, as well as all of our friends from Angola. If this will involve all of the locals from the valley, we will have to provide food and drinks for the mass of attendees, all in a few weeks."

"This will be easier than you think," replied Lucas. "Once the word is out, everyone at Nsanje will help get ready for the celebration. There's nothing like a celebration to generate enthusiasm, and there is plenty of space near the mission. The word probably will have already reached Nsanje long before we can arrive there."

The road followed the general path of the Shire River, often crossing higher plateaus to avoid the flooding waters. They were slowed by the multiple shallow overflows and the muddy terrain. As they proceeded along the road, passing multiple people walking along the roadside carrying various items, Angela saw that Lucas' truck was recognized by almost everyone, as the pedestrians waved and smiled as they proceeded along the seemingly endless pathway south to Nsanje.

"Is there anyone who doesn't know you?" she asked, as four hands immediately rose in greeting as they passed through the small town of Bangula.

"You're already renowned, honey. Just be nice and friendly. We should be there in another hour or so."

They came to a stop in the center of the town, the dirt road showed a crossroad with traffic on foot and an oxcart crossing before them. A smiling old man approached the unmoving truck and greeted Lucas, "Doctor Lucas, I see you have your future wife with you. We are all planning to come to the wedding celebration."

Angela smiled at the man in the tattered cap and misshaped shirt with dark stains. She mumbled to Lucas, "The jungle telegraph succeeds again. We just arrived and the news is here already."

The sign at the crossroad indicated a right hand turn "To Nsanje Mission Hospital, Sixty Kilometers." They turned right onto a dirt track and proceeded through the tall, green grass, moving slowly beside the parade of foot traffic headed south.

"Almost home." remarked Lucas, "and it's still light."

# 19
## Chapter

T he sixty kilometer drive between Bangula and the mission seemed to last only a few minutes as they moved through the emerald Southern Malawi countryside. Angela noted that a ridge of slate-colored mountains ran parallel to their path, some twenty kilometers to the west. Somewhere to the east the massive Shire River flowed a few kilometers from the dirt and gravel road, but its course was obscured by the virulent foliage growing on both sides of the track. Angela also noted the floodplain of extremely fertile soil stretching in all directions as they proceeded south along the road towards Nsanje.

It was apparent that this must be the location where much of the food is grown for the entire country, as the soil was dark and rich, with all types of crops growing in rich profusion. It was easy to see that everything was carefully cultivated with the neat rows of weed-free crops in full maturity.

"Yes," replied Lucas, when she commented on the agricultural region. "Farther north, near Thyolo, there are mountain ranges where you'll find many flourishing plantations and estates for growing coffee and tea. We can explore those a little later, when we have more time."

They continued to drive along the dusty gravel road, encountering no interruption in the steady flow of pedestrian traffic. This movement was interspersed with oxcarts and bicycles jostling in both directions, as the flow of traffic, carrying goods towards their destinations, made driving a constant hazard.

"Is traffic this dense most of the time?" asked Angela, as the people appeared to be walking not only on the margins of the road, but often on the track itself. In many places, there were clusters of individuals crowded closely together into clots, obstructing their truck's path.

"It's like this most of the time, honey. There is no other way the farmers can get their products to market. Even the occasional bus or truck would have to travel the same roads. This road from Bangula is almost the only route by which these crops can be moved north to feed the millions of hungry mouths in Northern Malawi."

Angela felt her excitement mounting as the distance to Lucas' home station shortened. She also noticed that as they came nearer to Nsanje, Lucas' truck seemed to be recognized by almost every person they passed on the road, and even some people sitting on the front porches of their houses extended some type of greeting as they drove past. Iuba gazed from the window at the panorama of Malawi as it passed before him.

"Big fish in a small pond," he laughed. "There aren't many doctors for hundreds of miles, so they all recognize me. We turn here."

They slowed to a crawl in the center of the small town square at a sign proclaiming, "Nsanje." Lucas made a sharp left and started down a short dirt road. At the end of the road, on the left, was a prominent white-painted, brick entranceway crowned by an iron arch, under which a white metal gate barred the road. Across the archway were the words "Nsanje Baptist Mission."

An elderly black man, wearing a dark green uniform stood up immediately upon seeing their truck, and with a huge grin that revealed many missing teeth he announced, as he pulled open the metal gate, "Ahhh, Doctor Lucas and the young lady. We were expecting you about now. An emergency was brought in a while ago and they are waiting for both of you in the operating theatre."

Lucas and Angela looked at each other and said in unison, "The jungle telegraph triumphs again," and started laughing.

After Lucas drove to the parking lot at the side of the hospital, both he and Angela got out of the truck. As he led her through the side door, Lucas remarked,

"It doesn't sound too serious. I don't see an ambulance in the parking lot. Probably just nicks and scratches. We'll go inside and see what it is. Usually, if there is serious damage, a big production would be in progress by now." Iuba followed behind them, after inspecting some of the shrubbery around the building.

As they walked the corridors towards the operating theatre, Angela estimated that the hospital had about three hundred beds and that the Nsanje Mission Hospital appeared to be at least twenty years old. She also noted that the building was exceptionally well-maintained with sparkling concrete-painted floors and clean patient rooms.

"Has it been like this as long have you've worked here?" she whispered as they entered the dressing room that served as an anteroom for the minor surgical suite.

"Only for the last year," he answered.

"As far as I can see, someone has taken excellent care of the facility. It seems brand new." Iuba followed his mistress into the dressing room and lay down in a corner.

"Yeah," he replied, as he pushed open the door and led her into the room with a patient lying on a bed. "We had the whole place repainted and repaired last year, so it's in fairly good shape."

"Doctor Lucas!" exclaimed a short, black, extremely obese nurse, her face lighting up as he and Angela came into the room. "We were expecting you! You've been missed greatly, and when we heard that you were on your way, we waited for you."

"Angie, this is Elvira, the Theatre Matron and boss of the Nsanje Mission Hospital operating room. Elvira, meet Angela."

A frown crossed the face of Elvira, as she looked at Angela. "So this is the future Mrs. Stuart? The rumors have already reached us. She looks undernourished to me. We'll have to get some sadza into her as soon as we finish the surgery," she said breaking into a wide smile.

Angela immediately liked the operating room supervisor. "I'm happy to meet you, Elvira. What can we do to help here?"

"Where's the patient's problem?" asked Lucas, good naturedly.

"Well, we have an HIV patient with an upper respiratory infection that has moved into his chest, and it's strangling him, Doctor." she replied. "He may need a tracheotomy."

The patient lay comatose on the table struggling to breathe.

Lucas immediately picked up a stethoscope lying on a nearby table and listened intently to the patient's chest. "This man definitely needs a trach," he said after a few seconds. "Let's get the tracheotomy set before he suffocates."

Five minutes later, with the tracheotomy in place, Lucas listened again to the man's chest, saying to the nurse, "He's exchanging air freely. He should be fine. Send him to a hospital bed, and start some intravenous antibiotics." He then turned to Angela, saying, "And we'd better get Iuba outta' here. He's contaminating the whole room!"

Iuba had followed Angela and Lucas into the hospital and then sneaked into the emergency suite when the door opened. He was now lying next to the doorway, showing his teeth silently when approached by anyone, refusing to move.

"Come on, ole boy!" Angela said calmly, opening the O.R. door and leading the now wagging-tailed dog into the dressing room. "You're not welcome in here, so just wait a few minutes and we'll get you some air."

Elvira noted that Iuba was limping and had some major scars, so she asked Lucas if the dog was healthy. After hearing about his encounter, she moved aside as Angela led him into the hall: "I don't want to mess with *that* animal. He can take care of himself!"

When they had finished in the operating theatre, Angela and Lucas returned to the dressing room to put on their street clothes and, with Iuba, made a brief tour of the hospital. They were warmly greeted by the entire staff at each ward. Lucas introduced Angela and Iuba with the warning that the dog would not attack, but was not to be fed or patted. Iuba's experiences from Angola had taught him about hospitals, and Lucas felt that he could have free access to the entire hospital, with the exception of the surgical suites. A brief discussion with the hospital administrator and director of nursing resulted in a reluctantly confirmed agreement to Iuba's universal access. At any other major African hospital, employees would have been surprised to see an eighty pound English Bull Terrier calmly patrolling the hospital wards and being greeted by nurses and patients alike, but this was Nsanje, Lucas' home mission, and so Iuba was tolerated. After a warm reunion with Lucas, the administrator cheerfully validated Angela's qualifications as Lucas' assistant. They were also pleasantly surprised to hear that she was his fiancée.

"It's time to see our living quarters, Angie. They have placed your accommodations in the nurses' quarters until we're married, so you won't be there for long. Iuba will stay with me," said Lucas, "as I have a house, and a nursing dormitory will not be the best place for him."

Lucas and Angela walked across the luxuriant grass behind the hospital toward a cottage about a quarter-mile from the hospital building. Iuba followed, as he had assumed his duty of investigating every bush and tree along the way. In the fading sunlight, the afterglow of the sunset produced an outline of the small building that made the house seem to reflect the light and leave a silhouette of extreme serenity as they approached it. No lights were apparent from within.

"Oh Lucas!" Angela remarked. "What a nice home. Have you been living here for the past years? No wonder you were so anxious to return to Nsanje."

Lucas opened the front door and entered the house behind Iuba, who decided to examine the building ahead of everyone else. They stood in the living room, which, while not pristine, was well ordered and clean.

"I see that the ladies have kept the place up," observed Lucas. Iuba answered his observation with a low growl, followed by a snarl, as he stood holding his ground in the living room.

"Conscience, is that you?" called Lucas, as he put his hand on Iuba's collar to hold him in check, knowing that the dog sensed there was someone within the building.

A petite lady appeared at the doorway that led to the living room from the kitchen, her black face aglow as she lit up with a smile.

"Doctor Lucas and the lady! We heard yesterday of your arrival in the country. Supper is almost ready, but I see you have brought another visitor. What's his name?"

"Good evening, Conscience. Thank you for thinking of us. This is Angela, who will soon be the mistress of the house. Iuba here is not too friendly to strangers, but will soon make friends when he gets used to you, so we'll leave him alone for a while until he knows you better."

Angela immediately felt a rapport with Conscience, who had taken care of Lucas for all these years. After he had introduced them, Lucas retrieved their luggage, moving the drugs and supplies from the truck into the hospital with the assistance of a few of the orderlies who had followed them from the hospital. They moved Angela's suitcases into the nurses' quarters, and fifteen minutes later he had returned to the house, leaving Angela to get acquainted with Conscience.

When he returned, he found Angela and Conscience sitting in the kitchen discussing domestic matters over tea and Iuba sleeping under Angela's chair, as was his custom.

"If Conscience has been running the cottage for all of these years, I'll do my best to get to know her and become friends," remarked Angela. "She knows your routine and I can learn from her."

"That won't be difficult. Conscience is friendly and easy to know," he laughed.

"Supper is in fifteen minutes," Conscience announced. "Miss Angela, you may be living with the nurses for a while, but we insist that you eat with us."

After a supper of sadza and beef, Iuba curled up in front of the burning fireplace, while Lucas and Angela settled into the comfortable chairs in the living room and sipped hot chocolate. In the evening, a chill could be felt when the sun went down here in the foothills of the Malawi Mountains, and the warm liquid warmed them as they sat and talked. It was time to discuss the future.

"If we have decided to be married in about three weeks, we'd better start to make a plan," said Angela. "Do we send invitations, and to whom?"

Lucas began to laugh. "Honey, this marriage will be an event for the whole Shire Valley. No invitations will be necessary for Malawi. Invited or not, everyone will show up for the party. Only relatives and friends from outside the country will have to receive an invitation."

"So we need a list of those we want to invite, including all of our friends and relatives in Europe and your relatives in America," replied Angela.

"The wedding itself will be at the mission church…maybe there's seating for a hundred or so…but the festivities afterwards will be a major event and will have to be held on the mission grounds," observed Lucas. "We won't serve alcohol, but food and drink will still be a major undertaking."

"But Lucas, if we're planning this wedding to be in three weeks or so, we're going to have to get our ideas organized now. Who are you going to ask to be the best man?" inquired Angela

"I have many friends in America," commented Lucas, "But I haven't seen them since I've been in Africa. On thinking about it, Ron would be a possibility, but why couldn't I ask Sir William, and he might bring Gayle along with him from England?"

"Yes, and my father and Tad will have to come from England, too. How to locate Jake could be a problem, as he's probably deep in the bush somewhere in Angola."

"We can't forget to invite Chauncey, and I'm sure the Rhodesian Selous Scouts will inform Sean, who I'll bet will appear out of some remote jungle camp. There's no way he'd forgive us if we made him miss a party like this!" laughed Angela. "I'd bet they all would enjoy coming to Malawi where it's peaceful and quiet."

"And bridesmaids?" asked Lucas.

"Becky Williamson has been my best friend for a long time. She and her father were forced by the war to flee to Luanda when the Lubalo Mission was raided. She'll be happy to be my Maid of Honor, but we need to locate her first. We know they were in Luanda before going on to Scotland, and the Presbyterian Mission Board in Edinburgh will know exactly where they are. Who is to marry us, Lucas?"

"Either your father or Reverend Williamson, your choice. I've not met either, but since you're the bride, you get to choose."

"If Dad is strong enough to come from England, he's the one whom I'd want to marry me."

After an evening spent going over the finer points of the wedding plans, Lucas yawned, and remarked, "Then it's all set. Tomorrow we can get started organizing the wedding. We have a lot to do tomorrow, and Elvira said the backlog at the hospital of patients waiting to be treated has been piling up.. Evidently the hospital was sending most of the serious cases to Blantyre for three months, but the non-emergency patients will need to be seen. It's time for bed. Let's take Iuba with us and I'll walk with you over to the nurse's residence so he'll get a chance to get some air. Then he can come back to the house with me for the night."

Angela reached down and patted Iuba, who, as usual, was sitting next to her with his head on her knee. "I know, ole' boy. It won't take long for you to get used to the Nsanje Mission, but with the influx of travelers for the wedding you're going to have to accept a lot of strangers." Angela knew that Iuba would be reluctant to stay every night for three weeks with Lucas, but there was no place in the nurses' quarters for him. He had been with Lucas every day, and after the marriage the problem would be over.

After leaving Angela at the nurses' residence, Lucas and Iuba found a bench next to the path leading back to his cottage. Sitting in the darkness, with the cool evening breeze blowing softly through the leaves of the surrounding trees, Lucas mused out loud to Iuba. "You know, Iuba," he said patting the dog and scratching his ears, "being married will really change my situation. I've always been responsible for only myself, and now I'll have a wife and, eventually, children to watch out for. That's an obligation for the rest of my life that I won't take lightly."

Iuba, realizing that Lucas was talking to him, stood up, and wagged his tail so vigorously that he was moving the whole back half of his body. He lifted his front paws onto Lucas' lap, so he was able to lick his face, and whined.

"Well, it appears that you are satisfied with the situation, Iuba, so it must be okay. Maybe we'd better head for bed."

Iuba refused to return to the cottage with Lucas, but trotted off to the front door of the nurses' residence, and finding a comfortable spot, he lay down to wait for Angela to emerge the following morning. Lucas knew that Iuba could be trusted to behave himself unless he thought his mistress was in danger, so he went home to get some rest.

Early the following morning, Lucas walked over to the hospital to review the backlog of pending cases and patients waiting to be evaluated. The list seemed endless, and as he reviewed each case he began to feel a twinge of guilt for having been in Angola for so long. "I didn't realize that so many of the natives needed medical treatment while I was gone," he thought as he reviewed the list.

Angela also rose early and went over to Lucas' house, sharing her breakfast with the ever-present Iuba, who had met her outside the dormitory. She began to work on the marriage invitations they had discussed the previous evening.

"This shouldn't take long," she confided to Iuba, as a few names appeared on Lucas' computer screen. As the minutes passed, the list grew longer. "We'll really need to invite these people from outside the country," she advised the sleeping dog at her feet. After working on the list, it became apparent that many of those invited would have to make plans to fly to Africa. "Making plans to fly to Africa will take some time. Perhaps three weeks won't be enough time," she concluded after an hour of work. She saved the list and headed for the hospital to help Lucas treat patients and to discuss the guests on the list with him.

Lucas arrived to find a long line of waiting patients outside of the clinic door, standing quietly anticipating treatment. This sedate row of people included all ages, from infants to the aged, and stretched across the grass and outside into the parking lot. Many of those waiting had come from fifty or a hundred miles away, walking on foot or riding buses after the mission had made it known to the general population that Lucas would soon return. They had begun to arrive two days ago and, without instructions, formed into a queue starting at the clinic door and stretching for hundreds of feet across the property of the mission. This was a silent, relaxed group, experienced and needing no regulation, with whole families sitting or standing in good order on the well-kept lawn. Almost every group had brought their own food and sleeping gear, anticipating the long wait for medical attention over the years. Even the younger children conformed to this well-ordered behavior pattern.

"Well," remarked Lucas upon inspecting the unusually long list of waiting patients as Angela arrived, "we'd better triage the group, so we'll be able to help the severely sick first, and then proceed to the rest."

After checking on the patients within the hospital, including the tracheotomy patient whom they had operated on the night before, Lucas started at the clinic door and proceeded to walk slowly along the line of patients, greeting many of them by name and asking what problem had brought them to Nsanje this morning. As he spoke Chewa fluently, there was no wasted time with interpretation or misunderstandings. The extremely diseased and those in the most pain were moved to the front of the line. No one objected to this policy, as this had been the strategy at the mission since Lucas had first arrived many years ago.

He greeted his nurse as she arrived and was unlocking the door to the clinic as she approached. "We seem to have collected a wide assortment of complaints, so you can help me organize them into priorities for treatment." She understood well his method of organization, but because of her lack of ability to speak *Chewa* one of the orderlies followed her to translate her questions.

Iuba, no stranger to mission hospitals and experienced with the process from Angola, found a shaded place under a large

Massasa tree in a remote corner of the front lawn and lay down quietly so he could observe Angela and still not be underfoot. The profuse cascade of patients continued uninterrupted until one o'clock, when Angela finally closed the clinic door. The many unexamined patients remaining inline were informed kindly that, "We will resume the clinic at seven tomorrow morning." She said this with a pleasant smile to those waiting at the front of the line.

"How many cases do we have for surgery this afternoon?" asked Lucas as they left the clinic for lunch.

"Only four or five minor cases," she replied, "But we have some issues to discuss about the wedding at lunch."

Iuba followed behind them as they sauntered across the gravel pathway to the cafeteria. As they sat at a table eating their lunch of vegetables and sadza, Angela explained that the number of people to attend the actual wedding would be relatively small compared to the masses, as Conscience had informed her, who would expect to be entertained at the reception following the wedding. Also, there was the time needed for guests to plan to attend, some coming from Europe.

"What do we do about the mob arriving from the whole valley and our obligation to feed and entertain them? How many should we expect to show up, Lucas?"

"No way to really know," Lucas calmly observed, as he swallowed his last few drops of hot tea. "The invited guests might be around 150, needing tables and chairs. The uninvited guests will likely exceed two thousand, including native dancers, chiefs, and the general population. George Patrick, a physician friend of mine, got hitched up in Mzuzu, in the northern part of the country, last spring. There must have been at least that many attendees."

"So, are we supposed to feed that entire group?" Angela asked incredulously.

"Yes, if we want to remain friends with the Valley people. We don't have to seat them, but it's the custom to provide food….. Probably kettles of sadza and gravy with some type of meat in it. It's no problem; Conscience has friends to do the cooking and distribution. We must remember to add the local and national politicians to the list of invited guests."

"I hate to think of the cost," mumbled Angela.

"Relax, honey. We'll only get married once, and you'll remember the wedding for the rest of your life. It isn't as expensive as it sounds. The 150 invited guests will be typical of any wedding, but the singing and chanting, drum pounding and tambourines contributed by our local indigenous friends will be unique, as will the native dress. It should be a lot of fun."

Angela got up from lunch and escorted Iuba outside to sit for a few minutes in the warm sun before going back into the depths of the hospital to do the surgeries. Finding a comfortable seat on a rock near a massive baobab tree, she sat down quietly scratching her ever-present companion's head. Feeling sleepy, she lay back on the grass, and drifted off to sleep, with the vigilant Iuba resting his head on her thigh. The two friends remained there peaceably for ten minutes until Iuba let out a low growl, followed by a nasty aggressive snarl. The threatening sound immediately woke Angela. Sitting up, she grasped the dog's collar and said, "Easy, Iuba. It's all right, boy!"

As she looked around, she could see no problem. In the surrounding area she saw not a single person, but the dog's threatening demeanor continued. As she watched Iuba's eyes, she noticed that the center of his concentration seemed to be on something behind her. She turned her head, and noticed a small mongoose sitting a few meters behind her, with its head high and front feet lifted up. Still she saw no cause for alarm, but Angela had grown up in a remote African location, and knew at the first glance that the mongoose was ready to pounce on some object.

She froze.

In a split second, a greenish-brown snake rose from the grass, striking three feet of head and body directly at Angela and Iuba. It never got there. The mongoose hit the back of the neck and head of the striking snake in mid-air, pulling it backwards and down as the small furry animal's razor sharp teeth penetrated the scales of the Gabon pit viper's neck. She heard a loud "crack" as the spine of the snake was broken and it writhed in its death agony. The mongoose calmly began to tear at the body of the snake, eating large chunks of the flesh.

"That mongoose saved both of us, Iuba" breathed Angela when she was able to speak. "The viper could easily have killed us. There's no way I could have known that it was there. A snake that size carries enough venom to kill a roomful of people."

Iuba, unaware of the service that the mongoose had given, was all for attacking the mongoose. Angela firmly pulled him to the gravel pathway, leaving the small animal to feast on his prize.

"You can't ever be sure about the bush," Lucas remarked when Angela related her story after she returned to the operating theatre. "I'm just glad that you were smart enough not to move so that Wilbur could kill the snake. That mongoose has been protecting the mission for a few years now. You can thank him later by leaving a piece of beef where he'll be able to find it. He's tame enough not to run at the sight of you, but no one has ever gotten close enough to touch him."

After finishing their work at the hospital, Lucas and Angela worked out a list of invitations to their wedding over supper. Some had to be sent by mail, but many of the guests could only be reached by phone or fax. It didn't take an extended length of time, so they sat together on the couch in Lucas' living room together afterwards for an hour or so, working out other wedding details.

"You know Angela, I really never knew that I needed someone until I met you," Lucas said as he softly kissed her on the mouth. "It was similar to my faith. I was content as things were, and then when He finally came into my life it was all consuming. Jesus took over my entire existence, the same as you have."

"I think that happens to many people. Until they meet Jesus, they really never know that they need the Lord."

"Well, it was the same with you, Angela. I was a content, happy bachelor until we met, and now it's hard to imagine living without you at my side."

Angela smiled and looked deeply into Lucas blue eyes, remarking, "Listen here, Doctor, you'd better get used to me because I'll be right next to you for the next fifty years or so."

Lucas pulled her close to him and said, "That's what I'm counting on, my sweet thing."

They laughed together and Lucas began to explain what she should expect at the indigenous wedding ceremony, even though in Angola she would have experienced many similar events.

"Malawi, of course, is not that far from Angola in statute miles, but there seem to be certain traditions unique to the Malawian people. If your father presides over the ceremony, it likely will be over in about a half-an-hour, but for the native traditional ceremony, which will follow, it will take another two hours of dancing, chanting, incantations, and certain bewitched blessings by the witch doctor. You shouldn't laugh during the native portion of the festivities, as the indigenous population takes it all very seriously. You'll get to smile and laugh when it's all over."

Angela now began to pay active attention to the coming local ceremony. "So explain what the *nanga*[1*] does in these two hours, Lucas."

Lucas held her tightly and kissed her repeatedly, saying, "You must wait and see! Just go along with whatever he does. But don't worry, there's no pain involved...I think..." He laughed wholeheartedly at her gullible expression. "I suggest that a good coating of cold crème on the skin won't be a mistake before you apply your wedding day makeup."

"From that remark, I assume that I get painted up?"

"The ladies will help you, and they will likely assist you out of your wedding dress and into some more comfortable clothes," Lucas said with a broad smile.

Acting casually, Angela asked, "Speaking of wedding dresses, where will I obtain a wedding dress around here, anyway?"

Lucas returned with a sly smile, "I already contacted Sir William at his home in London a few days ago, when we were in Zimbabwe, about your wedding dress. He and Gayle will be visiting us in two weeks. The dress is being made for you in London, and from his reply, the two of them are having a dress specifically made for you. They will bring it with them."

"You didn't! A girl should be entitled to pick her own dress." said Angela, offended by his audacity. Angela started to protest, but Lucas went on,

"I know, Gayle anticipated that you would object but she was certain that one of Sir William's dressmaker friends will be able to finish it on time and no one here could do it justice. I looked at one of your other dresses for the size and gave it to them."

Angela wasn't convinced by his argument, but he continued;

"Yeah, and you'd have picked some normal dress that was *affordable*. Those two will bring a garment that fits the occasion and will still be talked about for months after the service," laughed Lucas.

"It's kind of them, but I'm afraid of what the dress will look like…Say! How did you know what date to tell them to come?"

"I told them to prepare to stay with us for ten days, so that it will all work out. Gayle is bringing her personal hair dresser with them, too, so that you'll look even more stunning. He also does makeup, but I doubt that type of person will like Africa."

"It must be nice to be that wealthy," Angela replied jokingly. "Oh, and who else is coming with them?"

"Now that you asked, your father and brother will be on their private plane with them. They all met in London when Tad and your Dad returned to Scotland. Sir William located them through the Foreign Mission Board.

"So I don't even need to send them an invitation?"

"Well, it would be nice to send an invitation, but I assume the party is already getting organized," replied Lucas.

Angela was perturbed that Lucas had worked out this portion of the wedding without her assistance. But she was also positive that if Gayle and Sir William were selecting a dress to be made specifically for her in London, it would be the most magnificent creation that anyone in Malawi had ever seen.

"A hairdresser from London, in Africa? You've got to be kidding!" she moaned. "Please let me in on these little secrets ahead of time, Lucas. The wedding is for *both* of us, and a woman wants to plan her own ceremony, at least the traditional part, anyway."

Despite their dispute, they made up their differences easily and kissed passionately on the sofa. Then, Angela and Iuba headed for the nurses' quarters as Lucas had been called from the emergency room to evaluate a patient with an acute abdomen and in severe pain.

"So we'll have to begin organizing early tomorrow morning to send out invitations and decide specifics on the ceremony for Saturday three weeks from tomorrow, Iuba," Angela said to her four-footed companion as they walked to the front door of her building. Iuba said little, but he sensed the excitement in her voice as she patted his head after he lay down in his nightly spot next to the entrance to the nurses' apartment.

The next few weeks were filled with anxious organization as preparation for the big event progressed. The indigenous word from the mission went out all over the Shire Valley, and those not receiving a formal invitation made plans to visit the Nsanje Mission on the appointed day anyway. Dignitaries and politicians received formal invitations, as did their family members. Friends from outside the country were contacted by phone, as was Ron in Blantyre. Lucas' parents sent their sincere regrets as they would be in Europe, but Lucas' remark told the story,

"They didn't come to my graduation from college or Medical School and it would be a cold day in a very hot place before Mom would travel to remote Africa for anything."

"Heck, Lucas, by now, everyone in the Shire Valley is aware of the ceremony and we have guests coming from all over the country that I don't even know," remarked Angela one afternoon a few days before the ceremony. "It's strange that your Mom and Dad aren't coming, I hope to meet them later." She was aware that Lucas was uncomfortable about his parents' absence.

"Marriages seem to occur all the time, Angie, but the social interplay, as well as the free food and drink, are irresistible to a rural population, isolated and loving to have a good time. We should be happy that all of these people are coming to help us celebrate. I'll miss my family, but we should still have a nice time."

The preparations went smoothly, as the church had to be decorated and the mission grounds prepared for the massive influx of visitors. Food had to be purchased and prepared, and an overhead tarpaulin was constructed for the large mass of people, to fight off the glare of the sun, the blistering heat, or pounding rain.

The refrigerator space at the local butchery and restaurants was all utilized with the cooperation of the local merchants, as was the mission hospital. Water had to be made available, as well as campsites for the gathering crowd. It would have been a nightmare without the cooperation of the entire mission, community, and particularly, Conscience.

"How would we ever have gotten all this together without everyone's help?" Angela asked on the Wednesday before the big day. "Lucas, you have had to keep the mission hospital going while all of these preparations are going on. The plane from London is due in tomorrow morning with my family, Sir William and Gayle," reminded Angela.

Lucas paused for a second, and then asked, "Have we heard from your brother, Jake?"

"I received a wire, through Luanda, from Becky Williamson. She reports that the primary rebel camp, in the middle of the Angola bush, had received my message and that Jake would try to come, but there was no confirmation of it. I have no idea how Jake plans to get to Malawi, but if he knows about the wedding, he'll be here."

Arrivals for the wedding began to appear some three days prior to the wedding date. At first, a few scattered people were seen walking along the Shire Valley road toward the mission, and these people camped on the mission grounds after they arrived. By Friday, the day before the wedding, a virtual crowd had gathered on the mission grounds, already beginning the festivities, with dancing, singing and general celebration, along with the inevitable inebriation.

Plans had been made for Thursday morning to drive up to Blantyre to meet the plane. *It would be nice to see Sir William and Gayle, as well as her dad and Tad again*, Angela thought as she climbed into bed. Angela had decided on Wednesday evening that the preparations seemed to be going well, but she was still not really sure which of the guests from Europe would have arrived by Saturday. The best news was that Sir William and Gayle would stay here for a week after it was over, and that would be nice.

Thursday morning arrived somewhat cloudy, but the temperature remained warm and comfortable. The increasing foot traffic continued to flow into the mission grounds, with ox-carts, pedestrians and any number of other conveyances. Since this was going to be a celebration, the people from the Valley were prepared to have a good time. Food distribution, it was announced, would begin Friday afternoon, but this was not of much general concern, as most visitors brought their own victuals and gallons of the local opaque beer.

"We've got to drive through all these people just to get to the main road to Blantyre?" asked Angela, as they carefully maneuvered the truck through the traffic to the main highway. "I never suspected we would be married in front of a group this size."

"This is only Thursday, honey. Wait until Saturday morning."

The drive to Blantyre Cheleka Airport was uneventful. Sir William's private plane arrived on time from London, carrying Sir William, Gayle, Reverend Abercrombe, Tad, and Bruce, the hairdresser. Bruce was a piece of work, complete with purple pants, a neck scarf, pink shirt and a high, thin voice. Sir William was his usual jovial self and suggested that they all go to the Mount Souche Hotel for lunch. He had read about it in the travel brochure that had commended the venue. Angela was pleased to see her father and Tad again, and after the drive from the airport together, they had caught up with past events. Gayle remarked that Esther had returned to her family in America, who vowed she would never return to Africa under *any* circumstances. Although invited, Esther declined.

After lunch, as they were sitting around the table, Sir William asked, "So what has been done about the bachelor party tomorrow night? Who has organized it and where is it to be held?"

There was a long silence until Lucas said, "I don't believe there is going to be a bachelor party. It would have to be in Nsanje and that might be difficult."

Sir William winked broadly at Angela and said, "I bet we could organize a party Friday night! When we get to the mission, we'll get with a few of the local people and see what can be done."

Everyone laughed at his insinuation, and as they sat there enjoying the joke two tall, muscular men walked silently into the hotel dining room. It was Chauncey and Sean, dressed in army fatigues. They looked tired and were carrying their luggage in duffle bags over their shoulders.

"Where did you two come from?" smiled Angela as the two pulled up chairs from other tables. After the Castle beer had been poured into their glasses and the introductions concluded, Sean took a long drink and Chauncey began to speak. "Someone told me there was going to be a big bash on Saturday, down at the Nsanje Mission. I had to fly to Cheleka Airport to attend the soiree and I ran into a 'black' at a white Salisbury bar who had heard the same rumor. We decided to fly up here together to find out if the story was accurate. Have you all heard exactly where this brawl is going to be held?"

The group sat together and almost immediately everyone began to converse and get acquainted. They all seemed to enjoy meeting each other, and a convivial gathering was soon established. Before they were ready to leave, Angela reminded Lucas that a plane was supposed to arrive from Johannesburg, South Africa, earlier that morning, and perhaps the Williamsons, Becky and her father, Pastor Williamson, might have already arrived.

"How do we check on that?" asked Lucas.

"No problem," remarked Chauncey. "The manifest of the flight is supposed to be confidential, but the airport people know me well. I'll call the airport and find out."

Two minutes on the phone and Chauncey returned with a wide smile, as the rest of the group looked up at him expectantly.

"Okay, they've arrived. Since this is the primary hotel in town, they're probably here. All we need to do is ask for their room number."

An enquiry from the desk clerk, a phone call, and Angela returned to the group smiling happily. "They'll be down in a minute. How are we going to get this entire group into our truck to drive back to Nsanje?" she inquired.

Becky and her dad, Pastor Williamson, walked into the dining room. Angela and Becky embraced, each of them thinking that the other might have been injured or killed in the Angola war, and here they were being reunited safely. A few minutes later, after introductions had been given, the now large party had almost totally overtaken the small hotel dining room. Tad, Sean and Chauncey got along famously, as they all were involved in different wars of Southern Africa and had many common friends. Angela talked to her father, Becky and Reverend Williamson about their recent adventures, while Bruce sat quietly at one of the tables drinking Vodka. Sir William, Gayle and Lucas caught up with events of the world. The group moved out onto the manicured lawn and stood discussing the upcoming festivities and generally continued to get acquainted. Finally, Angela said, "It's getting towards afternoon and we need to leave for the mission so we don't end up driving in the dark. There are now eleven of us, so we'll need another vehicle."

"No problem," spoke up Sir William. "It just so happens that Gayle and I have leased a large VW Kombi and, with your truck, we can all travel together along with the luggage. The convoy leaves in fifteen minutes from the hotel front entrance," he said as he checked his pocket watch.

And so, fifteen minutes later the two vehicles set out for the southern part of Malawi. They were still getting to know each other as they drove along the roads. Bruce, the English hairdresser who had never been farther than the London City limits, was terrified of driving off into the bush, with what he thought was a totally uncivilized group of unsophisticated people, to God knows where. He was already yearning for the bustle of downtown London.

# 20
## Chapter

S unrise on Saturday was the beginning of the biggest day in Angela' and Lucas' lives. And what a beautiful sunrise it was. The yellow-orange glow on the horizon foretold of the clear skies to follow. Angela had thought fondly last night of her previous marriage and how different her relationship with Lucas was from the one she had shared with her former husband. She still thought about him from time to time, but now Lucas totally consumed her thoughts and desires.

By seven-thirty, Angela and Lucas were working on their final cup of coffee as they sat in his kitchen. Angela observed as she gazed out the window, "You know, I'm glad we closed the clinic and surgical suites for the weekend, since I see that the steady stream of visitors to the mission is now becoming a flood. No patients could even come in, and the mission grounds are already almost filled with visitors. More are coming, Lucas, where can we find a place for all of them?"

Lucas took a deep breath and looked from the window of the kitchen, as he drained the last remaining sip from his cup coffee.

He remarked that it was the largest number of people he had ever seen on the mission grounds at one time in twelve years. Conscience had agreed earlier that the mob exceeded any she had seen in the fifty-five years she had lived in Nsanje. She also said that it was nice to know that their wedding would be well attended, and that the Valley would long remember it.

Angela was beginning to become nervous, which she informed the other nurses when she returned to the dormitory. "I've only seen my wedding dress on a hanger once. Bruce insists that he needs to have me in a chair by eleven o'clock this morning to arrange my hair to work with the dress. It's the one Gayle and Sir William brought from England, and it has been pressed now, as it was boxed by the dressmakers before they left London. How are we going to get everything done by four-thirty for the ceremony?"

Lucas smiled at Angela, kissed her lightly on the cheek, and said sarcastically as he hugged her, "Angie, we have royalty from England, a totally competent bush pilot, a tough jungle fighter, as well as two Christian ministers experienced in African ceremonies to get this show organized. What possibly could go wrong? Relax and enjoy the fun!"

"I'm still worried about my brother Jake," replied Angela, frowning as she greeted Bruce, who motioned her to come into the living room for her sitting. "The bachelor party that Sean, Chauncey, and Sir William organized for you last night evidently gave everyone a good time, but Jake is still out in the Angolan jungle with Savimbi. Has he contacted anyone? I really need him here with us today. So far we haven't heard that word got to him in the Angolan jungles, and the news reports are that the fighting with the government has been intense for the last few days.

"Even if we haven't heard from Jake, I'm sure he'll come. It appears that my family in America is all on a trip to Europe and won't be here today, so I guess your family will have to do." remarked Lucas. He was sensitive that there would be no representative from his family at the wedding, but not surprised. At least Angela would have her family around her for the ceremony. He was relieved that Tad, Sean, and Chauncey had no trouble with camaraderie and were already spending time together.

The morning arrangements continued, as tents were being put up over tables with flower decorations, and silverware arranged for the invited guests. The formal table settings for the invited guests were supervised by Conscience, following suggestions given by Gayle, who seemed to Angela to be knowledgeable and extremely diplomatic about this sort of thing.

The smell of roasting beef and chicken pervaded the entire complex as the giant meal was being roasted over slow fires by teams of native cooks, with the drippings collecting in a large pots and being used again for basting the birds and beef as they turned slowly over the open fires. Meanwhile, the indigenous ceremony was largely being prepared and supervised by an ancient tribal chief named Ogou Wawa from the local Yao Tribe, who had been loosely associated with the Baptist Mission for decades, but had never seen fit to accept *any* deity as superior to his own ancestors.

"What is happening on the mission grounds?" Angela asked her father. She was really pleased that he had been able to come from England after all the trouble that had separated her family and friends. Now it was her big day and Becky and Reverend Williamson, as well as Tad, had all come to celebrate it with her.

"Oh, I suspect that the locals are just warming up for the ceremony tonight," he smiled knowingly. "As you know, in Angola it could easily take two days for the locals to get their feathers up for a major ceremony. Those drums sound like they're being tuned up for the big *makelele*. Your mother would have loved to help you prepare for this ceremony."

"It still makes me nervous, Dad." She really wanted to veer the conversation away from the thought of her mother, as it was depressing on a day this important "Those drums started last night and that constant beating keeps getting louder. I know any change in rhythm is significant."

"It's all in the preparation for an adoption into the tribe, Angie, honey. I wonder who the lucky person to be adopted is. Got any ideas?"

Angela turned pale. "You don't think…just because Lucas has been made a member of the Yao Tribe that they want to make *me* one? Lucas suggested the other day that…..Come on, Dad, this can't happen."

Reverend Abercrombe laughed openly, and then said, "The wife usually goes with her husband in the old Angolan tradition, honey. Now this is Malawi….You never can tell!"

The morning preparations continued as the hour for the ceremony approached. Work intensified both in the mission chapel and out on the expansive mission grounds. As the noon meal grew near, the natives built a massive fire in the center of the grounds in preparation for the ceremony. The male celebrants began to show signs of serious inebriation and a few lady members of the indigenous crowd did also. The drums now beat in a specific rhythm and dancing was beginning to expand into the mass of humanity. The dancing involved coordinated movements, that everyone seemed to know, and this fascinated Sir William as he watched from the window of the clinic.

"How do all those people move together? They can't possibly have practiced this, yet I see no faults in their steps."

"Probably all from the same Yao Tribe," Sean noted. "They learn it from childhood and return to repeat it at every celebration. Wait until the marriage starts and you'll really see something. It's called *diboka*."

The mission chapel was resplendent in floral decorations with gorgeous arrangements of frangipani, hibiscus, bougainvillea and flame lilies. Each pew exhibited these flowers at each end. The fragrances could be sensed over the entire building. Two pots of brunfelsia stood at the altar, one on each side. All of these flowers had been donated by the attending Valley population, and they made the chapel appear to be prepared for a typical African ceremony. The chapel was absolutely magnificent.

* * *

"I can't wear a dress this expensive!" remarked Angela as she looked in the mirror as the wedding dress was being fitted by Gayle in Lucas' bedroom. "These people are rural and this dress is made for a queen."

"Look at it this way," Gayle replied. "There is no telling what the Valley people will make you wear during the native ceremony, so you might as well look ravishing for the traditional part. Remember, you don't get married to Lucas but once."

The dress was made of pure white, layered satin, overlaid with tissue-thin taffeta, creating a sweeping, romantic drape, with spaghetti straps and genuine pearl beads at each layer. The veil, which was to cover her face, was of the finest, ethereal lace with an elegant diamond tiara adorned with crystals to crown her golden hair. The diamond tiara had been lent by Sir William's mother. Truly, Angela felt that the entire ensemble exceeded anything that she could have ever imagined in all of her daydreams.

"I don't know exactly how to thank you and Sir William for the dress." She was in tears as Gayle helped her try it on for size. It fit perfectly.

Bruce appeared at the door, and even he was impressed by the vision of beauty Angela portrayed in her wedding gown.

"You look enchanting, but we need to get your hair set. Let's get you out of the dress and into a chair."

Bruce moved a chair to the center of the room and pointed to it as Angela carefully removed the dress and hung it on a padded hanger. Now wearing a sweat suit, she submitted to Bruce's inspection and the washing of her hair as he talked to her about his first African experiences. It was evident to Angela that he was a highly trained professional who must have commanded a serious fee to travel from London to style her hair, and then stay for a week afterwards. He was also a licensed cosmetologist and had brought a large selection of foundations, powders, eye shadows, liners and whatever else in an alligator case.

She watched in one of Lucas' mirrors as her short, blonde hair was arranged and blown dry to accommodate the tiara. After Bruce had blown it dry and carefully combed it, working in all types of wonderful smelling hair products, he then added the flowers to accent the style.

"I've never had a formal hair dressing in my life," she said. "Bruce, you may be a neophyte in Africa, but you certainly know about ladies' hair."

It was now approaching two, and the flood of new arrivals had slowed to a trickle. The grounds of the mission had been rearranged to suit the indigenous chiefs, with three large ebony chairs made of finely carved wood, which had been brought by ox-cart and set at the center of the altar-like edifice that had been put before the now-surging bonfire. These chairs were draped with a lion skin on the center chair, a zebra skin and an elephant skin covering the chairs on either side. Large native spears adorned the altars' sides, their shafts hung with giraffe and hyena tails; the walking space in front was covered with multiple antelope skins. This was to be a genuine Yao tribal ceremony involving the three ruling tribal chiefs. It was evident that this would also include the highest *nganga* in the country by the plethora of magic gourds containing potions to be used during the rituals.

The crowd of waiting revelers was becoming more restless as the day progressed. The constant beat from the large, hollow logs as they continued their resonant echo, could be heard for miles, as the dancing and drinking continued into the early afternoon.

"Well, the formal arrangements are in place," sighed Gayle as she surveyed the immaculately set tables and the chapel. "I have no idea what we'll encounter if all those natives dancing around in the mission grounds continue, but that drumbeat is getting louder and more people are becoming intoxicated by the minute. No invited guests are expected for a few more hours, so we can get cleaned up and dressed for the formal wedding rites."

A little later, Angela watched Gayle and Becky Williamson get into their bridesmaids' gowns, which were matching off the shoulder, full length lavender silk with a draped bodice and faux wrap skirt. They had been made to match Angela's dress in the same shop with Angela's wedding outfit and were almost as magnificent as her white fantasia gown. Side by side they were staggering.

Lucas and the other men retired to his house for a few drinks and to prepare for the formal ceremony. Chauncey and Sean had no formal clothes, so they wore what they had brought: army fatigues. The rest of the party had formal clothes of varying origin, and Sir William looked regal in his tuxedo. Fortunately, he had brought a spare suit, which was somewhat tight on Lucas, but looked fine once he had gotten into it. The two ministers, Reverends Williamson and Abercrombe, sat down at the kitchen table and worked out a ritual that allowed each to speak and lead the sacrament, which they had divided into separate parts.

"You and I may be doing the formal parts, Reverend Williamson, but I suspect that the rituals to follow out on the grounds will be something else," quipped Angela's father. "If it's anything like the Angolan rites, it can run for hours, but everyone will have a good time."

The first formal guests to arrive were the government officials and their wives, at about three-thirty, in a convoy of shiny, new chauffeured Mercedes Benz limousines and a cloud of dust. They were dressed to the nines. These vehicles were followed by a long train of expensive cars owned by the upper class, mixed with farm trucks and other vehicles of lower value. These were driven by the shopkeepers and local business men, with their wives and families. Everyone seemed to know each other, and they stood and talked out in the cool sunshine, greeting old friends as they arrived. The tribal chiefs were well acquainted with the government people, and soon the congregation was thoroughly mixed, feathered headdresses next to formal top hats. Many of the government officials' wives were dressed in elaborate gowns, but nothing close to Angela's apparel.

Suddenly, a dull whirling sound that gradually increased in intensity was heard coming from the west. The informal talk stopped as the guests turned towards the source of the sound with wondering looks. "What *is* that noise?" asked one of the Malawi diplomats, standing with his associates.

Sean and Chauncey happened to be discussing the foliage with a group of ladies on the edge of the group. Ducking towards the ground instinctively, Sean exclaimed, "That sounds like a large helicopter, and it's approaching fast!"

"You bet!" returned Chauncey. "And by the sound of those rotor blades, it's heavy. It might even be carrying big time artillery." He crouched near the ground next to Sean.

Ten seconds later, the western horizon was filled by the silhouette of a huge military helicopter, armed with rockets and automatic weapons, and covered with military insignia. Since it was flying towards them from the west, the sun shone behind it and no one was able to recognize its insignia. All of the guests instinctively ducked.

"Hold on!" exclaimed Sean, shading part of his eyes to block them from the blazing sun as he stood up straight. "Those flags on the fuselage are Angolan!"

"What the heck is an Angolan military helicopter doing in Malawi airspace?" asked Chauncey as he stood up next to Sean and gaped at the now rapidly approaching aircraft.

"Look at those emblems again," repeated Sean. "That's the rebel Angola flag with the green stripe! He's way off course. Angola's a thousand miles from here."

"Well, at least eight hundred miles, anyway," corrected Chauncey.

The sizable airship continued its approach until it came to a halt, as it hovered over the mission at low altitude. The draft from the two large rotors created a wind that blew up a small dust storm below. Without a sound from the crowd, it moved two hundred meters to the south and then settled on a concrete pad next to the mission hospital.

Angela, hearing the commotion, looked out of the nurses' residence window and immediately surmised the situation accurately. "It's Jake! He came after all! No one else would be here in an Angolan warship with rebel insignia." She grabbed her robe, forgetting that she had no shoes, and ran to greet him, totally forgetting the crowd of people outside in her rush to see her brother.

The door to the nurses' residence opened and Iuba ran out with Angela as she moved towards the helicopter, now having settled next to the hospital. As the rotors slowed to a stop, the hatch to the body of the airship opened and a tall, thin man emerged wearing battle fatigues.

"You made it, Jake!" she cried as they embraced. "I just *knew* you'd be here!"

After the rotors stopped turning, the uniformed crew of the rebel Angolan helicopter disembarked and stood in a group next to their aircraft, quietly staying together. Among this knot of men was a short, thin black man with no badge of rank on his uniform. He said little but appeared to be treated with respect by the other crew members. Observing this short gentleman from a distance, the Malawian Minister of Foreign Affairs, who had been sent by President Hastings Banda as his representative at the wedding, walked leisurely in the direction of the helicopter until he stood next to the short man.

"Jonas, it's been a while since the African Council. We could have made arrangements for a more formal reception had President Banda known of your travel plans."

They shook hands warmly and the short man answered, "Herbert, I remember you well from the conference. I had not planned to come to Malawi until last evening, when one of my colonels requested leave to attend his sister's wedding. I thought that a trip to Malawi would be a good excuse to get a short break from the hostilities and perhaps speak to President Banda about the aide he has been sending. It's nice to meet again."

All of this conversation was held in a low voice with no sign given that the leader of the rebel Angolan forces was present at the mission. This was as Savimbi desired, but Angela, still in her bathrobe and holding Jake's arm, spotted the rebel leader standing near his aircraft and remarked to her brother, "I see the rebel leader came with you. We must be sure to make him feel welcome."

"Cool it, Angie," Jake whispered. "He was kind to come so I could fly here for a day. Most of these people have no idea who he is, and he wants it to remain that way."

Angela returned to the nurse's residence to finish preparation for the wedding, followed by the ever present Iuba, who didn't appreciate the crowd gathering on the mission grounds. Sean, now standing next to Chauncey, continued to overlook the gathering crowd waiting to enter the chapel.

"That short black dude by the helicopter talking to that government man ain't no Buck Private, Chauncey. Look at his manner and the way he carries himself, even though he shows no rank on his uniform. What do you think?"

"I think that you've spotted it right, Sean. I bet he's some big guy above the army ranking system, probably some type of

Angolan general or war lord," replied Chauncey, as they headed for the chapel to help in seating the invited guests. Tad and Jake joined the two as they walked the few hundred yards. Jake informed them that the 'short black dude' was Savimbi, commanding general of the Angolan revolution and not to be messed with.

The invited guests now began to file into the beautifully decorated chapel, finding seats in the pews. They were escorted and seated by Sean, Chauncey, Tad and Jake, who were ushers in name only. Most of the guests knew each other and conversed in low tones as they found places to sit in the informal atmosphere of the chapel. Close by, the constant beat of the indigenous drums continued in the background, and became louder as the clock at the back of the chapel showed four-fifteen. The natives had brought themselves up to a frenzy, as they prepared to begin their own ceremonies that would start a few minutes following the traditional rites now beginning in the chapel.

The murmur of conversation dwindled to a hush as Reverend Williamson walked into the chapel to the swell of the organ and stood before the dais. He was holding a Bible in his hands as he began to speak in clear tones, facing the gathered crowd. Conscience and a few uninvited Africans had quietly joined the congregation, standing at the back of the crowded chapel.

"Friends, we are gathered here to join in matrimony two people......" He went on for a full five minutes. Sir William, Jake, and Tad stood at the front of the chapel with Lucas, who appeared to be wearing a confident smile, but actually was terrified.

After this address, there was the singing of a few spirited Christian hymns and a short prayer by Reverend Williamson. The prayer was followed by a pronouncement by Chief Ogou Wawa, dressed in full ceremonial regalia, using a language that most of the audience readily understood, *Chinyanja*. The audience came to their feet as the respected chief concluded his short remarks at the front of the chapel.

As the organ music swelled to play the wedding march over the crescendo of the drum beat outside, a procession of ladies walked down the aisle, followed by Angela and her father. This included Gayle, and Becky Williamson. All three of the women were resplendent in their London custom-made dresses, but Angela's wedding gown was easily the most exquisite that the audience had ever seen. She carried a bouquet of apricot colored frangipani blossoms tied with a white satin ribbon in her hand. This was matched by the sprinkle of similar blossoms in her hair.

When the procession arrived at the front of the church, Reverend Williamson gave some opening remarks, including his review about the responsibilities of marriage and his long association with Angela from her birth. He then prayed for their union, peace for Malawi and a bright future for any offspring of Angela and Lucas. During this heartfelt prayer, Savimbi quietly slipped into the back of the chapel and found an empty seat in a pew in the back row. More traditional hymns followed.

"Who gives the woman in marriage?" Reverend Williamson finally asked.

Angela's father stepped forward and said in a loud, clear voice, "I do!"

He placed Angela's hand into the hand of Lucas, and then stepped forward next to Reverend Williamson, facing the couple and the audience. The vows were repeated smoothly and concluded with Angela's father declaring, "I now pronounce you man and wife!"

Reverend Abercrombe then gave a short sermon on the trials of marriage and how the Lord should be involved in the decisions of any successful couple. He concluded his remarks with this advice, "A successful marriage will have its ups and downs, but the final tally will not be on how well the marriage did during the easy times, but how the family manages during difficult times. All marriages have some periods of strain and you must anticipate these periods and be prepared for them when they face you. The Lord Jesus Christ will be present if you allow Him to remain with you throughout the marriage. God bless you both!"

The nuptials concluded, Lucas and Angela joined hands and walked towards the back of the chapel, smiling as the applause of the audience filled the building. At the door, they stood together greeting their guests as they moved to the reception area on the outside grounds. There was a thunderstorm of rice falling on the newly married couple as they proceeded to the reception area. The drums from the indigenous rites going on at the fire nearby now thundered, filling the retreating guests with their rhythmic cadence.

"So now we've seen the regular nuptials," remarked Sean to Chauncey. "I'll bet the African rites will be a lot more exciting. From the way those natives are getting themselves into a tizzy, you can bet Angela is in for a big time!"

Chauncey smiled wryly at the jungle fighter and remarked, "She's born and raised in Africa, Sean. Anything the natives have to offer will be tame stuff compared to what I'll bet she's seen in Angola. My money is on her."

Angela and Lucas walked over to the formally arranged tents where tables had been set out for the reception. A buffet had been arranged and after each invited guest had been served, Sir William made a few remarks before he toasted the couple with fruit juice. Immediately after his toast, a group of brightly costumed women from the group at the native fire came into the tent and escorted Angela over towards their small thatch hut to start the native ceremony.

Lucas looked up and smiled saying, "Does she have to be initiated into the Yao Tribe before the marriage ceremony?"

One of the ladies laughed and replied. "*Eya, munthu Yao fulumira msanga, Bwana!*" (You're a Yao, and very soon she'll be one too!)

Bidding the group in the tent goodbye, Lucas followed Angela over to the large circular fire, where hundreds of celebrants had gathered to partake in the native initiation and marriage. Many of the invited guests followed, knowing that the forthcoming activities would be worth watching, and many of them had never before had the opportunity to witness an initiation.

"Listen to those drums thunder!" remarked Sean. "It makes the ground shake."

The *thump-a, thump-a, thump, thump* continued as the chief strode out of the hut that had been constructed from the branches of a baobab tree, which he had been using as a residence at the celebration. He was dressed in his best ceremonial costume for the initiation and was indeed a startling vision as he stood before the wooden altar that the natives had built to address the waiting audience. He wore a robe of lion-skin, draped over his left shoulder with a necklace of crocodile teeth strung together on a golden chain around his neck At his waist was a ceremonial antelope skin skirt with beads and metal ornaments dangling from the hem, and in his right hand he carried a scepter of ivory, intricately carved, with a golden knob at the top and bottom. On his feet he wore shin-length boots made of animal skins, with intricately carved images of remote ancestors that only the witch doctor understood. His head was surrounded by a crown of rare bird feathers, skillfully woven into a headdress of bright colors. He stood there quietly waiting for the dancing and chatter to cease. His sub-chiefs sat proudly on either side of him on the ebony carved chairs.

At his right hand stood the *nganga*, the second most powerful man in the tribe, feared and respected by all. This *nganga* wore a mask made from the head of a hyena, and an irregularly arranged shirt and loincloth of animal skins. On his belt, he carried small pouches of herbs and potions, the purposes of which only he knew. In his left hand appeared a wooden rod that made groaning noises as he swished it defiantly through the air, as if to ward off evil spirits

The *nganga* stepped forward and held his rod high in the air before the now rapidly quieting crowd. The continued rhythmic beat of the drums could be heard, uninterrupted, as the natives sat before the fire, beating out a message on the large hollow logs in front of them. *"Doctor Lucas' partner will become a Yao Tribe woman,"* the drums repeated over and over for all the jungle as well as the fertile fields surrounding the mission to hear.

The witch doctor spoke in *Chinyanja*, "This is the flame of Ogou Wawa, hereditary chief of the lands surrounding this territory. Give ear to his pronouncements!"

The expectant crowd grew even more hushed as every eye watched the extraordinary figure of the chief step forward, his dignified stature exuding the confidence of an experienced leader of his people.

"We are here to initiate a new member to the Yao tribe!" the chief exclaimed in a loud clear voice that all could hear. He also spoke in the same Nyanja dialect. "She is to be the woman of our tribe member, Abambo (Lucas). How do you feel about her acceptance into our tribe as Te-Abambo?"

There was a brief silence, and then a roar came from the hundreds of throats of the tribe members. As they sat watching their chief, he stood in front of the wooden altar, and the blazing flames of the tribal fire flickered across his face in the fading light of the mission grounds.

The crowd responded in the Nyanja native ascension, a sound of traditional undulation - a singular noise made by allowing the tongue to flap against the roof of the mouth while giving voice to a high pitched tone. "Eyaaaaaaa, Eyaaaa ---lalalalalalala!" Given this sign of acceptance, the chief returned to his seat in front of the altar and signaled for the *nganga* to proceed with the initiation ceremony.

"I know that the wedding can only proceed after I become a tribe member," Angela whispered to Lucas, "but how much is involved? In Angola the ritual isn't all that long."

A group of the ruling tribal ladies came to Angela and led her to a bamboo enclosure constructed about thirty meters from the fire, and helping her out of her expensive wedding dress they placed tribal clothes on her body. They then painted her face and body with bright tribal markings, decorating her face, arms and torso.

"Oh no, you don't!" exclaimed Angela when the women attempted to take her underclothes and brassiere. "I need to keep *some* type of coverage."

Accommodation was accepted and Angela appeared before the tribal chiefs, as she was led from the enclosure, wearing a brightly colored Nyanga cotton cloth around her upper body and waist with a bare midriff. She was requested to kneel before the three chief's thrones as the drums came to a crescendo and then suddenly stopped for the first time in three hours. The silence was overwhelming.

"We come before the ancestor's spirits to induct a new member into the Yao Tribe this evening," proclaimed the *nganga* in the native dialect as he stood before the raging fire, his paint and copper adornments glittering in the firelight. "Do the spirits of our ancestors accept this postulant?"

Lucas could see from his point of observation near the fire that the witch doctor held a packet of dark powder cupped in his hand. The crowd of onlookers, sitting in front of the *nganga*, however, was unable to see this packet, as the witch doctor stood with his hands behind his back. At the conclusion of this question, he flipped the packet into the fire with a flick of his wrist, causing a minor explosion to come from within the fire. The reaction from the surrounding onlookers was to jump back and cringe. Angela lay flat on the ground, avoiding the flare of heat and flames extending in all directions.

After she resumed her kneeling position, twelve assistants to the *nganga* presented the symbols of life, each carrying one symbol before the fire and placing it on the table near the fire. These included wheat, pepper, salt, native brew, bitter herbs, water, a spoon, a pot, a broom, honey, a sharpened spear, and a shield. An African book was handed to Angela as a new incantation began, accompanied by the resumption of the rhythmic beating, which thundered out over the country side. The incantation was picked up by the watching indigenous crowd:

*"Dzinalanga ndi Angela. Ndifuna mundithadize Yao! Te-Abambo!"*

The incantation was also picked up by the wedding guests and translated to English, "Her name is no longer Angela. Make her a member of the Yao Tribe as Te-Abambo!"

As if by magic, a flame from nowhere flared up onto the table and, burning brightly, consumed or blackened the twelve symbols in only a few seconds. From his position, Lucas was able to confirm that the flame actually came from a metal bucket concealed underneath the table, reaching through an opening in the center, and igniting the offerings above it. In any case, the ceremony was impressive and certainly roused and excited the watching, awestruck audience.

"Our ancestors have accepted your sacrifices! You are now our sister! Rise and be welcomed to our family!" A necklace of animal bones was placed around her neck.

This salutation was followed by a loud cheer and as Angela stood in the flickering firelight among the painted, dancing, chanting natives, Lucas thought for just a second that his new wife almost appeared to have "gone native." Angela was embraced by everyone, and was absorbed into the mass of moving, undulating natives. She had now become a Yao tribeswoman. Jake and Tad, her two brothers, joined the dancing celebration group, as they were well used to these ceremonies and easily blended with the circle of natives as they circled the fire.

After fifteen minutes of dancing, the drums ceased and quiet spread throughout the crowd as they sat in a circle before the altar as Ogou Wawa stepped forward and raised his scepter for attention. "It is time to join two of our tribe in solemn matrimony," he intoned. "Let us begin the rite!"

It was now fully dark and the only visible lights were the glare from the light bulbs at the back of the mission hospital, far behind the congregation, and the glimmer of the fire as it continued as a full blaze.

The *nganga* stepped to the altar, and after a series of potions from his belt turning the flames first red, then blue and finally green, he intoned, "Who comes before our counsel to be joined as one, forever?"

Angela and Lucas stood before the altar with the fire behind them, surrounded by the members of the Yao Tribe sitting in a circle around them. "We do," they said in unison.

"If you agree to remain as one, following the rules of matrimony, loyal to each other and subservient to our ancestors' dictates, now is the time to say 'I do.'"

The hush of the onlookers was total, as the *nganga* raised his right hand and gestured at the fire with his rod. Ogou Wawa now stood next to the witch doctor, motioning with the scepter in his right hand. As the fire blazed into the night sky, a huge purple flame shot up from the fire and disappeared in a cloud

388

of smoke. Lucas was unable to discern its origin, but the staring crowd immediately stood and yelled at the top of their very loud voices, "The spirits have spoken, the two are now joined as one!"

Immediately the drums began their cadence, and as their throb engulfed the entire congregation the tribesmen began to turn and dance in place. Even those guests watching from the sidelines began to feel the enticing tempo, as the flickering light revealed the now-circling dancers, their feet stomping out the meter to the familiar sounds in perfect unison. The integrated chant of a thousand voices, now blended over centuries of repetition, echoed over the countryside, reverberating into the darkness.

"I guess we're married now, "quipped Angela as she moved with Lucas to the hypnotic beat of the drums and voices.

"Yes we are, honey, and there's no ceremony for divorce, so you're stuck with me for life!" he laughed.

Later in the evening Angela sat resting by the still blazing fire in native attire watching the party continue, and patting Iuba absent mindedly. Rubbing his ears, she thought to herself that this had been an important day in all of their lives. *It was really a blessing that my father and brothers were able to be here as well as many of our other friends. If only my mother had lived long enough to meet Lucas, I know she would have loved him as much as I do.* She stood and walked back to join the celebration, Iuba following loyally behind her.

The celebration lasted well into the early hours of the next morning, and by sunrise Lucas and Angela had snuck away from the crowd and were sitting on the front porch of their home, eating breakfast together for the first time as a married couple. Conscience had produced enough food for an army, and as they sat alone drinking tea, having pushed aside the remains of their repast, Lucas thoughtfully remarked, "You know, Honey, There's still a lot of suffering in the world from disease and lost faith. I know that we are only two people, but if enough others in the world felt a similar calling, perhaps some changes would come about to bring an improved outlook for those poor people without the advantages the rest of the world enjoys."

Angela, finishing her cup, stood up and said, "Lucas Dear, you're right, but it's time to see what little good we can do now right here in Nsanje. The weekend has produced another group of medical problems, so we have people to see."

Kissing him softly on the cheek, she left the porch and walked down the path towards the hospital, with the ever present Iuba, tail wagging, following her every footstep.

About Jonathan Marshall

Having served many years as a foreign medical missionary, Jonathan Marshall returned to the United States in 1990 and has been in active private practice as a urologic specialist and general surgeon since then. He and his wife Jenny, live on a cattle ranch in Central Texas and prefer to commute daily to work as, after living rurally in the African bush for so many years, city life just didn't cut it. His wife, Jenny, was born in Rhodesia (now Zimbabwe) to Scottish Presbyterian missionary parents and as a registered nurse, her training is highly valued on the mission field, particularly in the area of obstetrics and midwifery. She also earned a degree in legal studies. They continue to travel together frequently to foreign countries to work as short-term medical missionaries, most often in Southern Africa, where they are most familiar with the customs and languages.

Originally, Jonathan spent his early years in suburban Philadelphia, but as a boy of ten, the Marshall family moved to rural South Carolina to run the family cattle ranch. Most of his post-high school education was at Ivy League colleges and he obtained his Doctorate in Medicine from the University of Pennsylvania. As a urologic and surgical resident, he began to yearn to travel abroad in order to share his knowledge and expertise and became convinced of his higher calling as a medical missionary while on a tour to a Southern Baptist mission hospital, deep in the heart of southern Africa in 1970. This also compelled him to pursue a doctorate degree in Divinity in 1980 and later he earned a Ph.D. in Theology from Trinity Seminary.

CPSIA information can be obtained
at www.ICGtesting.com
Printed in the USA
LVHW112247120819
627434LV00001B/41/P

9 781682 135181